D0313114

Adam Blake is the pseudonym of an internationally bestselling novelist. He lives in London.

Also by Adam Blake

The Dead Sea Deception

THE
DEMON
CODE

ADAM BLAKE

SPHERE

First published in Great Britain as a paperback original
in 2012 by Sphere

Copyright © Adam Blake 2012

The moral right of the author has been asserted.

*All characters and events in this publication, other than those
clearly in the public domain, are fictitious and any resemblance
to real persons, living or dead, is purely coincidental.*

All rights reserved.
No part of this publication may be reproduced, stored in a
retrieval system, or transmitted, in any form or by any means, without
the prior permission in writing of the publisher, nor be otherwise circulated
in any form of binding or cover other than that in which it is published
and without a similar condition including this condition being
imposed on the subsequent purchaser.

A CIP catalogue record for this book
is available from the British Library.

ISBN B 978-0-7515-4578-4

Typeset in Sabon by M Rules
Printed and bound in Great Britain by
Clays Ltd, St Ives plc

Papers used by Sphere are from well-managed forests
and other responsible sources.

MIX
Paper from
responsible sources
FSC® C104740

Sphere
An imprint of
Little, Brown Book Group
100 Victoria Embankment
London EC4Y 0DY

An Hachette UK Company
www.hachette.co.uk

www.littlebrown.co.uk

To A. J. Lake, With All My Love

Prologue

The participants had been prepared.

Their captors had bound their hands and their feet, lined them up in the prescribed order and forced them to kneel on the cold stone floor, in the small room at the back of the old building. The room was really too narrow for the ritual that was to take place there. There were others that would have been much more suitable, but this one had been chosen by the prophet for esoteric reasons that few of them understood.

It was a warm night, the sun hiding just below the horizon, but the flagstones were still cold. Perhaps for that reason, or perhaps for other reasons that were equally valid, the men and women trembled as they waited on their knees.

Ber Lusim sent one of his men to tell the prophet that they were ready to proceed.

The man returned almost immediately, walking respectfully behind the holy one. Shekolni had attired himself in red robes hemmed with black – red for blood, black for mourning. Red braids were woven into the black of his beard, and on the slender palms of his hands, which were like the hands of a violinist or a doctor, the Aramaic words for life and death had been painted in red ink with black cartouches – signifying that God

1

had deputed to him both the power to preserve and the power to destroy.

The prophet held the holy book open in his hands, his head lowered as though he were reading from it. But his eyes were closed. The other men standing in the room knew better than to speak at such a time, but they swapped glances, unnerved and awed by this small sign of the prophet's otherness.

Ber Lusim bowed to the holy man – a low, prolonged obeisance – and the others all followed suit. Shekolni opened his eyes then and smiled at his old friend, an unaffected smile of warmth and shared joy.

'You've worked so long for this,' he said, in the language of their homeland. 'And now, here it is at last.'

'We all have,' Ber Lusim replied. 'May the One Name speed you, Avra. May the Host give strength to your hand.'

'Please! Tell us what you're going to do to us!'

It was one of the captives, a man, who had spoken. He was clearly terrified and trying desperately hard not to let that show. Ber Lusim respected the man's courage: he must already know a good part of the answer.

Although he ignored the question, Shekolni stared at the row of kneeling men and women long and thoughtfully. Ber Lusim stood by and waited, sparing speech: now that they were here, and every possible preparation made, he would take his cue from the prophet.

'I think their mouths should be stopped,' Shekolni said at last. 'There will be a great deal of noise otherwise. Indecent and extraneous noise. I think it will detract from the solemnity of the occasion.'

Ber Lusim nodded curtly to the nearest of his people. 'Do it.'

Two of his followers made their way down the line, fixing gags of wadded linen in the mouth of each of the sacrifices in turn. They were soon done. When the last of the twelve was effectively silenced, they saluted their chief with a clenched fist and the prophet with the sign of the noose. Then they withdrew to the doorway.

'Where is the blade?' Shekolni said. He knew where it was, of course: the question had the force of ritual.

So Ber Lusim answered it in a ritual fashion. He opened his jacket to show the multi-pocketed scabbard of woven hemp affixed to its lining and drew out one of his knives. In many places they would be called shanks, since they had no separate handle, only a slightly thickened stem that could safely be held, and a slender asymmetrical blade, rounded on one side close to the tip and sharp enough to part a hair.

'Here is the blade.' He reversed it in his hand and offered it to Shekolni.

The prophet took it and nodded his thanks. He turned to the kneeling men and women.

'Out of your sin will come a great goodness,' he told them, lapsing into their own language so that they would understand and be comforted. 'Out of your pain, a blessing beyond telling. And out of your deaths, life everlasting.'

He had been right about the noise. Even with the gags, and with Shekolni working as quickly as he could, the next twenty minutes were harrowing and exhausting. None of the onlookers were strangers to death, but death of this kind, with the victim helpless and full of panic because he can see it coming, is not a pleasant thing to watch.

But they did watch. Because they knew what the killing was for, and what hung on it.

The prophet rose at last, his hand shaking with tiredness. His robes were no longer red. In the shadowed room, the blood that saturated them had dyed them a uniform black. Ber

Lusim stepped forward to support Shekolni, taking some of that blood onto himself – literally, as it was already on him symbolically.

'The wheels begin to turn,' Shekolni said.

'And the wings to beat,' Ber Lusim replied.

'Amen.'

Ber Lusim signalled for the fire to be lit.

When they drove away, the old house was blazing. Not like a torch, but like a beacon in olden times, set on a hill to warn the sleeping citizenry of some impending crisis.

But no one would read it like that, Ber Lusim knew. The warning would go unheeded, until it was too late.

At that auspicious moment, a thought occurred to him. In his younger days, when his zeal had sometimes got the better of his discretion, he had earned the nickname *the Demon*. He was so more than that now.

But when the lid was torn from hell, and all the demons rose at once, perhaps the irony would be remembered.

PART ONE

A TRUMPET SPEAKING JUDGMENT

1

Heather Kennedy, formerly Detective Sergeant Kennedy 4031, of the London Metropolitan Police, Serious and Organised Crime Division, now without rank, stepped out of the foyer of Number 32 London Bridge, also known as the Shard, into brilliant summer sunlight. She walked down the steps briskly enough, but then, once she reached the bottom, she stood in the centre of the pavement, jostled by random passers-by, uncertain of what to do next.

Her right hand hurt.

Her right hand hurt because the knuckle was bleeding.

Her knuckle was bleeding because she had split it open on the jaw of the man who until five minutes ago had been her employer.

It was an equation whose final terms she was still working out.

Kennedy was chagrined at her intemperate outburst, and more than slightly surprised. Normally, if the client had made some sexist remark, tried for a casual grope, or even impugned her professional integrity, she would have dealt with the situation calmly and skilfully, and emerged unruffled. In no way, and under no circumstances, would she have punched him out.

But she couldn't remember the last time she'd felt normal.

Massaging the injured hand gingerly, she eased herself into the steady stream of commuters and tourists. She wanted to go home and get the hand into cold water. Then she wanted to have a good, stiff drink, followed by a badder, stiffer one.

The only problem with that formulation was Izzy. She wasn't sure how much further downhill the day could go without hitting bottom. Or what the consequences might be of walking in on Izzy in the middle of her working day, unannounced. The last time that had happened ...

Kennedy wrenched her thoughts forcibly off that track, but not before she saw all over again the mental image she'd been trying to avoid and was hit by the same feelings that it always inspired: bitter rage superimposed on terrifying emptiness like cheap whisky laid over ice.

So she didn't go home. She went to a bar – a characterless chain place with a faux-whimsical name that had firkins in it – and took that whisky straight instead of metaphorical. She nursed it gloomily, wondering what came next. The job at Sandhurst Ballantyne was meant to be the start of something good, but laying violent hands on your boss greatly reduces the chances of him recommending you to friends. So here she was, with a zero-calorie client list, an empty appointment book and an unfaithful (maybe serially unfaithful) girlfriend. The future looked bright.

Kennedy's statuesque good looks and long blonde hair attracted a fair amount of attention from the other daytime drinkers. Either that or it was the usual tedious business of a woman in a uniform. Hers was severe in the extreme – crisp police-blue security coveralls, black military boots – but for some men the fact of a uniform is enough.

She was just polishing off the whisky when her phone rang.

She fished it out with a momentary flare of hope: sometimes one door opened right when another one closed.

But it was Emil Gassan. He was an academic, a historian at a Scottish university who she'd got to know in the course of an old case – and that was the only thing he ever wanted to talk to her about. Kennedy refused the call and tossed the phone back into her bag.

She considered spending the day drifting around London: doing a gallery, taking in a film. But that would be ridiculous. She wasn't bunking school, she was out of work, and there was no point in putting things off. She squared her shoulders and headed for home.

Home was Pimlico – a short, elbowed hop by Tube, but then a fairly long walk up Vauxhall Bridge Road; long enough, anyway, that by the time Kennedy got to the front door of her flat, she'd revised that earlier rhetorical question. Where exactly *was* the bottom, these days? And did she really want to find out?

She made a lot of noise with the key in the lock, shuffled her feet on the floor and closed the door too loudly. When she was halfway up the hall, Izzy came out to greet her – from the lounge, not the bedroom, to Kennedy's relief.

Shorter and darker than Kennedy, Izzy was at the same time considerably more concentrated: a louche and limber ball of sex appeal, from which her fairly broad hips didn't detract in the slightest. Radiating both surprise and suspicion as she faced Kennedy down the length of the hall, she flicked a strand of hair from her chocolate-brown eyes.

'Hey,' she said.

'So you say,' Kennedy riposted.

'Do I get a kiss?'

It was a good question, but Kennedy didn't have a good

answer – or a good evasion. Hangdog, she advanced down the hall, kissed Izzy on the cheek, then carried on past her.

Izzy turned to watch her go. 'You're home early,' she pointed out. 'What, are you checking up on me now?'

'No,' Kennedy said. 'Why, should I be?'

'No.'

'Okay, then.'

They seemed to have reached the end of that conversational avenue. Kennedy went into the lounge, with a detour into the kitchen to put some ice in a glass. But when she opened the drinks cabinet and found herself meeting her own gaze in its mirrored back, she lost some of her enthusiasm. She already had one drink inside her. Getting smashed at eleven in the morning would feel a lot like a cry for help.

Izzy had followed her into the room. 'Is something the matter?' she asked. 'Aren't you meant to be at Shithouse Brigadoon this morning?'

'It's Sandhurst Ballantyne.'

'Yeah. Them.'

'I was.' Kennedy turned to face her, bottle in hand.

'And you gave in your report?'

'I tried to.'

Izzy cocked her head on one side and looked comically puzzled, which in another mood Kennedy would have found appealing. Right now it just irritated her.

'The client refused to be briefed. He told me not to submit the report. He offered to pay me a performance bonus if I binned it and gave his ratty little department a clean bill of health.'

'I don't get it,' Izzy said.

Kennedy shoved the whisky bottle back into the cabinet, then got it out again and poured herself a shot after all.

10

'Plausible deniability,' she muttered, as she did these things. 'The report says there's at least one and probably two people in the firm doing insider trading in client shares. If Kenwood knows about it, he's got to do something about it. And since one of the two crooks – the definite one, not the probable one – is his boss, he decided he'd rather not know.'

'Then why hire you in the first place?' Izzy demanded. 'That's stupid.'

Kennedy nodded, and took a swig of the harsh, blended whisky. She grimaced. Izzy's taste in booze was reliably horrendous. But she went ahead and drained the glass anyway. 'Compliance is part of his job. He had to look like he was doing something – but he was hoping I'd come back empty. Then when I didn't . . .'

She lapsed into silence.

'So did you take it?' Izzy asked.

'Did I take what?'

'The performance bonus?'

Kennedy sighed and put down the empty glass. 'No, Izzy, I didn't take it. He was getting himself off the hook by sticking me onto it. If I take the bribe, and then a year or so from now there's an internal inquiry or an FSA investigation, he can say I withheld information. Then he's in the clear and the fraud department comes after me.'

'Oh. Okay.' Izzy's expression changed. 'So?'

Kennedy showed her knuckles, covered in her own congealed blood. Izzy took the hand and kissed it. 'Good for you, babe,' she said. 'Unless he sues. Is he going to sue?'

'I don't think so. Whenever I'm in a one-to-one, I make voice-tapes. So I've got him making that indecent proposal on the record. And I'm sending the report in anyway, to him and his boss and the CEO. Unfortunately, he still owed me half my fee. And when I left, he wasn't reaching for his cheque book.'

'Any other clients in the pipeline?'

'The pipeline is dry all the way to the Caucasus, Izzy. This was meant to get me a lot of referrals to other city companies with security needs they couldn't meet in-house. Somehow, I don't think that's going to happen now.'

Izzy seemed perversely cheered by the bad news. 'Okay,' she said, 'so you can be a kept woman for a while. Live off my immoral earnings.'

She was joking, but Kennedy couldn't laugh, didn't feel able to cut Izzy the smallest amount of slack. 'Frankly,' she said, 'that sounds like one of the lower circles of hell.'

She realised at this point that what she'd come home for was an argument – a stand-up row about fidelity and responsibility that would probably feel really cathartic for the first five minutes and then after that would feel like she was force-feeding both herself and the woman she was supposed to love handfuls of broken glass. She had to get out of there. Nowhere to go, really, but she had to get out.

'I'm going downstairs,' she muttered. 'To box up some more of my dad's stuff. If I hang around here, I'll just put you off your stride.'

'Or inspire me,' Izzy said, but Kennedy was already heading for the door. 'Heather ...'

'I'm good.'

'I don't have to clock on just yet. We could ...'

'I said I'm good.'

She was aware of another sound that Izzy made. A sigh maybe, or just a catch in her breath. She didn't look back.

Downstairs, in her own flat, she threw random objects into boxes, opened wardrobe doors and slammed them shut again,

12

walked from room to room in a futile pantomime of bustle and purpose.

Moving in with Izzy had seemed like the logical thing to do, after Kennedy's father died. In the last year or so of his life, Izzy had been Peter Kennedy's de facto nurse, or maybe babysitter, or maybe both. That was what had brought them together. Kennedy was a rising star in the detective division of the Met: her hours were long and unpredictable, and she needed someone close at hand who could come in and pinch-hit at a moment's notice. Izzy was perfect, because although she already had a job, it was on a phone-sex line. Acting as a cheerleader for other people's masturbation was light work you could do from pretty much anywhere. All the equipment she needed was a mobile phone and a dirty mind, and she had both.

The process by which they became lovers was anything but inevitable. It had started around the time Kennedy was kicked out of the Met on her ear, which meant she was around the flat a lot more when Izzy was there. The relationship had developed through the months that followed and it had seemed natural when Peter finally died for Kennedy to move in with Izzy. The flat she'd shared with her father felt like an exhibit in a museum, its associations permanently fixed. Moving out – even though she was only moving upstairs – felt like escaping from at least some of those associations.

But escape depended on a lot of things, and it had its own rules. One of them was that you can't escape from stuff you're still carrying with you. Exploitative and degrading though Izzy's work was, she had never thought about quitting. She liked sex a lot, and when she wasn't having it she liked to talk about it.

And, as it turned out, she liked having it even when Kennedy wasn't around.

Their life together was now stalled: a perpetual tableau of *the adulterers discovered*, with Izzy scrambling to cover herself up, a sheepish young man trying to figure out what was going on, and Kennedy standing in the doorway, wide-eyed and reeling.

Izzy had never promised to be faithful, and in any case, she drew an absolute distinction between women and men. Women were lovers, partners, soul-mates. Men were an itch that she occasionally scratched. Kennedy had never thought that extorting promises was either necessary or desirable. In the patchy history of her sex life, *one* was the highest number of lovers she'd ever had on the boil at the same time, and it had generally felt like enough.

She ought to forgive Izzy. Or she ought to walk out with some cutting remark along the lines of 'check out what you're missing, babe'. She couldn't do either. The passive aggression of guilt, reproach and sullen withdrawal was the horrendous unexcluded middle.

Kennedy's phone rang. She glanced at the display, saw it was Emil Gassan again. She gave in and took the call, but only to tell him that this was a bad time.

Gassan got in first. 'Heather, I've been playing phone tag with you all day. I'm so glad I finally caught up with you.'

She tried to head him off. 'Professor—'

'Emil,' he countered. She ignored him. She didn't want to be on first-name terms with Gassan: on some level, it felt wrong that the dry, spiky academic should even have a first name. 'Professor, I really can't talk right now. I'm in the middle of something.'

'Oh.'

Gassan sounded more than usually cast down and Kennedy experienced a momentary compunction. She knew why he was calling and what it meant to him. It was all about that old case. The biggest find of his scholarly career was something that he could never discuss, on pain of death, except with her. Every so often, he had to vent. He had to tell her things that they both already knew and she had to listen – as a personal service. It gave her some sense of what Izzy must go through in the course of a working day.

'It's just ... you know ... pressure of work,' she temporised. 'I'll call you later in the week.'

'So your slate is full?' Gassan said. 'You wouldn't be free to accept a commission?'

'To accept ... ?' Kennedy was baffled, and – in spite of her sour mood – amused. 'What, you need a detective, Emil? You want me to track down a missing library book or something?'

'Yes. More or less. If you'd been free, I was going to ask you to take on some work – very sensitive and very well paid – for my current employer.'

Kennedy hesitated. It felt hypocritical and ridiculous to make such a rapid and shameless turn-around: but she really needed the money. Even more, she needed to have something that would keep her out of the flat until she could figure out what she wanted to do about Izzy.

'So who's your current employer, Professor?'

He told her and her eyebrows rose. It was definitely a step up from city sleaze.

'I'll come right over,' Kennedy said.

2

The Great Court of the British Museum was like a whispering gallery, magnifying sound from all around Kennedy so that she felt surrounded by and cocooned in other people's conversations. At the same time, sounds from close by seemed to come to her muffled and distorted: perfectly dysfunctional acoustics.

Or maybe she just hated the Great Court because when she'd come here with her father, as a young girl, it had been an actual courtyard, open to the air. She remembered clutching tightly onto his hand as he took her across the sunlit piazza into the cathedral of the past – a place where he'd been animated, happy and at home, and where just for once there was something he actually wanted to share with her.

Now the Great Court had a roof of diamond panes, radiating outwards from what had once been the reading room. The light inside this huge but sealed-off space was grey, like a winter afternoon with a threat of drizzle. It was an impressive feat of engineering, but she couldn't help thinking there was something perverse about it. Why hide the sky and then fake it?

Kennedy took a seat at one of the court's three coffee bars and started counting diamonds while she waited for Gassan. Knowing her man, she'd dressed formally in a light-blue trouser suit and grey boots, and pinned her unruly blonde hair back as severely as she could manage. Formality and order were big on Emil Gassan's list of cardinal virtues.

She saw him from a long way away, bustling across the huge space with the purposeful dignity of a head waiter. He was dressed a lot better than a waiter, though: his blue three-piece suit, with the unmistakable zigzag stitching of Enzo Tovare on the breast pocket, looked new and unashamedly expensive. Gassan thrust his hand out before he reached her, then kept it out so that it preceded him into the conversation.

'Heather, so good of you to come. I'm delighted to see you again.'

He really looked like he meant it, and she was disarmed by his beaming smile. She offered her own hand, had it grasped and engulfed and effusively wrung. 'Professor,' she said, and then, surrendering the point, 'Emil. It's been a long time. I had no idea you were working in London.'

He threw out his arms in a *search me* gesture. 'Neither did I. Until last week, I wasn't. I was still up in St Andrews – lecturing in early medieval history. But I was head-hunted.'

'In the space of a week?' Kennedy was as incredulous as he seemed to want her to be.

'In the space of a day. The museum board called and asked if I'd like to be in charge of the stored collection. Well, they didn't call me directly. It was Marilyn Milton from the Validus Trust, an independent body which has been sponsoring my research for the last two years. Validus is also a major sponsor for the British Museum and British Library. You know they used to be the same institution, until the library was moved in 1997?'

Kennedy shrugged non-committally. She wasn't sure if she'd known that or not, but in any case she didn't want to slow Gassan down by inviting further explanation.

17

'Anyway,' he told her, 'a position opened up – under somewhat tragic circumstances, I'm sorry to say. The previous incumbent, Karyl Leopold, had a serious stroke. And Marilyn contacted me to suggest that I apply – with a promise that she would let the appointments committee know I was Validus's approved candidate.

'I was going to say no. Leaving in the middle of a term, you understand – causes all kinds of disruptions. But in the end, the museum board were so keen to get me that they cut a separate deal with the university. Hired a lecturer to replace me until ... no, no, don't get up.' Kennedy had stood, indicating a willingness to go and get them both coffees and thereby stop the logorrhoeic flow. But Gassan would have none of it. He scooted off to the counter and when he returned, the tray he held had two slices of carrot cake on it, as well as coffees. Obviously he was seeing this as something of a celebration, and she was going to have to let him talk himself out before she got to be told why she was here.

'So,' she said. 'You're in charge of ... what was it again?'

'The stored collection.'

'And what is that, Emil?'

'Everything,' Gassan said happily. 'Well, almost everything. Everything that's not on the shelves. As you can imagine, the museum collection is absolutely vast. The part of it that's available for the public to see represents approximately one per cent of the total.'

Kennedy boggled politely. 'One per cent!'

'Count it,' he suggested playfully, holding up a bony finger. 'One. The rest of the collection spreads across more than twenty thousand square metres of storerooms, and it costs the Museum twelve million pounds a year to maintain and manage it.'

18

Kennedy took a sip of her coffee, but ignored the treacherous blandishments of the cake. Back when she was on the force, the stresses and physical rigours of the job had kept her slim no matter what she ate or drank. In the last few years, she'd had to learn abstinence. 'You must be very proud,' she said to Gassan. 'That they went to such lengths to get you.'

The professor went through a miniature pantomime of faux-modest shrugs and eye-rolls. 'It feels like a culmination, in a lot of ways,' he admitted. 'I've always felt that lecturing was a dilution of my contribution to the field. Now ... I'll be allowed, even encouraged, to publish, but I'll have no public duties at all.'

Kennedy considered that, and was reminded of what she'd said to Izzy about the circles of hell: the idea of spending her life in a subterranean vault, with no reason for stepping outside it, made Izzy's endless smut treadmill seem like the earthly paradise.

'So,' Kennedy said, cutting to the chase at last. 'Where do I fit in?'

Gassan had just taken a mouthful of cake, producing the short silence into which she had projected her question. Now he struggled to get it down so he could answer. 'There was a break-in,' he said at last, fastidiously wiping his lower lip with the corner of his serviette. 'A month ago. The night of Monday the twenty-fourth of July.'

'In the stacks?' Kennedy asked. 'The storerooms, rather than the museum proper?'

He nodded emphatically. 'In the stored collection, yes – which is now my responsibility. Whoever it was, they were very skilled. They were able to get in and out again without triggering a single alarm.'

'Then how did you know they'd been there? Wait, let me guess. From the gaps on the shelves.'

'Not at all,' Gassan assured her. 'In fact, as far as we can tell, nothing is missing. No, we found out about this several hours after the fact – and in a rather alarming way. The intruder left behind a knife. One of the security guards found it, the next morning, just lying on the floor. And it appeared to have been used. At least, there was blood on the blade. After that, they did a more thorough search for evidence and it transpired that a CCTV camera had caught the intruder climbing up through one of the panels of a false ceiling as he left.'

'Wait,' Kennedy said. 'So let me get this straight. You've got a break-in with nothing actually stolen and a bloody knife with nobody actually hurt?'

'Well, we assume that somebody must have been hurt. But it's true that there was no dead body at the scene – God forbid – and we have no way of knowing who was injured, or how. It's deeply troubling. And we've had a terrible time trying to keep the story out of the news. Something like this would generate the most sensationalistic coverage.'

'Yeah, I'd imagine,' Kennedy agreed. 'But you say you've got some closed-circuit footage of your burglar?'

'Yes, but he's masked, and it's hard to tell anything about him beyond the fact that he's male – and empty-handed. If you look at the image closely, he seems to be carrying a small satchel, but it couldn't have held more than a few items. And a quick stocktaking exercise showed nothing out of place. Although there are three and a quarter million artefacts in the collection, so it's entirely possible that we've missed something.'

Kennedy thought about this for a moment or two. A skilled burglar getting past a serious array of locks and alarms, to break into a collection presumably full of items both highly valuable and highly portable. But he didn't bother to bring a decent-sized shopping bag with him, and he didn't swipe anything prominent enough to be noticed. That meant iron self-control or a very specific mission statement. And then there was the knife. Was it a message of some kind? A threat? A bad practical joke? Whatever internal organ governs the detective instinct was making its presence felt. She had only come here as a favour to the professor, and for the money. Already, she had to admit, she was genuinely interested.

'What's my brief?' she asked Gassan.

The professor held up one hand, with the little finger folded down – then used the forefinger of the other hand to count off. 'It's three-fold,' he said. 'It *will* be three-fold, if you accept. First, we want to know how the break-in was accomplished, so we can close the security loophole.'

Kennedy nodded. She'd assumed as much.

'Second, we want to know what, if anything, was actually taken. And if the answer is nothing, we want to know what the intruder was doing during his – or her – time on our premises. If something was vandalised or interfered with, that could be every bit as serious as a theft. Oh, and we'd like to know who was injured, of course,' he added as an afterthought.

'And third?'

'We want you to find our intruder. And if appropriate, to secure an arrest.'

'I'm not a police officer any more, Emil.'

'I know that. Also, of course, I know why. We'd only ask you to put the full facts – the file, the evidence, everything you've found – into our hands. And then leave the rest to us. If we think it necessary, and desirable, we'll put the matter in the hands of the police.'

'Can I ask a stupid question?'

21

'Always.'

'Why aren't the police on the case now?'

Gassan toyed with what was left of his cake. 'This was a situation I inherited, obviously,' he said carefully. 'There was a police investigation, but it wasn't considered to be very productive. Trespassing isn't a crime unless actual damage is involved – and that was the only crime we could prove. The inquiry petered out, and the museum allowed it to do so. They'd already decided that it would be better to put the matter on a more discreet basis. Marilyn Milton was insistent that the museum's trustees wanted me to deal with this matter personally – and that they wanted it done without any further recourse to official bodies or agencies.'

Kennedy had to smile. 'So you thought of me?'

He returned the smile. 'The most unofficial person I know.'

'Okay,' she said. 'I'm going to need to bring up the subject of money, because—'

'Of course,' Gassan exclaimed. 'I apologise for not mentioning it sooner.' He reached into his pocket, took out a piece of paper and handed it across the table to her. It was a cheque, already made out in her name, from the bank account of the Validus Trust. The figure, which was printed rather than handwritten, was twenty thousand pounds. Kennedy stared at the four identical zeros. The fact that they had another number in front of them immediately distinguished this job from her previous one.

'Is that acceptable?' Gassan asked.

'Yes,' she said bluntly. 'Very. But I'd like a letter setting out the terms of my contract. No offence, but item three – finding your intruder – might turn out to be a tall order, if I can't get any other leads on him. I don't want to be working this case for ever. Or to have to give the money back.'

'That's perfectly reasonable. Marilyn indicated that this was a payment for four weeks of your time, on an exclusive basis insofar as that's feasible. But if you have other cases—'

'I don't have any other cases. That was just bullshit.'

'Oh. Well, you bullshit very well.'

'Thank you. Who would I report to?'

'You'll report to me and I'll report directly both to the museum board and to Validus. Their relationship to me is almost one of agency, in this respect – and the museum is very comfortable with that.

'As to powers, I believe what I'm proposing to do is to deputise you. So you'll be able to do anything that I could do. Talk to all of the staff. Have full run of the building. Full access to files and information.'

'Consult other people outside the museum?'

The professor's lips pursed slightly. 'Where appropriate. And so long as absolute discretion is maintained. I think that's a reasonable stipulation.'

'Entirely. I'll take the job.'

'I'm delighted to hear it.' Gassan threw his arms in the air and seemed almost to be about to lean over and hug her.

'Okay,' Kennedy said, forestalling that alarming possibility, 'do you want to show me the scene of the crime?'

'But of course.'

The professor stood and indicated with a sweep of his arm that Kennedy should follow him.

3

The picture of the museum's storerooms that Kennedy had had in her mind was a very romantic one, she now realised. She'd imagined vast underground halls with Gothic arched ceilings but ultra-modern steel doors like the doors of bank vaults. Either that or the colossal warehouse of the first Indiana Jones movie, with endless wonders sealed and stacked in endless identical packing crates: an Aladdin's Cave in camouflage colours.

The reality was much more mundane. The main storage facility wasn't even on the museum site: it was an entirely separate building, Ryegate House, on St Peter's Street in Islington, ten minutes away by cab. Kennedy wondered briefly why, in that case, Gassan had brought her to the British Museum at all, but the answer was obvious. He wanted to show off his good fortune, the prestige of his brand-new job, and he clearly felt that the Great Court made a better stage than the place they were now heading for.

He was right. The building in front of which the cab rolled to a stop was an anonymous brutalist block with a concrete façade only marginally enlivened by pebbledash. The effect might have been pleasant when the building was new: now, many of the rounded stones had fallen away, leaving recesses greened with moss. The effect was of a face pockmarked by disease.

Kennedy made some remark about the twelve-million-pound budget that Gassan had mentioned. It ought to run to a facelift, surely?

'Oh, it does,' the professor assured her earnestly. 'But we don't want to advertise what's here. We're very keen to be overlooked.'

He pointed to the sign beside the entrance. It simply read RYEGATE HOUSE, and it made no mention whatsoever of the British Museum. Yes, that had to count as effective camouflage.

Inside was a different story. The carpet in the foyer was deep and soft, and the doors were automatic, opening in front of them with a soft sigh of acquiescence. Kennedy could feel now how thick the concrete was under that erratic pebbledashing. It was there in the flatness of the acoustics, the instant deadening of all sounds both from within and from without.

The reception counter was the size of a small yacht. The woman on duty there was a stacked redhead whose white blouse was buttoned all the way up to the neck. She recognised Gassan and greeted him very civilly – even warmly – but she gave Kennedy a hesitant, searching look that bordered on open suspicion. Kennedy wondered whether the professor knew how big a hit he'd made in just one week. If the rest of the building was as keen on him as the reception desk was, he was sitting pretty.

Gassan introduced his guest with proprietorial pride. 'This is Sergeant Kennedy, Lorraine. She's here at the board's request, to investigate the break-in. Could you please buzz Glyn Thornedyke and tell him we'll need access to Room 37?'

They waited on the near side of a turnstile barrier. 'Security falls to my brief,' Gassan explained to Kennedy, 'but Thornedyke coordinates the actual rota and superintends on a day-to-day basis, reporting directly to me.' The speech seemed to Kennedy to be very much of a piece with Gassan introducing her as *sergeant*, despite the fact that she no longer had any rank at all: he liked to use the people around him as ramparts to build up his ego.

A door opened off to one side of them and a uniformed security guard appeared. He seemed to be barely out of his teens, with the overstretched rangy look that in girls is called coltish and in boys (if they're lucky) is politely overlooked. His fair hair was worn in a severe military crew cut, but his blue eyes had a baby-doll clarity of colour that undercut the effect. He all but saluted as he presented himself to Gassan.

'Rush, sir,' he said. 'Mr Thornedyke said you need me to open some doors.'

'Actually,' Kennedy said, 'I think what I really need before anything else is a tour of the building. Would that be okay, Professor?'

'By all means,' Gassan said.

The young man looked doubtful. 'I should be on the staff door,' he said. 'I should probably check in with Mr Thornedyke before I—'

'This is on my authority,' Gassan huffed, dismissing the objection. 'Sergeant Kennedy is a professional security consultant – an expert, with many years of police experience. We're very lucky to have her and we need to facilitate her investigation in any way we can.'

The tour took a lot longer than Kennedy had expected. It seemed to cover all or most of the building, but it was hard to tell because the interior structure of Ryegate House was homogenous to the point of nightmare. It consisted of dozens of more or less identical rooms, high-ceilinged, cool, with energy-efficient lighting that came on as gradual as a sunrise; hundreds of yards of corridor with ID-swipe checkpoints at every turn and angle, and occasional fire doors that closed down the corridors into short stretches like narrower rooms. There was a subtle but pervasive smell that was hard to identify. It was a little like the passenger cabin of an aeroplane, Kennedy decided at last: like the air had been recycled many times, and was going to be recycled a few times more before being allowed to go about its business.

As they trekked through the storage facility, Rush extolled its wonders. Kennedy felt that he was trying for the casual assurance of an old hand, but it sounded as though he were parroting stuff from an orientation lecture. The security systems were really good, he said. In most respects, state-of-the-art. There were pressure and breach alarms on all external doors and windows, movement sensors in most rooms and at nodal points throughout the building, full electronic records of every key usage and every entry and exit.

'CCTV?' Kennedy asked – she hadn't seen any cameras yet.

'Oh yeah, everywhere,' Rush assured her. 'But if you're looking for the cameras, you won't see them. They're built into corners, angles, mouldings and stuff. We use a system called CPTED, Sergeant Kennedy – Crime Prevention Through Environmental Design. It's like, you show people where your cameras are if you want to regulate behaviour in a big public space, right? In a shopping centre, say, or a multi-storey car park. Big Brother is watching you, sort of thing. But we camouflage our cameras, because this is a sealed facility. Nobody unauthorised is going to come through here unless they've broken in. So the CCTV is meant to catch criminals in the act.'

Including your own employees, Kennedy thought. Because conspicuous cameras would do both things – deter criminals and catch transgressions. What they wouldn't do was regulate the behaviour of people who worked with the collection on a day-to-day basis. This was a system that forestalled unpleasant surprises by treating everyone as the enemy.

What Rush never bothered to mention in the midst of all of these technological wonders was the collection itself; but as they moved from room to room, Kennedy couldn't keep her gaze from wandering, drawn by massive sculptures, Native American totem poles, bark canoes, suits of armour. The smaller items, as she'd expected, were safely stored in packing cases that lined the walls of the rooms or were neatly stacked in miles of grey-steel shelving. The big, uncompromising things were sitting right out in the open.

Room 37 was one of the least remarkable in this respect. It was full of shelf units and boxes and nothing else. They glanced inside but didn't go in, because Kennedy wasn't ready to focus in on it yet. She wanted to get a decent overview of the place first.

'Our environmental control is also state-of-the-art,' Gassan said, as they walked on. 'Temperature, humidity, light – they're all regulated and monitored in real time.'

'What are these?' Kennedy asked. She pointed to a grey box on the wall, right next to the more familiar red box that was the fire alarm. It was identical in size and shape, but was labelled SECURITY where the other was labelled FIRE. Like the fire alarm, it had a rectangular glass insert, bearing the words PRESS HERE.

'That's another security feature,' Gassan said. 'Installed by my predecessor, Dr Leopold. Breaking the glass or pressing the button triggers a lockdown. All internal doors are deactivated.

External doors and windows lock, and security shutters are lowered. It turns the building into a jailhouse, essentially.'

Rush was standing several yards further on, holding a door open for them. He fell in next to Kennedy, after Gassan had gone through. 'Not all that much use,' he told her, in a confidential murmur.

She looked at him. 'How come?'

'Well, it's manually operated, for starters. It's not tied to the movement sensors or the cameras. There's no automatic triggering.'

Sotto voce or not, Professor Gassan had overheard them. 'Because of the risk of injury to an intruder,' he said, giving Rush a look of schoolmasterly disapproval before he turned his attention back to Kennedy. 'We have legal and ethical responsibilities.'

'The alarm is linked to a local police station, sir,' Rush pointed out. 'And the average response time is twelve minutes.'

'The liability would still be ours,' said Gassan.

Rush walked on ahead again. He knew when he was beaten.

He rounded off the tour by taking them up onto the roof. He pointed out the pressure and movement alarms, CCTV rigs and the grid of outward-tilted razor wire around the whole roofspace to a height of five feet.

'This is all new,' Rush told Kennedy. 'We used to be pretty vulnerable up here. Now we're . . .' He hesitated.

'State-of-the-art?' she hazarded.

'Yeah, really. It's pretty amazing.'

Kennedy took a little wander, looking for any points of entry. There were air-conditioning ducts big enough to take a human body, but their mouths were covered by heavy metal grilles, riveted into place, and there was no sign that any of them had been touched. The door by which they'd accessed the roof was plate steel, with a combination lock, a key lock and three pad-lock-secured bolts. There wasn't even a handle on this side.

The two men were waiting patiently for her to complete her inspection. Kennedy walked to the edge of the roof, scanned the ground below and the approaches. The building had no near neighbours. It stood on its own ground, with at least six feet of clearance on all sides. No trees or telegraph poles or lamp stanchions for an intruder to shinny up. Drainpipes, obviously, but at intervals along their length Kennedy could see the spiky crowns of anti-climb brackets. She could also see the cameras swivelling back and forth on their mounts, quartering the landscape below them.

She went back to Rush and Gassan. 'You didn't catch anything on these, I assume?' she said, pointing at the cameras.

'From the night of the break-in, you mean?' Rush shook his head. 'No. We went through all the outside footage, right from when we locked the doors the night before. Nothing. Not a dicky bird.'

'Okay,' Kennedy said. 'I'm done up here. Thanks for waiting.'

'So did you figure anything out yet?' Rush asked her, almost shyly.

His faith in the detective's art was touching. 'Not yet,' Kennedy said. 'But I'd like to see the CCTV footage from Room 37 – the segment where your intruder shows up on camera. And then I'd like to go back in and take a proper look at the room itself.'

They went to the surveillance room, which was about the size of a broom closet. Rush opened up a locked steel cup-board and selected a disc from a hundred or so that were racked there.

There was only one seat, which Gassan insisted Kennedy

take, even though this meant Rush having to squat to operate the DVD playback. He slid the disc into a reader that was a blank steel slab without controls, opened up an interface window on the computer right next to it and typed in a time signature. A second window popped open on the screen: the camera playback, delivered in an area about the size of a credit card.

As the image resolved, Kennedy found herself looking at a space that could have been any one of the dozens of rooms she'd just walked through.

'Room 37,' Rush said, with just a hint of melodrama. 'Night of Monday the twenty-fourth.'

The point of view was from up near the ceiling. A shelving unit bisected the field of vision, so that they were looking down two parallel aisles. Everything was so still, the image might have been a freeze-frame except for the numbers of the time stamp cycling at top left.

'Can you make this any bigger?' Kennedy asked.

Rush fiddled with drop-down menus, but nothing happened. 'Sorry. I don't know the system that well.'

A figure came abruptly into view. Dressed from head to foot in black, with a black balaclava, it was the stereotype special ops agent of popular fiction. The eerie incongruity raised a slight prickle on Kennedy's scalp. Despite what Gassan had said earlier, it was impossible to tell whether she was looking at a man or a woman – although whoever it was must be young and strong. The figure scaled the shelf unit as though it were a ladder, pushed at something that was off-screen and then hauled itself through, out of sight.

The whole sequence covered no more than twenty seconds.

Rush rewound to the moment when the figure disappeared off the top of the screen, and froze the image.

'Ceiling panel,' he said, tapping the monitor. 'He went up into the drop ceiling.'

'And then?'

'No idea. We looked up there, but there was nothing, no trace of him.'

'And has anyone been allowed into the room since the break-in?' Kennedy asked.

'Well, we went in. The security team, I mean. Right after we saw the camera footage. Then the police came and made a search of the room. And while the police were still here, some clericals did a count to see if anything was missing – but that was under police supervision. Since then the room has been permanently off-limits.'

'Okay,' said Kennedy. 'Then I guess that's where we go next.'

4

It was at this point that Gassan peeled off, with apologies, to deal with some other work he had to finish before he left for the evening. He asked Kennedy to drop in on him when she was done with her inspection – an injunction that Kennedy pretended not to hear.

On the way down to Room 37, she tried to get Rush talking about himself. Most of the security guards she'd met had been ex-cops, ex-army or occasionally ex-criminals working on the poacher-turned-gamekeeper ticket. She was curious as to why someone would go into the job straight from school. But Rush was shy and wouldn't be drawn on that subject.

The room was just as unremarkable the second time around. Just row after row of wooden packing crates and cardboard boxes, with a stepladder leaning against one wall. There were none of the larger and more visually appealing items that had loomed above the shelf units in some of the other rooms.

Kennedy walked up and down the aisles. As she'd already been told, nothing appeared to have been touched. There were no tell-tale gaps on the shelves, no boxes out of place. Dust might have held fingerprints or indicated where something had been moved, but there was no dust. After three weeks of lockdown, the place was still spotless.

She returned to Rush, who was setting up the stepladder. 'There,' he said, pointing. 'That's where he climbed up. Cobbett and me went up to check, while we were waiting for the police to get here. Then the police sent their own people up, so I can't say nothing has been disturbed.'

He gave Kennedy an electric torch, which he'd brought with him from the CCTV room, and held the ladder steady while she ascended.

'Mind how you go,' he said.

Although Kennedy was wearing trousers, she noticed that the boy was keeping his face modestly averted from her ass – except for a sidelong glance as it bobbed past his eye level. Impeccable manners. Or more likely she was just too old for him.

The dropped ceiling was made of expanded polystyrene tiles in a rigid metal grid. She pressed her hands against the tile that Rush had indicated, pushing it up and then aside. From the top of the ladder, she was able to thrust her head and shoulders through into the narrow space above her. There was, she could see now, a gap of about three feet separating the drop ceiling from the real ceiling above.

She flashed the torch. It revealed an airless and featureless expanse only a couple of feet high but identical in its lateral dimensions, as far as she could tell by eye, with the room below. There were no vents, ducts, holes or grilles through which the intruder could have escaped.

'Am I missing something?' Kennedy called down to Rush. 'It doesn't look to me like there's any exit from up here.'

'We didn't find one either,' he shouted back. 'Walls are solid. Ceiling is solid. If he found a hole up there, he pulled it in after him.'

Kennedy did one more circuit with the torch, looking not for the intruder's escape route now but for anything even slightly out of place. There was nothing. She leaned forward to take a closer look at the nearest wall, which was just within her reach. She rapped her knuckles against it. Solid.

'Is it brick all the way round?' she called to Rush. 'No plasterboard?'

'No plasterboard. No voids. No hidden panels. Nothing but what you see, Sergeant.'

She looked down through the hole, meeting Rush's curious, slightly nervous gaze. 'It's not "Sergeant",' she said. 'Not any more.'

'Oh. Okay.'

'Heather will do fine.'

'Okay.'

There didn't seem to be any more sights worth seeing up in the ceiling space, so she came back down. When she was back on terra firma, she asked Rush to talk her through the whole sequence of events from the moment when the break-in was discovered.

He thought about it. 'There isn't that much to tell, to be honest,' he said. 'We found the knife – you heard about the knife, right? – first thing on Tuesday morning. But the break-in was the night before. The time signature on that footage you saw is 11.58 p.m.'

'How was the knife found?' she asked him. 'Do you check every room every day?'

'Yeah, we do. The duty officer clocks on at 6 a.m., signs the rest of us off on the rota and briefs us about anything special. Then we do vee-twos – visual verifications – of every room. I don't mean on the cameras, I mean we actually walk around the building. Steve Furness found the knife just lying on the floor there. Five- or six-inch blade. Really, really sharp. And it had been used. There was blood on it.'

'Did they find out whose?'

Rush shook his head. 'I suppose they tested it. But they didn't tell us what they found. Obviously we looked for a body, but there wasn't anything. Not even any more blood – only what was on the knife. Nobody was missing from our staff, or from the area – and you can see from the footage that the guy's not carting a body along with him when he leaves.'

'He doesn't seem to be carrying anything much.'

'No,' Rush agreed. 'And you know we didn't find anything missing. But the thing is, you're talking about hundreds of thousands of items, maybe even millions, and some of them are really tiny. Something could go missing and not be spotted for a long time. The clericals checked that all the boxes were still there and that the access seals on the important stuff hadn't been broken.'

'Is everything sealed?'

'No. Just the most valuable bits and pieces. Maybe ten, fifteen per cent of the collection. They did vee-twos on all of that stuff. But it's still possible they could have missed something. It's more than possible.'

Kennedy paced the room, looking from the shelf units to the ceiling and back again. 'How many cameras are in here?' she asked.

'Two.'

'Fixed?'

'All our cameras are fixed, Sergeant . . . Heather. If they were on swivel mounts, they'd have to be out in the open.'

She knew that she was missing something, some anomaly that was nuzzling at the edge of her attention. She decided to leave it there for now and let it announce itself in its own sweet time, rather than risk scaring it away by lunging for it.

'Did anything else happen on Monday or Tuesday?' she asked.

'Nothing that's relevant.'

'Forget relevance. What else was on your mind that day?'

Rush thought about that question for a moment or two. 'Mark Silver,' he said at last.

'Who?'

'One of the other security guys. He died on Sunday night, as it turned out. We found out about it on the Monday.'

'Died how?'

'Drunk driver hit him on a pelican crossing. Monday afternoon, some of the reception staff were going round taking up a collection. There was a pretty sombre mood. It was only a few weeks after Dr Leopold – he was the director before Professor Gassan – had his stroke. Everyone was talking about how bad news comes in threes. The break-in that night was number three.'

'This guy Silver was a friend of yours?'

'No. Not really. I knew him, but I never really talked to him much. I just felt bad that he died in such a stupid way.'

Kennedy asked a few more anodyne questions, steering the conversation back into emotionally neutral territory. None of this was coming together yet, but she could see that the boy found the topic distressing, and she didn't see any reason to make him dwell on it. 'Thanks for all your help,' she said at last. 'Tomorrow I'd like to look at the staff logs and staff profiles. I'm also going to do interviews with everyone who was on duty on that Monday. Could you drop into Professor Gassan's office and tell him that?'

'Okay,' Rush said. 'Sure. Or I could take you over there and you could tell him yourself.'

'No need,' she said quickly. 'I'm happy for you to pass the word along.'

*

As Kennedy left Ryegate House, three people watched her.

The first two were sitting in a silver Ford Mondeo – the most popular colour of a hugely popular car – fifty yards down from the building's front entrance. They were inconspicuously, even drably dressed, but there was a quiet intensity about them that compelled a second glance.

They waited while Kennedy flagged down a cab, and while the cab accelerated past them back towards the city centre. Then the man in the driver's seat started up the engine and eased in behind the taxi, with elaborate casualness. The man beside him checked the street, with a practised eye, to see if they were watched.

They were, but he didn't perceive that they were. Much further away, Diema stared down from the roof of a lock-up garage, through foliage that hid her from stray glances but gave her a more or less unimpeded view of the part of the street that concerned her.

She didn't follow. She was there to monitor for now, and to assess risk. Her current assessment was that there was very little. Neither Kennedy herself nor the people watching her were aware of Diema's presence, or that their own surveillance had been enfolded into something much larger.

When the time came to act, Diema would act. Those upon whom she acted would not see her coming.

5

When Kennedy got back to Izzy's apartment, let herself in and walked through to the living room, it was to the sound of these words: 'Oh God, I want you. I want you inside me, right now. Would you like that, baby? Would you like to fill me up? I bet I could take you, all the way ...'

This would have been alarming if Izzy hadn't been sitting right there in front of her, alone, watching *Coronation Street* with the sound turned down. She held her mobile in one hand, a mug of strong Yorkshire tea in the other, and though her face was screwed up into a grimace of arousal and urgency, she was draped over the chair in a very relaxed pose.

She was at work, in other words. Coaxing a stranger over the edge of the orgasmic precipice at the bargain rate of 80p a minute plus VAT. Since both of her hands were occupied, she waved to Kennedy with her left leg. *Tea in the pot*, she mouthed, raising the cup and nodding at it.

Kennedy didn't feel like tea. She fixed herself a whisky and water – in full stealth mode, making no sound that the phone might pick up. She took it through into the bedroom, shrugged her bag from her shoulder and let it fall onto the bed. She slumped down beside it, kicked off her shoes and stretched out full-length, resting her head against the annoying wrought-iron scrollwork of Izzy's headboard.

There was a TV in the bedroom, too. Automatically, she turned it on, just for the comfort of the sound. But it was set to ITV, like the one in the lounge, and the seventeenth retelling of how Frank Foster raped Carla Connor on the night before their wedding grated slightly on her soul. She surfed channels, bounced off a nature documentary and a stultifying studio quiz show before settling on the news.

As she lay there, she realised it was the knife that intrigued her most. Without that, the break-in was just a locked room puzzle – and most locked room puzzles had fairly mundane explanations once you cut away the dross. But the knife meant something else. There could be another, more serious crime dangling off the end of this investigation. She just didn't know what it could possibly be yet.

The TV news seemed to be all bad. A fire at a country house in the north of England had left a dozen people dead, even though the place was meant to be derelict. The police suspected arson. A terrorist group had planted a bomb in a German church and set it off during a Sunday mass. And a ground-to-air missile, accidentally launched from an IDF battery outside of Jerusalem, had sailed straight over the Dome of the Rock before it exploded in mid-air – and had therefore come within about a hangnail's width of starting the bloodiest religious war since the Third Crusade.

Too much. Too much craziness. She turned the box off again and focused her mind on Ryegate House. She would do the obvious things first, just so she could cross them off. Most obvious of all was Ralph Prentice.

Prentice picked up on the third ring, but he was brusque. 'I'm elbow deep in work, Heather. Short and sweet, or I'm hanging up.'

Since he worked in the police morgue attached to New Scotland Yard's forensics annexe on Dean Farrar Street, Kennedy tried not to think about what exactly it was that his elbows were deep in.

'Last month, Ralph. Night of Monday the twenty-fourth, into the Tuesday morning. Did you see any corpses presenting with knife wounds?'

A chair scraped and there was a barrage of rhythmical clicks at the other end of the line.

'No,' he said. 'According to the big book of everything, that was a pretty quiet night. Last quiet night I can remember. It's been apocalyptic since.'

'It has? Why?' Kennedy was interested in spite of herself. It was an unusual word for Prentice, normally a master of understatement, to use.

'Car bomb in Surrey Street. Aggravated shooting in Richmond. And then that fire in Yorkshire. You heard about that, right? Incendiary bombs – very professional kit, by all accounts. Anything with possible terrorist links, we've got a reciprocal arrangement. So a lot of our people are stuck up there, helping the local plod to count footprints.'

'But no knives.'

'Not for a while, to be honest. Plenty of random unpleasantness, but a bit of a lull in incised wounds.'

'Can you do me a favour, Ralph?'

'You mean, besides talking to you? Given how high they bounced you, Heather, this right here is already a favour.'

'I know. And I'm grateful. Really. But I'm trying to pin something down here and there's nobody else I can ask.'

Prentice sniffed. 'No, I should imagine not.' He didn't bother to say 'because you don't have any friends left in your own department': it was too obvious to need saying. Kennedy

41

had given evidence against two Met colleagues involved in an unlawful shooting, then lost two partners in quick succession in appalling bloodbaths. The bloodbaths were none of her fault, but in most people's eyes she was a snitch *and* a jinx. By the time they'd forced her out, it was a formality. Nobody would have agreed to work with her in any case.

She waited Prentice out. They'd had a really good relationship back when she was in the Met, and Kennedy had been careful not to presume on it too much since. By her own estimation, she still had plenty of emotional capital to draw on.

'Go on, then,' the forensics officer muttered at last. 'What do you need, Heather?'

'See if anything's come in from any of the hospitals,' she said. 'Malicious wounding, with a bladed weapon.'

'Same time frame?'

'Same time frame. Last Monday, or a day or so later.'

'Just London?'

'If you can pull the regionals, too, that would be great.'

'What did your last slave die of, Heather?'

'Sexual ecstasy, Ralph. That's what does for them all, in the end.'

Prentice sighed. 'I think it'll be cholesterol with me,' he said glumly. 'I'll see what I can do.'

The other easy call was to a man Kennedy knew by the name of Jonathan Partridge. He was an engineer who'd studied materials science at MIT. He was also a polymath who liked puzzles and he'd helped Kennedy out on a number of occasions with odd insights and esoteric connections. But Partridge wasn't home. All she could do was leave a message, after the Thatcher-esque matronly voice of the voicemail loop invited her to do so.

As she hung up, Izzy came into the room, grinning evilly and tapping her watch. 'Two and a half minutes,' she gloated. 'Counting from "What do they call you, lover?" to "Ohgodohgodohgod!" I wish talking dirty was an Olympic event. I could make my country proud.'

Kennedy lowered her phone. 'Don't you get paid by the minute?' she asked.

'Yeah. Of course I do.'

'Then the quicker you get the guy where he wants to go, the less you get paid.'

Izzy threw herself on the bed next to Kennedy and snuggled in close. 'It's not about the money, babe,' she said. 'I'm a professional.'

'Of course.'

'And my standards are very high.'

'I know that.'

'It's like you wouldn't respect a bullfighter who left a bull hanging on in agony instead of finishing it off.'

'Right. Because that would be inhumane.'

'Exactly. Or in a cockfight, if you got the cock all psyched up for the fight, and then—'

'Could we,' Kennedy asked, 'move away from the animal comparisons?'

Izzy rolled over on top of her and then sat up, smiling down at her, straddling her waist. 'But I didn't get to the bucking bronco.'

Kennedy raised the phone, like a barrister presenting evidence in court. 'I'm working,' she said.

'Uh-uh.' Izzy shook her head, still playful. 'When I'm on the phone, I'm working. When you're on the phone, you're getting other people to work for you.'

'Like you get other people to come for you,' Kennedy said.

43

Once it was said, it sounded a lot colder than when it was inside her head.

'Well, that's the name of the game, babe.' Izzy took one last shot at salvaging the mood: 'You want to help me beat my record?'

Kennedy felt claustrophobic, trapped not by Izzy's weight on top of her (which she could bear very easily; had often rejoiced in bearing) but by the invitation to pretend an easy intimacy that she couldn't feel right then. She hesitated. Words assembled themselves on her tongue that her mind refused to parse. She was about to say something horribly hurtful and destructive.

The phone saved her. It vibrated in her hand, giving off a sound like a hornet trapped under a glass. Kennedy shrugged a half-hearted apology to Izzy, who climbed off her and sat back.

'That was fast,' Kennedy said, after seeing the caller display.

'What can I do for you, ex-sergeant?' John Partridge asked.

She made a show of hesitation. 'Well, it's a big favour, John.' She let the words hang in the air for a moment, to see whether he'd stop her or encourage her.

'Go on, Heather. Coyness doesn't become you.'

That was all the encouragement she needed. She gave him a thumbnail sketch of the case, then came right to the point. 'You used to work at Swansea, didn't you, John?'

'I was in charge of their post-grad physics programme for three halcyon years. Before the Tories, when they still had funding. Why do you ask?'

'Do you think they'd let you borrow the Kelvin probe?'

Partridge laughed – a short, incredulous bark. 'It's not a case of borrowing the Kelvin, ex-sergeant. It's just a big barcode scanner with a computer attached. But there's no point having

44

the Kelvin without an operator. And those ladies and gentlemen are like the saints of a new religion. Generally whatever time they take off from research is booked six months in advance.'

'Okay,' she said. 'No harm in asking.'

'I didn't say no,' he pointed out. 'I'll see what I can do. But they'll laugh their legs off when I tell them they're investigating a break-in. Mass murders are more their style.'

'Thanks so much, John. You're an angel.'

'Fallen. Say hello to your lady love for me.'

'I will.' Kennedy hesitated. 'How's Leo these days?'

'Quiet.'

'That's good, right?'

'No, that's just Leo. He's quiet when he's bad, too. But in this instance, I think he's quiet because he's working. So perhaps "non-existent" would have been a better word. I haven't heard from him in months. If you need to get a message to him, though, there's a café in Clerkenwell that he uses as a poste restante. You're one of the three people I'm officially allowed to give the address to.'

'No need, thanks. But send him my love, next time you see him.'

'I will. And I'll let you know about the probe.' The line went dead: Partridge considered the formalities of leave-taking a waste of time.

'So what's the job?' Izzy asked. Kennedy looked up to see her leaning against the door frame, arms folded. The earlier flirtatiousness was gone. Izzy had had time to disengage and she clearly wasn't going to risk rejection a second time.

'It's hard to say,' Kennedy admitted. 'Investigating a crime that may not have happened.'

'I love it already. Tell me over a drink?'

*

45

They went to the Cask, on Charlwood Street. It was a fairly pricey pub, but it was close, and this early in the evening, it would still be possible to find a seat.

The conversation was desultory. After telling Izzy the basics, Kennedy stonewalled on all her questions. If she'd had the energy or the imagination to come up with another topic, she would have, but nothing occurred to her: Izzy tried to keep the conversation going on her own, but eventually they just wound down.

A few minutes into the silence, Izzy put out a hand and touched Kennedy's forearm.

'We're breaking up, aren't we?' she said. Her voice was calm, even resigned.

Kennedy stared at her. 'I don't know what we're doing,' she answered.

Izzy shook her head. 'Oh babe, you've got ninja lying skills, but not with me. You can't even look me in the eye any more. I'm talking to you and you're planning your getaway, right here.'

'I'm not planning anything, Izzy.'

'Okay, then do something for me.'

'What?'

'Kiss me.'

Kennedy looked around at the other tables, about half of which were occupied. 'We kind of stand out,' she said.

'Since when did you care? Kiss me or piss off, Heather. Don't hang around my place making me pay, day in and day out, because you're too lazy to pack a bag.'

To pack a bag? Kennedy's clothes, CDs and personal accoutrements had migrated slowly up the stairs to Izzy's place over a period of months. The point at which she'd moved in hadn't been formally marked. She'd assumed that her exit would be

46

similarly protracted: storming out and slamming the door so gradually that you'd need a stop-motion camera to catch it.

As soon as she realised that, she was ashamed, because everything that Izzy was saying was true. On the other hand, she reflected, it was also true that Izzy had been playing away – and with a man. So it was hard to sit there and take the lecture as though she had it coming.

'I don't know what we're doing,' she said again. 'Seriously, Izzy, I've been too busy trying to scrape together some work. But if I'd found the time, I guess I'd have thought that you might be prepared to give me the space, since it was you that was sleeping around.'

Izzy grimaced. 'Sleeping around? It was one guy. I was drunk, and I was horny, and I let one guy pick me up. I was alone for the best part of two years before you came along. I got pretty casual about stuff like that.'

Kennedy said nothing, but she let her feelings about this statement show on her face.

'I'm not a slut,' Izzy said.

'No.'

'When I don't have a partner, I still have a need to get laid every once in a while. I don't think that's a crime.'

'When you don't have a partner,' Kennedy said, 'then no, it isn't. But you've got me.'

'And it was a shitty thing to do, and I cried, and I said I was sorry – and I kicked the poor guy out without his shoes, if I remember right.'

'But on the upside, he got to keep his balls.'

Izzy grinned faintly at that, although Kennedy wasn't joking. If she'd still had her ARU licence, still had her gun, she might have done something stupid. She could picture it very easily. More easily than she could get her head around what

47

actually happened, which was that she stood there like a deer on the freeway and watched the knock-kneed little jerk haul his pants on, looking from her to Izzy and back again like he was trying to work out some equation in his head and he kept getting the square root of *huh*?

'I don't know what else I can do,' Izzy resumed. 'If you would've just unfrozen and let me back in, I think maybe I could have convinced you that I really do love you – and that a roll under the duvet with Shoeless Joe Jackson wasn't ever going to change that. But you didn't, so I couldn't, and here we are.' Her eyes were bright with tears by the time she finished this speech. One of them was starting to roll down her cheek.

'Wherever here is,' Kennedy said.

'Babe, we both know exactly where here is.'

Kennedy stood. They both had unfinished drinks, but the thought of having to carry on with the conversation just in order to finish them was suddenly unbearable. 'I'll sleep downstairs tonight,' she said, like someone saying *the time of death was 11.43 p.m.* 'I'll come and get my stuff tomorrow.'

'Or else we go back right now,' Izzy said, 'and I screw you so hard your brain melts and you don't remember what you were even mad at me for.'

'I . . .' Kennedy couldn't find any words. 'Izzy . . .'

'No,' Izzy said, holding up her hands in surrender. 'No need. No worries. I just thought it needed to be said. Do what you feel, Heather. And you hold that moral high ground against all comers, okay? You'll be fine so long as the oxygen holds out.'

The last words were hard to make out because she was crying so hard. Izzy turned and headed quickly for the door, ricocheting off an empty chair, then barging a guy whose expansive gestures put his almost-full pint directly in her path. The man's arm shook and beer slopped onto the floor.

'Clumsy bitch!' he shouted after her. 'Don't bloody drink it if you can't handle it.'

It was the sort of blunt-edged insult that Kennedy normally found easy to ignore. Normally, but not tonight. She took hold of the top of his glass and tipped it so that the rest of the pint was dumped over his END OF THE ROAD T-shirt. Then she brought her face up close to his. 'Words to live by,' she said.

The guy was still yelling as she left the pub and she half-expected him to follow her, but the look in her eyes as she stared him down had probably been a pretty scary one. There were no footsteps behind her.

And no Izzy up ahead.

Kennedy looked around, bewildered. She'd only been twenty seconds behind, and the street was clear in both directions. To the left, where Izzy should have gone, scaffold sheeting flapped around the fascia of the Windsor Court Hotel, whose SOON TO OPEN UNDER NEW MANAGEMENT sign was itself now in need of renovation. To the right, silent Georgian terraces extended into the middle distance, their doors raised above street level by steep arcades of steps, like a chorus line of dancing girls lifting their dresses to do a can-can.

The scrape of a heel on stone made her turn back towards the hotel, and this time she saw what she had missed. There was a body lying on the ground there, half-under the scaffolding that covered the whole front of the building.

Kennedy cried out and ran. In seconds she was kneeling beside the still form. It was Izzy, lying on her back, arms and legs asymmetrically sprawled. Her head was in deep shadow, but Kennedy knew her by a hundred other signs.

Don't move the body, she told herself. And the implications of that thought broke over her like a wave. *The body. Oh shit. Oh shit.* She felt for a pulse, found one, though it seemed weak. She looked for wounds and saw nothing.

'Izzy,' she babbled. 'Sweetheart, what happened?' She was rubbing Izzy's hand between hers, trying to wake her. 'What happened to you?'

Izzy didn't move or speak. She was deeply unconscious.

Kennedy got out her phone. She was dialling 999 when the scaffolding behind her head rattled, giving out a tinny music in the way that the vibrating rails next to a Tube platform announce the imminent arrival of a train.

She looked up. Over their heads, something black and angular was growing to eclipse the baleful street-lamp glow against which it was defined.

There was an instant in which to act, not time enough, really, except that Kennedy suddenly knew what this was and saw the punchline coming from a thousand Warner Bros cartoons. She threw herself on top of Izzy, gripped the lapels of her shabby-chic Marc-Jacob-alike leather jacket and rolled them both sideways with a furious, simultaneous shrug of every muscle she could enlist.

They did one complete roll, Izzy on top of her, beside her, then under her again. Right next to them, something struck the pavement like a colossal fist, the slap of impacted air hitting Kennedy full in the face. She gasped and her mouth filled with something thick and soft like talcum powder. An instant blizzard enveloped them both.

Through it, eventually, she heard voices. 'Holy *shit*.'

'My God, did you see?'

Kennedy tried to wave away the drifts and roils of white that were blinding and choking her. It had a bitter taste and it stung her eyes. As she levered herself upright, she felt a fine cakey dust crunch under her fingers. Hands came from both sides, helping her to her feet. People she vaguely recognised from the pub supported her arms, dusted off her clothes. 'Your friend,' someone exclaimed. 'Is she ...'

'I don't ...' Kennedy coughed, spat, tried again. 'I don't know how badly she's hurt. Call an ambulance. Please!'

There was a flurry of cellphones, everyone rummaging in bags and pockets and then drawing at once like the climax of a bad western.

Freed from the grip of the good Samaritans, Kennedy knelt again to examine Izzy, careful not to move her spine. The white powder, whatever it was, was settling on her face. Gently brushing it away, Kennedy found the contusion on Izzy's temple, already swelling, where she'd been hit. Horror filled her, and then white-hot anger.

She looked at what had fallen on them – or almost on them. It was lying a scant few inches from Izzy's head: a builder's pallet, with twelve sacks of cement piled on it, loosely tied with a single loop of rope. Some of the bags had ruptured. That was what was floating in the air and insinuating itself into their lungs.

It was the sort of thing that could look like a terrible accident, but clearly it was nothing of the kind. It was an ambush, hastily but efficiently improvised. Presumably the original plan had been to catch the both of them as they left the Cask and walked home together. But Izzy had left first, and the fact that she'd been enlisted as bait made it absolutely clear that Kennedy herself was the real target.

She looked up at the scaffolding above their heads. Nothing moved there, and it seemed unlikely that whoever had dropped the pallet had stayed to watch the after-effects. There was a ladder running up the side of the scaffolding to the first floor. That was probably how their unseen attacker had got up there. But he certainly hadn't come down again that way.

Kennedy picked a man almost at random, one of a group who all had the meticulously groomed scruffiness of students. She gripped his arm and pointed at Izzy. 'Don't let anyone touch her,' she said. 'Stay close to her until I get back. You and your friends. Stay with her. Surround her. Do you understand me?'

'All right,' the man said, 'but we don't—'

Kennedy didn't hear what else he said. She ran up the steps to the hotel entrance. A panel of thick particle board had been put there in place of the original door, but someone had prised it loose along the left-hand edge and pulled it away from the wall. She was able to squeeze in.

Nothing inside but darkness and silence. Kennedy stood still, listening, but heard only her own breathing. When her eyes had adjusted to the dark, she moved forward. The main stairs were right ahead of her. She rummaged in her bag until she found the pistol-grip pepper spray she always kept there. It was a military-issue Wildfire – illegal in the UK, but not nearly so illegal as an unlicensed gun.

She went for speed rather than stealth, taking the stairs three at a time. On the first floor, then the second, she paused and looked around. After the second, there was nowhere else to go – except the roof, presumably, and the stairs didn't go up that far.

She stepped aside into a patch of shadow. Light from the street lamp outside, which was level with the windows of these upstairs rooms, turned the scene in front of her into a black and white mosaic.

She'd just about decided that she was wasting her time

when something moved. It moved to the left of her, where there was nothing except the wall of the stairwell. It was a shadow: whatever had cast it was outside, on the top-most level of scaffolding. A window frame rattled and then creaked as it was opened from outside.

Kennedy waited until the man was halfway over the sill before she rushed him. She gave him a shot of the pepper spray right in the eyes, but a black mask covered his entire face and he didn't even react. He just dropped and twisted, turning the movement into a surprisingly graceful roll, and then he was inside the room with her.

She aimed a blow at his stomach as he scrambled to his feet, but the punch didn't connect. He leaned away from it with incredible speed, catching Kennedy's arm above and below the elbow, pulling her forward right off her balance and throwing her. She came down hard on the floorboards, stunned.

Through blurred, tearing eyes, she saw the man standing over her. He took something from his belt and she knew from the way it flashed in the yellow-white glow from the street lamp – dull-bright-dull, inside of a second – that it was a knife. She raised a clumsy block, but she couldn't protect her whole body, and stretched out on the floor as she was, she made an unmissable target. She was dead.

But the knife didn't come down. The man was staggering, clawing at his mask. The pepper spray had soaked through at last. It was burning his eyes and cutting off his breath, and because it was in the fabric of the mask there was no way for him to get away from it.

Kennedy got her feet under her and stood, but even blinded and hurting, he heard her step back. He advanced in a step-shuffle gait into the space she vacated, pressing her hard until the wall was right up against her shoulder blades.

Then he kicked her through it.

His foot connected with Kennedy's chest, with so much force behind it that it would probably have staved in her ribs if she'd been leaning against brick. But she was leaning against thin, stale, crumbly plaster pasted over wafer-thin laths. She went staggering and sprawling through into the next room, fell on her back and rolled aside, expecting him to follow through.

Nothing came through the wall. She got to her feet and staggered to the ragged-edged hole, cradling her chest and trying to suck in some air.

The man was gone. Kennedy pushed and stumbled her way back through to the room where they'd fought. Something lay on the floor, a dark and shapeless mass. Kennedy went to it and picked it up, then winced and held it far away from her face. Sodden, limp, sour with the stench of oleorosin, it was the man's face-mask, and he'd torn it half to ribbons in his haste to get it off.

On the street, the innocent bystanders had mostly dispersed like ghosts at cock-crow, their civic duty done and their curiosity satisfied, but the small group of students who Kennedy had summarily deputised stood in a slightly sheepish defensive ring around Izzy, who was still unconscious. Kennedy thanked them and released them back into civilian life. Then there was nothing else to do but wait until the ambulance arrived.

Izzy revived before the ambulance got to them. After a few seconds of not knowing where she was or what the hell was going on, she sat up – ignoring Kennedy's attempts to stop her – rubbed her eyes and looked around. She coughed, licked her lips and grimaced as she tasted the cement dust that had accreted on them.

'If you're trying to kill me for the insurance money, babe,' she said hoarsely, 'there isn't any. Hard to believe, but I'm worth more alive.'

Kennedy hugged her close. 'Shut up,' she muttered.

They were like that for a long time, sitting on the edge of the pavement, Izzy leaning awkwardly into Kennedy's embrace, as the dust settled all around them. A distant siren whooped and then was silent again, maybe their own ambulance, on its way.

'I like this,' Izzy murmured, her head pressed tight against Kennedy's bruised and aching chest. 'I like this a lot. I should have got the crap beaten out of me ages ago.'

6

Glyn Thornedyke, the security coordinator at Ryegate House, was a sort of corpulent wraith, badly overweight but pale and insubstantial and clearly very unwell. He seemed surprised that his approval was needed for a mass interrogation of the facility's staff – and in retrospect, Kennedy was sorry that she'd taken the time to ask him. It was already almost ten and her eyes had that itchy feeling that comes with the more serious kinds of tiredness. Giving statements to the police had kept both her and Izzy up until long after midnight. Then other things had kept them up. As a result, Kennedy felt both exhausted and full of urgency – a feeling like she needed to catch a bus that had already left.

'I'm going to want all the staff files,' she told Thornedyke. 'Hard copy or digital, whatever's quicker.'

'Yes. Very well.' Thornedyke cast his eye across the files and papers on his desk as though he suspected that what Kennedy was asking for might turn out to be right there in front of him. She wondered what kind of turf wars he'd already fought with Gassan – the professor had been very keen to claim the overview of site security as part of his own brief. 'I can certainly provide physical copies. Will you need anything else?'

The tone was balanced between hope and trepidation. Clearly, Thornedyke wanted her to say no and go away.

Kennedy had to disappoint him. 'Yes, Mr Thornedyke. I'll also want an office to conduct the interviews in. And someone to feed people through to me. I don't know anyone's face or where they work.'

'I can't allocate you a room,' Thornedyke said plaintively. 'Rooms are booked through the front desk. And if you take someone from my staff, I'll have a hole in the rota.'

'Well, how about if I take Ben Rush?' Kennedy said.

'The probationer?'

'Yeah. Him. Would that be a hole you can live with?'

Thornedyke thought about it. 'I suppose so. Yes. So long as it's just for one day.'

'Great. He'll come and collect the files from you as soon as I'm ready.'

The security coordinator still didn't look all that happy, but Kennedy left before he could raise any more objections.

Professor Gassan, only too eager to be of assistance – and maybe to demonstrate the size of his new empire – gave her the main boardroom to work out of. The space was about as big as a football field, with a conference table so long and wide it had obviously had to be brought up from the street in sections and assembled like a jigsaw. It was a vanity table, designed to make museum executives feel like they were wheeling and dealing in a serious, corporate world. The deep-pile carpet and thick, pleated curtains were identical shades of oatmeal.

Gassan also approved Kennedy's loan of Rush for the day, and the gangly boy turned up about fifteen minutes later with an armload of manila folders. He dumped them down on the table and mopped his brow, miming exhaustion.

'Thanks, Rush. Okay, you're seconded to me for the day. I hope that's okay. It's indoor work with no heavy lifting.'

Rush nodded equably. 'A change is as good as a rest.'

'Okay, then. I'm going to take an hour or so to go through these files and make notes. After that, I'll ask you to bring people in, one at a time, and act as chaperone while I interview them. In the meantime, did you get breakfast yet?'

Rush shrugged. 'Cup of tea. Round of toast.'

'Most important meal of the day, Rush. Is there anywhere around here that does coffee and bagels?'

Rush nodded. 'Sam Widge's, on Gerrard Road.'

'Lox and cream cheese and double espresso for me. Dealer's choice for you.'

She gave him a twenty pound note, and he was off.

The personnel files were as bare and banal as she expected them to be, and Kennedy was able to get through them easily inside the hour she'd allowed. The coffee helped. The flaccid bridge roll – 'no bagels left, sorry' – not so much.

All of Ryegate House's staff, both full-time and part-time, had impeccable employment records. None of them had any spent convictions or debt problems, or at least, any that had showed up at the fairly superficial level of investigation that the museum deployed. Most had been here since before the flood, and almost everyone above the entry level had been promoted internally.

On the face of it, a closet with no skeletons.

So Kennedy narrowed her search, looking for repeating patterns. It was standard police procedure with any possibility of conspiracy – or where you wanted to eliminate that possibility – to look for the common ground in which it could have grown: if two or more of the Ryegate House staffers had attended the same school or college, had worked together in another context, or were members of the same club or society, it would have been worth following up. But they didn't, hadn't, weren't. The only thing they had in common was Ryegate House itself.

Kennedy took a different tack, looking for hobbies or work experience that might translate into burglary skills. Not much there: two of the security team were ex-army, but their background – Royal Corps of Transport and Household Guard – didn't suggest that either had seen much in the way of special ops training.

Finally, without much more sense of direction than she'd had when she started out, she pushed the stack of files across the table at Rush. 'Shuffle and deal,' she said. 'Put them into some sort of order that makes sense to you and then feed them through to me one at a time.'

He seemed nervous with that much responsibility. 'Is alphabetical okay?' he asked.

'No,' said Kennedy, on an impulse. 'Surprise me.'

The next few hours were gruelling. With no steer from her, Rush sent in the top brass first. The topmost brass – excluding Emil Gassan – was a Valerie Parminter, who bore the title of Assistant Director. She was in her fifties and austerely attractive, with a well-maintained figure and pink-tinted hair that made a virtue of its unnaturalness. To judge from her face, she saw this interview as a huge affront to her dignity.

Parminter's responses to Kennedy's questions began as sparse sentences, but quickly degenerated into monosyllables. Her face said: I have to endure this, but I don't have to hide my contempt for it.

Kennedy went for the jugular without a qualm.

'So,' she said, 'this happened on your watch, so to speak. In the period between the departure of the old director and the arrival of Professor Gassan.'

Parminter stared at her, a cold, indignant stare. 'I don't think the timing is relevant to anything,' she said.

'Ah,' Kennedy said.

Those who live by the monosyllable shall die by the monosyllable. Parminter waited for more, and when it wasn't forthcoming she voided her hurt feelings into the accusing silence. 'For the record,' she said acidly, 'I suggested a full security review nine months ago. Dr Leopold said he'd take that under advisement. Which of course meant he'd sweep it under the carpet and forget it.'

'You had concerns about the adequacy of the security arrangements,' Kennedy summarised, scribbling notes as she spoke.

Parminter shifted in her seat. 'Yes.'

'But you only raised them on that one occasion. A pity, given the way things turned out.'

'I was ignored! You can only beat your head against a brick wall so many times.'

Kennedy pursed her lips. 'And these concerns. You voiced them in an email? A memo?'

'No.'

'At a minuted meeting, then.'

'No.' Parminter looked exasperated. 'It was a private conversation.'

'Which Dr Leopold will corroborate?'

The older woman laughed, astonished, indignant, faux-amused, but with a nervous edge underneath these things. 'Dr Leopold suffered a massive stroke. He can't even talk. But I'm not on trial here. Security is the Director's remit.'

'Of course,' Kennedy agreed. 'Nobody is on trial here. It's just that I was asked to submit a report on staff awareness and efficiency, in addition to the case-specific inquiry. I want to make sure I do you full justice.'

So start talking.

'This is absurd,' Parminter protested.

Kennedy shrugged sympathetically. 'I know.'

'We had a spate of attempted break-ins,' Parminter said. 'A cluster, all together, around seven months ago.'

'Attempted?'

'Yes.'

'No actual loss or damage?'

'No. But it made us all aware that in some ways we were falling short of best practice. I'd been on a course the year before where there were talks on how you should go about protecting very small and very valuable items.

'I pointed out to Dr Leopold that some museums and archives use a double-blind system for storage. When an item has to be brought out of the stacks into any other part of the building, a requisition form has to be filled in first. Assistants use the item code to generate a physical address from the computer and the box is brought up from the stacks, sealed. The curator who requested the box knows what's in it, but not where it is. The assistant knows where it is, but not what's in it.'

'Which has the effect of . . .'

'It makes targeted theft impossible. Our system, by contrast, depends on physical barriers and deterrents. Which are fine until somebody figures out a way to bypass them. And when they do, they know exactly where to look. Well, except for the books, of course.'

'The books?'

'The legacy collection from the old British Library. That's what Room 37 is full of, isn't it?'

Kennedy's interest quickened, despite the woman's lecturing delivery. Gassan had said that the British Library and the

British Museum used to share the same premises. At the time, she'd wondered where that random factoid had come from. 'Why?' she asked. 'What makes the books different?'

'Well, we don't have an extant catalogue for them,' Parminter said, as though stating the blindingly obvious. 'The catalogue and all the access codes went to the new library building on Euston Road. If they wanted to find a specific book, they'd have to give us a physical location – room, rack, position, box number. The only alternative would be to search every box until you found it.' The older woman smiled. 'It's ironic, really.'

'Is it?' Kennedy asked. 'How?'

'Well, the lack of a physical address means we've achieved a level of security for those books that goes beyond anything we've got for the other artefacts. And yet the books – at least the ones that were left with us after the move – are the least valuable part of the collection.'

'I'm not sure that counts as irony, exactly,' Kennedy said. 'But I take your point. Ms Parminter, what do you think the intruder was after?'

'Whatever he could get his hands on.' The answer sounded flip, but it was spoken with a definite emphasis.

'What, you don't think he had a plan? A specific target?'

'No. I don't.'

'Why is that?'

Parminter almost sneered. 'Well, let's just say that if he did, and if he ended up in that wing, in that room, he must have taken a wrong turning.' She stood up, without asking Kennedy if the interview was over, and headed for the door.

'He'd have had better luck going through our rubbish,' she said over her shoulder.

*

Before Kennedy could get to interviewee number two, Izzy called. She was still on the train.

'Hey, you,' Izzy said, trying to sound jaunty through the misery and the hurt. 'What you up to right now? Smiting evil-doers?'

'Interviewing witnesses,' Kennedy said. 'Smiting comes later. I thought you'd be there by now.'

'Train got held up outside Leicester. We'll be pulling in soon.'

There was a pregnant silence. 'Give them my love,' Kennedy said, for want of anything else to say that actually had any kind of a meaning attached.

'Obviously,' Izzy said. *They* were Izzy's brother Simon, his homophobic wife Caroline, who crossed her legs whenever Kennedy entered the room as though she feared her vagina was under direct threat, and their weirdly quiet but other-wise okay kids Hayley and Richard. They lived in a well-to-do suburb of Leicester, kept rabbits, and – considered as a family unit – had a Stepford kind of serenity that Kennedy observed with perplexity and mild suspicion. Caroline was something in the City, but at long-distance, making crazy money in a locked room at the top of the house that contained only a desk, a computer and three phones. Simon looked after the kids, the rabbits, the house and pretty much everything else.

It had been Kennedy's idea that Izzy should spend some time with her only sibling and his family – or at least, that she should get some distance from Kennedy until Kennedy was able to establish which chicken from her former life was coming home to roost. It had to be that. There was no con-ceivable way that the attack could have anything to do with her work at Ryegate House, which had barely begun. It was only the timing – and the unsettling visual echo of the black stealth-suit, so like the one she'd seen in the CCTV footage. But even if the Ryegate House intruder was crazy enough, and desperate enough, to commit a murder in order to hide a theft, there was no way that Kennedy presented a credible enough threat to motivate an attack like that. She knew nothing, had no leads and no ideas.

Izzy had been full of indignation and derision at the suggestion that she needed to be protected; but she thought it was hot as hell that Kennedy wanted to protect her, be her knight in shining armour. Once they were back in the comfort and privacy of Izzy's flat, the sex they'd had on the back of that particular conversation had reached heights and depths that surprised both of them.

But when it was over, and they were lying across each other in a snarl of knotted sheets like the victims of some very localised tornado, both of the elephants – the relationship one and the near-death-experience one – were still in the room. One hour of sweaty apotheosis didn't mean they were safely over the dead ground. And the fresh bandage on Izzy's forehead was a potent reminder that someone had just tried to cement their fate with actual cement.

Kennedy came up with the idea of a trial separation – partly so they could figure out how they felt about each other, partly so that Izzy could get out of harm's way while Kennedy tried to find out where the harm was coming from and shut it down.

It was a hard sell for Izzy. The great sex, and Kennedy's protectiveness, had completely changed her prognosis for the relationship. Now she wanted to capitalise on these game-changing events and get Kennedy to tell her that she was forgiven. 'Don't ask me to go to bloody Leicester!' she pleaded.

'I can stay out of trouble right here. I'll go and stay with Pauline and Kes, down in Brixton.'

'Too close, too current,' Kennedy told her bluntly. 'And you'd still be seeing all the people you normally see. Anyone who was halfway trying could find you inside of a day.'

'But what about my work?'

Kennedy picked up Izzy's phone from the arm of the sofa and waved it briefly in her face before dropping it into her handbag. 'That's your work. You can do it just as well from two hundred miles away. Better, you won't be tempted to invite a regular up for a face to face.'

It was deliberately cruel – a pre-emptive bid to end the discussion. And it worked really well, as far as that went. Izzy absorbed the low blow without a word and took over the packing for herself. When she left, an hour later, they embraced, but it was clumsy and tentative.

Just like their conversation now.

'I had a thought,' Izzy said.

'What about?'

'Sleeping around.'

'Izzy—'

'Hear me out, babe. I was thinking I could set you up with someone. Someone really cute. And you could, you know, be unfaithful right back. Get it out of your system. You wouldn't even have to enjoy it. It would just relieve the tension, you know? So we could get back to being us again.'

'Izzy, that's the stupidest thing I ever heard.'

'Okay.' Izzy abandoned the notion quickly, got some distance from it. 'I thought it was stupid. I just wanted to put it out there.'

'I've got to go.'

'Okay.'

'I'll call you tonight.'

'I love you.'

Kennedy hung up and grabbed the next file.

Second Assistant Director Allan Scholl – a Boris Johnson lookalike with a mop of blond hair he obviously thought was a selling point – was a whole lot smoother than Parminter and a whole lot more courteous. But he had even less to say. He was keen to stress his pivotal role on the day the break-in was discovered. It had been him who called the police, told security to seal off the room and organised the preliminary trawl through the collection to find out what had been stolen. He'd overseen the process himself, because his PA had been away sick and although he returned that day, he got in late.

'And you found that nothing was missing?' Kennedy said.

'Nothing that we could definitely verify,' Scholl corrected her. 'We've done a more detailed search since and everything appears to be where it belongs. But it's hard to be categorical on that point.'

'Why is that, Mr Scholl?' Kennedy knew the answer, but it never hurt to seem more clueless than you actually were: the Columbo principle.

'Because there are literally millions of items in the collection. To tick every one off the list would be hugely time-consuming. And visual verification might not be enough, in some cases. If you wanted to steal a very valuable artefact, and then to sell it on, one of the things you might do would be to replace the original with a copy so that its loss went undetected. Then there are the books . . .'

'Which aren't catalogued.'

'Which *were* catalogued, but the catalogue is both massively out of date and not here. It's at Euston Road, on completely separate premises. So yes, we think we dodged the bullet, and that's our public position, as it were. But privately, I'm agnostic.'

Kennedy thought back to the CCTV image of the man in black, with the tiny shoulder bag. Whatever he'd come for, it wasn't a bulky item. And he hadn't been on a random shopping trip, either.

So her position went beyond agnosticism. She was pretty near certain that something had been taken. The intruder had been picked up on camera and had dropped a knife (after he'd used it, which was a piece that didn't seem to fit anywhere in the puzzle), but he'd still got away clean, and she had no reason to assume that his mission was aborted.

What was the mission? And who was he? And how had he gotten in and out?

And in back of those questions: did he try to kill me last night?

As she went on through the morning, she got back into the rhythm of it. In her former life as a cop, she'd been good at this stuff. She'd understood, intuitively, that it wasn't about the questions. Not at first. You kept them bland and general, and people told you what was on their mind. The questions were like Rorschach inkblots.

'I got to work late that day,' said a man with bleach-blond hair, a dancer's narrow build and intense, over-large brown eyes.

Kennedy glanced at the corresponding file. Alex Wales. She made a connection in her mind. 'So you're Mr Scholl's PA?'

The man nodded at some length, as though Kennedy had made a point he profoundly agreed with, but he said nothing. Maybe his eyes weren't too big: they were just very much darker than his face, so that they drew your gaze.

'You were away from work all day on the Monday,' Kennedy said. 'Then you got in around eleven on the Tuesday. Why was that?'

There was a silence that was long enough for her to register it as awkward. 'I have pernicious anaemia,' Wales said. 'Every so often, I get fainting fits. I take pills to keep it under control – but even with the pills, the iron level in my blood fluctuates a lot. When it's really low, I can't even get out of bed.'

'So you took the Monday off because you were ill.'

Another pause. 'I just lay there all through Monday. And Tuesday morning, too. Then I got up.'

He seemed to be picking his words with care, as though afraid of being accused of something; faking a sickie, maybe.

'What was happening when you arrived on Tuesday?' Kennedy asked him.

'You mean, what was the first thing I saw on Tuesday?'

'Yes. Exactly.'

'The police were all over the place. Going through the rooms.'

'So what did you do?'

'I went to my desk. Logged onto my computer.'

'Just like normal?'

Wales nodded. 'Yes.'

'You weren't surprised to see that massive police presence? You didn't stop to ask them what was happening?'

'I thought they were probably investigating a break-in.'

'You thought that? Right away?'

Kennedy got another long, hard look from those big, dark eyes. 'Yes. Right away.'

'What made you think that?'

'Well, it seemed like the obvious explanation. But I suppose it could have been a lot of worse things.'

'Such as?'

Silence. Stare. Wait for it.

'Well,' Alex Wales said, 'it's not like the police ever come with good news, is it?'

She was finished before she knew it.

She was expecting one more clerk or curator to step timidly across the threshold, but when the door opened it was Rush instead.

'All done,' he said.

Kennedy looked down at the remaining file, sitting by itself next to the stack of those pertaining to people she'd already seen. 'What about Mark Silver?' she asked, and memory stirred as soon as she spoke the name aloud. She answered her own question. 'Mark Silver is dead.'

Rush nodded solemnly. 'Yeah. The weekend before the break-in.'

'Traffic accident.'

'Is correct.'

'So why did you give me his file?'

'Sorry,' Rush said. 'You said to put the files in some kind of order, and you said it couldn't be just alphabetical, so I went by start date. You know, when they came on-staff here. The people you saw first were the people who'd worked here the longest. So I was looking at the dates instead of the names. Otherwise I would have taken Mark out.'

There was a silence. Kennedy couldn't think of anything to fill it with.

'Do you want me to get you some more coffee?' Rush asked her.

'I'm fine,' she said. The truth was that she was too tired to move. As though she needed some excuse to go on sitting there, she opened up the cover of Silver's file and scanned the details. Born in Birmingham, educated in Walsall and Smethwick, and then buggered off to join the British Army on the Rhine. Obviously Mark had felt the need to shake off the dust of his home town and get out into the big world. Couldn't blame him for that.

As her gaze wandered across the page, Kennedy was struck by a mild sense of déjà vu. It was something recent, too. Dredging up the memory, she checked Silver's file against one of the others she'd just been looking at. Not a perfect match, but close enough. In order of start date, Rush had said.

Kennedy looked up at him. He was giving her a slightly puzzled stare, watching the expressions chasing each other across her face. 'Those break-ins,' she said.

'Break-in, you mean. Singular.'

'No. The other ones. The abortive attempts.'

Rush frowned. 'Oh, right. Those. That was a while ago now. We added some external cameras, up on the roof – you saw them yesterday. Whoever it was, they didn't come back.'

'Right.'

She almost had it now. Had some of it, anyway. Change the perspective, and the impossible becomes banal. Was that Columbo again, or Sherlock Holmes?

'Get your keys out,' she told Rush. 'I want to take another look at the room.'

7

Eight parallel aisles of boxes. No empty spaces on the shelves, although Gassan had told her the room was only at one third of its capacity. That was the first thing.

'So some of these boxes don't have anything in them, right?' Kennedy asked Rush.

'All the ones from about the end of aisle C onwards,' he confirmed. 'The clericals normally fill the space up from the front. But there's probably a few more empty boxes mixed in with the full ones – spaces that didn't get filled or things that were moved to new locations and left a gap.'

'So why bother to have boxes with nothing in them?'

Rush gave this question some thought. 'I suppose it's got some value as a smokescreen,' he said at last.

'You mean because it forces a burglar to open every box?'

'Yeah. But I think it was more about space, to be honest. The boxes are rigid, reinforced sides, high quality. They don't come flat-packed. So where else would we stack them? It'd be stupid to have rooms set aside for empty boxes when we can just fill the shelves here and then have everything set up ready for new stuff as it comes in.'

Kennedy nodded. 'Yeah. That *would* be stupid.'

She got Rush to show her the two fixed cameras, and with

his help she paced out the areas of the room that would be visible to each of them. The negative space, where the cameras couldn't see, was where she began.

He watched her for a while, opening boxes and peering into them. He was perplexed. 'Those ones are empty,' he told her.

'Yeah,' Kennedy agreed. 'And I bet nobody bothered to search them, right?'

'I don't know. There wouldn't be much point, would there?'

'Depends what you're looking for.'

Rush waited for more, but Kennedy didn't have any more to say. If she was wrong, she might as well be wrong off the record. There were hundreds of empty boxes on the endless shelves. The full ones were all the same size, since they all had the same contents: books from the British Library overspill. The empty boxes had just been put wherever there was space to put them, so they came in a variety of sizes to reflect the infinite variety of items in the museum's collection.

Kennedy was only bothering to open the largest ones, and she struck gold before she'd gotten halfway along aisle D.

She beckoned Rush over and pointed into the open box. He stared down and his eyes widened. The box contained a black sweater and a pair of black leggings. Black boots. A black balaclava designed to cover the entire face. And a large quantity of what looked like ash.

'Jesus,' he exclaimed. 'I don't get it. Is that what the intruder was wearing?'

'Yeah,' Kennedy said. 'It is.'

'Then why is it still here? We saw him leave the room.'

'No. We didn't. We saw him climb up into the ceiling space. But we both know there's no way out from up there. So whatever we saw, it wasn't the great escape. It was something else.'

Kennedy was still piecing it all together in her mind, but the fact that she'd gotten this part right gave her confidence to pursue the other, more elusive aspects of the crime. If it even *was* a crime.

'The room's been locked and off-limits ever since the day after the break-in,' she said – a statement rather than a question.

'Yeah,' Rush confirmed. 'I already told you that.'

'Clerical assistants did a tally of the contents, but they were watched the whole time. Nobody's been allowed to come in here alone.'

'Except the police.'

'Except the police. Take a note of the box number, would you, Rush? And then close up here. Leave everything exactly as it is.'

'Right.'

'And don't say a word to anyone.'

'Right.' He blinked rapidly, gave her a guarded look.

'I'll talk to the professor,' Kennedy said. 'And to Thornedyke. I'm not asking you to lie to your boss. Just don't talk to anyone else on the staff here, okay? Word will spread around, our suspect will get to hear about it, and then we'll be screwed. I think this is our chance to break this case.'

Rush seemed to like the word *our*, but he had to ask. 'We've got a suspect? As of when?'

'As of about five minutes ago. I won't give you a name – not just yet. If you see this person, you're going to need to behave absolutely normally, so as not to put them on their guard. But I promise you'll be the first to know after the professor.'

Back in the boardroom, Kennedy picked out the two relevant files and took them down to Gassan's office. She dropped them onto his desk and stood with arms folded while he read the names.

Gassan looked up at her, with blank amazement on his face. 'You're not saying these two had anything to do with the break-in?'

'Actually, Professor, I'm saying they did it. And I believe I know how they did it. One inside, one outside – probably the only way it could be done. But I need your help for the next part.'

'Which is?'

'Figuring out what it was they did.'

Gassan rubbed his forehead, as though he had a slight headache. Clearly the news that the break-in might have been an inside job didn't thrill him. He looked from one file to the other, then back to the first. 'I hate to point out the flaw in your reasoning, Heather,' he said at last, 'but Mark Silver was already dead when the break-in occurred. You must be mistaken.'

'Maybe,' she allowed. 'Get me the swipe records for that day and we'll know. Because if I'm right, they'll both have swiped out at the same time on the night of—'

Kennedy's phone played a few bars of ersatz jazz – an incoming text, not a call – and she paused while she checked the message. It was from John Partridge and it was good news.

Swansea said yes. Kelvin probe plus operator. One day only. Tomorrow.

She took the files back from Gassan. 'You don't have to believe me,' she said. 'Just let me run with it. We'll know a lot more tomorrow. Because tomorrow, we'll be able to go where they went. See what they looked at, what they touched. Find out what they took, if they took anything.'

Gassan looked at her with a very patrician scepticism, as though she'd just tried to sell him a timeshare. 'And how will we do that? By magic?'

'Pretty much,' Kennedy said.

8

'Isobel and Heather aren't here right now, but if you've got a message, go ahead and leave it after the beep. We'll be right back at you.'

Nobody had a message. There was no red light on the phone's base unit. Kennedy had only pressed the playback key so that she could hear Izzy's voice. The flat was haunted by her absence – an anti-poltergeist of inimical stillness.

She wandered from the living room into the bedroom, back out into the hall. None of these places felt as though they wanted her.

Ever since she first found out what gypsies were, back when she was about seven, Kennedy had nursed a secret fantasy that involved ditching everything except the clothes she stood up in and going on the road. When she was down, she tended to see rooms as prisons. That feeling came back to her now, stronger than it had ever been.

She took out her phone, looked at it as though expecting it to ring, or else defying it to. It didn't, but she noticed another text that she hadn't registered when she read Partridge's. It was from Ralph Prentice.

Might have something for you on the knife wounds. Just checking it out now. Probably be in touch tomorrow.

She keyed in Izzy's number, let her thumb hover over the call button for a good long while.

But in the end, she just put it back in her pocket.

The evening was a mausoleum. Kennedy tried – in quick, futile succession – to watch TV, read a book and tidy the flat. Her mind refused to focus down on anything. She ate supper – a defrosted lasagne and two stiff whiskies – then lay on the bed fully clothed, staring up at the plaster ceiling rose. The insane events of the night before sat undigested in her mind. Now that she'd seen it up close, the resemblance between the outfit modelled by the Ryegate House burglar and the one her own attacker had worn was even closer than she'd thought at first. Black is black, but the design of the balaclava was identical to the one she'd held in her hands after the attack on her and Izzy.

She had to face the possibility that someone wanted to halt her investigation – at a time when she barely had one. And wanted it badly enough to kill her. That thought shook loose a very disturbing memory. She'd met some people once who thought nothing of killing for a book. She really, really didn't want to meet them again.

The heat was oppressive. Kennedy went through into the living room and fixed herself another drink, then sat in front of the open window to feel the breeze. A thick bank of cloud hid the moon, but there were a few stars visible high up near the zenith of the sky. She imagined she was looking down from there – a psychological technique taught her by a crisis counsellor after the incident that had cost her the licence to carry. The exercise was meant to encourage a healthy decentring, putting your own problems in perspective. Kennedy found it useless in that respect, but it did give her a pleasant, mild sense of vertigo.

While she was still sitting there, trying to get lost in inconsequential thoughts as a defence against the scary ones, the end of the cloud bank unrolled with slow theatricality from the face of the moon. In its sudden spotlight, Kennedy saw something move on the roof of the building opposite. It was only for a second. Probably a cat, or nothing at all, a piece of garbage light enough to be lifted on the wind. Except that it was moving against the wind.

As casually as she could manage, Kennedy took another sip of her drink, set the glass aside and ambled away from the window, out of the door of the room into the hallway that ran the length of Izzy's flat. As soon as she was through the door and out of any possible line of sight from the roof, she sprinted down the hallway, took the stairs three at a time and got to the street door inside of twenty seconds.

Then she slowed and walked out onto the street at a casual pace, her head down, trusting to the darkness to cover her. She strolled away down the street, turned the corner, quickly crossed the road and took an alley that led behind the buildings on the opposite side.

The building directly facing Izzy's was another residential block. Kennedy was in luck: a teenaged boy and girl walked out of the back door as she approached it, and the girl obligingly held it open for her.

She found the stairs and climbed them, quickly but quietly. At the very top, there was an emergency door that led out onto the roof. Conveniently close to hand, a fire extinguisher sat in a niche on the wall. It was of the black CO_2 type, small enough and solid enough to make a reasonably good weapon. Kennedy snatched it up and slammed the door open.

And found she was facing the wrong way. The door opened towards the rear of the building, not its front. In the echo of the door's slamming, there were some other sounds – a scrape of stone or gravel, and then a rustling insinuation that died away quickly.

She ran out onto the roof and around the low housing in which the fire door was set. There was nothing else obstructing her view and no sign of anyone or anything that shouldn't be there.

Still wired, still suspicious, she patrolled the length of the roof, looking across directly at the windows of Izzy's flat. She could see where she'd been sitting, her empty glass still on the sill, and she tried to work out from that where the movement would have been.

She found it, in the end. The surface of the roof was gravel laid on green mineral felt and a small area of it bore both the scuff of footprints and the indentations of someone sitting or kneeling there for a long time.

Not paranoia. She was being watched.

And it seemed like the watcher must have wings, because there was no other way off the roof that she could see.

9

Partridge was waiting outside Ryegate House's main entrance when Kennedy arrived the next morning, with the smallest dog-end she had ever seen wedged between his index and fore-finger. He had two companions, both standing nervously upwind of Partridge's cigarette: a shy, slightly fey-looking young man and a serious, bespectacled woman, both in their early twenties and dressed in what looked like their Sunday best. Partridge himself wore a shabby donkey jacket over a plain white T-shirt and dark-blue trousers with more pockets than anyone could actually need. He took Kennedy's hand and greeted her with old-world civility.

Then he introduced the other two: 'Kathleen Sturdy and William Price, of the University of Swansea's School of Engineering.' They were standing to either side of a solid-looking steel box with rows of handles bolted to its sides and foam-rubber chocks affixed to each corner.

'This is the Kelvin probe?' Kennedy asked.

'This is just the scanning head,' Partridge said. 'There are a lot more components. They're parked in a van three streets away – closest we could get. My God, I hate this city.'

'That just makes you a bigger hero, John.' Kennedy turned

to the young man and woman. 'And I assume you two are the operators. Thanks so much for taking the time to do this.'

'Actually, we're graduate students,' the woman – Kathleen – answered. Her voice had a Welsh accent so delicate and musical that it sounded as though she were reciting a poem. 'But we're qualified to use the probe. We're both doing research in force microscopy.'

'And the university couldn't spare anyone from the faculty,' Partridge summed up. 'So William and Kathy kindly agreed to come down to the Smoke for the day and help you out. In exchange for their travelling expenses and a small per diem.'

'Of course,' Kennedy said. 'I'm grateful to you both. Really. This is just wonderful.' She didn't think Emil Gassan would object to the extra expense, but if he did, she would meet it herself out of the money she'd already been paid.

'Let's go in,' she suggested. 'I'll see about getting you some coffee, and then I'll explain what it is I need.'

'We might just as well skip the coffee,' Partridge suggested, as the two students hefted the steel case by its evenly spaced handles and raised it between them like pallbearers raising a coffin, 'and get straight down to business.'

But they couldn't do that without explaining to Gassan, and he was rattled all over again when he realised what he was signing up to. 'Are we sure that this is legal, Heather?' he asked, drawing Kennedy aside. 'It sounds as though it might raise issues of privacy and freedom of information.'

'These are your premises,' she explained. 'All we're doing is examining them for evidence of unauthorised access. We're not assuming criminality, only trespass. We're going to look around Room 37 and find out what was done there. Then when we brace our suspect, we'll have some ammunition. This

81

was a professional job, Emil. He won't cave, he'll stonewall you to the last inch. If you want to have any chance of finding out what happened that night, you'll need to have a good part of the answer before you ask the question.'

She waited while Gassan thought it through, but she knew she was right and she didn't have any doubt as to what he'd eventually decide. 'All right,' he said at last. 'Let's do this.'

At Kennedy's suggestion, they brought Rush in to help the two students ferry the rest of the components from Partridge's van. While they were unpacking and setting up, Kennedy tried to explain to Gassan what the probe actually did, but very soon ran into the limits of her own understanding, and Partridge had to come to her rescue.

'In the 1980s,' he told Gassan, 'two Swiss scientists developed a new kind of microscope, one that could scan at an atomic level. They called it AFM, atomic force microscopy. And they did great things with it. It could resolve images down to nanometer scales, with enormous accuracy. The only problem was that the image size, even for a single-pass scan, was colossal. So unless you were looking at incredibly tiny areas, it wasn't feasible to use an AFM device.'

Away in the background, Kennedy could see Rush standing a little aside from the students. He was helping them whenever they needed him, passing them components from the boxes, holding the main body of the probe steady while Sturdy or Price connected a cable or a bracket to it. It was obvious that he was attracted to Sturdy – and that he had no chance at all because Sturdy and Price were already an item. *The follies of youth*, Kennedy thought.

She wrenched her attention back to Partridge, who was still talking about the Kelvin probe and its short but illustrious history. 'But then,' he said, 'the University of Swansea got stuck into the original design and started to come up with some really sweet variations. They more or less invented a science called nanopotentiometry. It measures minute changes in electrical potential. The probe looks at the conductivity of an object's surface. It creates a map of that electrical potential.'

Gassan was nodding, but his eyes were a little glazed.

'You can use it for fingerprints,' Kennedy told him, cutting to the chase. 'It does a million other things, too, but for police it's a fingerprint machine.'

Partridge looked pained at this oversimplification, but he nodded. 'Traditional fingerprinting produces an image using oily residues from the skin surface. But those same residues alter the electro-magnetic profile of any object that you touch with your hands. So the Kelvin probe cuts out the middle man and looks at the conductivity of the object's surface. It creates a map of electrical potential – on which fingerprints stand out like mile-high beacon fires. No need for developing or resolving agents. No need to touch the surface at all, so no danger of destroying or contaminating other kinds of evidence like DNA while you're looking for a latent print. And you can programme it to recognise and respond to a specific print – your prime suspect, say. It's like a magic lamp. Except it's bloody hard to use, because you've got to adjust the sensitivity of the reader to a minute degree of accuracy to screen out other kinds of random or systemic variation in the electric field forces. Hence these two enthusiastic young people working their arses off in uncomplaining silence behind me.'

Kathy Sturdy and Will Price looked up, awkward and embarrassed, as Partridge gave them this accolade. They'd unpacked the components of the probe and assembled it beside its steel housing. Now Price was adjusting brackets and screws on its outer case, while Sturdy was taking readings from a small tablet computer that she'd attached to the device via an HDMI cable. Rush watched them, or at least he watched Sturdy, his expression rapt.

The scanning Kelvin probe didn't look like a magic lamp. It didn't look like a microscope, either. It looked like an artist's impression of a vacuum cleaner from a sci-fi pulp published before vacuum cleaners had actually been invented. Every single component looked ramshackle and jury-rigged. The only high-tech thing about it was the image on the tablet PC, which formed and reformed itself out of bright-green grid lines from moment to moment.

Sturdy tweaked the image using virtual slide controls over-laid on it. She did this for a long time, before finally nodding to Price. He took the business end of the device – a scanning head about as long and thick as a foot ruler, attached to a three-metre length of cable – and ran it across a fire extin-guisher mounted on the wall beside him.

The screen blanked, the gridlines reassembled themselves and a new image appeared. It was hard to make out what it was. Its planes of coagulated colour defied interpretation, until Sturdy, with a sweep of her hand across one of the sliders, caused the image to zoom out wide, revealing the curved sur-face of the fire extinguisher.

She zoomed in again and the surface dissolved into level upon level of fractal complexity.

'Twenty?' Price muttered to her. 'Twenty-five?'

'Twenty-five,' she confirmed. 'I'm going to heighten the con-trast by half a per cent.'

'Okay. Shall I hold steady?'

'No, slow sweep. There. Up. Up by a couple of ... stop.'

Price was pointing the scanner at the base of the fire

extinguisher. Sturdy tapped and stroked with the tip of her index finger on the virtual controls. The screen blanked and remade itself in squares of a couple of centimetres on a side, settling to a preset level of magnification. Kennedy and Gassan found themselves staring at the raised whorls and ridges of a fingerprint.

'And Bob's your uncle,' said Partridge, with some satisfaction.

'My word,' said Gassan, after a pause for genuine awe.

'But that's only the first battle,' Kennedy reminded him – and the students. 'There are going to be lots of prints in here. We're looking for a particular set, and we're going to give you a match in advance. Rush?'

'Oh. Right.' Rush reluctantly tore his gaze away from Sturdy. He reached into his pocket and removed a stainless steel fountain pen in a plastic evidence baggie. Kennedy had told him to go for something metallic if he could. The greater the electrical conductivity of a surface, the better the Kelvin scanner worked on it.

She took the bag and handed it to Sturdy. 'How does this part work?' Rush asked the student.

'We find a print on the pen,' she said, holding the bag gingerly by its corner, 'and we enter it on the recognition software. Then we set the scanner to ignore anything that isn't a match. Hopefully we'll be able to get a full print off the pen, because then we've got the widest range for identifying partials.'

Kennedy turned to Professor Gassan. 'And from that,' she said to him, 'we make an action-map of the room. We find out exactly where your intruder went and what he touched.'

'Although that still won't tell us if anything was taken,' Gassan said doubtfully. 'As we already discussed, Heather, this room is overspill from the British Library collection. We don't have a catalogue.'

'You busy, Rush?' Kennedy asked.

Rush's head snapped up. 'Me?' he said.

'You.'

'I . . . no. I'm good. What do you want?'

'Go get me a catalogue,' Kennedy told him.

10

It took three hours. Nobody at the British Library seemed to have the slightest idea what Rush was talking about when he mentioned the relic collection at Ryegate House. Or else they did, but they didn't see any reason to let his problem become their crisis.

Finally, a bored clerical assistant found a third-generation photocopy of some pages marked on the first sheet in scrawled handwriting with the single word BOXED. 'It might be this,' he said.

It looked right, because it was broken down by room and the rooms were thirty-four to forty-one. It also looked piss-poor, because it was *only* broken down by room – not by aisle or box. But it was the best Rush was going to get, so he took it and went back to Ryegate House.

He found Partridge and the two students still scanning Room 37 while Kennedy was walking along the aisles laying Post-it notes down on the floor or affixing them to the shelf units, marking up the places where the Kelvin probe had already found matching fingerprints. Professor Gassan seemed to be present in a supervisory capacity – standing in a corner and watching with a mixture of fascination and concern.

Rush gave Kennedy the list and waited for her to fulminate in her turn, but she seemed unsurprised. She just nodded and handed it back to him.

'Not a lot of use,' he observed.

'No,' Kennedy said. 'But I'd have been really surprised at this stage to get anything better.' She glanced across at Sturdy and Price, who'd reached the end of the last shelf unit and were now scanning the further wall. 'We're almost done,' she said. 'We'll go over this stuff right here, then we'll bring our suspect up to the boardroom and brace him. I want you there, Rush – and Professor Gassan, and maybe your boss, Thornedyke. Apart from that, we're still saying nothing to everyone else until we've got the full story.'

'Okay,' Rush said.

At the other end of the room, Sturdy looked around at them and waited politely to be taken notice of. 'I think we're finished,' she said.

Kennedy went over and conferred with her, while Rush scanned the room. For the first time, he thought about what it was he was seeing here: a three-dimensional map of the intruder's movements around this space. Or maybe four-dimensional, since the clustering of the Post-it notes presumably indicated how long he'd spent in each part of the room.

He looked at Kennedy, who had caught his glance and read it correctly. 'It's interesting, isn't it?' she said. 'Everything comes back to this one area.' She indicated the very end of aisle B, where Post-its grew in bristling thickets. 'Whatever our intruder was interested in, it was definitely somewhere in this stretch. But he didn't know exactly where.'

'Seven boxes were handled extensively,' Sturdy chimed in. 'These seven here, all sequential, all grouped together. The rest weren't touched at all, except for this one, right next to the others – a broad palm-print, which I think might mean that it was pushed to one side, out of the way.'

She looked at Kennedy as she said this, a little nervously, as though hypothesising might be Kennedy's prerogative. Kennedy nodded encouragement. 'That's what I'd have said. So?'

'So he knew what he was looking for, but not exactly where it was.'

Because he was working from this list, Rush realised, suddenly. *And it breaks the books down by room, but not by box. Maybe he started at a random point, or maybe he took a guess based on the length of the overall list and the position on the list of the thing he wanted.*

Which meant . . .

It came to Rush, then, that he'd had the whole thing arse-backwards all this time. He'd been assuming that the intruder had passed through Room 37 on his way out of the building and that his real business had been conducted somewhere else. But the clustering was a smoking gun.

The intruder was after a book, or maybe several books.

'And the fact that he stopped after seven boxes,' Kennedy pointed out, their thoughts running on parallel tracks, 'means that he got what he came for.'

'In box seven.'

'This one.' Kennedy laid her hand on the lid of it. 'Emil, do you mind?'

'Of course, of course.' Gassan had been absorbing all this in fascinated, perturbed silence. He waved her on hurriedly. Kennedy opened up the box and slid out the first volume. It wasn't really a book: it was a slender pamphlet, the paper foxed with age and ragged along every edge, in a stiff Mylar sleeve.

She held it up and showed it to them all. It was hard to tell what the title was. Everything was in the same font, but in a wide variety of point sizes, with italics thrown in seemingly at random.

A New-yeers Gift
FOR THE

PARLIAMENT
AND

ARMIE:
SHEWING,
What the KINGLY *Power is;*
And that the CAUSE of those
They call

DIGGERS
Is the life and marrow of that Cause
the Parliament hath Declared for,
and the Army Fought for

'A New Year's gift for the Parliament,' Kennedy read aloud.

'By Gerrard Winstanley,' Gassan finished.

Kennedy scanned down the cover. 'Yeah,' she confirmed. 'That's the one. Do you know him?'

'Winstanley was a Digger. They were proto-communists, at the time of the English Civil War. They believed in shared ownership of the land.'

Rush consulted the list. He found the pamphlet reasonably quickly. 'Middle of the seventeenth century,' he confirmed. 'Sixteen fifty-two, according to this.'

Kennedy went back to the box and fished out the next book. Another pamphlet, very similar to the first both in appearance and in general condition: *The Law of Freedom in a Platform*, Rush read over her shoulder. She slid it back and took out another book, square-bound and obviously a lot more modern, entitled *Political and Religious Extremism in the Interregnum*. She turned it sideways on to read the catalogue number on its spine.

'We might be in luck,' she said. 'It looks as though the books were put in the box in catalogue order. Now that we've got the list to cross-reference against, we've got a good chance of figuring out if anything is missing.'

'Then let's continue,' Gassan said. He took the list from Rush's hands, laying claim to it.

Kennedy took the box, Gassan read aloud from the list, Rush, Price and Sturdy watched in solemn silence and John Partridge retired into a corner of the room to light up a strictly illegal cigarette. It only took them ten minutes to get to the first missing item.

> Title: *A Trumpet Speaking Judgment, or God's Plan Revealed in Sundry Signes*
> Author: Johann Toller
> Catalogue number: 174583/762
> Date: 1658

It was the only missing item. From there to the end of the box, everything was in apple-pie order.

Rush was amazed. Mostly at the power and versatility of the Kelvin probe, but underneath that, he was amazed that anyone would go to so much trouble for a book.

'I suppose it's valuable,' Kennedy mused. 'It's getting on for four hundred years old.'

'Which is nothing,' Partridge said drily. 'I don't know very much about the antiques business, obviously – not my field at all – but at a generous estimate I'd say that a book from that time would be worth … well, no more than a hundred thousand pounds or so. Professor Gassan, would you agree?'

'I'm hardly an expert on the market value of these things,' Gassan protested. 'But I'd be surprised if that book was insured for more than fifty or sixty thousand.'

Rush thought about that. There were any number of other books in the box whose worth was likely to be at least as great, and they didn't weigh all that much, so it would have been easy for the intruder to grab a handful of them and hit the road.

But they all knew, from the evidence of the fingerprints, that that wasn't what had happened. You search through seven boxes, take one item, then stop: obviously, that one item was what you came for.

And then what? You *burn* it? Because what Rush had seen in that other box, a couple of aisles over, was definitely ash.

Gassan was looking at Kennedy expectantly. Now that she'd brought off this miracle, his expectations of her were clearly running very high.

'Very well, Heather,' he said. 'You've gathered your evidence. I presume you have a plan for how to use it?'

'I think we're ready to meet our suspect,' Kennedy said. 'We'll need to use the boardroom again.'

'The boardroom?' Gassan frowned. 'Perhaps my office would be more discreet?'

'I bet it would,' Kennedy agreed. 'But I don't see any harm in having a little shock and awe on our side.'

11

'You started here six months ago,' Kennedy said.

She'd positioned Alex Wales so he'd get the full court-of-the-star-chamber effect, his chair facing theirs across the intimidating rampart of the boardroom table. Kennedy herself, Emil Gassan and the security guy, Thornedyke, sat in a row more or less at the centre of the long table. On Kennedy's orders, Rush stood off to one side, right at Wales's shoulder, to ram home how serious and official this all was. But Wales didn't seem troubled. There was nothing in his bearing that suggested he had anything to hide. He stood erect, ignoring the chair, arms at his sides and head slightly lowered, like an actor at an audition.

'Yes,' he confirmed.

'And prior to that, you were working at the British Library.' Rush thought the 'prior' was a nice touch. Kennedy was going for a forensic style.

'Yes,' Wales said again.

'But you didn't say so on your application. You hid that connection, even though it might have been considered relevant experience. Why was that?'

'I wasn't there for very long,' Wales said, with a shrug. 'And I left for private reasons. Reasons that were nothing to do with my conditions of employment. I didn't really want to answer questions about that.'

'Right,' Kennedy agreed. 'And what about your friend, Mark Silver? What was his reason for not saying that he'd worked there?'

Wales looked to Professor Gassan, and then to Thornedyke, as though the question were unfair and he expected that one or other of them might step in to defend him. 'Mark Silver wasn't my friend,' he said. The heavy emphasis on the last word left them to infer that there was a relationship there, but it wasn't one he was going to elaborate on without being asked.

'No?' Kennedy's tone was politely sceptical. 'You arrived at the British Library together. You worked together. You left together. Then you both got jobs here within a few weeks of each other.'

'Did we?' Wales asked. 'Mark must have worked in a different department from me.'

'He was a security guard,' Kennedy said. 'It would have been hard to miss him.'

Wales didn't answer – but then, she hadn't phrased it as a question.

'There was actually a gap in time between the two of you resigning from your jobs at the library and the start of your employment here,' Kennedy took up again.

'I was out of work for seven weeks,' Wales said.

'And in that gap – back in February – there were a number of attempts to break into Ryegate House. Attempts that failed.'

'Really?'

'Really.'

'There's nothing to link me to those attempts,' Wales said.

'Maybe not,' Kennedy allowed.

She glanced at the file in front of her, flicked through its pages and checked them against another sheet on the desk: a yellow carbon copy from a multi-part document.

'But I was curious about the timing,' she said, 'and I wondered whether either you or Mark Silver had any prior convictions for breaking and entering. I didn't want to rely on something that might turn out to be complete coincidence. So I went back to the police background check that the Library ran on you when you started there. Do you know what I found?'

'I've never been in any trouble with the police.'

'Alex Wales has never been in any trouble with the police,' Kennedy corrected him. 'But you're not him, are you? The real Alex Wales lived in Preston, until he left home three years ago, aged sixteen. His family reported him missing, but that was as far as it went. A routine security search would only be looking for convictions, so it wouldn't pick up that missing persons report. You were safe unless the real Alex Wales popped up and asked for his identity back, and what were the odds of that?'

Kennedy stood. 'I want to show you something,' she said, crossing to a far corner of the room, where an object stood swathed in a green tarpaulin. She hauled the tarpaulin away and threw it aside, revealing a large cardboard box.

Wales stared at the box. A frown suffused his face in slow motion. Encouraged, Kennedy let the silence stretch out until it was really uncomfortable, but Wales said nothing.

'So there were those attempted break-ins, back in February,' Kennedy resumed at last. 'And then there was an actual break-in, a few weeks ago. Quite a professional one. The police couldn't offer any explanation as to how someone had managed to get past all the security to waltz into a locked room. The answer, of course, is that he didn't. The burglar was already in the building when the annexe closed for the night. Already in the room, in fact. Curled up inside that box.'

Wales smiled coldly. 'That doesn't seem very likely,' he said.

'No,' Kennedy agreed. 'It doesn't, does it? You'd expect the swipe records to show that someone didn't go home that night. A Friday night, for the record.'

'The break-in took place on Monday night or Tuesday morning.' It was the first time Professor Gassan had spoken. He looked a little out of his depth, clearly not fully briefed, but trying to seem as though he were on top of everything anyway.

Kennedy gave the professor a brief glance, shook her head. 'No, Professor, it didn't. That's how it looked. But it only looked that way because it went wrong. Mr Wales here got into position on Friday, just before the evening lockdown. He swiped into Room 37 at 4.53 p.m. Seven minutes later, right on time, he swiped out for the day and – to all appearances – went home. But you didn't, did you, Mr Wales? You handed your swipe card to your friend Mark Silver at the door of Room 37. He swiped you out at the end of the day, while you went to the box, carefully chosen to be outside the field of vision of the two CCTV cameras, climbed inside and waited for everything to go quiet. Easy enough to arrange, and so long as Silver chooses his moment, nobody's likely to notice one man swiping out with two cards, one after the other. All he had to do was swipe out as himself, then curse as though the machine didn't recognise the card and swipe out again as you.'

Kennedy opened the lid of the box and tilted it to show the interior to Wales, and then to each of the others in turn.

She turned it in her hands so that they could see the discarded clothes and the thin layer of ash around and under them.

Wales murmured something under his breath. Rush couldn't be sure, but it sounded like a foreign language.

Kennedy stared at the man curiously. 'What did you say?'

Wales didn't answer.

'Not much to show for a three-day occupancy,' she went on, tapping the box. 'Did you fit yourself with a catheter or were you just wearing a nappy? Either way, it still meant three days without eating or drinking too much, because there's a limit to what you can carry away with you.'

Wales met Kennedy's gaze full on. 'There are limits to most things,' he said. His bland tone undercut the implied threat.

'Mr Wales wanted to be alone with the books, for however long it took,' Kennedy said, ignoring the remark. 'His intention – his sole purpose for being there – was to search, box by box, for a particular item. Once he'd found it, all he had to do was to wait out the weekend. Because at start of day on Monday, Mark Silver was going to come back, swipe Wales in at the main entrance, then come to Room 37 to let him out.'

'Heather,' Gassan protested, 'what are we assuming here? That these two men went looking for the Toller book at the British Library and followed its trail back to here?'

'That's exactly what I'm assuming.' Kennedy was watching Wales's face, which had changed at the mention of Johann Toller – his expression becoming first more intense and then more closed and guarded. 'But all they could find at the library was the same list that Rush got for us. That got them as far as Room 37. From there on in, they were on their own.

'And that was where things started to go wrong. Because

Mark Silver didn't come back on the Monday. He'd been killed, over the course of the weekend, by a hit-and-run driver. The kind of million-to-one accident you can't plan for. Mr Wales had the book in his possession by then – the one that he'd been looking for all along—'

'*A Trumpet Speaking Judgment, or God's Plan Revealed in Sundry Signes*,' Glyn Thornedyke read aloud from the piece of notepaper in front of him, in a tone that sounded slightly pained.

'—but zero hour rolled round and Silver didn't show.' Kennedy turned back to Wales. 'You didn't know he was dead, of course, but you knew he'd miscarried. So now you had to come up with another way of getting clear.'

'I really don't understand,' Thornedyke protested. 'This book dates from the seventeenth century. I'm sure it's quite rare, but it's not as though this were a … a Gutenberg Bible or a Caxton hymnal. What was the point?'

'Yes,' Kennedy agreed. 'What was the point, Mr Wales? Care to tell us? I'm wondering about the ashes in the box, particularly. Did you steal the book or did you burn it?'

Wales had had his arms at his sides all this time. Now he folded them and bowed his head again with a sigh of what sounded like resignation.

'It would be impossible to make you understand,' he said.

'Well, we'll get to that,' Kennedy said. 'Anyway, there you were. Mission accomplished, but stuck in your box with no way of getting out again. Plan A had obviously gone up in smoke. Plan B was the knife, wasn't it? The knife with blood on it. Interesting that you were carrying a knife in the first place – and I'm sure I don't need to remind you that armed robbery is a whole different animal from breaking and entering. But anyway, the knife was what got you out of that room.

'I couldn't figure out, at first, how someone who obviously knew where the CCTV cameras were, and stayed out of their way the whole time he was in the room, would screw up so spectacularly right at the end. Screw up twice, in fact – letting the camera see him just that one time and leaving the knife behind.

'But by now, making sure you were seen was the whole point. You waited until night. Then you cut yourself – on the arm or the leg, maybe. Somewhere that wouldn't be too visible. You left the knife right out in the open where it would be certain to be found. And you walked into the eye-line of the camera, as you climbed up into the ceiling space. It was all improvised, but it was really good stuff. It looked like you were making your getaway.

'In reality, you came down in a different part of the room, where you knew the cameras couldn't see you. And all you had to do after that was to climb back into your box and wait until morning. In the morning the security team found the knife and raised the alarm, which was what you needed them to do. Because the only way you could walk out of Room 37 without Mark Silver's help was if the normal swipe-in-swipe-out restrictions had been lifted. And they had to be lifted to let the police come in and search the room.'

Kennedy had been holding the box all this time. She let it fall now and it made a hollow, funereal thud as it hit the floor.

'So that was why you weren't there on Monday, or first-thing on Tuesday morning, but then suddenly you popped up again in the middle of the day. I don't know how you picked your moment to climb out of the box. I'm guessing you just waited for silence and took a punt. Then you either walked on out before you could be challenged, or you stayed right there in the room as though you were part of the search. You had to leave your outfit in the box, but of course you'd brought a change of clothes in any case. It was just a shame that the room was sealed after that and you couldn't get back inside, unsupervised, to grab your blacks and dispose of them. Am I close?'

Wales smiled – a smile that saw what was coming and welcomed it. 'Very close,' he admitted. 'Very close indeed.'

Something was wrong.

Kennedy had questioned scores of suspects during her years in the Met, and had sat in on the questioning of many more. She'd honed her skills both at piling on the pressure and at reading the body language of the man or woman she was interrogating – because pretty much everything, in a good interrogation, comes down to the accuracy of that reading and how you let it shape the questions.

Alex Wales's body language was flat-out wrong. Fear or arrogance would both have been fine, and there was a whole range in-between that Kennedy would have recognised and known what to do with. But what Wales was radiating, despite his best efforts to disguise it, was something else entirely. It was *anticipation*.

Every now and then, he would lift himself up very slightly onto the balls of his feet, just for a moment or two, and there was a residual tension in his posture even when he was pantomiming dismay or resignation. He was tense and excited about something that was coming, something that he knew would happen soon. But Kennedy had no idea what that something was, right up to the point where she mentioned Mark Silver's death.

Then something happened to Alex Wales's eyes and Kennedy felt a jolt of pure shock rush through her from the centre on out to the extremities, as though someone had just plugged her heart into a live socket.

Wales's eyes reddened.

They became bloodshot with a suddenness that was almost surreal. It was as though blood were welling up in them like tears, waiting to be shed.

She had seen this before. *Haemolacria*. It was the side effect of kelalit, a very potent drug in the methamphetamine family. Three years earlier, back when she was still a cop, Kennedy had run across a group of people who all took the drug, and all displayed the same unsettling trait. They called themselves *Elohim*, or Messengers, and they were the holy assassins of a secret tribe of humanity – the Judas People. It occurred to Kennedy now that when Wales had seen the ashes in the box, when he'd murmured under his breath, his expression had changed – become for a moment much more serious, even solemn. He'd looked like a man in church, kneeling at the altar for holy communion. And she was sure that whatever it was he'd said, he'd been speaking to the ashes, rather than to anyone else in the room.

If Alex Wales was on kelalit, the reddening of his eyes indicated that his system was preparing for sudden, violent action. The drug would give him the speed and the strength to kill like a demon unleashed from hell.

She knew this because she had seen it happen. She had watched her own partner cut down by one of these monsters – had faced them herself, in a case where their conscienceless atrocities had been triggered by something as banal and trivial as the translation of a lost gospel. So if she and Gassan and Thornedyke and poor puppy-like Rush were going to survive past the next few seconds, Kennedy would have to pull something out of her ass real fast.

And in the meantime, she just kept talking. Because if Wales had wanted to kill them straight out, they'd be dead already. There had to be something else he wanted, too.

'You had me guessing, at first,' Kennedy said, improvising recklessly, 'about the target. The book. What was so special about it. Why you'd gone to all that trouble to find it and acquire it. False identities. Breaking and entering. Camping out in a box. Then I realised that it might not be about the book at all.'

Wales scowled in slow motion. Obviously that guess had gone way wide. It *was* all about the book. But Wales was still listening.

You want to know what we know, Kennedy thought. *You want to be absolutely sure we're still blind before you pull the plug on this. Or else you want to know who else, besides us, has to be taken down.*

And maybe it would slow you down a little if you thought that might be a long list.

'So at this point,' she said, pushing back her chair and standing up, 'I started to call in some favours. People I still knew in the Met. Academics. Acquaintances in the intelligence community. I shared data with friends and gave them the whole story. Your name. Silver's name. The title of the book, and my guesses as to who you really are under that *nom de guerre*.'

Gassan made an audible gasp. He was staring at Kennedy in horror. 'Heather,' he protested weakly. 'We stipulated discretion.'

'Yes,' she said. 'You did.' She was moving now, around the edge of the table, and Wales was turning his head to keep her in sight.

'You have no idea who we are,' he said. And his voice had changed. The humility had fallen away, the naked edge of something completely other showing through.

'I know this much,' Kennedy said, still ambling towards the

head of the table – not even looking at the door, although it lay full in her path. 'I know that you and Mark Silver don't regard anything you did as a crime, and you don't feel any sense of guilt for it. Even if you'd had to kill, as you more than half-expected you might, you'd have been ready for—'

That was as far as she got. Wales saw where Kennedy was heading or else just guessed – as Kennedy had guessed – that something wasn't playing out as it should. He stepped into her path and suddenly, as his hands unfolded from his chest, he had a knife balanced in each of them.

The second shock was as painful as the first. Kennedy knew the knives, too: handleless sica blades. Their unsettling, asymmetrical shape cropped up in her nightmares.

'Thornedyke,' she shouted. 'Do it!' It meant nothing, it was just a distraction. Thornedyke scrambled up and staggered back from the table, utterly terrified. Professor Gassan, with more presence of mind, lunged for the phone.

Rush went for Wales and the speed of his reflexes was what saved Kennedy from dying in that first moment. He charged the man from behind, trying to pin his arms to his sides. For a moment he succeeded, but Wales bent from the knees, dropping cleanly out of Rush's grip, then jabbed up and back with his left arm. His elbow slammed into Rush's crotch and the boy folded with a whuff of agonised breath. Wales rose as he fell, the elbow still extended so that it hit Rush in the face with solid, sickening force.

By that time, Gassan had the phone receiver to his ear and his hand on the key pad. As he pressed 1 – for an external line – Wales's right arm straightened like a whip and the knife that had been in his hand was in Gassan's chest. The professor sat back down again, eyes wide, hands fluttering in uncoordinated protest.

Kennedy threw herself forward before Wales could recover his balance, and grappled with him. It wasn't an attack, it was more of an embrace. She was hoping to trap Wales's arms against his body, as Rush had, and stop him from using the remaining knife.

He twisted against her and Kennedy could feel his intimidating strength. She couldn't maintain the hold. Wales's left arm came free and he slammed her hard against the wall. But they were so close together now that it was hard for him to bring the blade to bear against her. He stepped back.

Rush – amazingly, still in the fight – kicked at Wales's legs. It was a glancing blow, with almost no leverage behind it, but Wales stumbled, and it took him a fraction of a second to right himself – long enough for Kennedy to throw her left arm out, smashing the glass on the security alarm. The sound of the thin plate breaking was almost inaudible.

The sound of all the room's door locks cycling was much louder.

Wales drove her into the wall with the full weight of his body and kicked her legs out from under her as she fell. At the same time, the shutters came down across the windows with a grinding shriek of metal on metal, taking out most of the light.

'Lockdown,' Kennedy gasped. She was on her stomach, pressed painfully into the angle of wall and floor, Wales's knee in the small of her back, his body overlaid on hers so that every movement she might have made seemed to be forestalled in a different way. Wales held the knife right up against her throat: she felt the sting as it broke her skin and something like the heat of a blush as a little of her spilled blood trickled down into the hollow of her breastbone. 'No way in or out, Alex. So whatever you do or don't do to us, you're not walking away from this.'

The man was bending low over her, his face almost on the same level as Kennedy's and an inch or so away. His wide eyes, alien and inscrutable, stared sidelong into her own. The red tide brimmed behind them, threatening to spill down his cheeks.

'The average response time is twelve minutes,' Kennedy wheezed, fighting the urge to pull away from the blade – as though the man were a cat and any movement from his prey would trigger instincts so strong that conscious thought wouldn't come into it.

Rush was still down, or down again, folded around his injured crotch. Emil Gassan had slumped back in his chair, hands clasped to his chest in an incongruous attitude of devotion. Thornedyke had backed away until he hit the wall and stood frozen, watching, his lower jaw hanging down in mute horror and dismay. 'And there's what,' Kennedy said, forcing the words out from lungs that felt hollowed out like gourds, 'six or seven doors between you and the street? How good are you with locks?'

It was impossible to tell what was going on behind the red-rimmed, open wounds that were Wales's eyes. He said nothing, and the razor edge at Kennedy's throat didn't move. But the expression on his face, now, was one of serious thought.

Rush spoke for the first time, from behind them. Kennedy didn't dare turn to see what the boy was doing or if he'd managed to get upright again. His voice was strained and tremulous. 'Alex,' he said, 'listen to me. What you've done . . . it's just breaking and entering. Maybe theft. You might not even go to jail. But if Professor Gassan dies, that's murder. You've got to stop this. Give yourself up. Don't be stupid. Nobody cares that you nicked a bloody book.'

Footsteps sounded from outside and someone knocked on

the door – tentative at first, then more loudly. A second later there was an answering knock from one of the other doors. The room was surrounded, and the police were coming.

Wales seemed to weigh these things in the balance. He let out a long, slow, steady breath, but his left arm tensed. The blade bit a fraction of an inch deeper into Kennedy's flesh, making her flinch and stiffen.

'I swear to God,' Rush said again, desperately, 'you won't go to jail.'

Wales straightened, removing his weight from Kennedy's back. 'No,' he agreed. 'I won't.'

He drew the knife across his own throat.

12

Some hours – maybe four, maybe five – went by in fuzzy staccato. Disconnected freeze-frames, the intervals between them filled with endless replays of that one indelible instant. Kennedy tried to shut it out with other thoughts, but it ran over and under and through them, the way Alex Wales's blood had run over the knife blade and his shirt and the table and the oatmeal carpet and Kennedy's hands and Rush's hands as they tried to stanch the endless flow.

And through it all, Wales had smiled at them, contemptuously amused by their futile attempts to keep him alive against his will.

Kennedy had given two statements to the police, one to the regular Met, the second to one of the many anti-terrorist agencies, all of whom were on high alert because of the recent spate of fires, explosions and car-bombings. There was no question of her being blamed for the death. Rush's testimony agreed with hers on every count, and the investigating officers were seeing these events in the light of the attack on her, two nights ago, where it now seemed more likely than not that Wales had been the aggressor. Thornedyke and Gassan would corroborate Kennedy's story, too, no doubt, but neither could be approached for an opinion right then. Thornedyke had gone into screaming hysterics immediately after Wales's suicide, had continued to show signs of distress and panic through the removal of the body, and on arrival at the hospital had been put under sedation. Emil Gassan was in intensive care and might not survive.

The forensics, too, supported an assumption of suicide. The angle of the gash in Alex Wales's throat was consistent with a self-inflicted wound and although nobody had said so to Kennedy, they would obviously have checked the knife-hilt for prints by this time and found only those of Wales himself.

But the emergency room staff were if anything even more reluctant to let go of Kennedy than the police were, convinced first that some of the blood that had dried and caked on her must be her own and then that she must be suffering from shock.

And maybe she was, at that, but hot, sweet tea wasn't going to help her out of it. She had to get away from solicitous bystanders and professionally neutral cops, and work out for herself what all this meant.

The Judas People. The Judas People running headlong into her and Emil Gassan. How could such a thing happen? What mechanism could even begin to explain it?

She had to call Izzy. Make sure Izzy was okay. Okay, maybe it didn't make too much sense, when you looked at it closely – why wouldn't she be? – but the instinct was too strong. Impatient of getting herself discharged from the hospital, or of persuading the friendly, inquiring detectives to tell her she was free to go, she went to the bathroom and called from inside a locked toilet.

Izzy didn't answer and Kennedy started to panic. But as she was in the process of dialling again to leave a message, the phone registered an incoming call.

'Sorry, babe,' Izzy said. 'Missed you by a second, there. Everything okay?'

Everything wasn't, but Kennedy was suddenly tongue-tied. Izzy was still safest where she was. And telling her what had happened would mean an argument, because she'd want to come back and look after Kennedy, be there for her, and that was the last thing that Kennedy wanted right then. The assassins of the Judas People didn't work alone, they worked in twos or threes. The man who'd called himself Alex Wales was down and he wasn't getting up again, but there could be – would be – others.

Kennedy stammered through a few minutes' worth of banal lies about how everything was okay and how nothing at all, either good or bad, had happened to her.

'Well, God knows, I can sympathise,' Izzy said, sounding glum. 'A game of Trivial Pursuit with Hayley and Richard has been the highlight of my trip so far. And it was the family edition, babe, so they took me to the cleaners. Have *you* ever heard of Frankie Cocozza?'

'No,' Kennedy said. 'Izzy, I've got to go. Someone just came in.'

'Okay. What's that echo? It sounds like you're in the loo. If you're in the loo, and someone just came in, you've got a harassment suit right there.'

'I'm ... in a hallway.' Kennedy's mind was still firing randomly and she realised suddenly that the next day's papers would be full of the violent suicide at Ryegate House. There was no way Izzy wasn't going to get to hear about it. So she switched horses in mid-banality, came clean and gave Izzy a heavily redacted version of recent events that amounted to: someone died.

'Right in front of you?' Izzy demanded. 'Someone just died, with you standing there? I don't get it.'

'It was ... it's hard to explain, Izzy. But I'm fine. I'm totally fine. He killed himself.'

'He what?'

'He killed himself. It was the guy who broke into the museum storeroom. We caught him. But he killed himself.'

'Oh my God.' The long silence at the other end of the line indicated how nonplussed Izzy was: silence wasn't normally her thing. 'So it's over?'

'*That* part of it's over.'

'Then it's safe for me to pack up and—'

'No. No, it's not. Give me a couple more days.'

'Seriously?'

'Seriously.'

'A couple of days is how long I'm gonna last, Heather, with the wicked witch giving me the evil eye every time I use a bad word.'

'All right.'

'You know how many bad words I use.'

'All right, Izzy.'

'No, babe. It's not. It's not all right. You're telling me you're fine, but you don't sound fine, and I know how you lock things down inside. God knows, I paid a lot to find out. Say the word and I'm there. I'm there right now.'

'No, Izzy. Stay where you are. I'll call you tomorrow.'

'Okay. Okay. Heather?'

'Yes?'

'Call me tomorrow.'

'I will.'

'Promise.'

'I promise I will.'

'You know, some people find dirty phone calls cathartic. If you need my professional services ...'

110

'Oh, for the love of God! Tomorrow, Izzy.' Kennedy hung up, even more restless and distracted than she'd been before the call. She missed Izzy, still resented her, was afraid for her, wanted never to see her again and wanted to see her right then.

And then there were the Judas People, who still made no sense. No sense at all.

When the doctors and nurses were done with their scattershot solicitude, they reluctantly agreed to release Kennedy on her own recognisance.

Before she left, she asked about the others. Both Gassan and Thornedyke were unconscious, one was stable, and there wouldn't be any more news before morning. Rush had been released a couple of hours before.

But he hadn't gotten far. When Kennedy walked out onto the street, he was waiting for her right by the entrance – leaning on a sign which told her that this was University College Hospital, on Euston Road. She hadn't even thought to ask, and if anyone had told her, the news hadn't sunk in.

Rush looked haggard and punch-drunk with tiredness. The right side of his face was swollen, the eye mostly closed.

'I want to talk this over,' he told her.

'Tonight?' Kennedy asked.

'Tonight.'

'It can't wait?'

Rush shrugged – a gesture that took in his injury, hers, the hospital, the whole crazy situation. 'Well, you tell me.'

Kennedy hesitated. Of all the questions he might ask her, there were only a few she'd be happy to answer. But she had to admit that there were a whole lot more that he was entitled to ask. She looked at her watch: it was 9.30 p.m. The night was – grotesquely and impossibly – still young.

'All right,' she said. 'Let's talk.'

They took a cab back into town. Kennedy had it drop them off at a pub on Upper St Martin's Lane, the Salisbury. They could have walked, but the presence of the cabbie constrained conversation and gave Kennedy time to think about what she was going to say to Rush.

The boy tried to buy the round. Kennedy sent him to find some seats instead, got the drinks – a pint of lager for him, Jack Daniels over ice for her – and went and joined him. He'd chosen a corner table, was sitting with his eyes on the door. His hands, as he drank off half the pint in one long swallow, were shaking. His battered face was drawing more than a few curious or uneasy glances from people at the tables around them.

'So how are you holding up?' she asked.

Rush just shook his head. She took that to mean that the jury was still out.

'You saw it coming,' he said. 'Some of it. You knew what Wales was going to do.'

'I had no idea what he was going to do.'

Rush took another sip, put the mostly empty glass down. 'But you knew he was dangerous. That he had a weapon. You were moving towards the alarm before he pulled those knives. So I'm thinking you could tell me what the hell it was I saw today. Because right now, I feel like I'm drowning. I don't know what just happened to me. I almost died, and it's like a meteor fell out of the sky and hit me in the head, or something. It makes about that much sense to me, you know?'

Kennedy swirled the glass, let the ice clink against its sides, but felt no inclination to drink. Her stomach was as tight as a fist.

'You're in mild shock,' she said. 'Maybe you shouldn't go

back into work. If I were you, I'd take a few days off. What you've just been through wasn't business as usual.'

He stared at her, bemused and unhappy. 'Is that what you're going to do? Take a few days off?'

'No,' Kennedy admitted.

'No. Because there's something bigger behind this, isn't there?'

'Yes.'

His good eye widened. 'I knew it. I knew it from your face. I want you to tell me about it.'

'I can't do that, Rush.'

'Can't?'

'Won't, then. Trust me, it's a lot better for you if you don't know. If you don't get any closer to this than you already are.'

'What does that mean?' Rush asked.

Kennedy tried to pick her words with care, but she felt stupid and tongue-tied. 'It's the sort of thing ... once you know it, you can't just walk away. There are consequences.' It was the wrong thing to say, she could see from his face.

'I'll take my chances,' he said.

'No,' she said. 'Look, I do feel like I owe you something, Rush. But it's not an explanation, it's a warning. You asked me if I knew who Alex Wales was.'

'Do you?'

'I know his ... family. I've met them before and I know what they're like. They're going to be looking for payback for what happened to him. From everyone who was in that room, just as soon as they find out who was there. So your best bet is to get far away from Ryegate House for a while and let this die down.'

'And you think if they really want to find me, they won't keep looking?'

113

Damn. Good question. 'No,' she admitted. 'They'll keep looking.'

'Exactly. And you're going straight back in there tomorrow morning and picking up the investigation, right? I'm not stupid, Heather. Not as stupid as I look, anyway. I know there's stuff you didn't work out. Questions you still need to get answered.'

Kennedy's heart sank. 'Rush, questions are pretty much all I've got,' she said, allowing her exasperation to show through in her voice. 'These people broke into Aladdin's cave and stole a single book. Or maybe they didn't. Maybe they broke in and *burned* a book. Can you come up with a plausible explanation for that? Because I can't. And that's before we even get to the part where I let Emil Gassan, who I kind of count as a friend, get stabbed – maybe fatally – right in front of me. So yes, I'm still hired. I'm still on the job. But your job description is a little different from mine.'

'I didn't even mean any of that,' Rush said.

'No? Then what did you mean?'

'I mean why was Wales still there? He stole – okay, stole or else destroyed – that book three weeks ago. If the job was finished, he should have cut and run.'

'So?'

'So the job wasn't done. He came back because he had unfinished business, and whatever it was, it was something that made it worth the risk of sticking around through a police investigation.'

Kennedy had reached the same conclusion, but she didn't want to have this conversation with Rush. She just wanted him to understand how close he was to the edge of a precipice and to have the sense to walk in the opposite direction.

'Have you got any holiday coming?' she asked.

'Holiday?' Rush was derisory. 'I haven't even finished my probation yet. I'm casual labour.'

'Then be casual about it,' Kennedy said. 'Don't turn up for work tomorrow. If they bounce you, shake it off and walk away. You're young. You'll bounce right back. Stay away from Ryegate House. And if anyone asks you about what went down today, don't answer.'

'What if it's the police?' Rush demanded sardonically.

'If it's the police, stonewall them. You don't remember, you didn't see, nobody told you a thing. You're just poor bloody infantry.'

'You're making a lot of assumptions.'

'Like what?'

'Like that death means the same thing to me that it does to you.'

'Death means the same thing to everyone,' Kennedy said sharply. 'It means your hearts stops, your brain cools and people start referring to you as "the body". There's no such thing as a good death, Rush. There are just some that are worse than others.'

Rush tapped his beer glass with his thumbnail, watching it rather than looking at her. 'My best mate died in a knife fight at school,' he said, in a tone that was almost conversational. 'He got stabbed. And my first girlfriend killed herself with sleeping pills because her step-dad raped her. She sent me a text to say goodbye and I couldn't get there in time. She must have known I wouldn't, but she wrote that message anyway. I still have it. I went after him and almost killed him, except that when I had him on the ground I couldn't do it. Didn't have the right mindset, I suppose.'

'Did any of this come up in your job interview?' Kennedy asked laconically.

He shrugged. 'It was a long time ago.'

She sighed. 'Okay, I get it. You're telling me you know about this dark, grown-up stuff. Well, maybe you do, at that. If you're sure you want the truth, I'll give it to you.'

'I want it,' he said at once.

So she told him the whole story – or at least, as much of it as was hers to tell.

She started with the death of Chris Harper, her partner, who bled out in her arms after taking a wound from one of the Messengers' poisoned knives. It was hard for her to keep her voice steady. Even after three years, it still hurt to remember.

She talked about the Judas People for what must have been an hour or more. She told Rush how they lived as a separate tribe within the mass of humanity. How they hid in the cities of the Earth, choosing places where there was sufficient density of population to hide them, and how they'd perfected the arts of camouflage to the point where they left no footprint on history, no record of their comings or their goings.

Rush kept quiet for most of it and let her talk.

'And they really believe they're descended from the serpent of Eden?' he asked, when she'd finished.

'By way of Cain and Judas,' Kennedy said.

'But the serpent was the Devil.'

Kennedy shrugged. 'That's our version. Their version is that he was an emissary of the true God who stands above and outside creation. So Cain was special, and all Cain's offspring are special, whereas Eve begat a lineage of sinners and wastrels. But they name themselves after Judas because he's the one who made the covenant with God on their behalf.'

'And the deal was?'

'Three thousand years in the wilderness. For all that time,

the children of Adam are the stewards of God's Creation. But after that time is up, the faithful – the true heirs of Cain and Judas – will be given their reward. Which is everything. Dominion over the whole world.'

Rush absorbed this for a few moments in silence. 'Three thousand years counting from when?' he asked at last.

'Well, let's just say that God should have called by now. Judas made the covenant about two thousand years ago, but the date that was used as a reference point was around a thousand years BC. The unification of the tribes of Israel, under King David. That was the cornerstone of history, as far as Judas was concerned. The one moment in time that everybody knew and nobody was going to argue about. So that was what he and Christ used as a reference point. At least, that's what the Judas Gospel says.'

'And they waited all that time . . .' Rush mused.

'They're still waiting. They're not happy about it, but at this point they don't have a lot of choice. The thing is, there aren't that many of them. And three thousand years is a long time as far as genetic inbreeding goes. So they come out into the world every so often. I mean, some of them do.'

Rush was looking at her with a baffled kind of expression, so Kennedy went on, picking her words carefully. This part of the story belonged to others. It wasn't for her to tell how Leo Tillman's family had been stolen from him, and how he'd later killed his own sons, at Dovecote Farm in Surrey, without knowing who they were. That secret, at least, she intended to take to her grave. 'They send women out, to get pregnant. To bring in new genes. The women meet Adamite men, get married and raise families with them.'

'Adamite?' Rush said, with a grimace. 'What? What's that? The rest of us?'

117

'That's the rest of us, yeah. And these women, these "vessels" – the *Kelim* – get pregnant three times. As soon as the third child is old enough to travel, they just disappear. They go back to the tribe, taking the children with them. Mission accomplished.'

'You're putting me on,' Rush protested. 'Nobody would do that. It's sick.'

'Getting into this stuff,' Kennedy said, deadpan, 'it's like stepping into another world, Rush. They've got their own rules. Their own way of seeing things. And it does the job. Stops them all dying from double recessives. But anything could happen to a woman out in the world by herself. A woman raised in seclusion, totally lacking in street smarts. So there are others. Agents. Operatives. People who act like guardian angels for the *Kelim*, and to some extent for the whole tribe. They're called the *Elohim*, which is Aramaic for "Messengers", and if they think someone knows too much . . . well, their speciality is accidental death, but they're comfortable with straight murder, too. That's what Alex Wales was.'

When she finally ran out of words, Rush stared at her for a few moments in complete silence.

'I don't know why I sat through all that lunacy,' he said at last.

'Yeah, you do,' Kennedy said. 'It was because you saw a man kill himself right in front of you today and you can't get the picture out of your head. You're willing to listen to any amount of lunacy if it will help you to understand that.'

'That'd be great if it actually worked. But I'm not understanding any of this. It's a stupid story.'

'Yeah, isn't it?'

'But you say it happened to you.'

'And to you, Rush, as of today. You were in the room. With any luck, they won't know that, but maybe it's just as well you

118

made me tell you all this. At least now, you might be that little bit more paranoid at a time when you've actually got something to be paranoid about.'

'Thanks,' Rush said glumly. 'Anything particular I ought to watch out for?'

'What happened to Wales's eyes, that's something they seem to do a lot. When they kill. When they're thinking about killing. Or sometimes just as a response to stress or emotion. It's called haemolacria. They weep blood.'

'Jesus.'

'It's because of the drug they take. It's toxic and in the end it kills them, but it makes them faster and stronger and more resistant to pain. Believe me, it takes a lot to put one of them down.'

'Like you said,' he reminded her, 'I was in the room.' He pondered, staring into his empty glass. 'But why didn't he just kill us all, then? Wales, I mean. It wouldn't have been all that hard.'

Kennedy felt the weight of that guilt and unease settle on her. 'He could have done, if he'd wanted to. But I think he didn't want to be questioned. They hide from the light. I threw that into the mix and hoped he'd run away. It didn't occur to me that he'd kill himself to avoid answering awkward questions.'

She picked up her bag, straightened her jacket and generally did the premonitory things that mean you're about to leave. Rush ignored the signals.

'What do we do now?' he asked her.

Kennedy frowned. 'We don't do anything now,' she said. 'We go to bed and sleep. Neither of us is in any shape for life-or-death decisions.'

Rush laughed hollowly. 'You think it's going to be up to us to decide? Really?'

Kennedy got to her feet. 'I think we wait and see,' she said. 'If we're lucky, this is where it ends.'

But it wouldn't be. Of course it wouldn't. That was why she'd told Izzy not to come home yet, and why she'd told Rush enough to put him on his guard. It wasn't over. It couldn't be.

Herself, and Emil Gassan. No coincidence. She'd been rolled up into something, by a force that she couldn't see or define. She was in this mess for a reason and it sure as hell wasn't her own reason.

'We'll talk tomorrow,' she told Rush. 'I have to sleep.'

'Okay.'

'You're staying?'

'I need another drink.'

'Just make sure you can still walk home,' she said. 'I'll see you tomorrow.'

But as she turned, he called her name again. She looked back over her shoulder.

'It's Ben,' he said.

His voice was slurred enough that she didn't understand at first. 'It's what?' she demanded.

'Benjamin. Ben. My given name. I was christened—'

'Okay.' She waved him to silence. 'Sorry. It's way too late for that. You're Rush now.'

He sighed deeply.

'What's the secret of a good joke?' he asked Kennedy.

'Timing.'

'Right. So I guess I'm a bad one.'

She just about had time to jump on the Piccadilly Line at Leicester Square, then drop down to Pimlico on the last south-bound train.

Kennedy's feet were heavy and she was irresolute all the way

120

back about where she was going to sleep. The night before, Izzy's bed without Izzy in it had felt like an alien planet. But she suspected that her own would feel like a crypt.

In the end she went for Izzy's because at least the bed was made and she could just fall into it. Whether she'd sleep was a question that would answer itself in due course.

She opened the door and stepped inside, wondering for a moment why the action of the lock seemed a little looser than usual, the cylinder rattling slightly in its housing.

As she stepped across the threshold, she saw the living room door ahead of her standing open. She knew she'd left it closed that morning, so now she knew why the lock was loose.

Stand or run? A professional wouldn't give her a chance to run in any case, and if it was a casual burglar – please, God – she could probably take him. She reached into her bag for the pepper spray.

Arms locked around her from behind, pinning her hands to her sides. Something was pressed to her face and though she struggled not to inhale, consciousness slipped away before she could even register the smell of the drug.

13

The world came back piecemeal, a lot more slowly than it had gone away.

Kennedy was aware of sounds first: slow, discrete, shifted toward the bass register. Not words, as such – and they carried on not being words no matter how hard she focused on them.

Then a sourness that was half-smell, half-taste welled up from everywhere and nowhere, around and inside her. She balked.

'Mistakh he. He met e'ver.'

'Ne riveh te zi'et. Hu vihel veh le tzadeh.'

Hands clasped her head and shoulder. She tried to pull away from them, but they just turned her onto her side. Her stomach tightened, sending a peristaltic wave through her upper body. She retched weakly, felt warm liquid run over her lips and tongue.

Cloth beneath her cheek, beneath her body. Soft, and cool. It had rocked slightly when she moved. She was on a bed.

A blurred dot of light appeared, more or less centred in her field of vision. It expanded and there was movement in front of it, across and across.

'Can you hear me? Can you hear what I'm saying?' A man's voice, deep and mellifluous.

Kennedy played dead as she laboriously assembled her recent memories into some kind of sequence. The stairs. The door. The bed. No, she was missing a step. Someone moving behind her, arms pinning her arms, the handkerchief pressed to her face. And then the bed. Fine.

Not fine at all.

'I think she's awake.' A different voice, not harsher but deader, affectless: a voice that actually scared her, given the implications of why she was lying on a bed, why she'd been attacked at all.

'Then let's get started.'

Hands were laid on her once more. She was too weak and sick to resist as she was rolled onto her back again and her arms were pulled up over her head. Something closed on her left wrist with a snap. There was a metallic clanking and scraping, then *clack*, something bit into her right wrist, hard and sudden enough to make her flinch. When she tried to flex her legs, she discovered that they were already immobilised in some way. She was spread-eagled on the bed, and absolutely defenceless.

'*Ni met venim, ye sichedur.*'

'*Nhamim.*'

If that language, whatever it was, was what her assailants spoke to one another, Kennedy wondered for a moment why they'd shifted into English. The answer came to her at once: 'Let's get started' was something she was meant to hear and be frightened by. Seeing through the ruse gave her some crumb of comfort.

She opened her eyes now. There didn't seem to be anything to be gained by faking unconsciousness any longer.

The biggest surprise – although it shouldn't have been a surprise at all – was that she was in Izzy's bedroom. She probably

123

hadn't been out that long and there was very little point in ambushing her at the flat if her assailants then had to take her to someplace else entirely. But still, the familiar surroundings accentuated the weirdness and her terror at what was happening.

There were just the two of them – the ones she'd already differentiated by their voices. Both were young, but one was very young, perhaps still in his teens or early twenties. He was slightly built, handsome, with shoulder-length black hair and a short, neat moustache and beard.

The other was bigger and stockier, with a sullen baby face. Black hair, again, but this man wore it short and in a curiously retro style, with an off-centre parting.

Both were dressed in rough-weave linen suits in a colour that might be called a light tan, and both had the unnatural pallor of the Judas tribe, whose life was lived mostly underground. Both were staring at her with solemn intensity – accompanied in the case of the bigger man by something like disgust.

'We're going to ask you some questions, Miss Kennedy,' the bearded man said gently. Unsurprisingly, he was the one with the attractive, cultured voice. *The designated nice cop*, Kennedy thought. But she wasn't about to give him the benefit of any doubts on that account. 'About the job you were called in to do at the British Museum and about the events of this afternoon.'

Kennedy didn't answer. She twisted her head to look up and then down, taking in what they'd done to her. Her wrists were cuffed – with a single pair of handcuffs threaded through the bed's wrought-iron headboard. Pink, furry handcuffs: bondage gear. Her legs were locked in their wide-open position by some sort of hobble bar. But she was fully clothed. They hadn't even taken off her jacket. The mixed signals were confusing. Why prep her for rape and then stop halfway?

'Don't know ... what you're talking ... about,' Kennedy mumbled. Her mouth and lower face were still numb from the drug and it was hard to form the words. But in any case, it seemed like a good idea to let them come to her.

The bigger man uttered an oath she didn't catch. He reached into his jacket and drew out a knife. Kennedy's heart hammered as she saw the asymmetrical shape of it, the curved spur where the blade ought to narrow to a point and the blunt, rough tang, the exact same metal as the blade, that served it as a hilt. It was the sica again.

These men were Messengers – the professional assassins of the Judas tribe.

The big man pressed the knife to Kennedy's cheek. 'Listen to me, filth,' he said, between clenched teeth. 'Every time you lie to us, I will cut you. Every time you don't answer quickly enough, I will cut you. Every time I don't like the answer you give, I will cut you. And when I have no more questions, I will cut your throat.'

'Samal.' The younger man spoke the word softly, but his partner tensed at once and looked to him, settling for Kennedy the question – which had been open up until then – of the pecking order. He made a gesture and the heavy-set man took the knife away from Kennedy's face, lowered it to his side. Nice cop outranked nasty cop.

The younger man sat down beside her on the bed, arranging himself almost primly, and stared into her eyes. He smiled – and the smile was a lot more unsettling than the big man's ferocity. It was the smile of someone so sure of his own rectitude that guilt and shame couldn't land a punch on him.

'My name is Abydos,' he told her. 'And that man there, with

the knife, he is my friend, Samal. Samal is a man who – as you might imagine from his manner – doesn't flinch from unpleasant work. But despite what he says, it will be I who will question you. And I will only allow Samal to hurt you if you force my hand. By that I mean, if you make me believe that hurting you will bring you to tell us more or keep you from lying. You understand me? If you cooperate, there will be less pain. Perhaps no pain at all. And the end, when it comes, will come more quickly and more easily.'

He paused, as though he expected her to reply. When she didn't, he resumed. 'I can, besides, offer you one further consolation. At the moment – with only a little more stage management – your death will seem like a sexual game that escalated out of control. But if you tell us the truth, without prompting, then before we leave here we'll remove these . . .' he gestured, with a tight, uncomfortable smile '. . . accessories from your body and leave it fully clothed. You won't be dishonoured.'

'Yeah, I'll still be dead, though,' Kennedy said. 'I hate to sound ungrateful, but . . . you know.' It hurt her throat to speak, she discovered, and her voice came out as an unlovely croak.

The young man shrugged. 'You're an intelligent woman,' he said. 'If I promised to let you live, it would be meaningless. We'd both know it for a lie and then you wouldn't believe anything else I told you.'

Kennedy licked her dry lips, muttered something low and far back in her throat. When the young man obligingly leaned forward to try to catch her words, she spat in his eye. It was all the defiance she could muster, but she saw from the horror and disgust that flared in his face that it had done the job.

The man took out a handkerchief and wiped his cheek with

it. 'Well, then,' he said, his mouth twisted, 'perhaps I was mistaken. Perhaps it will be impossible, after all, to conduct this conversation along rational lines.' He looked to the other man, who still stood ready with the knife in his hand. 'Samal, take a finger.'

The big man bent over her. Contradictory expressions – eagerness, revulsion, fear, hate – chased themselves across his face.

'I'll talk,' Kennedy said quickly. 'You don't need to cut me. I'll tell you what you want to know.'

Abydos gestured, and Samal paused again. He hadn't even touched her and he seemed relieved not to have to, even though she saw how easily the knife sat in his hand. She was sure he'd killed before. She was equally sure that torture held no particular terrors for him. There was nothing like mercy in his face, and if anything, he seemed to feel a visceral loathing for her. On an impulse, she struggled against the cuffs and let her forearm, as if by accident, touch the back of Samal's hand. The man jumped as if he'd been stung.

Women, Kennedy thought. *You're scared of women.*

'Very well,' Abydos said. 'Let's begin with this afternoon. You called a meeting, at Ryegate House. What happened there?'

Kennedy licked her dry lips and tried her hardest to keep her voice steady. 'I accused a man, Alex Wales, of theft.'

'Theft of what?'

'A book.'

'Name the book.' Abydos's emphasis was so precise that Kennedy hesitated, forewarned. She knew how important the written word was for the Judas People. Actually, she'd been told in counter-terrorism seminars back when she was still a cop, that the same thing went for most religious fanatics. To the fundamentalist mindset, the word was literally flesh and any harm or disrespect offered to it was a direct assault on the godhead.

So, out of some half-explored instinct, she lied. 'We weren't able to find that out,' she said. 'We just knew that there was a discrepancy. That one of the boxes in that room was light. Something had been stolen.'

'And you knew that Alex Wales had stolen it.'

'Yes.' Again, they had to know this much. Their agent, the other member of their cell, hadn't reported in – had dropped off the map. His death would hit the news soon enough, if it hadn't already. Lying wouldn't help her.

'*How* did you know?' Abydos asked.

Kennedy stumbled through an explanation. The chiming dates in the personnel files. The inside-man hypothesis. The coincidence of Silver's death.

'Very good,' Abydos acknowledged, as though he were a teacher, or else a priest coaching her in her catechism. 'And you put these things to him. To Wales.'

'I questioned him. Yes.'

'How did he reply?'

'He didn't. He refused to answer any of my questions. And then, when I locked him in the room and called the police, he killed himself with his own knife.'

Samal made a sound, an ululating moan, deep in his throat. Abydos glared at him and admonished him in whatever their language was. '*Ne eyar v'shteh. De beyoshin lekot.*' It certainly sounded a lot like the bastard Aramaic of the Judas People.

'*Ma es'irim shud ekol—*' Samal answered, his face as tragic and imploring as a whipped dog's.

Abydos cut him off with a curt, commanding gesture. Then

128

he turned back to Kennedy, as though there'd been no interruption. 'But it won't do,' he told her. 'You're very careful to say "*I* did this" and "He wouldn't answer *me*". As if the two of you were alone in that room. But you weren't. You will tell us, please, who else was there.'

Kennedy realised with a cold, sudden shock that this – all of this, everything that was happening to her now and was about to happen – was the reason why Alex Wales hadn't killed her when he could. Once he'd decided on his own death, it became essential to allow Kennedy to live so that these men could question her.

'I thought Wales might be more likely to talk if I spoke to him alone,' she said. Her voice cracked, zigzagged raggedly up the scale, and there was nothing she could do to stop it.

'No,' Abydos said. 'I don't think so.'

'It's the truth.'

There was a long pause. 'I ask you again, Miss Kennedy. Who else was there? Tell me, and spare yourself this pain.'

'It's the truth,' she said again.

'Well,' Abydos said. He nodded to Samal.

Kennedy braced herself, but she knew enough about torture to be sure that any preparations she made in advance would be useless as soon as it started.

She thought the man might take a few moments to screw up his courage, but he just stuck the knife deep into her left side, until it touched the rib and ground against the bone. Kennedy opened her mouth to scream. Abydos, who had been expecting this, pushed a piece of cloth – a handkerchief, maybe – deeply into her throat. The scream became a soggy yodel, more vibration than sound. The man watched her closely, clinically, as she struggled and gurgled into the gag.

'Again,' he said.

Samal lowered the blade and Kennedy went into futile spasms, panic and terror shutting out all rational thought.

But the knife didn't touch her, because the two men had both frozen at a sudden sound, absurd and extraneous, from outside the room. Five hollow knocks, in quick succession, in the sequence universally known as shave-and-a-haircut.

'Izzy?' It was a woman's voice, young and slightly querulous, coming from the other end of the hall – from the flat's front door. 'Lover? Are you in there?'

14

Abydos responded a little quicker than Kennedy, and that slight difference was crucial. As she tensed her body for some movement violent enough to warn this newcomer off, he gripped her wrists tightly in his hands and whispered a single word to Samal.

'*Rishkert.*'

By that time, Kennedy's legs were lifting off the bed, but Samal caught her ankles in mid-air and forced them down again slowly and inexorably. She couldn't produce any more noise than the writhing of her upper body against the sheets.

'Izzy? Are you in here?' The voice seemed a little wary and unhappy. 'The door wasn't locked . . .' Abydos gave Samal a smouldering glare and Samal turned his face away from it as though from a slap.

Footsteps in the hall, getting closer. 'Izzy?' By now, whoever it was had to have seen the light streaming from under the door. But you wouldn't just wander into someone's bedroom, uninvited. Nobody would be insane or brazen or crass enough to do that, unless they were pretty sure they had an open invitation.

The door handle turned and the door opened an inch. 'Okayyy . . .' The voice had changed from tentative to teasing, although there was still an undertone of uncertainty. 'If you've got someone in there, I'm giving you a full ten seconds to get under the covers. Nine ... eight ... seven ... Nah, to hell with it.'

The door was pushed fully open and a young woman – a *very* young woman – stepped into the room. She couldn't have been more than nineteen, and even in her extreme panic, a part of Kennedy's mind found time for wonder and outrage.

Jesus, Izzy.

The woman was wearing jeans and a white T-shirt – plain, even drab – and black wrestling boots that hadn't been in style for so long that they had to be a retro affectation. Her hair was short and dark and tightly curled, her eyes were violet, and right then they were as wide as saucers because whatever she was expecting to be looking at, what she was actually seeing was two stony-faced men and a tied-up woman, and Samal had stood and swung round to face her, a gun in his hand now (replacing the knife – when had that happened?) pointing directly at the mid-point of her body.

'I ... I ...' she faltered. 'I was—'

'Come into the room,' Abydos said. 'Come. We won't hurt you.' His voice was firm, but with a slow, even cadence, reassuring. He made no move towards her, but his gaze was fixed on her eyes. 'Come in, or this woman will die.'

The girl looked from Abydos to Samal, then to the gun. Her face was the face of a trauma victim, dull with shock. *Run*, Kennedy thought, and tried to say, but the only sound that came through the gag was a desperate, almost voiceless growl.

'Come inside,' Abydos said, in the same gentling voice. 'Close the door.'

The girl took a step. At least, her foot moved forward, but her body stayed where it was, on the threshold, frozen.

'My mum knows I'm here,' she said, but she said it with a rising pitch, as a question or a plea.

'All right,' Abydos said. 'It's all right. Close the door.'

But the girl seemed to have run out of motive force. 'I just wanted ...' she said. 'I was gonna give Izzy her books back.'

She held up something that Kennedy hadn't seen until then: brightly coloured, even garish, and with a high gloss over which the light of the lamp played in a momentary flash of Morse.

It was a porno mag. *Bush League*. Two mostly naked women entwined on its cover, pelvis grinding against pelvis, the body of one twisted ridiculously to display her gigantic breasts to the best effect.

'You want to see?' the girl said, holding it out. Samal recoiled from the image as though it were a snake. And then a number of impossible things happened in swift sequence.

From under the magazine, which tilted suddenly in the girl's hand, two glittering threads arced up to hit Samal in the centre of his chest.

There was a sound like a clock ticking, but too fast and too loud. Samal did a clumsy moonwalk, moving backwards across the room in three jerky half-steps, until his shoulders hit the wall. He slid down it, expelling breath in a grunt of agony.

Meanwhile, Abydos had lunged for some weapon of his own, but the young girl had dropped both the porno mag and the spent Taser, leaped across the bed like a hurdler and was up in his face, darting whip-swift punches at him that forced him to use both hands to defend himself.

Both hands were enough, at first, but the girl was in constant movement, her body swaying back and forth, her flickering hands weaving in and out like the shuttle on a loom, forcing Abydos back. Then there was a moment when he warded off two low blows, leaving his upper body undefended. The girl stepped into the gap and drove her forehead into his face.

Abydos staggered back, blinded and in pain, and the girl pirouetted, her left leg swinging round with balletic grace to smack into the side of his head with a muffled crunch. He sank to his knees, then toppled full length.

A movement closer to hand diverted Kennedy's attention. Samal was groping for the fallen gun. Acting purely on instinct, Kennedy twisted round on the bed and dropped her legs over his head. Then she drew up her knees, so that the hobble bar hit him in the throat.

If he hadn't been groggy from the Taser, he'd have dealt with the clumsy assault in a heartbeat. As it was, he had to wrestle with Kennedy's dead weight for a few seconds before he succeeded in lifting her bodily and throwing her off. In that time, the girl had crossed the room again, snatching up Izzy's bedside lamp *en passant*. She hadn't even slowed to look at the lamp, it seemed to Kennedy, but with its stainless steel base, its weight and its heft, it fitted her needs exactly. She swung it back behind her like a bowler, then brought it round and up, gathering her body under it, and delivered it with appalling force to the point of Samal's chin. The blow lifted him an inch off the ground and dropped him flat on his back on the bedroom floor, which shook under his weight.

The girl circled him cautiously. The big man was still conscious. He rolled to his side, trying to get up yet again. Unhurriedly but with clinical precision, she delivered three devastating blows to the back of his head, which drove him into Izzy's shag-pile carpeting like a hammer driving a nail into a board. After a moment's further appraisal, she hit him again.

Then, finally, she dropped the lamp and flexed her hands as though gripping it so tightly had hurt her a little.

Somewhere during those last, terrifying seconds Kennedy had drawn in a panic breath so deep and sudden that she'd partially inhaled Abydos's handkerchief. Now she was suffocating on it. She writhed on the bed, trying to draw in air that wasn't there.

The girl was checking the two sprawled bodies with quiet, detached interest, but she noticed Kennedy's plight at last. She put down the lamp and reached into Kennedy's mouth to fish out the handkerchief by the end that was still visible.

Kennedy took a raw, shuddering breath, converted – when she let it out again – into the ragged sobs of shock.

'You're fine,' the girl said, sounding exactly as Abydos had sounded a moment or two before. 'It's over. But you have to go.'

'Who . . .' Kennedy wheezed, '. . . are . . . you?'

'I'm Diema,' the girl said simply. She was searching Samal's pockets, and then Abydos's, for a key, but Kennedy didn't make the connection until she saw it, until the girl was unlocking the cuffs at her wrists, the bar at her ankles. 'You need to get out of here,' the girl repeated as she worked. 'These men came here alone, but there will be others. Probably soon.'

Kennedy sat up and began to massage some life back into her numbed hands and forearms. She glanced down at Samal, afraid in spite of what she'd seen, in spite of what her rational mind was telling her, that he might rise up and attack her again. 'I'm sorry but I'm not getting this,' she said, when she felt she could trust her voice. 'Who are you? Why did you help me? Are you – are you really a friend of Izzy's?'

The girl gave her a slightly startled look, momentarily thrown. 'A friend of your lover? Don't be ridiculous. Just listen to what I'm telling you. Find a place they don't know about. And then another place, and another. Keep moving. Change your habits. Don't give them an easy target.'

The police, Kennedy thought. *I've got to call the police.*

The bedside table had gone over and the phone was lying on the floor. She reached for it, but the girl's foot came down on her wrist before she could touch it. She let all her weight fall onto Kennedy's hand, making Kennedy gasp in pain and shock.

'No,' the girl said.

Pinioned, Kennedy looked up at her. The girl's face, calm and detached despite the violence she'd just meted out, was folded into an uncompromising frown.

'You know who I am?' she asked Kennedy. 'Where I've come from?'

Kennedy pushed the answer out through clenched teeth. 'No. I r-really don't.'

The girl's eyes flicked momentarily to the bodies on the floor, then back to Kennedy. 'The same place *they* came from. And we're all sworn to keep that place a secret. So you know what I'd have to do to you if you picked up that phone and dialled.'

She took her foot away. Gingerly, Kennedy flexed the fingers of her hand. They hurt like hell and she could barely make them move, but none were broken.

'Think about this,' the girl said. 'These men came here to question you and then to kill you. They failed, so others will be sent. Assuming you did speak to the authorities, I doubt they could help you very much. It would be hard for them even to believe you. Get out now. Leave behind everything you don't need. Think about where you go. Who you talk to. The trail you'll be leaving behind you. Because there will be people following that trail, people who are very skilled at what they do.'

'So I shouldn't go back to Ryegate House?' Kennedy asked. 'You're warning me off?'

The girl's frown deepened. She stared at Kennedy as if she were mad.

'Of course you should go back. Finish the job you were given. Find the book and do what has to be done. Why do you think I've been wasting my time watching your back? Why else would you be worth saving?'

She turned on her heel and left, treading the porno mag underfoot with contemptuous disregard.

15

In Scotland, four clergymen reported missing are found dead. Their deaths mirror the deaths of four of the twelve apostles of Jesus: Matthew (stabbed through with a spear, in this case an athletics javelin), Thaddaeus (beaten to death with a rock), James (beheaded) and Peter (crucified upside down). Scottish police classify the murders as hate crimes.

In Umbria, a road bridge collapses. Cars fall like heavy rain into a steep gorge, at the bottom of which there is another road, carpeted with rush-hour traffic. Two hundred are killed.

In California, every warm-blooded animal in the San Diego zoo dies over a three-day period, showing symptoms similar to Ebola. When the viral agents are isolated, they are found to be different for almost every species, individually tailored or adapted for maximum susceptibility. The birds are simply gone, one morning, their cages open to the sky. A state-wide search fails to find a single one.

In Beijing, the Tiananmen Gate, its structure weakened in some way that defies analysis, disaggregates into several massive blocks of stone, which crush a party of German tourists and three students cycling to college. The pulped bodies are removed in buckets, prompting protests from relatives about the insensitive handling of their loved ones' remains.

Seven young cavers in Auckland enter a beginners' cave with a maximum depth of seven metres. All are found dead from severe decompression sickness and arterial gas embolisms, consistent with a dive to a thousand metres and an almost instantaneous return to the surface.

Across the world, the ripples were spreading. *But that is precisely the wrong metaphor*, Ber Lusim thought. Ripples get weaker and weaker, the further they get from their source. This – he observed with a certain pleasure – was more like a tsunami building, or like a riptide dragging more and more unwary swimmers into its invisible, deadly channels.

It was not that he relished pain and degradation for their own sake. Once, perhaps. A little. But he was no longer that man, no longer purely and simply the Demon. The prophet's words had changed him in his essence, without altering his trajectory by the smallest fraction. He did all the things that he had always done, mortifying flesh and spirit, but different meanings now attached to his actions. That was Shekolni's miracle, and proof enough that he was touched with the divine.

The prophet found his old friend sitting on the cot bed in his sleeping quarters. The room was as bare as a monk's cell, so in fact there was nowhere else to sit. Easily and unselfconsciously, Shekolni seated himself on the stone floor in front of Ber Lusim.

Ber Lusim had been reading, but now he jumped to his feet and offered the bed to Shekolni – who declined it with a wave of the hand. Ber Lusim took his seat again, closed the book and set it to one side. It was *the* book, of course: the book that had become the focal point of their lives and their aspirations, their rock of salvation and their stern taskmaster.

'Why so thoughtful, Ber Lusim?' the prophet asked. 'You've

pulled the trigger, now, and the bullet has gone out into the world. You can't alter its flight.'

Ber Lusim raised an eyebrow. 'Such things are my province rather than yours, Holy One. And I'm not sure I agree. With a bullet, as you say, all the thought and the care is taken before it's fired. Afterwards, you can only watch and see what comes.'

'So? Isn't that what we're doing?'

'Your pardon, Holy One, but this thing that we do is more like torture. A series of careful and painstaking interventions to achieve a cumulative effect.'

Shekolni smiled. 'And it's this that creases your brow? Are you having second thoughts?'

'Not at all!' Ber Lusim was shocked at the implication. 'Torture is something I'm very well versed in. I'm not taking issue with the plan, only trying to comprehend it.'

Ber Lusim stared at Shekolni, there in the darkness of the cell, which was unrelieved apart from the flames of three candles, burning in a niche beside the bed. The shadows covered the prophet's face as if with a veil, so his expression could not be read.

'Do you ever think of our childhood?' he demanded at last. *When you were only a man*, he meant. *When there were still mysteries you couldn't pierce.* But he didn't say those things. Tact and humility were important, when dealing with the incarnate divine.

The prophet laughed. 'I wasn't even alive in those times. I don't remember them at all. My life began on the day when I saw my first vision. Nothing before that has any meaning for me.'

Ber Lusim nodded as though he understood, although the statement showed how utterly different the two men were. Both of them by the violence of their natures and the force of their will had marked themselves out for peculiar destinies. But whereas Ber Lusim had embraced that violence and made it his garment, Shekolni had opened it like a door, passed through it into a place that was unknowable.

'Children are cruel,' Ber Lusim murmured. He was thinking of himself – his first experiments with the pain thresholds of others, that had permitted him to know himself.

'All men are cruel,' the prophet said. 'And all women, too. If we were not, then we would not need God.'

He climbed to his feet again. His movements were uncannily like those of an old man, although there was not a month between his age and that of Ber Lusim. Perhaps the mantle of holiness was heavier than ordinary men imagined.

'It's important to comprehend,' he said. 'To have a mental model for one's actions that takes everything into account and answers all objections. I'm about to preach to your comrades in arms. You should come and listen.'

'I invite you to think of a miracle,' the prophet said, his words rolling out across the vast hall almost like physical things, each cradled in a tangle of echoes. A hundred men watched him and listened to him, eager for revelation, immune to weakness and doubt. 'The miracle of birth.'

'None of you have wives or children. None of you ever will, now, not through any weakness or failing in you but because of the accident of history and the unalterable shape of the Plan.

'But let me assure you that birth, seen from up close, is a very ugly thing. The mother, in her birth-agonies, fills the air with her screams – with animal bleats and bellows. Sometimes she loses control of her bowels. The newborn child, when he comes at last, is covered with the filth of his mother's entrails, and more often than not with her blood. Scarcely human, he

141

looks, as he's held aloft. To be human, he has to be cleansed. To be human, he has to breathe. And to be human, he has to be separated from the womb that bore him and nourished him. Cut free with a knife.

'Does the doctor who wields the knife see the glory or does he see the ruck and ruin of blood? Does he smell incense or excrement? Does he hear screams or angels singing?'

Avra Shekolni paused theatrically, for the answers that would not come.

'You are that doctor. And the future, the thing that is waiting to be born, depends entirely on your readiness with the knife, your skill. It needs you to cut away what once was so very precious, so very much needed, and now is only dead weight. It needs you to see past the blood, however high it rises, to the light – the endless, endless light.'

He fell silent, and his arms, which had been thrown out as though to embrace them all, dropped to his sides. The followers of Ber Lusim fell to their knees as one. Most were weeping, and all were making the sign of the noose.

Ber Lusim knelt too, his heart singing, his blood drumming in his ears.

He had served heaven at one remove – God's commandments trickling down through the minds and voices of fallible men.

Now he was a word that God spoke.

PART TWO

A SOLDIER

16

It had never occurred to the girl that she would be chosen. Once, perhaps, she had toyed with the possibility, back when she was still in the usual age range for such things. People she knew had been taken at twelve, thirteen, fourteen.

But she reached sixteen, and nobody came. And then there was the great upheaval, the *y'siath*, when the People left the place where they'd lived for seven generations and travelled to the new city.

Once there, they unpacked their things again and tried to make it be home. But it wasn't home. The girl herself, along with all the People she knew (she didn't know all that many; she was solitary by nature), felt restless and unsettled. Everything seemed to have ended and nothing seemed to have begun again. Life's rhythms, which in the end are life itself, had been interrupted.

The girl had tried to express that feeling in the paintings and sculptures she made – and she'd waited for the normal sense of things, the unbroken skein of thoughts and associations and actions that made up her world, to heal her.

Chaos in the Sima, the council of elders. Voices raised in the Em Hadderek, the place of gathering. Normality circled at a distance, like a bird that has left its nest because of some perturbation and now can't settle again.

The girl was armoured against the chaos around her, at least to some extent, but it was hard not to be troubled when wise man and fool shouted anger at each other and everyone voiced disdain for the elders. Love was both the foundation of society and its mortar: if that failed them, what would be left?

The dissenting voices said that the People shouldn't have left Ginat'Dania, the Eden Garden that had been their home, that God hadn't sanctioned it. This led on inexorably to debates about what exactly God *had* sanctioned, and about the failings of the Messengers, or rather of their supreme shepherd and commander, Kuutma-that-was. He had betrayed the People, the rumours went, by falling in love with a woman in his charge, and by mourning her too much when she was dead. His judgement had become infected. He had let the enemies of the People live and grow stronger, and ally with one another. Until finally he himself had fallen in battle against the strongest of those enemies, the out-father Leo Tillman and the *rhaka,* the she-wolf Heather Kennedy. It was because of these failures that the People had had to move, in a caravan of sealed trucks, from their old home beneath Mexico City to the present Ginat'Dania thousands of miles north and east of that place.

The new Kuutma stood aloof from such allegations, mindful of the dignity of his office.

But the rumblings of protest grew, and finally they split the Sima itself. One of the three council elders had voiced the most terrible of heresies, the abomination of abominations. His peers had had no choice but to expel him from the chamber, and later that day it was learned that he had left the city – had gone out into the world, unsanctioned, unaccompanied, without name or blessing or commission.

Whereupon the city rocked crazily, like a boat when someone has stepped from its belly onto the shore and left it too light, too high in the water. The People were frozen and breathless, listening to echoes from a sound no one had heard.

And then, inexplicably, long after she'd stopped thinking of such a thing as being possible, the girl was summoned. Not by the council of elders but by Kuutma himself, known as 'the Brand' – the leader and commander of the *Elohim*, who held all truth in his heart and all vengeance in his hand.

The summons came at a time when she was least prepared to answer it. She was working on a massive canvas, the largest she had ever attempted. Standing at the top of a ladder, spattered and splotched with paint from head to knees, she was painting an angel's face when two angels appeared to her.

They were Alus and Taria, Kuutma's own personal attendants, and bodyguards. Their sudden arrival in the girl's studio almost made her fall off her ladder with shock.

'You're wanted,' Alus said simply.

They waited in silence while she washed herself, nervous and a little ashamed to be naked before them.

Walking between the two women, through the busy streets around the Em Hadderek, and then down the massive stairway beyond, the girl looked shyly but yearningly first at one and then at the other.

'See anything you fancy?' Taria asked her brazenly.

The girl blushed to the roots of her hair. 'I'd like to paint you,' she said. 'Your muscles are so beautiful.'

The angels thought that was hilarious, and said that they might consider sitting for the girl some day when they were free. But then in a more serious tone Alus reminded her that it was Kuutma she was going to see, and it would be better right now to keep her thoughts focused on that.

They took her to Kuutma's quarters, on the city's lowest level – which in the street argot of the People was sometimes called *het retoyet*, 'the dregs'. Kuutma had a modest apartment there, far less than he was entitled to. But like his predecessor, he was a man of modest tastes.

He was, moreover, a warrior, who had lasted in the ranks of the *Elohim* longer than most, and had the scars to prove it. Not on his body: though this Kuutma had been called on to kill many in the world outside, he had never (so far as anyone knew) taken wound or hurt. The scars were on his soul and the girl could see them there when first she looked into his eyes.

He was a solid, compact man, a little under average height but broad across the shoulders and with a sense of massiveness about him that, like the wounds, was not purely or even primarily physical. True, his hands were huge, and his forearms roped with muscle: but his broad, flat face – unusual among the People, and perhaps suggesting a Slavic out-father somewhere in his ancestry – had about it the stillness of profound meditation. He was bald, as the last Kuutma had been, but what had seemed martial in his predecessor looked on this man like the *askesis* of a monk or a hermit: a humbling of bodily pride, a stripping down to basics.

'Thank you for coming,' he said to the girl. His voice had a curious accent to it, the vowels forward and elongated – probably a survival from his last field posting, which would fade soon enough now that he was at home again among the People.

'Of course,' the girl said, blushing a little, caught unawares by Kuutma's gentleness and consideration.

What he said next surprised her even more. 'I owe you an apology.'

That seemed unlikely. He was Kuutma, after all. He was one of the names, and he held the fate of the People in his hands. Uncertain what to say, the girl simply shook her head.

'Yes,' Kuutma said. 'I do. On behalf of the last Kuutma. You were assessed and the results were impressive. You should have been called into service, as your brothers were called. Your mind and temperament fit you well for it. You have the resilience to survive outside Ginat'Dania. To adapt, among the unchosen, without losing yourself to their ways. You also have, very obviously, a powerful imagination that will enable you to innovate in situations for which your training has not adequately prepared you. In any event, I called for you today to right the omission that has allowed you to languish here, unused.'

The girl's heartbeat suddenly became perceptible to her, rising from unfelt background to a heavy hammering in her chest. It was hard to draw a breath. *Not the Kelim*, she prayed, to a God she seldom troubled. *Please, please, not the Kelim. Don't let my life go the way of my mother's life.*

'I feel that what I do here is valuable,' she said, in a voice that sounded in her own ears despicably weak, almost pleading.

'Of course,' Kuutma said, still gentle. 'That's in your nature. Wherever you are, and whatever you do, you will find a way to be useful. But there are places where you're needed more than you're needed here.'

Please.

'And so I have decided that you will become one of my *Elohim*.'

Almost, the girl shuddered. Relief flooded her, and then

149

joy. She was called – and to a vocation to which she could give herself without reservation. The *Kelim* served the People with their womb alone, and in the process were lessened (though everybody pretended otherwise). The *Elohim* served with hearts and minds and hands. A knife or a gun, she imagined, was only like any other tool – like the brushes she used when she painted, except that they were limited to the one effect, the one colour. She wasn't afraid of violence. Painting was already violence. She was full of violence, as far as that went.

Her acceptance wasn't required: she was being informed of a decision, not an offer. But still she said, 'I accept, Kuutma. I accept with joy.'

'I'm pleased,' Kuutma said solemnly. 'These are not joyful times. We are uncertain, and divided. But it may be, little sister, that you'll be the one to raise us up again.'

'Only tell me what I have to do,' the girl said.

Kuutma smiled at the urgency in her tone, not a patronising smile, but a recognition – an acknowledgement – of the passion that filled her. 'First, you must be taught,' he said. 'And that's no small thing. Then ... well, I have a plan, and you are a part of it. When you're ready, I'll explain it to you. And then I'll send you out.' He stood, and indicated that she should follow, but for a moment she couldn't move.

'If it please you, Kuutma,' she asked him. 'Send me where?'

He regarded her with a complex, unreadable expression. He took her two hands in his and pressed them together as though he were conferring a blessing, or else inviting her to join him in prayer.

'To your ordeal, little sister,' he said solemnly, even sadly. 'To the task and the testing that is yours and yours alone.'

17

Kuutma had said that the training would be no small thing. In fact it was an ordeal that almost broke her.

The girl discovered, as she had expected, that neither the mechanics nor the ethics of killing were daunting. She'd always preferred a solitary life, with few and fleeting human attachments: she had the sense that not many things lasted, and that romantic and familial loves were either comforting illusions or self-consciously played games. So it was possible for her to learn – in exacting detail – a great many ways of ending lives, without her emotions or her conscience becoming engaged. It was all theory, so far, but it was theory to which she applied herself with guiltless enthusiasm.

The physical demands of the training were another matter. The girl had to endure seventeen-hour days of drilling and practice, of gym and exercise regimens, of classes in sabotage, use and maintenance of weapons, infiltration, unarmed combat systems, battlefield survival, tracking and surveillance.

Then these lessons would stop and another sequence would start: world history, politics, languages, psychology, sociology, non-verbal communications, even fashion. The girl knew the purpose of these soft and seemingly trivial disciplines, and she didn't protest. When another of the students made some

151

contemptuous comment, the trainer, Ushana, made him stand up in front of the other recruits and rebuked him mercilessly.

'You might live among the unchosen for ten years,' Ushana said, 'and kill once. So tell me, child, how you would allocate time between combat and infiltration.'

The girl kept her head down and applied herself assiduously to the learning of things that seemed both foolish and impenetrable, the nonsense syllables of an alien language. And gradually the dead ground between the disparate facts filled up with more facts. Pathways of logic opened up through the mad hinterlands and she began to see the wider, Adamite world outside Ginat'Dania for what it was: a horrifically distorted reflection of the real world in which she lived.

Also – and this was the only thing that actually frightened her – she was brought to see the differences of scale. The People lived in a space a handful of miles across and many levels deep – a great city that for most of them was in effect the whole world. But they knew that there was another world, which God had gifted to the children of Adam, but had promised in the fullness of time to render to his true chosen.

What the girl had never appreciated up until then was just how much bigger that other world was than the world she knew. As she explored it in wide games that began in the immediate environs of Ginat'Dania and then took her further and further afield, she saw the truth of it. The world was so big that it seemed to go on for ever, country opening on country and then on further countries into a distance that her mind was, at least at first, simply unable to fathom.

Kuutma told her, later, that this was common and far from trivial. Many young men and women in Messenger training experienced a sort of conceptual paralysis when they first stepped out of Ginat'Dania into the immensity of the Adamite nations. Some never got over it, and therefore were never able to join the *Elohim*. Some seemed to adapt, but then descended into psychosis once they were outside. It was a problem that seemed, if anything, to become more acute with each generation – perhaps because the gulf between Ginat'Dania and the world of the unchosen became ever greater over time.

The girl survived the existential crisis by looking at the world as an aesthetic composition. Scale was a device that an artist could deploy in the service of an effect. How great was God, then, who had painted on a canvas so huge that thousands of millions of men and women could live out their lives upon it.

The teaching continued. Each week, each day, it seemed she drew further and further ahead of those she trained with. In unarmed combat, she routinely humbled opponents much bigger and stronger than her. Her will was like a wire wound over and back on itself a million times within her compact body, so that her smallness concealed a great, unyielding immensity.

She excelled in use of weapons.

She excelled in tactical and strategic thinking.

She excelled in stamina.

She excelled in intelligence and in the retention of information.

It became, for her classmates, a matter of extreme pride to keep pace with the girl in anything. To best her, even temporarily, was an achievement to be boasted about for months.

Many of the boys in the group expressed a romantic interest in her – and many of the girls, likewise, since the People had no taboos about what the Adamites called homosexuality. The girl made it clear in every case that these attentions were unwelcome. In fact, she feared intimacy as others seemed to fear loneliness. To let someone into her life and into her bed, to speak unguarded thoughts in the heat of unguarded acts – it was an idea that thrilled her and nauseated her in equal measure. But close up, as soon as she felt any quickening of interest in anyone, boy or girl (more usually boy), the nausea overwhelmed the excitement. She could imagine the physical act of sex, the rest was too unnerving to contemplate.

When she finally gave herself, it seemed more an act of violence than of love. She was on the third and last day of a competitive field test, matched against a superior team that had had them outmanoeuvred from the start. If the girl herself had been team leader, she knew she could still have pulled things together – forced a victory or at the very worst a draw. But the leaders had been chosen by random lot, and her team's, an impulsive and excitable boy named Desh Nahir, was not equal to the task.

So on the third day, the girl's squad was trapped in an indefensible position at the bottom of a shallow gully and wiped out by a sustained enfilade attack that left them covered from head to foot in the red paint that was standing in for blood.

Subsequently, the girl had to spend three hours lying still in the place where she'd been shot, before the whistle sounded for the end of the day's combat.

As soon as she was able to move, she found her team leader disrobing in the locker room and tackled him. She didn't punch or kick or slap him, she just pressed her body against his so that his uniform would be saturated with the red paint and he'd be obliged to take a share of the dishonour that was by rights his, not hers.

But the tumult of her feelings, though it was dominated by anger and frustration, had other components, too. The pressure of her body against Nahir's began to arouse feelings that were not entirely unpleasant, and when he kissed her, tentative, terrified of her rebuke, she responded.

Their relationship lasted for five weeks, long enough for the girl to decide that she'd been right in the first place: the annoyances and provocations caused by letting someone get that close to you far outweighed any possible pleasures. She told Nahir that it was over, much to his chagrin, and when he so far forgot his dignity as to plead with her, she walked away.

There was another fling, with a girl four years older than her, which she undertook in order to make sure that she hadn't just picked the wrong someone. The results were much the same, although that relationship lasted a little longer and ended a little more stormily.

The girl trained for three years. It wasn't, in any sense, long enough, but she knew that time was short. She could tell this from the way their teachers drove them, and from the fact that sometimes when she looked up from her exercises in the arena or in the classroom, she would see either Kuutma himself or one of his two angels watching her closely, with a grave, absorbed expression.

The teachers were not troubled by the high rates of attrition. One by one, the students fell away after failing this or that test, or else simply stopped attending classes for no reason that the girl could see.

As the third year wore on, they began to take the drug, kelalit. The first time the girl took it, letting just a tiny drop of the clear liquid fall from the eye-dropper onto her tongue, it was like being splashed across the brain with liquid nitrogen. Everything became incredibly sharp-edged, incredibly clear – and incredibly slow. She felt both strong and dead, as though what had been her body had been filled with molten metal, which had now cooled and hardened into some terrible machine in her exact shape.

They put her into the arena and sent three opponents against her at once – all *Elohim* like herself, but without the benefit of the pharmacon. The fight lasted nineteen seconds.

Afterwards the girl puked her guts up, and then lay awake for most of the night, trembling and sweating.

'It's poison,' the teacher Ushana told her, when she asked. 'The exact formula is known only to the chemists who make it, but all of its nearest cousins are utterly lethal. Adamites take them for pleasure and become addicted to them. They take larger and larger doses, and in the end their minds and bodies are destroyed by the cumulative effects of the toxins.'

The girl was shocked and afraid in spite of herself. Loss of control was high on her personal list of deadly sins. 'How is the way we use the drug different?' she asked, hoping to be reassured.

'We take no pleasure in it,' Ushana said.

No, Kuutma told her later, there's more than that. The drug we take, kelalit, *the curse and the blessing*, is not a single substance. It's a compound, made of many drugs, and some of them are at war with each other. The core compound induces a rush of euphoria, a feeling of omnipotence, but it clouds the mind and dulls the senses. Kelalit, by contrast, heightens the senses and speeds up physiological processes. The flow of information through the nerves of the body is hugely enhanced, which means that both perception

156

and action are much quicker. Of that core sense of power and joy, meanwhile, enough is maintained to make the user shrug off pain that would normally distract or even incapacitate. Out of a filthy and shameful indulgence, the craftsmen of the People had fashioned a warrior's tool, flexible and powerful.

But still deadly. Most of the *Elohim* who died out among the Nations did so from the cumulative effects of kelalit.

Over weeks and months, the girl became habituated to the use of this double-edged tool, this treacherously mixed blessing. By the summer of the third year, she could endure a full dose of kelalit, despite her relatively small body mass, and function at the heightened level of perception and action for hours at a time. She grew more adept, also, at handling the physiological and emotional crash that always followed.

Once again, she was the example held up to all the others, the model they followed and fashioned themselves upon. When another trainee, Esali, died of a kelalit overdose, and her stiff, grey body was brought through the dormitory in a deafening silence of disbelief and denial, the girl realised that being top of the class had its downside. Esali had been trying to become more like her.

The girl kept to herself more than ever after that. She hadn't ever encouraged her classmates' cult of hero worship, but now she repelled all advances with deliberate rudeness. She wanted no more deaths queuing up at the gates of her conscience, no matter how strongly those gates were defended.

She endured. She won out. She took all that her teachers could give her, internalised it, and like a spider gave it back as a single thread of woven silk. Only the oldest teacher, Rithuel, who taught some of the psychology classes, gave her a less than exemplary mark. In fact, he gave her a fail. When the girl sought him out to ask him why, he was blunt but – to the girl's mind – enigmatic.

'To make you pause,' was all he said.

'To make me pause in what?' she demanded.

Rithuel opened his palms and held them out to her, empty. 'I don't know,' he admitted.

'Then—'

'Inaction can be as important as action. The pause before you act is filled with many things, and one of them is truth.'

'But I didn't fail your tests,' the girl protested. 'I answered every question. I don't believe I made any significant errors.'

'You made no errors at all. That was precisely what troubled me. I think it may help you, some day, to know that you're not perfect. To be so close to perfect can sometimes be a dangerous thing. Dangerous for the soul, I mean.'

And there was yet one more test, one about which all the students exchanged wild rumours, empty speculation and tasteless jokes. It would come when they least expected it, the students mostly agreed. And you could fail it by a single word or movement out of place.

One evening, after eating her evening meal in the refectory, the girl was sought out by a runner who said that Ushana was waiting for her in the gymnasium. When she got there, she found the teacher waiting in the dark. At her feet there knelt a man – a boy, rather. His hands and feet had been fastened with short lengths of chain to the tallest of the vaulting horses, where iron rings had been set – presumably, the girl now realised, for this purpose. The boy was her own age, but with the white-blond hair almost never seen among the People. He was slightly overweight, and dressed outlandishly in short trousers and a sleeveless tunic that bore the meaningless legend

HOME-BREWED FOR FULLER FLAVOUR! He was terrified, the marks of recent tears on his cheeks.

The girl knew at once what was expected of her, but she said nothing. She presented herself to her teacher with a respectful bow, ignoring the boy utterly, until Ushana nodded in his direction. 'That is Ronald Stephen Pinkus,' she said. 'Say hello to him, in his own language.'

'What is his language, *Tannanu*?' the girl asked. She knew better than to assume that the boy spoke English, just because that was the language of the words on his shirt.

'English,' Ushana said. There was approval in her tone.

The girl turned. 'Good evening to you, Ronald Stephen Pinkus,' she said.

The boy's face underwent a convulsion of surprise and hope. 'Shit,' he yelped. 'You speak English! Oh, thank God! Listen, there's been some kind of a mistake. They think I'm someone else, but I'm not anybody. They took me right off the street, and it's like – I don't know. I don't know what they want.'

The girl turned from him again, looked to Ushana.

'Kill him,' Ushana said.

The girl bowed her head in acquiescence, but she didn't move. She wanted to be sure. 'For what crime?' she asked.

The boy had no idea what was being said. He looked from her to Ushana and back again. Perhaps he thought that she was passing on what he'd said to her.

'For no crime. Kill him because I tell you to.'

And she did. With her bare hands, because no weapon had been specified. Afterwards, though she wept, she wept in silence, and nobody in the dormitory had any inkling of it.

Ronald Stephen Pinkus was not of the People. It was wrong

to cry for him, and it was shaming. Next time, she promised herself, she would do better.

And so, in due course, she was sent back to Kuutma, with a note from her teachers that was notable for its brevity: 'She's ready.'

He welcomed her with a fatherly embrace, expressing great satisfaction in her accomplishments. The girl thanked him graciously. Neither of them mentioned the mark that Rithuel had given her for psychology, and so she was saved from the necessity of criticising one of her teachers.

Kuutma gave her fresh fruit and water spiced with cloves and cinnamon. He offered her wine, too, but the girl wasn't fond of wine. Alcohol interfered with her body's uptake of kelalit, slowing it down unpredictably.

They sat in companionable silence for a while, in the same room in which they had met, three years before.

That meeting was on Kuutma's mind, too. 'I told you once that I had a plan for you,' he said to her. 'It's time, now, for that plan to be put into effect.'

The girl experienced a moment of very pleasurable disorientation, a shifting of her mental perspectives sudden enough to induce mild vertigo. If Kuutma had summoned her here to command her into action, then she was now a Messenger. Those simple words were her graduation ceremony, her induction into the ranks of his *Elohim*.

'I'm ready,' she said.

'Good.' He filled her glass with water, then his own. The wine, it seemed, had been brought only in case she wanted it. 'But you need to know that this is an unusual assignment – an unusual situation, in every respect – and you'll be within your rights to refuse it.'

160

The girl nodded. She wondered what Kuutma could possibly ask of her, in the name of the city and the People, that she would refuse – or would even hesitate before accepting.

'You know that one of the elders has left us. An elder, I should say, in name only. He is younger than me, in fact.'

'Yes,' the girl said. And then, 'Of course.'

'He was the *Yedimah*,' Kuutma said. 'The Seed. The one who, in the sittings of the Sima, is deputed to look to the future and argue in favour of change. But he has forfeited that position, of course, and the name. He is who he was. Avra Shekolni.

'Shekolni took his writ too far with the rest of the Council of Elders, bringing into question the most profound and sacred of the principles by which we live. His premise, essentially, was that the People have misinterpreted the nature of the bargain God made with us – that our entire way of life is founded on a misunderstanding. God promised us the Earth, Shekolni said, but He didn't promise to deliver it to us: He expected us to take action ourselves to accomplish His will. You see the problem with this position, sister?'

The girl did, and said so.

'Then expound it for me.'

'The Adamites outnumber us by many thousands to one. And their history is one of uninterrupted war, so their weapons are advanced far beyond anything we can match. That's why we hide. If we tried to fight, we couldn't possibly win. So we wait. We wait for God's judgement.'

'An excellent summary,' said Kuutma. 'And the council spoke to Shekolni in that wise, seeking to correct his thinking. But, as you know, he wouldn't take correction. He was expelled from the Sima. And then he left Ginat'Dania itself. It's not known how he was able to get out of the city without sanction or permission, but it's certain that he did. We've searched far and wide for him since, but found no trace.'

The girl nodded, but didn't speak. She would ask questions only if she was invited to.

'Bad as this was,' Kuutma went on, 'we now know that there is worse. Shekolni made contact, out among the Nations, with a Messenger – or rather a Summoner, a commander of Messengers – who seems to share his unsanctioned views. The commander in question, Ber Lusim, was a great man in his time – so formidable, and I might venture to say, so cruel a warrior that he was sometimes called, by those who knew him, the Demon. The previous Kuutma relied on him absolutely. But then, perhaps ten years ago, Lusim fell into disgrace. He failed in his sacred duties. There were deaths – from among our number, not Adamite deaths – that could have been avoided.

'The old Kuutma called Ber Lusim back so that he could be punished, but he refused to come. When Messengers were sent to recall him, he disappeared. It was only then that we realised how strong a cult of personality had grown up around him – for a great many Messengers who knew him and had sojourned with him among the Nations now followed him into exile. They dropped from our radar – went native, we thought, although if anything the truth seems to be the opposite of that. They hold themselves aloof, still, from the Adamites, even though they've foresworn all contact with the People and with Ginat'Dania. Theirs must be an intolerably lonely existence.

'But somehow, as I said, Avra Shekolni found Ber Lusim. At first this was only a guess: Shekolni disappeared so completely, we theorised that he must have had help. Then Ber Lusim contacted us himself and said that Shekolni had been sent to

162

him and his followers by God – and he thanked us for being instrumental in the forwarding of that gift. He warned us not to look for Shekolni and he told us – I quote exactly – to hold ourselves ready for judgement.'

Kuutma paused for a moment and took a sip of his water. He swirled it in his mouth, as though trying to rid himself of a sour taste. Then he swallowed.

'I sent a reply to Ber Lusim,' he said, in a low voice. 'Or at least, I sent forth one of my *Elohim* at a time and in a place where I guessed – correctly – that Ber Lusim would be sure to intercept him. I warned Lusim that Shekolni was a heretic. And I urged him to come back into Ginat'Dania, among the People, where he belongs.'

'He ignored the summons,' the girl guessed.

'Yes, he did. But more. This will distress you, sister. Remember that God ordains all things and brings forth good from evil. Ber Lusim scarred the face of my emissary with blades and hot irons, making him so hideous that all who saw him flinched and looked away. Branding my servant in this way was an insult aimed at me. This innocent man's face was only the paper on which Lusim chose to write his message.'

The girl was inured to violence, but this still shocked her to the core. Her stomach convulsed and her gorge rose sour in her throat. She missed some of Kuutma's words as she struggled to regain her equanimity.

'—of course impossible, now, for that man to go back out into the world. He was forced to forsake his calling. And beyond that, the shame is very great. He's asked leave to kill himself, but I've told him to reflect a little and to spend time with family and friends. I hope that will be enough to draw him back into the normal business of life, which has an enormous healing power in itself.'

'This Ber Lusim is a monster,' the girl said, her throat still tight and sore from the acid she'd forced back down.

'Perhaps.' Kuutma sighed heavily. 'After this atrocity, we spoke the *hrach bishat*, the execration, over him. As you know, that curse was once reserved for those thought to be possessed. It meant that Ber Lusim was henceforward to be considered a demon, rather than a man. He had finally earned the title that had already been accorded him.' Kuutma seemed to hesitate. 'Tell me, little sister, when you were growing up, in the orphan house, did you ever experience cruelty, or discrimination, on account of your origins?'

The girl stared at him, false-footed by the sudden change of topic. 'Sometimes,' she said, at last. And then, 'That was a long time ago.'

'The other children called you names?'

The girl thought back. Yes, of course they had, but it had meant very little. It was the teacher-nurses who'd hurt her, by their coldness and contempt. Until she learned to find the place inside herself that they couldn't touch – and to love colour and tone and texture and pattern more than she loved people.

'What did they call you?' Kuutma asked.

'It was a long time ago,' the girl said again.

'But you remember, I'm sure,' he prompted her.

'They called me bastard.' And mixer, by-blow, whore-sore, bleed, drop-in, mongrel, *Kelim*-fart, crossbreed, Adam's apple. A hundred things, all variations on the same thing. *Your mother went out into the world and spread her legs, waited for some passer-by to impregnate her, and now here you are.*

'Ber Lusim was also the child of a *Kelim* woman. It may be that the abuse he suffered as a result was what hardened his heart against the *Kelim*.'

164

Kuutma raised his glass, as though to take another sip of his water, but then merely stared into it, and for the longest time said nothing.

'Perhaps Shekolni was right, in one respect,' he murmured at last. 'Change ... change may come to us, whether we want it or not. I'm not even sure that this would be a bad thing. Stagnation is possibly our worst enemy at this point. Stagnation and decadence.'

He shook off the sombre mood with a visible effort, looked at the girl and raised the glass a little higher in a salute. 'I shouldn't speak this way,' he said, 'on this day of your triumph. I've watched you through your training. I don't know if you were aware of that?'

She was very well aware, of course, but she made some modest disclaimer.

'Yes,' Kuutma said. 'I've watched you and I've been pleased. Proud. Delighted. You've suffered all that's worst in us, and you embody all that's best. I hope to live to see you rise to the heights you deserve.'

The girl was uncomfortable with so much praise. 'What am I to do?' she asked, both as a way of changing the subject and because she was desperate to know.

'I'm sending you against Avra Shekolni and Ber Lusim,' Kuutma said simply. 'I want you to find out how many men now follow them, and where they are, and what they're doing.'

'And bring them home to be judged?'

'No.' Kuutma shook his head. There was a sheen of sweat on his bald forehead, which made it gleam even in the room's dim light. 'Or at least, not immediately. Ber Lusim is a formidable opponent in his own right, and we don't know for certain how many others stand with him. You could scarcely hope to prevail against them alone. Consider how you would be handicapped, in any such meeting. Consider how little you could hope to achieve.'

'Then give me helpmeets strong enough for the task,' the girl said. It never occurred to her to doubt that she'd be the leader of any such team: she didn't underestimate her own abilities, and in any event Kuutma wouldn't be talking in this way to a mere footsoldier.

'Yes,' he said. 'I will.' And as he explained his plan to her, she began to realise why he had offered her the option of saying no to this. But she had no intention of refusing. She knew that Kuutma's scruples on her behalf were mistaken and that the things he thought would be hard for her would come more easily than he could ever imagine.

He finished his speech and waited in silence for her to respond.

'I'll need a new name,' she said at last.

Kuutma was taken aback at this apparent non sequitur.

'None of this will work if I tell them who I am,' the girl explained, holding his gaze to show how little the specifics of her brief had shaken or abashed her.

Kuutma appeared to consider. 'No,' he allowed. 'Perhaps you're right.'

'So I'll be Diema,' the girl said. It meant sycamore seed, something light that travels a long way on the wind. She meant it both literally and ironically. She would be going a long way, but she intended to move by her own volition.

She'd never liked the name Tabe, in any case. It reminded her too much of her mother.

18

Diema went among the Nations and she learned their ways. She thought she already knew them, but there was a difference, she now found, between the self-contained trips conducted by her teachers and this – she searched for a word – this *odyssey*, this great journeying into the unknown.

To survive in the Adamite world, completely alone for much of the time, Diema had no choice but to match velocities with it – which was bruising and existentially terrifying. She immersed herself in random encounters, casual social gatherings, loose and trivial connections. Self-help groups, speed-dating parties, karaoke nights, business seminars, rock concerts, evening classes, public meetings and prayer circles: she shot through them like an exotic particle through a bubble tank, accreting mass and spin, learning her role.

Being young and (it seemed) fairly attractive, and not yet entirely in control of the social signals she was sending, she found herself more than once in situations where she might have been in danger of rape or assault. But she was adept at curbing the men who threatened her and judicious in her response, leaving them damaged but not crippled. Each of these incidents was a learning experience. She had never guessed how important sex was as social currency among the

Nations, how large a part of their everyday interaction was based on it.

This part of Diema's task, which Kuutma had called acclimatisation, was open-ended. It was up to the girl herself to decide when she was ready to move on. She took three months. Part of her rebelled against the loss of time and impetus, but she'd learned from her teachers how crucial it could be when you fought to have a firm footing. If you leaned outside of your centre of gravity, even a weak adversary could topple you. She wasn't going to make that basic mistake.

Or perhaps she was just stalling. Some of the things she'd discovered out here, in the wasteland that was the Nations, affected her in wholly unexpected ways.

Television, for example. The first time she turned on a TV in a hotel bedroom, feeling the need for some background noise, and found herself staring at a stylised cat chasing a stylised mouse through a house that was magically endless, she stood there for five minutes like somebody hypnotised. How could these anarchic, insane little masterpieces exist? What idiot savants made them?

Cartoons became Diema's one vice. Whenever she had to kill time in any place where there was a TV, she'd flick through the channels until she found some children's network and sit for hours, guiltily but thoroughly absorbed in this world of talking rabbits and ducks, bombs labelled BOMB, non-permanent death, tragicomic peripateias and the wonderful Acme company, which made everything you could ever want and sent it to wherever you were.

The cartoons were a barricade, sometimes successful and sometimes not, against the nightmares. She dreamed most nights about killing the boy (whose name, Ronald Stephen Pinkus, she could not make herself forget). Except that in her dreams, his death was a Sisyphean labour that always had to be begun again as soon as it was done. She woke with tears on her face and hated herself for them. They were the visible sign of some terrible inner flaw, that she had to isolate and eradicate. Ronald Stephen Pinkus had set some tiny part of her at war with the rest. But she was strong, and resilient, and she was confident she could defeat that rogue fragment. She would know she'd won when the dreams stopped coming.

And eventually, nightmares aside, she decided she was ready. She had read the briefing documents that Kuutma had given her – endlessly and obsessively, until she had them by heart – and she'd chosen her entry point.

The foremost sacrament of the Messengers was the taking of kelalit. Ber Lusim and his followers would not have forgone it, and though they could obtain weapons and supplies from anywhere they liked, the base ingredients of the lethal, indispensable pharmacon were very hard to source. Diema considered a number of merchants who Ber Lusim would know and picked one – one known for his discretion and who had been used by Kuutma-that-was in the days when Ber Lusim was still among the chosen.

That first choice bore no fruit, and nor did the second. But the magic of threes worked in her favour. At the third house, in Paris, she hadn't been watching a week when she saw Ber Lusim's messenger (a man known to her from Kuutma's files) come to collect a purchase. Following him at a distance, she found the building site whose portakabin huts housed the Demon's French residence.

She went in, cautiously and slowly. She took nothing for granted. She watched and tabulated and bided her time. She was a soldier, now, and her heart rejoiced in the task that had been set her.

169

Over several months, she built up a picture of Ber Lusim's network.

It was much smaller than Kuutma's network, of course: it had to be, since it consisted mainly of the members of his own cell who'd broken away from the People at the same time as him.

Diema learned about that schism by listening to their conversations. She had a US Army ScopeNet directional amplifier, jacked with layer after layer of intelligent noise filters. She could adjust the settings to correct for two or three intervening walls and windows, and for her own angle to each new speaker. She did most of her eavesdropping lying on her stomach on the roof of Ber Lusim's various safe houses and waystations, eyes closed, shutting out the world, focusing herself down to the fluting, sussurating soundscape.

She got what she needed.

She mapped Ber Lusim's command structure, which was massively decentralised. The troops at his disposal numbered far fewer than the numbers of the legitimate *Elohim*, though still more than she'd guessed. Shockingly, he'd been able to recruit other Messengers previously thought faithful. Evidently, Shekolni was far from alone in his dissatisfaction with the new Ginat'Dania.

She learned that Ber Lusim relied very heavily on two lieutenants – Elias Shud, who was as blunt and brutal and dangerous as a runaway train, and Hifela, the 'Face of the Skull', who was a great deal more dangerous again and almost as fast as Ber Lusim himself.

She learned about Toller's book, which perhaps ought to have come as no surprise. Toller was known to the *Elohim* already, and his appeal to a mind like Ber Lusim's was obvious.

But it wasn't Lusim who was driving this. It was Shekolni,

the disgraced elder (although Lusim and his people referred to Shekolni simply as 'the prophet'). Lusim seemed to have been relegated to the lesser role of taskmaster, with his own consent, and the perverse but fierce loyalty of his own followers had been transferred to the other man. Shekolni's word had come to them, when they needed it. They treated him with hungry reverence, and they obeyed his every word.

The astonishing thing was what he was telling them to do.

Diema went back to Kuutma and told him what she'd discovered. That the renegade *Elohim* were burning every copy of Toller's book that existed in the world, except their own, and killing everyone outside their ranks who might have read it.

Kuutma didn't even pretend to be surprised. 'We've done similar things to protect our own scriptures,' he reminded her.

'To protect them, yes,' Diema agreed. 'This goes far beyond protection.' Then she told him what it was that Shekolni was doing and what he hoped to achieve by it.

And Kuutma laughed. But it was a bitter, incredulous laugh. 'It's wonderful,' he said. 'So many thousands, at one stroke. Millions, perhaps. He dares God to intervene, even while he pretends to bow to God's word. It's a game of chicken, played against heaven.'

'A game of what?' Diema asked. And Kuutma explained to her the rules of that game. How two men embark on a course of action that will destroy both of them – for example, driving cars towards one another, at a speed great enough for a fatal crash. And the loser is the one who swerves aside.

'I don't believe that God plays chicken,' she said grimly.

'Little sister,' Kuutma said, 'he most assuredly does. But he does not drive the car himself. He chooses proxies. At this point, let there be no misunderstanding, he has chosen you.'

'You chose me, *Tannanu*.'

'True, as far as it goes. But the circumstances that made you the right choice? That wasn't my doing, nor yours. Providence moves through us, in its own direction, which is so much at odds with our directions that – good and evil alike – its passage can hurt us past saving. We can only hope to be whole, when His will has been done. We can't ask to understand.'

He was looking at Diema closely and thoughtfully. 'You've achieved great things, in a relatively short time.'

'Thank you, *Tannanu*.'

'But one thing that you've done does not make me happy, little sister. It fills me with alarm.'

Diema kept her face impassive, though her stomach clenched. 'I've done nothing to compromise your plan, *Tannanu*,' she said – a minimal defence, at best.

'Of course you haven't,' he agreed. 'But at certain points, in your travels, you've stepped aside from your task to look into a matter that has no relevance.'

Diema bowed her head, partly to hide her face so he couldn't read her guilt in it, and partly out of genuine shame.

'It won't happen again,' she said tightly.

'Ronald Stephen Pinkus,' Kuutma said, placing audible gaps between the three words of the name. 'The boy you killed. You've been investigating his family. His parents, and his surviving sister. Why would you do such a thing?'

Diema forced herself to meet Kuutma's gaze. 'Out of an idle interest, only,' she said. 'Nothing more. Our teachers taught us to be curious about how systems work, in the Adamite world. The boy's family is a system. My action changed it. I wanted to see how it had reacted to that change.'

'No more than that?'

'No more than that, *Tannanu*.'

Kuutma nodded. 'You named yourself the sycamore seed,'

he reminded her. 'Study it. Lightness is the virtue that will serve you best. To float through their lives, without touching or being touched. I say this not to chide you, but to help you.'

'What do I do now?' Diema asked, desperate to change the subject.

'Bring your team together,' Kuutma said briskly. 'All of them, in the prescribed pattern and order, as we discussed.'

And she did. She let Providence do its work.

She let the hammer meet the nail.

PART THREE

PART THREE

THE HAMMER

19

Southampton Row at half-past seven in the morning was already busy. Shops had their shutters half-raised so employees could limbo underneath and start stacking shelves. Upmarket cafés and breakfast bars were packed with early birds heading for the shops and offices of the West End, cheaper ones with tired cleaners and security staff clocking off from night shifts.

Kennedy walked between them, a transient, belonging neither to the night world nor the day. Fatigue and fretfulness distanced her from everything. She felt as though the surface of her brain had been roughly polished up with a scouring pad, and that this process had loosened it enough in her skull for it to jar when she walked.

She'd left Izzy's the night before with nothing but the clothes she was wearing. Both of her attackers were still profoundly unconscious, and Samal in particular looked like he'd need a lot of medical attention if he was ever going to play the piano again – or form a sentence with more than one syllable in it. But Kennedy's nerves were shot and she couldn't bring herself to pack a suitcase with the two men lying there, stepping over their inert bodies as she hunted out her own blouses and slacks from among Izzy's cocktail dresses and sexy lingerie.

So she just got out of there, locking the door behind her.

She made a quick pit-stop at her own apartment on the floor below, where she threw some underwear and shirts into a shoulder bag.

She'd told Izzy about the need to break her own pattern. When you were being hunted, the worst thing you could do was to stick to known contacts and established habits. Otherwise, sooner or later, at a bend in some familiar path there'd be a tripwire and a pit with sharpened bamboo stakes at the bottom. She took her own advice. She walked half a mile from the apartment before grabbing a taxi.

'Where to, love?' the cabbie asked.

'Where did you pick up your last fare?' Kennedy asked him.

'Eh?' The cabbie seemed to find something sinister in the question.

'Whoever was in here last. Where were they coming from?'

'Talbot Square, innit. Out by Paddington Station.'

'Great. Take me there.'

It was a good choice, as far as that went. Talbot Square opened off Sussex Gardens, where every second house was a hotel. Kennedy grabbed some emergency supplies from an all-night mini-market on Praed Street, then checked into one of the hotels, reassuringly named the Bastion, with mildewed pilasters framing the door and a sign jammed into the lower corner of the window that promised FREE WIRELESS INTERN. Presumably an E and a T were hidden by the angle of the frame.

She paid for her room with cash. The desk clerk wanted to see some ID in the name of Conroy, which was the name Kennedy had given, but she deflected his curiosity in that regard with a couple of twenties.

The room was an odd, indented shape, seemingly made up

out of pieces cut from other, adjacent rooms. Kennedy snatched a couple of hours of shallow sleep in the narrow single bed, but the pain in her wounded side woke her every time she shifted position. In the end she gave up and just lay unmoving on her back, staring at the mottled plaster of the ceiling and trying to figure out how things had gotten so screwed up so quickly.

Not by accident. Not by serendipity. Not by blind chance. Lightning didn't strike the same spot twice without a bloody good reason.

The Judas tribe had sent their Messengers, their *Elohim*, to kill her.

But the girl who'd saved her had identified herself as a Messenger, too.

There were wheels within wheels, and fires within fires.

When dawn filtered through the paisley-pattern curtains, she got up and showered. The water only ran lukewarm, but it was still enough to start the shallow wound in her side bleeding again, marbling the water at her feet with red ripples. Kennedy felt an incongruous sense of relief. The wound had scabbed and was only bleeding now because she'd opened it again. She was lucky that the Messengers used different blades for torture: the ones they used for murder had usually been anointed with a powerful anti-coagulant that made even shallow wounds potentially fatal.

She dried herself, ruining the towel in the process, and then disinfected and dressed the wound. Time to face the day. And to put herself fairly and squarely back in the crosshairs again.

Because her first stop was going to be Leo Tillman.

The Pantheon Café on Montague Street had a frontage so narrow and unassuming that its name had to be intended as some kind of ironic gesture. When Kennedy stepped inside, she found that she was the only customer in the place, but then again it would only have held about eight people when full. Two tables covered with tartan-patterned plastic tablecloths stood just inside the door, to balance the two outside. Beyond them there was a cooler that was too big for the tiny space and blocked half of the tiny counter. On the wall opposite the drinks machine, a much-smeared whiteboard advertised the specials of the day – falafel in pitta bread, dolmades, feta salad. For a Greek café, they didn't sound all that special.

At the counter, a man with a slim, athletic build, slicked-down hair and a bandito moustache that looked like it had just blown in from someone else's face was arranging slices of baklava into a crude mosaic on an oval tray.

'Hi,' Kennedy said. 'I'm trying to get in touch with Leo. Leo Tillman.'

The man didn't look up from his work. 'Yes,' he said. 'And?'

'And I was told that I could leave a message for him here.'

'Ah.'

Kennedy waited, but that seemed to be it. 'So if I leave a message with you,' she continued, 'maybe you could pass it on to Leo the next time he comes through. If that wouldn't be too much trouble.'

'Ah,' the man said again. 'If.'

'Look,' said Kennedy. 'Do you know Leo or not? If it's not, I'm out of your life.'

The man looked at her for the first time – an appraising, appreciative stare. 'You are not *in* my life, my lovely,' he told her solemnly. 'I see this man, I tell him you're looking for him.' He shrugged and gave her a sad smile. 'All I can do.'

180

Kennedy locked eyes with him. 'So what are you going to tell him? I didn't even give you my name.'

'I tell him that a very beautiful woman is looking for him. And I describe your lovely face, your lovely body to him in such detail that he knows who I mean.'

Kennedy's tolerance for this kind of talk was low. She opened her mouth, already lining up a row of curse words to fire out of it, but then she noticed that the man was looking over her shoulder.

Tillman was behind her, leaning in the doorway, heavy hands deep in his pockets.

'It's good to see you, Heather,' he said. 'Come on into my office.'

Kennedy thought Tillman meant the diner, but as it turned out, his office was Coram's Fields – a more or less perfectly X-shaped patch of greenery just west of Gray's Inn Road. In the days when Coram's was a foundling hospital, the fields would have been its grounds, awash with urban orphans discovering what grass felt like. These days it was mostly filled with foreign students from London House and solicitors' clerks on their lunch breaks.

Tillman sat on a bench at the top of a grassy bank and motioned to Kennedy to sit next to him. For the moment, she ignored the invitation. Tillman looked pretty good, she had to admit. Or maybe it was just that the first time she'd met him, he'd been running on empty, twelve years into a mono-maniacal quest that was disintegrating his mind and his body an atom at a time. He still looked like an Irish docker with an anger management problem, but now he looked like an Irish docker on his way to church, instead of on the third day of a suicidal bender. He sat with his huge hands resting demurely on his knees. His sandy hair – now fuse-wire silver at the temples – was combed back into some kind of a shape, instead of spiking and rolling randomly like a freeze-frame of a brushfire.

'Okay,' Kennedy said. 'I just wanted to drop off a message. I was told that the Pantheon was your mailbox. But you saw me coming, right?'

'John told me you were looking to get up with me,' Tillman admitted.

'And then what? You decided to camp out at that café until I showed? If you've got that much time to waste, Leo, good for you. I don't. Why didn't you just call me?'

'Manolis is helping me with something,' Tillman said. 'A project I've got going on. Calling you was the next thing I was going to do, Heather. As soon as I got done with this.'

His tone was mild, calming. The truth was that her anger had nothing to do with him. She'd been helpless the night before, tied to a bed with her legs spread wide, while two men threatened and brutalised her. True, she'd then seen her attackers beaten flatter than a dirty postcard, but that hadn't done much to reconcile her to her own pain and humiliation.

'I'm having a bad week,' she told Tillman. 'I'm sorry. It's good to see you, too.'

She sat down next to him, stifling the restless urge that wanted her to stay upright and moving.

He made no attempt to touch her. He wasn't a man who did hugs and kisses all that much. Back when he was searching for his family, he'd lived like a monk for long enough to make solitude his natural state. You didn't put something like that down lightly, once you'd let it get into the grain of you the way Leo had. And he didn't try to coax her to talk, either. He just waited, knowing that she'd get to it in her own time.

'So what *were* you doing back there at the café?' she asked again. 'John Partridge said you were on a job. What does that mean for you, these days?'

Tillman laughed softly. 'It never seems to mean the same thing twice. But this isn't work, exactly. More like a side effect of work. Someone's been watching me. I'm trying to figure out who it might be and what they're looking to do, but they're good enough that I can never seem to catch them at it.'

Kennedy was perturbed and he saw it in her face. Again, he waited quietly for her to explain.

'Okay,' she said. 'I don't like that one bit. It might be completely unconnected with what brought me here, but I don't think that's very likely.'

She told Tillman about the events of the last few days, concisely but with as much circumstantial detail as she could provide. She wanted him to see it all from the same perspective from which she'd seen it, as the pieces all came together and screamed the impossible, unwelcome conclusion at her. But she stopped with the death of Alex Wales. She couldn't talk about what had happened after that, after she left the hospital and went home. Not to Tillman. Not yet.

'The Judas People,' Tillman murmured, when she'd finished. He said it with a kind of dulled wonder, as though it were somehow both unexpected and obvious at the same time – like the favourite in a horse race romping home after you'd bet on a hundred-to-one outsider.

'Yes,' Kennedy said, a little piqued by his calm. 'The Judas People, Leo. The ones who killed my partner, stole your family from you, and almost—' She reined herself in, catching a hysterical edge in her own voice. 'I'm not dealing with this all that well,' she said, stating the obvious. 'It's been three

183

years, and I did my best to forget the whole thing. Now – it's like it never went away. Like we never came back from Mexico.'

'But we did,' he reminded her. He gave her a remorseless stare. 'Heather, they threw everything they had at us and we came out of it still on our feet. This isn't like that. This is you walking across the edge of something they're involved in. They may not even have put two and two together. They may not know it's you. That you're ... someone who already knows about them.'

'I wish I could believe that,' Kennedy said bleakly. 'But I don't. And neither do you. If it was just me, I'd buy it. Maybe. It could be the lousiest of lousy luck. But it's not just me, it's me and Emil Gassan. Two of the three people in the world who know that the Judas tribe are out there. That kind of changes the odds, doesn't it?'

Tillman blew out his cheek. 'Maybe.'

'Maybe?'

'I could make a case. All of this seems to be about that book, somehow, doesn't it? And Gassan's speciality is deciphering old texts. So I don't see it as too much of a stretch that he was close to hand when the book was stolen. Or destroyed. Or whatever happened to it.'

'Except that he wasn't. He was drafted in afterwards, like me.'

'Still. Old texts are his discipline. It makes some sense for him to be there. And when they asked him to bring in a private investigator, how long do you think his shortlist was? It was you, Heather. You're the only person he knows with that background.'

'Just coincidence, then.'

'Just coincidence. Because the alternative is to think that the universe folds itself out of shape just for you. And once you start thinking that, you're well on your way to some kind of serious personality disorder.'

Kennedy didn't say word one about either pots or kettles. 'Well, thanks for coming up with a rational explanation, Leo,' she said. 'But that isn't how it looks from where I'm sitting. There must have been a hundred palaeographers the museum could have gone to. And the guy in charge of the collection getting a stroke right then, and the theft happening right then . . . I'd say we're operating right out at the limits of coincidence here.' She steeled herself. 'Anyway,' she said, in a low voice, 'there's more.'

'You think I couldn't see that in your face? Go on.'

'They came after me last night. When I got back home, they were waiting for me.'

Tillman's eyebrows went up a fraction, which for him was expressive of extreme astonishment. 'Knowing their fieldcraft,' he said, 'you were lucky to spot them.'

'I didn't spot them,' Kennedy said. 'I walked right into it. They were going to kill me. Question me first, and then kill me when they had all the answers. But then this . . . this *girl* turned up. And bear in mind, Leo, I don't call women girls all that often. She was young. And she was better than they were. She saved my life. Left these two Messengers more dead than alive. And mostly she just used her bare hands and the bedroom furniture.'

She let that sink in for a few moments. Tillman's face showed that he was weighing up what it meant. But Kennedy drew the conclusion for him anyway. 'She was one of them. One of the *Elohim*.'

He tapped his thumb against the back of the bench, looking off into the distance. Not randomly, Kennedy realised. He'd

185

chosen this spot because of the view it commanded, and he'd been monitoring all the people who'd walked by while they were talking. He was still doing it, making sure they weren't being watched or eavesdropped on, checking lines of sight and patterns of movement.

'Two factions,' he said at last, after a long silence.

'That's the obvious conclusion,' Kennedy agreed. 'But what the hell would it mean? A breakaway group from the Judas tribe, the way the Provos broke away from the original IRA? These people kept their shit together for two thousand years. What's so special about now?'

'We know they decamped. Relocated their hidden city from Mexico to someplace else. That would have created a lot of stress. Hundreds of thousands of people on the move, leaving behind everything they knew. Having to build their homes again, from scratch. It's probably safe to assume that they're going through some social upheaval right now. Choppy waters for the chosen people.'

'It was three years ago,' Kennedy pointed out.

'Doesn't matter. The shockwaves might take a whole generation to die down. Longer even. Anything that big, Heather, it happens too slowly to measure. Believe me. A lot of my assignments for Xe were what they call *après-war*, so I got to see a lot of people – a lot of cultures – working through a lot of bad stuff. Everything gets thrown up in the air and comes down again in the wrong order. This wasn't a war, obviously; it was an exodus. But I bet it was comparable in some ways.'

Kennedy found herself rebelling against this argument. Maybe sympathising with the bastards who'd done so much to ruin Tillman's life and tried to end hers was just too big a feat of moral gymnastics for her to pull off. 'Comparable to

186

a *war*? The only way it would be comparable would be if they'd gotten so hidebound – so rigid in the way they think and the way they live – that any kind of change would break them.'

'Well,' Tillman said, looking away again, 'it's only a hypothesis. The facts on the ground suggest that they're fighting against each other. We can agree on that much. The reasons ... well, we're never going to know, one way or the other, are we? If you asked them, and they told you, they'd have to kill you right after.'

He said it lightly, but Kennedy didn't laugh – and Tillman wasn't really joking. He stood up and stared down at her in silence.

'What?' Kennedy said.

'What is it you want from me, Heather?'

'Right now? Nothing. I'm just warning you, because it seems to me that if they're really dusting off unfinished business – if this is more than just coincidence – then they'll be coming after you next. And now it looks like they already did. I bet it's them who are watching you.'

'No,' Tillman said.

'What do you mean, no? The one person they hate more than me would have to be you, so it's kind of inevit—'

'I mean, you didn't come here to warn me.'

'I didn't?'

'Well, not just for that. Tell me the rest. You want me to ride shotgun for you?'

Kennedy was appalled. 'No,' she said. 'Leo, no. Jesus, after what you've been through? I'm not trying to pull you back in. Not ...' *Not to fight them*, she wanted to say. *Not to kill any more of them.* But if she followed that chain of ideas, with Tillman right there in front of her, there was no way of knowing what her face might give away. He still had no idea that the two Messengers he'd killed at Dovecote Farm had been his own sons. She was determined that he'd never find out.

In fact there was only one conceivable counterbalance to that determination, and this was the real reason why she'd come: outweighing the two dead sons, the one living daughter. Tabe. Because it was impossible, looking at the girl's face and hearing her speak, not to see the resemblances, hear the echoes. But she'd been with Diema so briefly, at a time when her thoughts had been in turmoil. She could easily be mistaken. The age was about right, but what the hell did that mean? All of the Messengers were young. The drugs they took to increase their strength and speed killed them before they got old.

'There's something else,' she admitted. 'Something I'm going to need to tell you about, only I can't do it yet. I don't know if I'm right, and if I'm wrong it would be ...' She tailed off. This had strayed onto really dangerous ground, really fast. 'I swear, Leo,' she said, aware of the hollow reverb on her weasel words, 'as soon as I'm sure, I'll tell you. And then – well, yeah, then I'd want you to get involved. Then you'd *have* to get involved.'

'And until then, I just have to trust your instincts?'

'Yes.'

'Fine,' Tillman said. 'Because I do.' He let out his breath in a long sigh. 'It's funny. For a long time, I thought I was at peace. I knew that Rebecca was dead. I knew how she died, and why. I knew my kids were doing okay, that they were happy, even if they were with those maniacs. I thought that was enough. But lately it's been troubling me. Like, how could I know they were out there and not try to find them? Even if

I only saw them from a distance, it would mean so much. You coming to see me ... it's strange, but it's strange in a good way. It's as though everything I thought we laid to rest is waking up again.'

Not quite everything, Kennedy thought. *Not Ezei, or Cephas.* This was why she was terrified of letting him get too close. It magnified the risk that he'd find out what he'd done, and she was sure beyond any shadow of a doubt that the knowledge would break him. 'Leo,' she said, trying to head him off, 'we found their home once and they uprooted it and moved it. There's no way they'd let you find it again. I think you should put that out of your mind. And believe me, please, I really didn't come here to drag you into my mess. I came to warn you to watch your back, and ... No, that's all. Just watch your back. If you've got the option of going to ground somewhere, do it. When it's over, I'll leave a message at that café, or wherever. I'll come over and tell you what happened. Maybe – maybe I'll have some news to tell you.'

'Heather,' Tillman said mildly, 'with respect – and I hope you know how much I respect you – I don't think that's how this will work. Even if I was happy to sit it out, I'm the only one you can ask for help who knows how these bastards work.'

'I'm not,' Kennedy said, a little desperate now. 'I'm not asking you for help. Actually, I'm asking you not to help. I've got ... I'm setting something up. Something complicated. If you come barging in, you might wreck it. Please, Leo. Keep your distance until I'm done.'

'Something complicated.'

'Yes.'

'A sting of some kind?'

'I'd tell you if I could.'

Tillman laughed. 'Damn, Heather. How could you be a murder cop all those years and not get good at lying? You can't even look me in the eye. Look, you need me, and I'm offering. Of my own free will. You don't have to say yes or no right now. Just keep in touch, and when I'm done with this other stuff I'm doing, I'll be available for any kind of back-up or heavy lifting you need done. Where are you staying? Not at home, I'm assuming?'

'No,' Kennedy said. 'Nowhere anyone could find me.'

'Well, don't get too comfortable, all the same,' he warned her. 'But we should stay in touch, even if you don't want me elbowing in on your play. *Especially* if you don't want me in on it. You've got pen and paper? Write your address down for me.'

So nobody with long-range listeners pointed in this direction could hear her say it out loud, Kennedy realised. She hesitated, but really there was no good reason not to give Tillman the address of the Bastion. If something did happen – if the *Elohim* popped up in his life, too – it would be better if he could let her know about it quickly. She wrote the name and address of the hotel on the back of a till receipt that she found in her purse. She handed it to Tillman and he thrust it into his pocket without looking at it. 'We'll do this again soon,' he promised her.

'I'll yell out if I need you,' Kennedy counter-offered. 'I'll leave a message at the café. Stay away from me and away from all of this, until you hear from me.'

'No promises,' he said. 'But let's stay in touch anyway. It's best if each of us knows roughly where the other is, at least – in case anything happens. So I'll assume I can reach you at this address unless you tell me you're going to be somewhere else. Okay?'

Kennedy nodded. 'Okay.'

'And I'll let you know if I find out anything about the people who've been tailing me. Might be unconnected, like you said. Just unfinished business from my misspent youth. If it's not, I'll keep you in the loop.'

They said goodbye, but as Kennedy was walking away, he called out to her. 'Heather.'

She turned.

'Just like old times,' he said.

Gassan's exact words, Kennedy thought. At the time, she'd disagreed. 'Yeah,' she said glumly. 'Pretty much.'

20

From Coram's, Kennedy went on to Ryegate House. It was past 9.30 a.m., now, but the building was still closed to the world, with steel shutters down over the sliding doors of the front entrance and three police cars parked in a row outside. She rang the bell a few times without eliciting any response at all. Then she went around the back of the building, found the staff entrance that Rush had mentioned and hammered on the steel-plated door as loud as she could.

Eventually, the racket produced a result. There was a rattling of keys from inside the door. It swung open and a uniformed guard stared blankly at Kennedy from the inside. 'This is the staff entrance,' he said coldly.

She stepped in past him without giving him time to react. 'I'm on staff,' she said. 'I work for Professor Gassan.'

'ID, please,' the guard demanded belatedly.

Kennedy showed her driver's licence.

'I mean, internal ID. Are you on our system? If not—'

'I'll vouch for her,' Ben Rush said, walking up to join them in the narrow service corridor. 'It's all right, Cobbett. She's investigating this.'

'I thought the police were investigating,' the other man said. Being sidestepped didn't seem to have done much for his mood.

'She's private. Reports direct to the professor.'

Rush took possession of her and led her away. 'Only that would be a neat trick right now,' he muttered grimly.

'Any word there?' Kennedy asked him. She was ashamed that she hadn't tried to call the hospital herself, but survival had had to be the first item on the day's agenda.

'Nothing good. Lorraine called ten times already. They won't tell her much, because she's not family, but it sounds as though they're having a hard time getting him stable. Police are all over the place, but they won't give us the time of day. Mr Thornedyke's still under sedation, and Valerie Parminter is away on a course, so there's nobody taking decisions about anything – there's just the police and the headless chickens. Lorraine will fix you up with a day pass, and we'll take it from there.'

He took Kennedy through a labyrinth of corridors and stairwells and finally through a double door into the foyer. Lorraine was standing at the reception desk with her fists clenched at her sides, hiccupping out huge, body-shaking sobs.

The receptionist seemed unable to formulate a complete sentence, but from the fragments she did manage to get out, Kennedy gathered that Emil Gassan was dead, from a combination of toxaemia and blood loss, both probably exacerbated by an unidentified alkaloid on the blade of Alex Wales's knife. Valerie Parminter wasn't answering her phone. Maybe she was dead, too, Lorraine wailed. Maybe everybody was dead.

Rush deadended the switchboard to a *call again later* message while Kennedy got the distraught woman calmed down a little. Dredging her memory of the staff interviews she'd done, she suggested that Lorraine go find Allan Scholl, the next in the pecking order, and tell him he was in the big chair for the day.

All of this displacement activity helped Kennedy to keep her own emotions at arm's length until she felt a bit more ready to deal with them. She'd known this was possible from the moment when Gassan took the wound, so she felt little surprise. What she felt instead was a sickening sense of guilt and shame that she'd let it happen – that Gassan had died because she'd been so completely unprepared. Because she'd blithely and unthinkingly set a trap for a rabbit and had no game plan when she realised she'd caught a tiger.

Once Lorraine had left, Rush turned to Kennedy again. 'We won't get near Alex Wales's desk,' he told her. 'The police bagged everything and took it away, then they went and bagged the desk, too. It's wrapped up in that plastic they use at airports for busted suitcases, and police tape all on top of that.'

Kennedy forced herself to think about practicalities. 'What about his computer?' she asked.

'They took that first.'

'And his locker?'

'Oh yeah. They're way ahead of us.'

It would have been surprising and even mildly scandalous if they weren't. They'd had the whole night to work in, after all, and this was their job. Kennedy had to remind herself that it wasn't hers, any more. Not now that it had become a murder investigation. The only sane thing to do was to walk away.

And spend the rest of her life seeing Gassan take that knife in the chest, in endless action replay.

'You still want in on this?' she asked Rush.

'Doesn't matter what I want,' he told her. '*In* is what I've got.'

Kennedy couldn't fault the logic, especially now. With Gassan's death, the stakes seemed a lot clearer than they had

194

the night before. The Messengers were already trying to kill her, and they'd be coming for Rush the moment they figured out he was involved. 'Okay,' she said. 'Do you know anyone in the IT department here?'

The boy thought long and hard. 'I sort of know Matthew Jukes. I mean, we've had a few drinks now and again.'

Kennedy took out her wallet, drew two fifty-pound notes out of it and handed them over. 'If your computer network has some kind of back-up storage, we may be able to get at Wales's files that way. See if this Jukes guy will take a bribe.'

'And if he won't?'

'Roll him and steal his passwords.'

Rush whistled. 'Going down the slippery slope real fast here, aren't we?'

'See what a bribe will do, anyway,' Kennedy told him. 'We'll come up with another way in later, if that doesn't work. Call me when you've got anything to tell me, and we'll meet up – somewhere else, not here.'

She left the way she'd come. The staff door was unattended, but the guard who'd challenged her on the way in was having a cigarette break in the courtyard just outside. Discipline was going to hell.

21

After Kennedy left him, Tillman went back to the Pantheon Café. Manolis's wife Caitlin was at the counter. She gave him a nod that was on the ragged edge of civil and unlocked the door to the back room.

Tillman knew better than to ask her whether Manolis had called. Caitlin regarded Tillman as belonging to a disreputable past that her husband should have stepped away from long before now, and his recent reappearance in Manolis's life had been the cause of more than one snarled and muttered argument that Tillman had tactfully pretended not to over-hear.

But Manolis was one of the best covert surveillance men he knew. There certainly wasn't his equal in London – or at least, not walking around free – so Tillman had approached him, with some qualms, and offered him a one-off payment for a short, probably risk-free job.

All of this pre-dated Kennedy's call, but what she'd just told him fitted with disturbing neatness into his own ongoing problems – and that was the real reason why he hadn't pressed her for further information. He already had some pertinent facts in his possession and was in the process of acquiring more.

In the back room, he sat at a fly-specked table and played

patience with a deck of cards that was missing the two of clubs. It was pretty pointless as a game, but it had a certain value from the point of view of Zen meditation. After three hands, the door opened and Manolis entered, still in his bike leathers and helmet. He dumped a rucksack on the table in front of Tillman.

Tillman put the cards back in his pocket.

'Well?' he asked.

Manolis nodded.

'She had a tail?'

Manolis held up his hand, the thumb and forefinger a half-inch apart. 'A little one,' he said. 'Cottontail, like a rabbit. Pretty much definite, Leo. Was the same girl that was following you two nights ago. I didn't get a clear shot of her face, but the height, the build – identical. Let me show you.'

He took off his gloves and then his helmet. From inside the helmet he removed, with great care, a small lozenge of black plastic that had been affixed there by two steel brackets clipped to the helmet's inside rim. At one end of the device, the only break in its smooth surface, there was a tiny glass bulb: the micro-camera's lens.

From the lozenge, Manolis detached the even smaller plastic wafer that was the memory card. He booted up the computer in the corner of the tiny room, and slid the card into a reader built into the front fascia.

A window opened and began to fill with thumbnails. Manolis leaned close to the screen, squinting at the tiny images with furious concentration. 'Here,' he said at last. He clicked the mouse and one of the images expanded. It showed the part of Hunter Street that ran behind Coram's Fields. The image was tilted slightly, which wasn't surprising, since it had been taken from a moving motorcycle. What was surprising was that there was no motion blur of any kind, only a little fish-eye distortion, because of the curvature of the lens. Manolis knew his kit and what it was capable of.

He zoomed in on a corner of the image. A woman – Heather Kennedy – was walking away from the camera, her face turned in profile. Fifty yards behind her was a shorter figure, a girl, very slight in build, wearing black jeans and a white T-shirt. She had her back to the camera, her face not visible at all.

Manolis tapped the mouse and the screen flickered, one image replacing another so that the figures moved forward in jerky freeze-frame. At the same time, the angles and relationships shifted. Manolis had overtaken the girl and continued to take pictures as he passed her. The image tilted even further, but the focus stayed pin-sharp even when he zoomed in to the point where her head filled the screen.

Her head, but not her face. As though she could sense the camera, she turned away from it, so Manolis had got only the back of her neck, the curve of her cheek.

'I would have gone back for another pass,' he said to Tillman apologetically. 'But I didn't think I'd get away with it. You know, you can just tell, sometimes, if someone's got their radar out, and it felt like she did. I didn't want to scare her off. But she looks like the same one to me.'

'Same one,' Tillman said. 'Definitely. And she hasn't let me get a clear look at her face, either. So she was tailing me and now she's tailing Heather. Did you manage to follow her back to source?'

Manolis clenched and unclenched his fists, and bowed his bullet head. 'Sorry, Leo. I lost her. I don't think she saw me, I think she just has good tradecraft. She zigs and zags a lot, and I was in traffic. She went down Onslow Street. There are steps down from the main road. Steep. I can't drive down there. And if I ditch the bike and follow, she sees me, she knows why I come. I had to let her go. So then I go round by Saffron Hill, but there's no sign. She's already gone.'

'Don't worry about it, Mano. What you've got is good. Very good. But stay free. I may need you to do one more thing for me.'

'It's all in the price. You've got me for three more days.'

'You've given me everything I asked for. If you do this, I'll pay you a bonus. But I'm absolutely fine if you say no, because the risk profile just changed radically.'

'I never said I wanted to keep my head down, Leo. Only way to avoid *all* the risks is to be dead. What do you want me to do?'

'Nothing, just yet,' Tillman said. 'Heather said she was attacked last night, and this girl pulled her irons out of the fire. I want to go look over that ground. Might pick up something that we can use. Because what I really want to do, right now, is to meet this kid and ask her what it is she thinks she's doing.'

Manolis shrugged. 'I'm here when you need me,' he said. 'But one thing, Leo. If you need to see your friend again, better make it somewhere else.'

Tillman was surprised. 'Why's that, Mano? I'd have thought Heather would be just your type.'

'Yeah, exactly,' Manolis agreed. 'Caitlin thinks so, too.'

22

Matthew Jukes caved in very quickly once money was mentioned, but the list of Alex Wales's files that he handed to Rush furtively in the alcove that housed the coffee machine ran to over fifty pages, and the file names mostly gave no clue at all as to their contents.

'Is there any way to get these files back up on another computer?' Rush asked Jukes.

'Anywhere you like,' Jukes said. He was a sour-faced bugger, normally, but the combination of money and an opportunity to show off had rendered him magically cordial. 'All this stuff is in the mainframe. Even if you save to your own C or D drive, there's a hundred per cent back-up at the end of the day. That's standard policy.'

'So you can set me up with Wales's files, on my own machine?'

'It would be my pleasure.'

In fact, Jukes went one better than that. He faked a temporary administrator ID for Rush, which gave him full access not just to Alex Wales's files but also to his usage stats. That meant Rush could see what he'd done and when he'd done it, which files he'd kept open for longest, even which ones he'd printed out.

And the results were surprising. As Allan Scholl's PA, most of Wales's time should have been divided between Scholl's diary and Scholl's inbox. In fact, Wales seemed to have gotten that bread-and-butter stuff out of the way right at the start of each day, logging on as early as 7 a.m. After that, he let the emails lie wherever they fell, while he trawled through pages and pages of what looked like gibberish – random screeds of numbers and letters separated by occasional backslashes.

'Database logs,' Jukes said carelessly. 'They look like that unless you go in through the client server. You can't open them up as files like you can with Word docs and stuff like that.'

'Why not?'

'Because of the architecture. It's event-driven.'

'Jukes, I have no idea what you just said.'

'That's obvious,' Jukes sneered, his natural obnoxiousness bobbing briefly to the surface. 'All right. Say you ask a question like how many people are there in the world?'

'Okay. Say I do.'

'So what's the answer?'

'There isn't any answer,' Rush said. 'It's changing all the time. It's changed in the time it takes you to ask me the question.'

'Exactly. Same with this stuff. Event-driven architecture just means that the system keeps adjusting itself in real time. External events trigger updates. So every time you ask the question, you get a different answer. You can't open the file because there isn't a file. There's a data set that keeps changing.'

Rush scrolled through pages and pages of the same kind of nonsense. Occasionally he saw something that looked like a surname with initials attached. MILTONTF. LUBINSKIJJ. SPEEDWELLNM. The rest was impenetrable, just alphanumeric vomit.

'So what question was he asking?' Rush demanded. 'Is there any way we can tell?'

'Maybe.' Jukes waved him up out of the seat and took his place. For a few minutes, he opened windows on the screen and watched while white-on-black text scrolled through them. Occasionally he typed strings of letters in response to cursor prompts.

What he ended up with was another array of random symbols, but he nodded as though it made sense. 'There,' he said, pointing.

The tip of his finger touched the word USERS?, followed by a dozen or so numbers. Rush could see now that it recurred all the way down the screen, at least once in every two or three lines.

'Users of what?' he asked.

Jukes tapped some more, leaning close in to the screen as though he stood a better chance of prising loose its secrets if he cut down the distance.

'I don't know,' he admitted at last. 'Wait. No. Yeah, I do. This is old data. Like, completely defunct. No wonder Alex was able to get into it so easy.'

'This was easy?'

'Try getting at the live stuff. You'll see. This is ... yeah, it's part of the British Library database.'

Rush's heart did something surprising and alarming inside his chest. 'Which part?' he asked.

Jukes threw him a curious glance. 'Getting excited now, are we?'

'Which part, Jukes?'

Tap. Tap. Tap. 'Users,' he said.

'Shit, I got that much.'

'Keep your hair on, will you? It means people who called a

book up, from the stacks. Wales was trying to generate a complete list, but the system wouldn't let him because the data wasn't live any more. It had been disaggregated, taken out of the data set that you can use to populate a form. Anyone in IT admin could have just changed the flag and brought them back again, but Wales didn't have the pass codes.'

'So? I'm getting about a third of this, by the way.'

'So he had to dive down into the data set and do it low-tech. He looked for the identifying code for that one book and then wherever it cropped up he trawled the user stats until he found out who requisitioned it.' Jukes looked up at Rush, blinking rapidly and arrhythmically – his tell when he was thinking hard. 'I mean, back when it was in the stacks. Before they closed the reading room at the British Museum and took the circus down the road. There would have been a handwritten form that the user took to the desk. Then whoever was on the desk would scan their ID and—'

'No,' Rush said. 'No, Jukes. Don't try to talk me through your whole system. Just tell me if I'm right. Wales was trying to make a list of the names of everyone who'd ever read a particular book.'

'No.'

'No?'

'He was trying to make a list of everyone who ever even filled in a form so they could see it. They wouldn't have had to read it.'

'Right. You're right. Okay, so now tell me if he succeeded. Is the finished list in here somewhere?'

Jukes blinked some more. 'I don't know,' he said. 'I suppose we could input some of these user names as strings and search the rest of Wales's files to see if they turn up anywhere else.'

'So do it.'

Jukes did it. 'Nope. Nothing. Maybe he wrote it up by hand. Or maybe ... wait. Let me look at his deleted files.'

'You can do that?'

Jukes chuckled evilly. 'Oh yeah. Unless you use a shredder program like Eraser, hitting delete is just hitting "save for later". And nobody here is allowed to put non-authorised software on their machines, so usually everything just ends up ... Okay, here.'

A pop-up farm of windows opened on the screen. Jukes culled them back again methodically, until there was only one left.

'There's your list,' he said.

Rush could tell one thing at a glance: *A Trumpet Speaking Judgment* had never been a smoking bestseller. There were only about twenty names on the list, and if the dates next to them were the dates when they'd accessed the book, the time span he was looking at covered more than fifty years. The earliest name, FOSSMANH, was listed against the date 17/4/46; the latest, DECLERKJO, against 2/9/98.

'Is there any way we can get addresses and telephone numbers for these people?' Rush asked.

'Oh yeah,' Jukes said. 'Two ways, actually.'

Rush waited. 'Well? What are they?'

'A telephone book, or another ton. Your credit just expired, mate.'

23

The street door of number 276 Vincent Square, Pimlico, was controlled by a buzzer system, but someone – presumably the two killers who'd stopped by the night before – had disabled it so that it hung an inch open in the frame, refusing to latch. *Should have spotted that, Heather*, Tillman thought. *You're slipping.*

Isobel James's flat, he knew, was number 11, which was on the third floor. The lock here had been picked, rather than forced, and Tillman was prepared to use his own lock-picks, but he didn't have to. He found a spare key underneath a potted palm that stood in the window recess next to the door: the third most likely place after the mat and the door sill.

Inside, silence and stillness and a penumbral gloom. The flat's hallway had no windows and didn't look onto the world outside at any point. Tillman took out a flashlight and clicked it on, casting it around the confined space. Nothing moved, and there was nothing to see that wasn't bland and obvious. Bookcase. Hall table with a nude sculpture based on Klimt's *The Kiss*. A few coats hanging on hooks on the wall.

The still air had a slightly stale, trapped smell. All the same, once Tillman had closed the door, he did a quick preliminary search, moving down the hall with a stealth that belied his sheer bulk to peer into each room and around each angle. He was checking for ambushes, but the air hadn't lied. He was alone in the flat.

Tillman was reasonably confident now that he wouldn't be disturbed, but he still kept to the agenda he'd decided on beforehand: start at the scene of the crime and work outwards. He went straight to the bedroom and stepped inside.

There were no bodies there, alive or dead. Again, this was only confirming what his nose had already told him. If Kennedy's attackers had died here, and their bodies hadn't been removed, the complex aromas of decay would already have been detectable.

But they could still have died and been carried away by someone else. Tillman surveyed the ruck and debris in the room and began to read it. The blood on the sheets he assumed was Kennedy's. There was a large, dark stain about a third of the way down from headboard to foot, consistent with a wide, shallow wound to the upper body. She'd seemed to favour her left side a little when they'd met. Now he knew why.

More blood on the carpet, in two areas. Right beside him, between the bed and the door, and over on the far side of the room next to the wall.

Nearest first. He knelt to look at the dark dots and stipples on the beige carpet: the discreet Morse code of spectacular violence. Tillman saw several distinct clusters of dark spots and one extended spray of clotted streaks that widened from a point near to the bedside table. Someone had been hit repeatedly on this spot, probably with more than one weapon and from more than one angle. Wide variation in the area and angle of scatter suggested that the victim had been standing when the assault began, but that it had gone on – maybe for some time – after he'd fallen.

206

Tillman crossed the room to examine the other bloodstains. There were fewer of them and they told a different story. A wide sprinkle of near-invisibly small flecks, irregularly distributed with wide gaps: a blow to upper body or more likely to the head, in a space where objects – objects no longer present – occluded the blood spatter. He saw a fast, furious fight, a lucky or well-aimed blow breaking the septum of one fighter's nose, or else a cut to the cheek or forehead.

On the wall immediately behind the blood spatter there was an area of damage, a roughly circular area, just below Tillman's head height, where something had smashed into the plaster hard enough to leave an impact crater. Someone's fist, or the back of someone's head.

Now that he could see how narrow and restricted a space this was, he marvelled all over again at the skill the unknown girl had shown. To take down two armed opponents, when one of them is already pointing a gun at you ... that's something of a challenge even when you've got all the free space you could wish for. In this small bedroom, where the battlefield included the splayed body of the woman she'd come to rescue, it was only a hair's breadth short of a miracle.

But she had one advantage over them. She was a wolf in sheep's clothing.

Something brightly coloured caught Tillman's gaze, tucked right up under the bed where it would have been invisible from most angles. He knelt and retrieved it. It was a torn corner of glossy paper, showing part of a photograph, the curve of a woman's breast and part of her shoulder.

Not just helplessness. Her disguise had gone further than that. Knowing she was dealing with – what? Ascetics? Misogynists? Religious zealots? All of the above seemed to fit the bill – she'd armoured herself in unrighteousness and carried her Taser into the room behind the makeshift screen of a pornographic magazine.

So where had she gotten it? Tillman looked around, found the rest of the skin-mag where it had fallen or been thrown behind a chest of drawers. *Bush League. Hot amazon action. Mandy and Celeste get dirty with toys – and boys!* There was no price sticker, nothing to provide a clue as to the magazine's origin.

He backtracked into the hall, flicking the flashlight around the floor. After a few moments he found a wrinkled skein of torn shrink-wrap. At one corner was a green label, smearily printed with the words *US hardcore: only £3.99*.

Paydirt. So to speak. This was a local product, snatched up to meet the needs of the occasion.

Tillman found the shop around the corner in Fynes Street. It called itself a newsagents, confectioner's and tobacconist's, but it was also a general store in a half-hearted way, boasting a single shelf unit stacked with tins of baked beans, Green Giant sweetcorn, Vesta curry sauces, digestive biscuits and bottles of washing-up liquid old enough to have wept fluorescent green tears a third of the way down their plastic sides. One wall, behind the counter, was stacked high with cigarettes. The wall opposite was a magazine rack, whose top two shelves were a cornucopia of T&A. A closed-circuit camera on a jointed steel arm leaned down from the ceiling at a crazy angle. The angle was because the housing was loose and the supposedly tamper-proof unit had slid halfway out of it – but it looked as though the camera was in the grip of a voyeuristic impulse, coming in close to ogle the porn.

Between the cigarettes and the magazines sat a bored, flabby man with thick glasses and a pock-scarred, glassy-eyed face. He was slumped in on himself as though he was cowering away from his own cash register. Then Tillman realised that both the man's expression and his posture had the same explanation. He was watching a tiny portable TV, an antique model shaped like a rectangular telescope. The TV spoke in waves of murmured static, but presumably there were words or music of some kind underneath.

'You sell this?' Tillman asked the man. He held up the magazine and the man leaned forward to peer at it. He kept looking for a lot longer than seemed necessary, first taking in the cover image and then – judging by the movements of his eyes – reading not just the title but also the rest of the copy.

'Could be,' he said at last. 'We sell a lot of 'em.'

'Mostly to men, though,' Tillman said. 'Right?'

The man switched his gaze from the passionately entwined amazons to Tillman's face.

'Of course to men,' he said. 'I don't sell to kids, do I? Are you from the council?'

'No, I'm not. Were you working here last night?'

'Yeah.'

'Until midnight?'

'We're open all hours. It says so on the sign.'

'Well, last night you sold this to a woman. A young woman.'

The man blinked and his Adam's apple bobbed a little. 'Oh,' he said. 'Her. All right, yeah. I remember now.'

'What do you remember?' Tillman asked.

'Sour-faced little madam, wasn't she.'

'Go on.'

'Well, I tried to have a bit of a laugh with her. I can't remember what I said, but something harmless, you know. Something a bit light-hearted. And she give me a look like I was something under her shoe.'

'Kids of today, eh?' Tillman said, stony-faced. 'So does that thing work?' he nodded up towards the camera, and the shop-keeper followed his gaze.

'Yeah, it works.'

'And it was working last night?'

'It's on all the time. It's on a loop.'

'I'd like to take a look at the tape.'

The man looked scandalised. 'I can't do that. My customers value their privacy.'

'Is that why they buy their porn in a sweet shop? What if I told you she was underage?'

A flicker of uncertainty crossed the man's face, but he rallied quickly. 'I asked her to show ID,' he said. 'It looked good enough to me.'

'And that's on the tape too, is it?' Tillman asked.

'It ... I ... yes ... I think, that might have been on another occasion, when she ...' the man floundered, looking for a safe haven to sail his white lie into.

'I'm not from the council,' Tillman said. 'And I don't care what you sold her. I'm just her social worker and I want to make sure it was actually her. Show me the tape, I'm on my way.'

'It's digital,' the man said. 'On a disc. I don't understand it myself. I'll have to get our Kevin.'

Tillman nodded. 'Good call,' he said.

The screen on the portable TV was about three inches square and the picture was every bit as good as the sound. It offered a glimpse into a fragile, beleaguered world, canted slightly off the true and periodically overwhelmed by waves of interference like pixellated blizzards.

The slight, speechless teenager who answered – or more usually failed to answer – to 'our Kevin' messed with the controls on the TV, the playback machine, the TV again. The picture swam into and out of focus, but after a while it was obvious that sharpening it up any further would just add more contrast rather than more detail. They fast-forwarded through the previous day's footage, telescoping twelve hours of lived time into a couple of minutes of jerky stop-motion. The man with the bottle-glass spectacles seemed to have been on duty for the whole of that time, apart from a couple of toilet breaks lasting four or five frames each, during which his part was played by our Kevin.

'There,' the man said at last, jabbing his stubby index finger at the screen.

Kevin froze the image, but he froze it between frames, so that the girl danced in and out of the shop's entrance, her foot over the threshold, then back, then over it again. The boy swore to himself a little, pressing PLAY and PAUSE alternately until the image stabilised.

But the resolution was so bad that freezing the picture just removed one layer of information. Tillman reached past Kevin and hit PLAY again, watching the whole short sequence through from start to finish. You could tell more about the girl while she was in motion. There was a care and an economy in her movements, the tightness of a coiled spring, or of a dancer waiting for her cue.

He rewound to the beginning, watched again as the girl entered the shop, picked up the magazine – after a quick, detached scan of the top shelf – and presented it to the man at the counter.

'So is it her?' the man asked Tillman. 'The one you're look-ing for?'

'Does it zoom?' Tillman asked Kevin, ignoring the question.

'A little,' the boy muttered. He held down a button and the

central part of the image swelled until the girl's face, seen from above and off to one side, filled the screen.

It was a reasonably attractive face, as far as Tillman could tell from this soup of pixels, heart-shaped, with large dark eyes, framed by a barbed wire tangle of short, spiked hair. She was too pale, though – pale enough that you might think she was anaemic, or recovering from a recent illness. *Or that she grew up underground*, Tillman thought, *in a city that was never open to the sun and saw nothing unnatural in that deprivation.*

So what do you make of the outside world, princess? Not a whole lot, probably, since they only let you out to hunt.

He rewound and watched again, but he went too far, past the point where the girl entered the shop. Outside the front window, in shot but barely visible, horizontal blurs were succeeded by vertical blurs. Then the door opened and the girl stepped inside, quick, methodical, racing against time – on her way to save Heather Kennedy's life.

What had he just seen?

He rewound again and pondered those blurs. Something moving on the pavement or on the road. Moving sidelong into sight. Then a bob, or a dip: the sense of a quick, downward movement, ended as soon as it was begun.

Then the door opening.

Again. He still couldn't make sense of it. Again. He turned the sound up, hoping for another contextual clue, and heard a rumble like a slowed-down road drill. It stopped before the girl came into the shop. In fact, it stopped just before that quick dip.

Of course it did.

Tillman turned to the shopkeeper. 'She was on a motorbike when she arrived,' he said. 'Yes?'

The man's face lit up with sudden animation. 'Yes,' he agreed. 'She was. I remember that, because she didn't have a helmet on. That was what I said to her. I said, you'll come a cropper one of these days, riding without a helmet. And she just give me a look, like I didn't have the right to even talk to her.'

'Do you remember anything about the bike?'

The man shrugged. 'Sorry. I don't know nothing about them things.'

'Anything at all? The colour? Decorative trim? One exhaust or two?'

The man shrugged again. 'It was just a bike.'

'Actually,' Kevin said, 'it was a Ducati Multistrada 1200. The Sport version, in red and silver, with a hybrid frame. Pirelli Scorpion Trail tyres, front and back. And she had the side panniers, too.'

There was a pause while both older men stared at him, the shopkeeper in blank astonishment and Tillman with something like respect.

Kevin blushed furiously under this close surveillance. 'But she'd taken the windshield off,' he mumbled.

24

H. Fossman. N.O. DeClerk. P. Giuliani. S. Rake. J. Leavis. D. Wednesbury. A. Davies. And so on.

Rush didn't have much to go on, at first, but he reasoned that most of the people who went looking for *A Trumpet Speaking Judgment* would do so for professional rather than recreational purposes. Camped out in Emil Gassan's office, where he figured he was unlikely to be disturbed, he started off by typing each of the names into a meta-search engine along with a number of additional terms such as 'Civil War', 'English history' and 'seventeenth century'.

A fair few of them turned out to fit right into that framework. They were historians with published works including a biography of Oliver Cromwell (Nigel DeClerk), a history of religious dissenters in northern Europe (Phyllida Giuliani) and a racy study of the British interregnum called *The Headless Kingdom* (Stephen Rake). The rest didn't appear to be famous in any field that Google cared about. They were stubborn enigmas until Rush remembered that they had to have taken other books out of the British Library, too, and would probably still be on the main user database. That gave him full names and contact details, and opened up a lot of other options.

Most of which then closed again, pretty quickly.

When Rush saw the pattern emerging, he swore under his breath. He called Kennedy in a state of barely suppressed hysteria and told her that he had something he needed to talk over with her right then. She told him to meet her at the Union Chapel, so he grabbed his coat and sprinted most of the way there.

She was sitting right under the pulpit, with her backside on the back of one pew and her feet on the seat of the pew behind. Even in a deconsecrated church, that felt slightly shocking to Rush, whose Catholic upbringing furnished him with enough devils and guilt for any three ordinary people.

She was talking on the phone, and judging by the half of the conversation he could hear, it was to a boyfriend.

'No, of course I miss you. It's just that I'm still . . . if I could get up to see you, I would. You know I would.'

Squeak and rattle of the boyfriend's voice. He sounded shrill.

'I get that, babe. But I don't know and I can't promise.'

Squeak. Rattle rattle squeak. 'Izzy,' Kennedy said, interrupting the flow. 'Isobel. Stop. I've got to go. I'll call you later.' Rattle. 'Yeah. Love you, too. Well, hold that thought and we'll work on it soon.'

She snapped the phone shut and put it away. Rush stared at her. He'd registered that the boyfriend was a girlfriend and was trying to process the information.

'What?' Kennedy said.

He pulled himself together and handed her the sheaf of printouts he was carrying. 'Wales was obsessed with that book,' he said. '*God's Plan Revealed*, and the talking trumpet, and all the rest of it. He was trying to work up a list of everyone who'd read it or even taken it out of the stacks. So then I tried to find out who these people were. Some of them are dead, but that's—'

'Recently?' Kennedy broke in quickly.

She was instantly alert, in a way that told Rush this news wouldn't have come as much of a surprise to her.

'No,' he said. 'Not recently. Why?'

'Never mind. Go on.'

'Well, these were people who took the book out back in the forties and fifties. It would be a bit surprising if they were still around. But here's the weird thing. Some of the names kept coming up in archived news reports. I ignored them, at first – thought they were probably just coincidence. But I started noticing that all the news items were about people going missing. Around about a dozen of the people who were on Wales's list have disappeared. And you see the dates? They're all this year, within a couple of months of each other. That doesn't sound like a coincidence.'

'No. It sounds like a conspiracy. But mass kidnapping?'

'A minute ago, you looked like you were ready to buy mass murder,' Rush said. 'What's the difference?'

Kennedy shrugged. 'Mass murder is part of the Judas People's regular MO,' she said. 'But usually they cover their tracks and make it look like an accident. People going missing means other people going looking for them.'

Rush gave her a bewildered and slightly scandalised stare. 'You're telling me they'd kill people just because they happened to read a particular book?'

'It's fair to say, even on my limited experience, that that's the core of their remit,' Kennedy told him.

'Seriously?'

'Seriously. Rush, I told you what you were getting into. If you want to back out, now's a really good time. They came after me last night and I was lucky to get away in one piece.'

She told him about the two *Elohim* and the scary ninja girl.

216

Rush was both shaken and fascinated, and stopped her with frequent questions. When she'd finished, he shook his head as though to clear it.

'Jesus,' he said. 'So what do we do now?'

'It's pretty obvious, isn't it?' Kennedy said. 'We read the book.'

25

'This,' Manolis said, 'is going to be a ram raid.'

Tillman chewed down on the words and found he didn't like them much. 'There's no way to do it with finesse?' he asked. 'Get in, get out again, nobody the wiser?'

They were in the back room at the Pantheon and Manolis was once again sitting at his command deck. He'd thrown away the Linux interface he usually defaulted to and taken the system back to the bare bone of some prompt-and-command structure that displayed in green text on black background moving up the screen too fast for the eye to follow. The screens, plural: there were whole recursive nests of them, opening out of each other and then falling back again in a fractal cascade.

'I wish,' he muttered distractedly. 'But there's nobody who's meant to have access to this data in real time. Not even the government. You must understand, Leo, this is not one system of cameras. It's thousands of systems, millions of individual machines, most of them set up by local councils for traffic control or to monitor public order hotspots. The police, the army, MI5 and MI6 and NaCTSO, they all make search requests on these systems, all the time, and they're accommodated. But they follow protocols, they go through channels, and they take their time. What we do is different. What we do is to interrogate all the systems simultaneously.'

'And you can make that work?' Tillman asked.

Manolis blew out a breath with an audible puff. 'Damn yes, I can make it work. But not for long. As soon as I'm in, every system will report a breach and every operator will try first to shut me out and then to backtrack the query and find me. This they will succeed in doing, definitely, if we give them long enough. Proxy servers – even the best proxy servers – are not designed to stand up under that level of interrogation. So before they obtain our real-world location, we get what we need and we close down. The numbers, please.'

Tillman gave him a sheet of folded paper, on which he'd written five different registration numbers. Manolis entered them one by one into a small search window at the bottom right of the screen. He did it with scrupulous care, referring back to the paper after each tap on the keyboard. All of the numbers belonged to motorcycles purchased in the UK in the last six months: specifically, all of them belonged to red-on-silver Ducati Multistrada Sports with side panniers and Pirelli Scorpion Trail tyres fitted front and back. Tillman had heard the absolute conviction in Kevin's voice, along with the wistfulness and the hunger, and would have staked his life on the accuracy of that description. Even in its basic configuration, the Multistrada was an expensive toy, and the machine that had made such an impression on Kevin was bespoke, not off the rack. That was the only thing that gave them a fighting chance on this.

There were 4.2 million CCTV cameras mounted on the streets of Britain, with more coming online all the time. And a very large proportion of them used some form of optical recognition system for vehicle licence plates. So in theory, if they pooled all the log listings for the CCTV camera networks that Manolis could hack into, they should end up with five dotted lines spun out across space and time, with each line representing the path taken by one of the five bikes. Only one of the five lines would intersect the Smoker's Paradise newsagent's shop in Fynes Street, Pimlico, and that one would be their target.

Manolis turned a slightly tense face to Tillman. 'Ready?'

'What do you mean, am I ready? All I've got to do is stand here, Mano. Take it away whenever the spirit moves inside you.'

Manolis tapped a key. 'I'm an atheist,' he murmured. 'But I'm a very bad atheist. Let's hope God takes that into account.'

The windows on the screen now seemed to be shuffling themselves like cards in a deck, the stack reshaping itself in peristaltic ripples with each screen refresh.

'Are we in?' Tillman asked.

'Some hold-outs. But yes, mostly we're in. And wait … wait … yes, already we have a winner, I think.'

'We do?'

Manolis dragged one of the windows away from the stack. 'These are central London feeds,' he said. 'And this bike – TC62 BGZ – is all over everywhere.'

'Was it in Pimlico last night?'

'I'll tell you as soon as I know. But it was in Clerkenwell the day before. It's her, Leo. I feel it in my soul.'

'Your atheist soul.'

'You think Christians have the monopoly? Yes, my atheist soul.' Manolis was silent for a moment, then he swore. 'Buggering shit.'

'What's the matter?' Tillman demanded, but he could see that the deck was thinning out.

'They see me already. Good security. Too good to take the

candy I offer. They're not bothering to backtrack, they're just shutting the systems down and rebooting, to break the connection. So ...'

'So?'

'Ram raid becomes hijack.' The Greek's long, elegant fingers flicked at the keyboard with ethereal delicacy. 'I am now the traffic controller for the whole of the Greater London area. Congratulate me, Leo.'

'You're the man for the job,' Tillman said tersely. 'Doesn't it make us easier to find, though?'

'Yes. Once I let go. Right now ...' Manolis fell silent again, concentrating on the input from the screens and the information flows he was managing to control and merge moment by moment into a single data dump. Tillman said nothing, just let him work.

'Done,' Manolis said at last. 'Almost done. Leo, remove the flash drive, there, from the machine, when I tell you to.'

The flash drive was bright yellow and bore the smiling face of a cartoon duck. It wasn't an ironic statement, it was just part of a job lot that Manolis had bought cheaply from a wholesaler. Their capacity interested him more than their aesthetic. Tillman took the small wedge of plastic between finger and thumb, then waited until Manolis said 'Now.'

He tugged the drive free. In the same moment, Manolis spread both of his hands over the keyboard and pressed down four or five keys simultaneously. He held the pose while the remaining windows popped like soap bubbles, one by one, until only one was left. On this one, the actor Wilfrid Brambell mouthed silently against a backdrop of metal bedframes and discarded tyres.

Manolis raised his hands from the keys and flexed his fingers. 'There,' he said. 'Death to tyrants.'

'Death?' Tillman echoed.

Manolis shrugged brusquely. 'Well, not death, exactly. It depends on your opinion of classic British sitcoms. I personally think *Steptoe and Son* was a highlight. So I'm giving the traffic control computers a free download of the first and second seasons. This should prevent them from completing a trace on us. It's very hard to swim upstream, even when the stream is running through fibre-optic cable.'

With the command deck effectively offline, Manolis had to break out a battered old laptop to examine the data they'd stolen. His initial instincts proved correct: the licence plate TC62 BGZ had been recorded by a camera in Vincent Square at 11.30 p.m. the previous evening. There was no camera in Fynes Street itself, but that was close enough – and the bike's movements over the past two days gave ample confirmation. It had been clocked half a dozen times in Islington, on St Peter's Street, and it had been in Onslow Street that same afternoon.

'No wonder you lost her,' Tillman said. 'You thought she was still on foot. And while you were taking the long way round, she switched to the bike. Probably drove right past you.'

'No, probably not,' Manolis protested. 'Some things I might miss. I wouldn't miss this bike.'

'Sorry,' Tillman said dryly. 'I didn't mean to question your professional expertise. Okay, Mano, let's work out the clusters. I want an introduction to this girl. How close can you get me?'

'I land you in her bedroom. Soft as thistledown.'

Which made Tillman wince a little, both because the girl was less than half his age and because he'd seen from the blood evidence what she was capable of in the bedroom.

'I'll settle for the front door,' he said. 'And I'll wear hobnail boots so she hears me coming. I'm not in the mood for suicide.'

The phone rang and Manolis picked up. He said 'Yes' twice, then held the phone out to Tillman. 'Your friend,' he said.

'Which friend?' Tillman demanded.

'The one my wife wouldn't approve of.'

Tillman took the phone. 'Hello, Heather.'

'You said to tell you if I was moving.'

'So where are you moving to?'

'Avranches. Normandy. A day trip.'

'Okay. Check in when you get back.'

'Will do, Leo.'

Tillman rang off and gave the phone back. 'Caitlin doesn't have to worry,' he told Manolis. 'Heather has refined tastes.'

Manolis shook his head sorrowfully. 'A pity. We would have been good together.'

'Throw yourself into your work,' Tillman suggested gravely.

Manolis did. And Tillman played fifty-one-card patience for three hours while his old comms sergeant worked through the endless data streams, eliminating and collating.

'Here,' he said at last. 'I think I have it, Leo. This is the place where your girl has spent most of her time over the last three days – all of the time when she wasn't watching you or the refined blonde.'

'Where is it?' Tillman asked, putting the cards away. 'Where does she live?'

'In a warehouse, apparently,' Manolis said, with a good deal less confidence. 'On an industrial estate in Hayes.' He gave Tillman a doubtful look. 'Perhaps this is her day job.'

26

Kennedy met with a lot more trouble than she expected in tracking down a copy of Johann Toller's book to read. Borrowing a computer at the Charing Cross Library, and trying not to disturb the sleeping winos who used the reading room as a flophouse, she was able to find twenty-three copies of *A Trumpet Speaking Judgment* that had been listed at one time or another in the catalogues of the libraries of the world. That made it marginally less scarce than a Gutenberg Bible.

But actually it was a whole lot scarcer, because once Kennedy started calling around she discovered that every single one of those copies had been bought, burned, stolen or just plain mislaid in the space of the last few years. There wasn't a copy of Toller's book to be had for love or money.

Well, maybe for money. She called John Partridge, who grumbled that Kennedy was asking him to search for a needle in a haystack and that he'd get round to it when he could, and then called her back, less than an hour later, to report that he'd found a copy of the book. Or, he added, scrupulously, something almost as good.

'What does that mean?' Kennedy asked suspiciously.

'Well, I tried the obvious,' Partridge told her. 'I thought it would be the easiest thing in the world to find either a scan of the book or an e-version. Most books that are out of copyright have been put through the OCR mincing machine and made available online. But I hit a brick wall. And it wasn't for lack of trying. A lot of links that should have led to your book turned out to be dead-ends. The sites had been completely erased. Viral markers on the search engines, nothing at all at the URLs.'

'So?'

'Digital slash-and-burn, Heather, my love. Someone went after those sites with malice aforethought, tore them down and then sowed the ground with salt.'

'Could be nothing to do with our text, of course,' Kennedy thought aloud.

'If it was one site, the odds would favour coincidence. After half a dozen, you pay your money and take your choice.'

'And how many times did you come across this, John?'

'A lot more than half a dozen. In the end, I got lucky – up to a point, anyway – by specifically targeting non-live data. In other words, old stored downloads of data sets from defunct sites or sites that don't offer direct internet access. And that's where we come to the good news.'

'There's good news?'

'The place where I found the abstract was the Scriptorial at Avranches, in northern France. They haven't got an actual copy of the book, but they've got a full typed transcript.'

'And they can send it to me? That's brilliant.'

'Hold your horses, ex-sergeant. They absolutely refuse to make the transcript available online or to send it out in file form because they no longer have the original text to compare it with. They used to have a copy of the actual book, but it was ruined in an accident a few years ago. There's no way of verifying the authenticity of the transcript and the curators

225

don't want to be responsible for bad scholarship. But they will let you examine the transcript, if you turn up in the flesh. The head of the preservation department there is a man named Gilles Bouchard. He's a friend of a friend of a friend of someone I used to be very friendly with, once upon a time. For her sake, he'll bend the rules a little for you.'

'Did I just hear a subliminal love story, John?' Kennedy asked. 'No, I know, a gentleman never tells. Listen, this is great. Really. If I owed you a pint before, I owe you a brewery now.'

'Distillery, please. My poison of choice is usquebaugh.'

'Single malt or blended?'

'Surprise me. But not too far north. The winters are murder on my arthritis.'

Kennedy hung up and made some more calls. The last of these was to Rush.

'So now what?' he asked her. 'You're going to France?'

'Already booked. It's a long haul. Eurostar to Paris, then regular train out to Rennes and another fifty miles from there in a rental car. I'll be back tomorrow.'

'You should take me along.' Rush kept his tone light and sardonic, but she could hear the yearning. 'You'll need someone to stand on the running board and take potshots at them if they catch up with you again.'

'Yeah,' Kennedy told him, 'but I can't afford your fare.' *Or any more deaths on my conscience.* 'See what you can dig up about Johann Toller's life,' she suggested.

'His life, Kennedy?'

'Yeah. Think about it. I chase the work, you chase the man. We're the horns of the buffalo, Ben.'

'You're the horns of the buffalo. I'm the swishing tail of the buffalo, swatting away a few flies. The horns of the buffalo don't look stuff up on Wikipedia. Because that's what you're asking me to do.'

'I'm serious,' Kennedy said. 'I think we can assume that Toller is important to the Judas People for some reason. If we knew who he was, we might have a chance of figuring out what that reason is.'

Rush still wasn't happy, but he allowed himself to be persuaded. And Kennedy didn't begrudge the time it took to persuade him because he was essentially right about her motives. She was sending him to do make-work while she got on with the investigation.

That was the plan, anyway.

27

As far as the internet was concerned, Johann Toller was an enigma. But buried in the search engine dross, Rush found a few nuggets of fact. One of these was an encyclopedia entry that appeared again and again, endlessly recycled from one site to another with no citation of the original author.

> Johann Toller (????–1660), rose to prominence as a member of the Fifth Monarchy movement, a group of religious and political dissenters in seventeenth-century England with links to similar groups spread across Continental Europe. Little is known about his early life. Toller wrote several books and pamphlets criticising the post-revolutionary government of Oliver Cromwell for its failure to legislate for complete religious freedom. He was executed in 1660 after a failed attempt to assassinate Sir Gilbert Gerard, the former paymaster of the Parliamentary Army.

Wherever Rush looked, that same bald summary stared back at him. Nobody bothered to list Toller's several works, or to say anything further about how the man had lived and died.

Switching to IMAGES, he found that a single picture predominated. It wasn't a picture of Toller, it was a reproduction of the frontispiece of his book. Below the title, there was a carving or etching of a hill with a small town nestled at its base. It looked vaguely familiar.

The picture was captioned with a few words in a very ornate, almost unreadable typeface. *De agoni ventro veni, atque de austio terrae patente.* Rush parsed them as foreign and almost gave up at that point, but he fed them back into Babelfish to see what came out. *Out of the belly of the beast I come, and from the open mouth of the Earth.*

He looked up the Fifth Monarchists and found out they were just one of about a hundred radical religious movements in seventeenth-century England, routinely persecuted and marginalised for their beliefs. They didn't sound that radical at all to Rush, but he got lost among the details. Mostly they just seemed to be saying that the second coming of Christ would happen at 2 p.m. on Tuesday. Or maybe three in the morning on Thursday. Or watch this space. Hadn't every age had its end-of-the-world nut-jobs? Or was it something that happened cyclically, like locusts?

At this point he struck a richer lode of data from a man named Robert Blackborne, another member of the Fifth Monarchy movement. Blackborne had all kinds of anecdotes about Toller. Like, he claimed to have been 'born in darkness and delivered into light', and to have regular conversations with angels. And despite his accent and manner of speech, Blackborne seemed sure that Toller was born somewhere exotic, because he had this peculiar way of making the sign of the cross, which he tried to make the other Fifth Monarchists adopt. *He put his hand to his throat, thence to his heart, and his stomach, and so in a circle back to where it began. And when I tasked him with this, and shewed him the right way, he said the blessing was thus practised by the angels in high heaven, and he could not choose but to honour it.*

Blackborne also kind of had an origin story for Toller. It seemed he was travelling through the Alps this one time, and he fell down a ravine and almost died. *He was sore wounded, and likewise constrained in a strait and terrible place, that he thought he would not see another day. So he commended his soul to God, and gave himself to solemn prayer, that he might prepare himself to stand before the seat of judgment.*

But then an angel appeared and told Toller eternal truths, which he felt he had to pass on to the rest of humanity.

Rush copied it all into a master file. He was starting to feel like he was getting somewhere, and he considered walking over to the British Library and seeing what he could turn up there – ideally under a false name, given what had happened to everyone else who expressed an interest in Toller's life and works.

Then it occurred to him that he had another option. It was stupid on the face of it, but ridiculously easy to do.

He went down to Room 37. Three times along the way, he passed police either standing and talking or walking in a different direction, but they only acknowledged him with wordless nods.

He swiped himself into the room and went straight to the box that Alex Wales had raided.

As he'd already noticed, it contained a mixture of old source texts and modern commentaries. He helped himself to a grab-bag of what seemed to be relevant histories and biographies, and beat a quick retreat.

But once back in Gassan's office, he found himself unable to read. He was suddenly struck by the ghoulishness of what he was doing – the fact that he was sitting at a dead man's desk, when the man wasn't even in the ground yet.

It was as though he hadn't really registered until then that Gassan was really dead. It had been abstract and now it was suddenly concrete: it was this room, and this desk, and this silence. From a photo in a silver frame, the professor smiled out at him, incongruously triumphant, holding up a bronze plaque. Maybe he got third prize in some archaeological bake-off.

The more Rush looked at the picture, the more sinister the smile became. *I know something you don't*, Gassan seemed to be saying.

All you know is what it's like to be dead, Rush told the picture.

And everyone gets to find that out.

28

From the Eurostar terminal onto the train, then to Paris, then to Rennes via Le Mans and Laval on an SNCF stopping train: it was, as Kennedy had told Ben Rush, a long haul. She'd intended to keep herself occupied by reading the abstract of Toller's book supplied by the Avranches Scriptorial via John Partridge, but when she finally broke the file open on the tiny netbook that he'd loaned to her, it was a much slighter affair than she'd been expecting.

In the hermetically sealed tube, crossing the English Channel a hundred metres below the ocean bottom at a speed of 200 miles an hour, she read this:

> The author states as his theme the end of human history and the beginning of Christ's reign on Earth. He asserts that this is imminent, based on observations drawn from recent history.
>
> Toller then moves to the prediction of the events that will occur as the year 1666 (referred to, he claims, in the Book of Revelations) approaches. The 'sundry signes' of the title are these future events, which will herald and foreshadow Christ's return to Earth.

There was more, but it was all on the same abstract level. Predictions about things that had or (the smart money said) hadn't happened three and a half centuries before. If you were looking for a definition of futility, you pretty much had it right there.

Once she was out of the tunnel on the French side, Kennedy checked her emails. All but one of them were from Izzy. Read in sequence, they made up a riveting saga of frustrations, humiliations and atrocities. The characters – wicked witch Caroline, pussy-whipped Simon, Hayley and Ben co-starring as the babes in the wood – were larger than life but painted with real conviction. It was better than a Christmas pantomime. Or it would have been, if the subtext hadn't been so loud and clear: *I'm your girlfriend, get me out of here.*

And she couldn't. After what had happened at the flat the night before, she didn't even dare to send a reply. There was no telling which parts of her life the Judas People were tracking. Izzy had almost died once already. Putting her back in the line of fire at this point was something Kennedy couldn't bring herself to think about.

So she turned to the remaining email, which was from Ralph Prentice.

Okay, he wrote. I said I might have something for you on the knife wounds. I didn't want to say any more than that until I'd checked it myself, because we seem to be going through a silly season. Lots of nasty incidents, but some of them less nasty than completely baffling. Who's got time to cut the heads off a thousand rats? Where would you get the rats from in the first place?

But I digress. You remember we talked about the fire-bombing up in Yorkshire? It was a listed building –

Nunappleton Hall. A convent, at one time, then a stately home, then empty and supposedly derelict. Empty right up to the time of the fire, in fact.

Local police are treating it as a terrorist attack, because the munitions that were used were extremely sophisticated. They called in the Met to assist with forensics, and a lot of the paperwork went across my desk – including the autopsy reports.

You might be wondering why there'd be any autopsy reports when the fire was in an abandoned building. Answer seems to be that the terrorists brought some hostages along with them and killed them on the spot. The method of execution – and I use the word advisedly – was with a knife, in each case. Severe damage to the eyes, too, possibly done with the same implement. But cause of death for all twelve was a single deeply incised wound to the throat. A very sharp knife drawn right across.

Prentice didn't shy away from the grisly details of the post mortem examination, and hardened as she was Kennedy found the saliva drying in her mouth as she read. The victims had been gagged. Their hands and feet tied. Probably killed as they knelt, side by side, in a confined space – a stone larder behind the house's main kitchen. Blinded and then slaughtered, most likely one at a time because some of the bodies had fallen so that limbs overlapped in ways that would be improbable if all twelve of these anonymous men and women had been killed at the same time.

They weren't anonymous, though. All of the bodies had been identified either by DNA or by dentition. Kennedy scanned the names briefly, but they meant nothing to her, or at least, they meant far less than the terrible, indelible image of

234

twelve people waiting in terrified, enforced silence as the butcher worked his way down the line.

She closed the email. Was this connected in some way with the theft of Toller's book? Was there a single strand of insane logic connecting the Ryegate House break-in with this slaughter that had happened two hundred miles distant? Steal a book, then massacre a roomful of men and women? For most people, those crimes didn't belong in the same paradigm – but for the Messengers of the Judas tribe, who'd been killing for centuries to protect the sanctity of their gospel, it could easily be possible.

A horrible suspicion came to her. She reached into her pocket again and brought out Ben Rush's list: the names of British Library users who'd accessed Toller's book and then vanished. She compared it to the casualties at Nunappleton Hall. Toller's list of the disappeared was identical to Ralph Prentice's list of the dead.

Kennedy had a strong stomach. It was her head that rebelled against this atrocity. Not kidnapping, then. It was mass murder, after all. And carried out with hideous care and precision. The Judas People, who saw their murders as sanctified rather than sinful, were loose in the world again.

No. They'd never left. She looked up Nunappleton Hall online. She wasn't the slightest bit surprised to find that it had changed from being a convent to an estate right after the English Civil War, when one of Cromwell's ex-generals had been looking for a place to settle down and grow roses up the door and when Johann Toller had begun preaching across England about Christ's Second Coming.

She did one more thing. She searched for 'rats with heads cut off'. She had had no idea what Prentice had been talking about, but the search engine showed it as a trending topic in the news and on social media. Someone had carpeted Whitehall, in London, with decapitated rats – about a thousand of them. The police were saying it was either an animal rights protest or some sick student prank. The rats had been carefully positioned in front of a building called the Banqueting House, which had been designed by Inigo Jones, some of the news reports noted, and completed in 1622.

It felt to Kennedy as though she were seeing pieces of a pattern, individual stones in a complex mosaic, but she was too close to it to see what was actually represented there. It meant something. She just had to find the vantage point from which the crazy little details coalesced into a face, a word, an answer. There was a level on which all of this made sense.

That thought, when she dragged it up into the light and looked at it, was the scariest thing of all.

29

Tillman lay in thick undergrowth and watched the warehouse through his field glasses. He lay on his stomach and kept himself as still as he could. The broken splotches of colour on his camouflage suit would hide him from a casual glance, but until the sky darkened completely, movement could still betray him.

The warehouse wasn't exactly a ferment of activity, but people were moving in there. Twice during the day a truck had arrived and been allowed inside through a freight bay just left of centre in his line of sight. One of the two had emerged again, with a different man at the wheel, and driven away along the sliproad, passing within ten feet of Tillman. The other was still inside. Presumably it was being either loaded or unloaded, but the rolling door of the bay had been pulled down and locked, so it was impossible to tell which.

Throughout the day, people moved behind the windows, quickly and purposefully. In the forecourt, seven cars – all fairly new but nondescript – stood side by side. They had to belong to the warehouse staff or managers, since they'd been there the whole time that Tillman had been watching and nobody had approached them in that time.

This was where Manolis had traced the bike to, but there

was no sign of it here – or the girl, for that matter. There was a margin of error, of course, and Mano had been keen to stress that this was only a best guess. The cameras hadn't logged the place where the bike spent its nights. The warehouse was just the nexus of its last recorded positions for each day. Sometimes the girl had approached it from the west, more usually from the north or east, but she'd come here every day, towards midnight or a little after, and the bike hadn't shown up on camera anywhere after that until six or seven the next morning. If she wasn't at the warehouse, she was somewhere close enough to it that the building itself was worth more than a passing glance.

On paper, the warehouse belonged to a freight haulage company, High Energy Haulage. The name and logo of the firm were blazoned over the front and rear door of the building. The logo looked like one of the trilithons at Stonehenge: a broad horizontal bar, with two vertical bars of about equal length extending downwards. The bar on the right touched the top stroke, but there was a narrow gap at the top of the left-hand bar. Tillman wasn't sure what it was meant to be, but it tugged annoyingly at his memory. He'd seen it, or something like it, before, and he hadn't liked it then, either.

In fact, there wasn't much he liked about this place. The fact that it was full of busy people, but with almost nothing coming in or going out, stank out loud. He had a hankering to see what they were up to, and he knew that his only chance was going to be at night. That was why he was still here, out in the long grass, with cramps in his legs and jagged-edged pebbles pressing into his chest.

He trained the field glasses on the rear door and the freight bay, the windows, the roof. There were security cameras, but he could see a couple of approaches that would take him safely through them. An alarm system, but it didn't look like anything that would give him too much trouble. The external hub was labelled WESTMAN SECURITY SYSTEMS. Tillman knew pretty much what was inside that box and what it would do, and what it wouldn't do. So long as it hadn't been tweaked from base specs, it was going to be a dog that failed to bark.

But most likely there'd be dogs, too. And guards. There might even be a night shift, in which case he'd have to think again.

But as the sky darkened, and one by one the warehouse staff walked out to their cars, shrugging on jackets or overcoats, and drove away, Tillman became more sanguine about his chances.

The forecourt was empty now, but he still waited. After fifteen minutes, a man in a black uniform came out through the rear door, locking it behind him, did a perimeter walk that took him two and a half minutes, and went back in again. He did the same thing again an hour later.

This time, when the door closed, Tillman got to his feet, massaging his aching muscles, and started to walk towards the building.

Diema watched him as she had watched Kennedy, from far enough away that he could only be made aware of her through some gross error of her own. She was sitting a quarter of a mile away, behind a rampart of discarded crates and boxes on a piece of wasteground left to stand between two identikit business units – one dedicated to anti-theft devices for cars, the other to the manufacture of breast implants from medical-grade silicon. The whole logic of the Adamite world, served up like the moral in a fable.

She liked that simile. But she wasn't feeling the detached

contempt and superiority that it implied. The truth, though it exasperated her to see such weakness in herself, was that Tillman made her uneasy.

She knew who he was, of course. Kuutma had told her everything, arming her in advance against surprises. Tillman was the father of her flesh. It was him who had impregnated Diema's mother, Rebecca Beit Evrom, when she was sent into the world as one of the *Kelim*, completing a purpose that was above and beyond him. He was, in this, like a donkey carrying one of the faithful to pray. The donkey has no clue what the weight on its back really signifies, the meaning of its labour. It plays its part, controlled by whip and words, and then it's put to pasture.

Diema had spent her whole life among the People, the fathers and mothers of her soul. Though her sire was a heathen and her mother had died when she was too young even to grieve for her, she dwelled among the chosen and she was of their number. The least of their number, it was true, and she had been made to feel that. But still, that truth outweighed all other truths. It was the grounding and the purpose and the very meat of her. So it wasn't that she felt any kinship with Tillman, because of some animal task he'd performed adequately nineteen years before. If anything, the contemplation of his role in her conception filled her with disgust and something like shame – the sense of having touched, at one remove, something foul.

But she couldn't help herself. She was surprised and even a little shaken at what he had managed to do here. He had realised that she was following him and somehow he'd found out enough about her to follow her right back. Except that by good fortune, she hadn't been back to the safe house even once in the last three days. She'd divided her time between

following Tillman and the *rhaka* and watching this place –
which she was almost certain was Ber Lusim's.

So now Tillman was investigating *her* investigation, which,
of course, was all part of Kuutma's master plan. But still, he
made her uneasy. And the unease and the disgust were like oil
and water: they didn't mix.

She imagined killing him. That helped a little.

30

Most of the drive from Rennes to Avranches was on main roads through the ruined industrial hinterlands around Fougères. But when Kennedy got to the coast, she saw the vast expanse of the estuary stretching away on both sides and the fairy-tale castle of Mont Saint-Michel hanging behind her shoulder.

She stole a look out across the bay, a tidal plain so wide she couldn't see its edges. Mont Saint-Michel guarded it with anachronistic zeal, its lower slopes crusted with the barnacles of cheap restaurants and souvenir shops, but the abbey of La Merveille standing proud and clean at the top like an angel on a dunghill.

She should have brought Izzy here. Izzy wouldn't have gone walking on that pottery-clay beach for a million euros and a pink Cadillac, but she would have trudged up to the abbey and back, complaining all the way, and she would have drunk apple brandy with Kennedy in one of the local dives until Kennedy had to half-carry her back to the hotel for holiday sex that was wild and clumsy and heart-stopping like the first time ever.

The Scriptorial wasn't hard to find. The road took Kennedy straight into town, and the building was right there in front of her. An angle of the old city wall enfolded it on two sides, and an ancient square tower rose right behind it, but the Scriptorial itself was a triangular tumulus with rounded corners, like a man-made anthill.

The bulk of the space, Kennedy knew, was a standing exhibition devoted to the history of books and book-binding, and the literally crowning glory on the building's top floor was a selection of the books rescued from the library of La Merveille around the time when the revolutionary government decided that bibles made good kindling.

Kennedy reported to the desk, and while she waited, cast her eye over the exhibits. There were models of La Merveille showing the stages by which it had been built over the space of a handful of centuries, stone sculptures and wooden carvings looted from its chapel, and maps of the area at different times in its history. But she was too tired from the drive and too restless to take in much of what she was seeing.

'Miss Kennedy.'

The voice was cultured and with the merest trace of an accent – just enough to turn the i of *miss* into an ee. Kennedy turned and Gilles Bouchard extended a hand.

Long acquaintance with Emil Gassan had conditioned her to expect someone both dry and dapper. But Bouchard was young – maybe her own age – robustly built and dressed very casually in a grey polo neck sweater and snow-white jeans. His hair was long, fine and blond, his narrow face tanned like a movie star's.

She took the hand and shook it. 'Yes, I'm Heather Kennedy. And you're Dr Bouchard?'

'Gilles.'

'Gilles. Thank you for agreeing to see me at such short notice.'

'It's my pleasure. I believe I may be repaying a favour, by a fairly Byzantine route.'

243

Kennedy grinned. 'Yes, so I was led to believe.'

'I was also told you might not have much time.'

'I'm here on your terms. But if you've got the book ready to hand, I'd love to take a look at it.'

'The book,' Bouchard said. He gave the word a slightly satirical edge. 'Yes. Well, I'll show you what we have, and I'll explain how we come to have it. Please, come this way.'

He led her away from the timeline and the lower slopes of the exhibition to a door, which opened onto a stairwell with red-painted walls. The stairs were steel, and rang under their feet.

'The Scriptorial within the Scriptorial,' Bouchard said. 'It runs clockwise, where the public rooms run counter-clockwise – or widdershins, to use the charming English word. We call this space *le filetage administratif*; the administrative thread. You understand the metaphor? Like the thread of a screw.' He gestured with his index finger, moving it in a spiral.

'I understand the metaphor,' she confirmed.

'This is where we keep the bulk of our collection,' he told her, 'along with facilities dedicated to their preservation and repair. Many of our books came from the abbey, as you probably know – and our bias, perhaps for that reason, is towards religious works. Here. I have set this room aside for you.'

He unlocked a door and ushered her into a room that was no more than a cubicle. The desk and straight-backed chair that it contained more or less filled it. Behind the desk there was a single wall-mounted shelf. The walls and ceiling were painted in a soul-sapping hospital green.

The room was narrow enough that if Bouchard had followed her, he would have been standing uncomfortably close, so he stayed in the doorway, hands in pockets, and indicated with a nod of the head the slender document that lay dead centre on the desk.

'The book,' he said, with the same slightly mocking inflection as before.

Kennedy sat and pulled it towards her. It was a bundle of A4 sheets, a little ragged and feathery at the edges, held together by a bulldog clip at the top-left corner. The title *A TRUMPET SPEAKING JUDGMENT* was roughly centred on the page, typed in 12-point Courier.

'And this is a full transcript?' she asked.

'Yes, we think so. But we don't know. It's an anomaly, to be honest. We would probably have thrown it away except that we lost our only copy of the book – the actual printed book – in bizarre circumstances, and were unable to replace it. Since this is all we have, we keep it. And since it's lacking even the most basic authentication, we don't advertise the fact.'

He excused himself politely, aware of her tension and urgency but too polite to comment on them, and left her with the transcript.

Kennedy removed the clip and turned the page – or rather lifted the page, since the typescript wasn't bound. She was surprised to find that the second sheet was a muddy photocopy of what must have been the original book's frontispiece. It was a line drawing, done with indifferent skill, of a cliff wall with a town at its base. Underneath the picture, there was an epigram in Latin. *De agoni ventro veni, atque de austio terrae patente.* Kennedy's Latin was just about good enough for *those who are about to die salute you*, and she'd never liked that sentiment much in any case.

She turned to the next sheet, which was numbered 1.

Since this New Worlde proves to be so very like the Old, and since our new-minted Rulers are of base metal, that a man may bite and see the mark of his

Teethe in the coine, I say now: I have done with them,
for all and ever. I and every Manne of Sense. And so I
stand upon the Muses' Mountain, asking Inspiration of
all, though my true Muse be Godde the Higheste. And
here He doth deliver, through me unworthy, His final
Judgment.

For Christes Kingdome is upon us, and indeed has
come later than some sages conjudged. And now,
because He loves His servants, He lets me see his
footprintes wheresoever I look. He will walk on
English souls and eat of English bread, and ye that
read me will see it, whether looking out from Munsters
spire or from Westminsters darkened casements. Ye
cannot choose, for he will speak at first in Fire and
Water and last in Earthe and Air.

The wordes of the psalmist (114:4) shall be proved
correct. No less so the words of John (1:12 and 5:6).
And also, be mindful and listen, as John likewise saide:
he that hath ears to heare, God has enjoined him to
heare. It matters not a whit whether he wish it or noe.

Kennedy looked ahead. The last sheet in the stack was
number 86. It was going to be a sod of a long night.

31

Tillman made his approach along a route that took him between the lines of sight of the security cameras. There might be nobody watching the monitor in any case, or the monitor might be set to flick cyclically through the camera feeds, but he took as few chances as he could.

He went to a place he'd already chosen from a long way out – the angle of a wall, where a dead zone for the cameras corresponded with a thick patch of shadow between two arc lights. He pressed himself in against the wall, partially shielded to his left by a downpipe, and waited.

The next time the guard made his rounds, Tillman was ready. He let the man walk right past him.

'Hey,' he said. 'Got the time?'

He wasn't being a smart-ass. Rotational force increased your chances of a clean knock-out, because when you turn quickly, your brain, in its bubble of protective fluid, floats relatively stationary inside your turning skull. As the guard swung round to face him, Tillman smacked him across the side of the head with a sap. The man's knees buckled. Tillman caught him as he folded and lowered him carefully to the ground.

He quickly took the guard's jacket and cap. Keys were in the jacket pocket, ready to hand: good. There was no time to take the trousers. If anyone *was* watching the camera feed, the gap before he emerged again had to be short enough not to arouse suspicions. He tied the guard's hands and feet with plasticated wire and gagged him with duct tape. Rough and ready, but it would hold for a while.

Then he stepped out into the light, head turned slightly away from the watching cameras, and ambled around the back of the building towards the door.

He was putting his money on there being a straightforward lock that one of the guard's keys would fit, and even then he knew he needed to get it right on the first or second try. Otherwise, he'd have to shoot the lock-plate off and take his chances with whoever was inside. He had his gun, a Mateba Unica, unholstered in his hand as he stepped up to the door.

But his luck was in. The guard hadn't just left the door unlocked, he'd placed a wooden chock on the ground to wedge it open. That level of sloppiness and stupidity was a gift from God, and Tillman took it. He didn't even break stride as he pushed the door wide and stepped in.

On the other side of the door, there was a narrow vestibule, completely empty apart from a time clock on the wall and a rack of punch-cards. The time clock showed six o'clock, and had presumably done so for quite a while. The cards had a patina of dust, some had fallen out of their pigeonholes onto the floor, and there were bootmarks laid across them. Whoever was staffing this place now, they didn't bother with clocking in and clocking out.

There was a double swing-door ahead of Tillman, light spilling out from the crack between the two doors. He pushed it open and walked right through.

Into a much larger space, flood-lit. Huge wood-and-steel-framed shelf units towered past the floodlights into the darkness of a ceiling void that had to be forty feet above him. On the shelves, crates and drums and bulky objects swathed in plastic fibre-wrap.

Closer to hand, another guard turned as the door slammed against the wall.

'What took—' he said.

Then he registered Tillman's camouflage trousers, or maybe just Tillman's cold, stern face. His eyes widened.

Tillman hit him across the jaw with the butt of the Unica, knocking him backward into the nearest rack of shelves. It was very solidly built and didn't even shake. The guard managed to stay on his feet, but he made the mistake of scrambling for the gun at his side. Tillman kicked his legs out from under him.

There was no need for another punch. Tillman got the guard in a throat-lock, his free left hand holding the guy's arm against his side so he couldn't bring the gun up, and applied steady pressure.

After thirty seconds, the guard wasn't moving any more. After forty, Tillman set him down, tied him up and gagged him like the other one, and put him out of the way on one of the floor-level shelves.

No way were these guys *Elohim*: they were local hire, and not very good at that.

Now, belatedly, Tillman did the reconnaissance that in a perfect world he would have done before going in. First of all, he checked for interior CCTV hook-ups, or wiring for pressure or contact alarms. There were none, which didn't surprise him now that he'd seen the standard of the security staff. Next, he found the other doors out of this massive, hangar-like room – there were seven, in all – locked the ones that would lock with

249

the guard's keys, and marked the locations of the others. One led through to an inner office whose floor-to-ceiling window was designed to allow whoever sat there to oversee everything that went on in the warehouse. It was dark, now, and empty.

Tillman checked the rolling door of the freight bay, too. It wasn't a separate space but an area within the bigger room, with a built-up platform beside it and an unloading ramp for big items. An overhead crane hoist hung above it. In silhouette, it looked like the bowed head of a sleeping tyrannosaur.

So why would our girl spend her nights here? he wondered. *And why isn't she here right now?*

But maybe a bigger question was: where *is* here?

He went to the nearest shelves and took a look at their contents. The bulky, wrapped items looked to be machine parts, but it wasn't easy to guess what the machines might be. He slashed some of the boxes open with the German paratrooper's gravity knife that he wore in a boot-sheath. They contained metal mouldings, screws and gaskets – the lowest common denominator of garages and workshops the world over.

But in a garage or a workshop, some of these boxes would be open and in use. Even in a wholesale warehouse, you'd expect some of them to have been broken out from under plastic seals to fulfil part-orders. Tillman ran his spread fingers over box after box. The dust was thick enough to ruck under his touch, and apart from the places where his hand fell, it was pristine.

So whatever was going on here, the stuff on these shelves was a front. For what, though?

Tillman thought of one place he could go to for an answer: the truck. If it was being loaded, it wasn't with this stuff. He went over to the freight bay and tried the truck's rear doors. Padlocked. But it didn't take long to find a crowbar, and the hasp of the padlock broke open on the third tug. He threw the doors open.

The dark interior of the truck was piled high with boxes. He took a torch from his pack, flicked it on and played the beam over the labels on the nearer boxes.

$C(CH2OH)$ 4 PENT
B-HMX 95% HANDLE WITH CARE
1,3 BUTADIENE BULK ELAST
AMM NITR. CONC CAKE

He sucked in his breath. Not nice at all. Some of this stuff – like the ammonium nitrate, which made up a large percentage of most commercial fertilisers – might have looked reasonably innocent by itself. But there was only one context in which all of these substances would ever crop up together, and that was bomb-manufacture.

The truck was a bespoke bomb factory on wheels.

But it wasn't only that, Tillman discovered as he widened his search. There were wooden longboxes, too, of a type he immediately recognised from his mercenary days. They were the crates in which guns and rifles were sometimes transported, wrapped in grease and plastic to keep them rust-proof for long-term storage. He broke one open, opened up the inner seal and pulled out a shining FN Mark 16 assault rifle. He counted six in the box. Another, smaller box in the adjacent stack contained forty-millimetre grenade launchers. They looked like a good fit for the FNs. And moving that box brought him face to face with another box, whose sides bore military stencils: CBU-94/B TMD SOFT. The TMD in that mouthful of acronyms stood for Tactical Munitions Dispenser. Cluster bombs, in other words, with launchers.

Bombs. Guns. Portable munitions. Everything you needed to start your own war. Tillman backtracked. The busy little beavers who'd been filling this truck with high-tech death for most of the afternoon probably hadn't been carrying the crates and boxes far. With some of this stuff, you minimised human contact as far as you could, on the grounds that if someone's hand slipped you suddenly didn't have humans any more – just runny chuck steak. So somewhere close by, and probably in this room, there was a cache.

Once he knew that, it was absurdly easy to find. At one end of the room, separate from the fixed shelving, he found a set of moving racks of the kind used for library storage. These were packed as tight as sardines, with no aisles between them. But each unit ran on tracks and had a wheel fitted so it could be moved to left or right, creating an aisle wherever it was needed.

Wheeling the racks into all their various permutations, Tillman found what he had expected to find: a trapdoor set flush with the floor, with three keyholes evenly spaced along one of its edges.

Risking the noise, Tillman shot out the locks one by one. Then he lifted the trap part-way. Striplights flickered on automatically down below, illuminating a lower chamber as big – but not nearly as high – as the one he stood in. Quarry tiles on the floor, some of them cracked, white-limed walls. Broad, sturdy wooden steps led down to it, and alongside them there was a mechanical chain-hoist. A smell compounded of mildew, packing grease and bleach rose to greet Tillman, strong and dank and insinuating.

He thought for a moment or two. He wanted to go on down and find out the worst. But this place – not just the hidden basement, but the building as a whole – could easily turn into a trap. He had to take a few minimal precautions, at least, his own version of a tripwire tied to a few tin cans. The instinct was too deeply ingrained in him to ignore.

Tillman let the trapdoor fall all the way open. It hit the wall, where a wooden stay-bar had been bolted into place for it to rest on. He walked back across to the freight bay looking for something he could use.

Seven miles away, a red light winked on a board, to the accelerating pulse of an electronic alarm.

32

Diema muttered an oath. It wasn't much of an oath, since the People viewed profanity as a wound to the soul of the utterer, but there was a lot of feeling behind it.

The warehouse's alarm was silent, but the red light flashing on the tell-tale unit just over the loading bay doors showed that Tillman had tripped it – probably by forcing a lock or stepping in front of a motion sensor. It was only a matter of time, now. He could still get out of there before they came, but only if he knew what he'd done, moved now and moved fast.

The girl waited, edgily, for the inevitable consequences to play out. It took eleven minutes before a black van, high-sided and windowless, pulled off the A312 onto the deserted industrial estate, drove halfway down the approach road to the warehouse and stopped, effectively blocking it. The only other way out was across open ground to the south or east.

A minute later, a Volvo S60, also black, rolled up behind the van. Whereupon the van drove over the lip of the kerb and into the wasteground, trundling slowly around to the other side of the building.

Diema watched this disaster unfolding with a mixture of exasperation and fatalism. She still needed more from Tillman, so his death right now would be a major stumbling block. On the other hand, it would show perhaps how flawed he was – how much less than she'd been told. There was a great deal of report and speculation in Kuutma's files about Tillman's unique talents – his combat skills, his intuition, his dogged courage, his endless, insane resourcefulness. Now it seemed he was falling at the first hurdle, and in such an obvious way! Couldn't he have checked for alarms? Couldn't he have taken the time to do proper recon?

Men – only men, no women – were stepping out of the van and the car now, and walking towards the warehouse. Most were the same men who'd been working there earlier in the day, but among them Diema saw two who were of a different order. The skeletally thin man with the ash-white hair was Hifela, the Face of the Skull, and the muscular man beside him, who looked like an oaf or a butcher, was Elias Shud. They were hand-trained executioners, answerable only to Ber Lusim himself.

So it was over. Unless she risked everything to go in and rescue Tillman from the mess he'd made. And even then . . .

She counted ten. Ten *Elohim* – two of them among the best the People had ever raised.

It was over, whether she went or stayed.

33

What Tillman found in the lower room came as no surprise, but only because he'd already had the big surprise when he opened up the truck. Along with more explosives and raw materials for explosives, there were RPG-Komar shoulder-mounted missiles, self-igniting phosphorus grenades, Belgian army issue Tatang combat knives, M2 backpack flamethrowers and – looking almost ashamed of the shabby company it was keeping – a box of digital alarm clocks ready to be filleted for timing mechanisms. It was an arsenal of enormous extent and terrifying variety, assembled by someone who knew what they wanted to cook up (presumably Armageddon) and exactly what the recipe called for.

Tillman wasn't given to letting his imagination run wild, but found himself playing out in his mind the scenarios that would arise if this Pandora's Box were opened and a tenth of its contents saw the light of day.

But this was an ongoing operation. It didn't look like a survivalist stockpile assembled against a future apocalypse. Quite the opposite. Two trucks had rolled in, one had rolled out again. The other had been stacked to the roof with instruments of death and mayhem and was in the freight bay ready to roll.

Perturbed, Tillman retreated to the upper level.

He was remembering the petite, self-contained girl he'd watched on the CCTV feed at the newsagents' in Pimlico. It was hard to reconcile that pretty, solemn face with this house of horrors. But then again, from what Kennedy had said, the girl was as much beast as beauty.

Shaking his head to clear it of the ammoniac stink, Tillman crossed to the office. He didn't bother to try keys this time, since there was no way his visit here was going to pass unnoticed. He just kicked the flimsy door off its hinges and walked in.

A dark-green filing cabinet stood demurely in the corner of the room. Tillman tried the top drawer, found it locked. Again, he thought, *To hell with subtlety*. He still had the crowbar in his hand and he used it to bend the front of the top file drawer out and down.

The file hangers inside were labelled with alphanumerics – TN1, GF3, KB14. He hauled papers out and scanned them. Most were bills of lading, invoices and paperwork for shipments out of the warehouse. Screws, bolts, belts and gaskets going to Bergen, Berlin, Bogota, Brussels, Brisbane. Either there were no As or they were filed out of sequence. The High Energy Haulage logo was on every sheet, its head office given each time as a different address in a different city, all of them a long way from Hayes, Middlesex.

Tillman opened up the next drawer, and the next. He found more of the same. Nothing incriminating, nothing that related in any way to the real business of this place. But why would there be? He scanned more and more of the paperwork, trying to get a feel for what this operation might be about from the items that had been sent out and the places they'd been sent to.

But there was no rhyme or reason. Most of the destinations were big cities, but some were towns he'd barely heard of. San

257

Gimignano. Bardwell, Kentucky. Darling, South Africa. La Orotava. He glanced across at the desk in the office. Two computers sat there, side by side. Maybe a better bet.

But as he crossed to the desk and leaned in to turn on the nearer of the two machines, he heard a loud, metallic clattering from behind him, the unmusical tolling of empty paint and lube cans. He'd wired up all the doors in that way, but the direction of the sound suggested it had come from the double doors through which he'd entered.

He was all out of time.

34

Diema waited and watched.

There was nothing else she could do.

She saw Hifela and his hit squad walk into the warehouse through its rear doors. She saw most of them come out again and walk around to the front of the building, presumably to catch Tillman between two fronts.

A minute or two passed without further sound.

And then there was a single, resonating boom.

Leo Tillman had just been dispatched, execution-style.

Diema thought about this and tried to decide how she felt about him being dead before circumstances had even obliged her to speak to him. But as she considered, she frowned.

No, that made no sense. Her first guess had to be wrong.

35

Elias Shud thought often about the parable of the talents. Maybe too much, if he were honest with himself. In the parable, the man who didn't use what God gave him was rebuked: the Lord's blessings went to those who diligently exploited what they already had.

Shud's own talents were mostly kept hidden, these days, because he had chosen to follow Ber Lusim into exile – and in the decade that followed, Ber Lusim had sent him only against the softest of targets.

So a man who was capable of going up against the mightiest fighters in the Nations, and coming away with their blood on his hands, had been used instead to dispatch men, women – even, occasionally, children – who didn't even know that they were targets and either died unknowing or died surprised. And then, more recently, as Shekolni had preached his gospel of pre-emption, he had created terror on a larger scale, but still without any personal engagement worthy of the name.

So Shud had come to think of himself, in recent years, as a man whose service to the Word consisted chiefly in the abasement of his pride – in the glory that comes from forsaking glory.

Today felt no different. They were responding to an alarm

call from the warehouse. Ten of them. A *minyan* of Messengers! Rushing to respond to a wire chewed by a rat or a security guard whose chair had toppled over while he dozed.

But as soon as they came within sight of the building's rear entrance, they knew it wasn't that. The door had been left open, which told them immediately that the yokels on-site had miscarried in some way.

Hifela commanded his men with gestures to fan out to left and right of the door, and chose two to lead. But there was no attack as they went in. The way through the small room beyond was clear.

Shud went in next and saw what they'd missed: one of the guards, bound and gagged and rolled out of sight in the corner of the room, behind a stack of fibreboard panels. He was barely conscious, but Shud slapped him awake and ripped the gag from his mouth.

'How many?' he rasped.

'One,' the man mumbled. 'I . . . I only saw one.'

The number meant nothing in itself. It was far safer to assume they were facing a team. But now, at least, they knew there was someone ranged against them. Their time hadn't been completely wasted.

'Armed?' Hifela asked, behind him.

The guard nodded. 'I think . . . yes. A gun. He hit me with the butt of a gun.'

Hifela looked at the double doors that stood before them. To push them open and walk straight through was obviously an option. They had superior numbers, after all, and they were *Elohim*, warriors in the service of the Name.

But they were not fools. In battle, they knew, to throw away an advantage when you don't need to is a sin – usually a mortal one.

261

Speaking with his hands again, Hifela designated two to watch the doors. The rest he took with him, back through the rear door and around the side of the building.

The warehouse space was huge. It took up most of the interior of the building, and there were half a dozen ways or more of approaching it. Two of them were doors opening off parallel corridors that were easily reached from a side entrance.

Hifela led the way there and let them in using a master key. They entered, separated into two groups, and – on Hifela's signal – moved quickly and silently down the corridors to the two doors. Hifela opened one with the master key. Shud broke the other open with a single thrust of his shoulder.

They surged into the warehouse from two sides and scattered widely, looking for the enemy.

There was no enemy, but there was a fire.

In the middle of the floor, a green steel drum blazed: brilliant blue flames, with a rippling heat haze towering above them like a genie in the still air.

And just below them, Shud knew, not to mention in the truck parked on the far side of the vast room, there were crates and barrels of high explosive, both stable and unstable; cubane, nitrocellulose, half a dozen varieties of plastique and toluenes.

'Put it out,' Hifela hissed.

That wasn't the mistake. Two men moved forward quickly, the others coming up behind to cover them. One of the two dragged a fire blanket down from an emergency point without breaking stride.

But as they got closer to the burning drum, their footsteps faltered. One of them fell to his knees, the other staggered and clutched his throat.

Shud suddenly realised something that he should have registered before: the colour of the flames.

'Don't go any closer!' he bellowed, in the tongue of the People. 'Stay away from it. That's paracyanogen. There's cyanide gas in the—'

A shadow occulted the light, directly above his head. He dived and rolled even before he thought about it, and so was saved. Something slammed down out of empty air like the slamming of a door, and the two men to his left were no longer there.

Staying down, Shud took in the scene in a series of quick glances. The shattered packing crate, full of steel ball-bearings that were now rolling freely across the floor. The two men under it, the one clearly dead, the other horribly crushed but still moving, trying to free himself.

Above them, the jib of the overhead crane still rocking, its jaws wide and empty. All their enemy had had to do was position it above the burning drum and wait for them to come.

And that was when the shooting started.

36

These things occurred to Diema, in this order.

First, that the sound she'd heard at first couldn't have been a gunshot, because only a lunatic would fire a gun in a warehouse full of high explosives.

Then, that the sounds she was now hearing definitely *were* gunshots.

And then, and therefore, that someone inside the building either didn't care about consequences or was so sure of his aim that he was prepared to take the risk.

Leo Tillman was making a fight of it. Against ten *Elohim*. It was the most perfect, the most complete insanity.

But as madness went, there was something admirable about it.

37

From his position on the floor, Elias Shud had two major advantages.

The first was that the remains of the broken packing crate gave him effective cover. The second was that the toxic gas coming off the burning drum of paracyanogen was both hotter and lighter than the air in the warehouse, so he wasn't in danger of inadvertently taking in a gulp of invisible and odourless death.

He was well placed, therefore, to admire the precision of the shots that killed several of his comrades.

They were coming from high up and over to his left, and they were spaced far enough apart to indicate a handgun set on full manual. Heavy, too: a .454 Casull load, or something very similar. The tool of a craftsman, in other words. Three men fell in the space of about ten seconds, each taken out by a single shot.

In combat, Shud kept his emotions firmly in check, but he was aware that one of the emotions he was shutting down was the thrill of meeting – after so long an interval – a worthy opponent.

He saw his comrade and leader, Hifela, kneeling behind the angle of a wall, triangulating – just as Shud himself had done –

the point of origin of the shots. Hifela caught Shud's gaze, gestured him to wait, took out his phone.

Shud turned his head, slowly and smoothly, to take in the area of the freight bay. There were very few places that would allow both for cover and for a clean line of fire. And obviously the shooter had started off by being *there*, in that corner, where the controls for the overhead crane were dangling on the end of their free line.

Hifela was talking in a murmur to the two men outside, the ones he'd left covering the rear doors. He put the phone away, signalled to Shud *be ready*.

Shud had a sica blade in one hand and a gun – a Jericho 941 loaded with low-penetration hollow-point ammo – in the other. Aside from being flat on his back, he was as ready as it was possible to be.

When the doors burst open, he was already rising into a crouch. Their man would be facing a vicious enfilade out of nowhere: he'd have to move or die, and any move away from this fresh attack would take him in Shud's direction.

The whipstitch whine of semi-automatics was his signal. Shud was on his feet and running, Hifela running too on the other side of the shelving rack, staking out the dead ground between them without any need for discussion or signals.

Shud actually saw his man, just for a moment, wedged into the corner of the freight bay with nowhere to run. He brought up his arm and squeezed off a shot without even slowing, and felt a surge of satisfaction when the intruder jerked, half-turned around by the force of the bullet. He'd taken the shot either in the shoulder or high up on his chest.

Then the neon strips stuttered and stalled, and the room was plunged into complete darkness. Acting on honed instinct, Shud shifted left and slowed, breaking his stride. Bullets snarled against concrete beside him, where he'd been. So the enemy was hurt, but not down, and still working every advantage he had.

But the darkness helped Shud just as much as it helped his quarry. Knowing that Hifela was perfectly placed to fire if the man moved away from the wall and betrayed his position out in the open, he ran forward another ten feet, ducked and rolled, so that he was right up against the rear wheel of the truck. At this distance, even going by hearing alone, he could hardly miss. He waited for his enemy to move.

But nothing moved. And now Shud was skewered on the same dilemma, afraid of giving away his own position by an incautious sound or movement.

He considered. The man had to be very close. If he'd run towards Hifela or the others, there would have been shots or scuffles by now. So he'd remained in the freight bay, holding perfectly still just as Shud was, waiting for his moment.

The man had very few options, at this point. He could go around the front of the truck, between its bumper and the drop-down doors; around the rear, into the open – and into Hifela's line of sight; under the truck, over it, or into it.

It struck Shud that by putting out the lights, the man had given away his decision. In the dark he was moving out, now, across the floor of the room. He was in the open, advancing as silently as he could between his attackers, taking the only chance he had to make it out of the trap he'd dug for himself and reach one of the doors.

Shud rose to his feet. Ten steps away, at the mouth of the freight bay, was the main bank of light switches. He took those steps slowly, soundlessly, shifting his weight with infinite care so that not even the rustling of the fabric of his own clothes would give him away.

Beside the cab of the truck, he paused again. There was no movement, yet, from anywhere else in the room. He reached out, still slowly, still silently, and found the lower edge of the panel of light switches, smooth steel bolted to split and weathered plywood board. His fingers traced the switches. He knew them by their relative positions. External lights. Bay lights. Main strips.

But before he could flick the switches, something cold and hard touched the back of his neck.

From inside the cab of the truck, whose windows must have been rolled down all this time, the man's voice murmured right in his ear.

'Sorry. Lights were just bait.'

On the first word, Shud was already moving. But the man shot him high in the chest, the bullet heading down through his body at a steep angle. It was not just the bullet, it seemed, but the whole world that attacked him. The wall charged him, knocking him off his feet, and then the floor reared up to slam against his splayed body, full-length.

Shud heard the truck's engine start, saw through bleared eyes its lights opening like the eyes of a dragon started from sleep.

The engine noise swelled to a roar and the truck leaped backwards, smashing into the nearest racks of shelving, sending them tumbling and crashing against their neighbours. The chain reaction toppled the burning drum of paracyanogen and a wave of blue fire spread across the room, lighting up a scene of chaos and destruction – running men, falling crates and toppling walls of shelving.

Then the truck reversed direction and rushed on Shud, and the darkness followed in due course.

38

The truck punched its way through the drop-down door of the freight bay without slowing, bringing it down from its housing in the brickwork and ripping out a steel supporting joist along with it. The debris rained down on the truck, which was already slewing around towards the slip road.

There was a moment when the light from one of the security spots shone directly into the cab, showing the driver, beyond any possibility of a doubt, to be Leo Tillman.

Diema felt an astonishment that had a prickle of awe in it. Ten Messengers, one Adamite man. It was like a Zen koan: there was no meaning in it that her mind could grasp.

The truck drove up the slip road, gathering speed. When it got to the car that had been left there as a road block, Tillman pulled suddenly to the left to hit it at an angle, spinning it off the road and over onto its side, its roof, its other side. It was still a terrific and damaging impact, but the truck, rocking like a boat in a tempest, kept right on going.

Three men – Hifela and two others – ran out through the ruined freight bay doors, guns in their hands, and took aim. To get to the main road, the truck would have to turn broadside on to them for a space of fifty yards, making the driver a relatively easy target.

Diema fired low. Her first two shots missed, but the third hit one of the shooters in the knee. He fell, clutching his leg, and a second later his scream floated past her on the light wind.

A lacework of shots forced Hifela and the other man to retreat behind the angle of the warehouse wall, carrying the wounded man between them. They returned fire, for the sake of their self-respect, but out in the dark of the wasteground Diema was an impossible target.

When the truck was out of sight, she slipped from her covert and retreated quickly back to the fence that separated this site from the next. She was about to lie down on her belly and slide through a hole in the base of the fence when the night turned to summer noon.

The explosion was an assault against each of her senses in turn. After the fireball, the shockwave hit her like a wrecking ball and threw her down onto the ground. The sound – a great, prolonged roar – mauled her as she lay there, stunned, and then a searing, chemical miasma invaded her lungs along with her sudden, shaking breath and tore at her from the inside.

It was whole minutes before she could make herself move again. She felt as though every inch of her skin had been separately squeezed and pummelled. The fire was still lighting up the sky brighter than daylight, but the smoke had now rolled across her and everything that was near at hand was cloaked and distorted by it.

Breathing as shallowly as she could, she crawled through the hole in the fence. On the far side, she stowed her rifle in a battered-looking sports bag, changed quickly into the clothes she thought of as her homeless street urchin disguise, and cleaned most – but not all – of the camouflage dirt off her face with moist wipes.

When she walked away, she was both anonymous and

vaguely unclean. In the Adamite world, she found this to be the best disguise of all. The eye glanced off her because it didn't want to see.

Not that anybody was likely to be looking, right then. The wrath of God had fallen on Ber Lusim and his people. And with supreme, inscrutable irony, it had worn the face of Leo Tillman.

Tillman drove for about five miles – sticking to back roads and country lanes – before he found a place where he could stow the truck. It was a derelict petrol station, right on the main road, with an equally abandoned-looking cottage alongside it. Possibly the cottage was attached to the property – live-in accommodation for the manager of the station, until the completion of the M25 left him beached an unfeasible six or seven miles from the passing trade.

Tillman steered the truck between the rusting pumps and the blind eyes of the kiosk, and rammed it slowly and carefully through a decorative latticework fence into the cottage's back garden. Then he got out and propped the fence back up again. The cottage hid the truck from the road, which was something, but it was as conspicuous as hell from the station forecourt. Given the obscene potential of its cargo, he'd have to come back soon and put it somewhere safer. But this would do for now. He still had to trek back overland and retrieve his own car, which was a mile or so from the warehouse in a stand of trees.

Sitting on the truck's running board, Tillman stripped off his jacket and then slowly, with his left hand, undid the straps of the Kevlar vest. His shoulder was aching and starting to cramp. Examining the impact site, he realised that he was lucky to have gotten off so lightly. The deepening purple bruise was centred a bare inch from the edge of the vest.

Tillman pushed air through his clenched teeth, consumed for a moment by utter self-disgust. It had been bloody amateur hour all the way, and it was a miracle he'd gotten away as clean as he had. He remembered a barracks in Angola, more than a decade earlier. Field Sergeant Bennie Vermeulens holding forth as he sewed up a massive knife wound in his thigh with fishing line. 'Improvising is the last tool in the box, Leo. It's what you do when your plans run out. So every time you do it, ask yourself if you should have had more plans.'

If that last man – the one who'd looked too big to run so fast – had aimed an inch to the right, the hollow-point shell would have gone into Tillman's shoulder, and its casing would have broken into molten meteors spraying out and down through his chest. Or if the guy had loaded a more penetrating round, at that distance the vest might not even have stopped it.

And if there'd been no handy tub of stabilised paracyanogen gel? No overhead crane? No truck?

He should have had more plans. Definitely.

But that wasn't all. He'd left men standing and given them a clear shot when he ran. He'd been saved by another shooter, firing from the other side of the warehouse, away from the road. Someone, therefore, who must have already been in position when the kill squad rolled up, probably even earlier, when Tillman was doing his own recon. As he watched the warehouse through his field glasses, another pair of eyes had been trained on his back.

Friendly eyes? Best not to take anything for granted at this point. The hand that picks you up out of the fire may just be saving you for the frying pan. But friendly or not, he knew who they belonged to and how elegantly he'd been set up. He just didn't know why. Or how she'd guessed that he'd track the bike and use it to get back on her. Or why she'd bothered, once he was in the trap, to help him get out again.

What are you up to, girl? And how do you even know me, let alone know me so well?

Unless it was all chance. All screw-up. Maybe she'd been watching the warehouse, too, and that was why she'd spent so much time there.

Like Kennedy, he had a sudden, uneasy feeling that he was a piece in a pattern he couldn't perceive. Not acting, but acted on. And that the pattern, when he finally saw it, might be one he wouldn't like much at all.

39

And the False word wille die, and the True worde live. As on the threshing Floor, when Chaff is sorted from Wheat, that all who worke dilligently and earn their Hire may finally eat. The Infidels who soile the Holy Worde will bewaile their Blindness, and repent. Even in the House of the faithlesse Soldier they will repent. And in Münsters Churche, so, and likewise, they will repent. But such repentance wille come too late and Helles Fires will take holde on them.

Gods Angel will stand over Zion with a flaming Sworde outstretched in his hand, ready to doe Execution. But his first Stroke he will withholde awhile, because the Houre is not yet come.

Where the Highest bled, the Lowest wille likewise bleed. Even the vermin, that all shunne and disdaine. Shall it not be below as it was above? God has even promised this (Matthew 6:10).
The water of Ister will runne red, as with Blood – a greate Wonder, and one that all will attest. They that touche it will be stained. They that drinke it will be cursed.

Kennedy shoved the thin sheaf of typewritten pages away from her and massaged her eyes with the heels of her hands.

She'd learned a lot about Johann Toller in the last three hours, but was starting to wonder how much more she could take.

Toller described the source of his revelations as an angel made all of fire, with six wings and multiple pairs of eyes under each wing – Revelation 4:8, he had helpfully added. The angel had appeared to him when he was close to death, and recounted the prophecies to him.

And they were deeply strange. They soared and plunged from the sublime and the cosmic to the sordid and the petty. God would deal out vengeance upon the nations that denied him, but also on specific, named people: minor officials in Cromwell's Barebones Parliament and its successors, quarter-masters in the New Model Army and even clerks in government ministries.

But riding behind the local details was a religious fervour freed from the confines of workaday sanity. Toller believed that Christ was on his way, ready to keep a date he'd made with the faithful long before. He was already late. He was already looked for. If you held your breath and closed your eyes, you could hear his footsteps.

A conviction grew in Kennedy as she read. The terms of Toller's rhetoric were so similar to the Judas Gospel, as Emil Gassan had once read it to her, that she knew, somewhere beneath or beyond reason, that the echoes meant something. Like Toller, the Judas People were obsessed with timing and haunted by the fear that the Lord might have turned his face away from them – that their precious covenant might come, in the end, to nothing.

The similarities were too close to be accidental. Toller even mentioned the same figure of three thousand years, which was central to the Judas tribe's theology but made very little sense to regular Christians. A three-millennia cycle was about to close, Toller said, and once it was complete, everyone would see God's final purpose. Which was exactly what Kennedy had read, three years before, in the forbidden pages of the Judas Gospel.

While she was still trying to make sense of this discovery, the door behind her opened. Gilles Bouchard stepped inside and skirted the little desk to stare down at her, moving with the silence of a monk in a cloister. She gave him a nod of acknowledgement, and saw Bouchard measuring with an expert eye the number of pages she'd turned.

'You should skip to the climax, Ms Kennedy,' he said, smiling. 'There is, I promise you, a great deal of repetition along the way.'

Actually, Kennedy had already skipped ahead to the last page. It was the same as the rest, maybe a little more wilfully opaque and fantastic in its imagery, but cut from the same cloth as the rest of the book.

And the Stone shall be rolled away from the Tombe, as it was the Time before. Then will a VOICE be heard, crying 'The Hour, the Hour is at Hand' and all Menne will see what heretofore was hidden. The Betrayer will condemne a great Multitude with a single Breathe. On the Island that was given for an Island, in the presence of the Son and of the Spirit, hee will speake the Names of the thousand thousand that will be sacrificed. And from his Throne in the Heavens, the Lord Jesus who is our Glory and our Life will speake the Names of the few that will be Saved.

Kyrie eleison. Christe eleison. Kyrie eleison.
Amen.

'It's an unfathomable and pointless book,' Bouchard murmured. 'But typical of its time.'

Kennedy put down the page she was reading and swivelled on the chair to face Bouchard, resting an arm across its back. 'Is it?' she asked. 'How, exactly?' She was looking for reassurance, she realised. If all this madness was in the air back then, the eerie parallels she was seeing would be a lot less disturbing.

Bouchard made a non-committal gesture. 'I didn't mean anything profound,' he assured her. 'I just meant that Toller's argument would have been far less controversial in the 1600s than it sounds today.'

'The religious mania?'

'The second coming of Christ. Specifically that. A great many people, in Toller's time, took it as a given that the Day of Judgment was at hand. Not sad, troubled men with sandwich boards, but influential thinkers. Entire religious movements, in fact.'

Bouchard leaned back against the wall, since there was nowhere in the room that he could sit. 'It's strange, in some ways,' he said, 'and very understandable in others. Strange in the timing. The word "millenarian", by its etymology, explicitly addresses a phenomenon that happens at the end of a millennium – the end of a great swathe of time, which is easy to mistake for the end of time itself. The late seventeenth century was a long way away from one of those watershed moments. But it seemed like an ending for other reasons.'

'What reasons?' Kennedy asked. Dry as the subject was, she was keenly, even urgently, interested.

'You're inviting me to give you a lecture,' Bouchard warned. 'You may come to regret that.'

'Go ahead,' Kennedy told him. 'You don't scare me.'

Bouchard grinned, and spread his arms in a declamatory gesture. 'It was the best of times, it was the worst of times,' he said. 'Well, mostly it was just the worst of times. Or at any rate, the most unsettled. The most unstable. The upheavals of the seventeenth century had the feel of a great and irreversible change, a culmination of human history. In Britain, the monarchy was overthrown and the king beheaded by his own people. In Europe, the Lutheran challenge to the Roman church seemed to echo the cataclysmic battles promised by St John in his Apocalypse. If Mother Church could be attacked, undermined, forced to fight for her survival, then what was safe?'

'So there was acid in the Kool-Aid,' Kennedy summed up. 'For a century or so. Across a whole continent.'

Bouchard shrugged, seeming unconvinced by the metaphor. 'Johann Toller belonged to a group called the Fifth Monarchists,' he said. 'Have you heard of them?'

Kennedy shook her head. 'I'm probably not going to have heard of any of this stuff. Assume I'm completely ignorant. I won't be offended.'

'They were one of many, many radical organisations at that time. Religious zealots – and as part and parcel of that, political dissidents. They came from many different backgrounds – prominent politicians, magistrates, writers and high-ranking army officers – but they were united by a single article of faith. They believed that there was a shape to human history, which the wise and the good could analyse and understand.'

'What shape?'

'A cyclical one. They believed that there had been four great monarchies or empires, each ruling over a particular age, and that each in its turn had been conquered and overturned by the next. I believe the four were Babylon, Persia, Macedonia, and then Rome.'

'So where was the fifth monarchy?'

'Not where,' Bouchard said. 'When. The fifth monarchy was the one that was about to dawn. The new king would be Christ, and his reign would last for ever. They backed this theory up with close reference to Biblical texts. There was a very heavy emphasis on the Revelation of St John, which famously gives the number of the beast as 666. Many argued that the year 1666 would be the last year of the earthly calendar. They liked the Book of Daniel, too. In that book, Daniel receives a vision of four great beasts who will have dominion over the Earth, and then, after "a time, and times, and half a time" will be cast down. That will be the signal that the son of man was about to ascend his throne.'

Again, Kennedy heard a definite and scary echo of the Judas tribe's world view, with its insistence on thousand-year-long cycles and its infatuation with St John. The only extant version of their secret gospel had been encoded in a copy of his.

'And Toller was part of this group?'

'A leading figure, along with the likes of John Carew, Vavasor Powell and Robert Blackborne. Blackborne was the first secretary of the admiralty, by the way. Their modern-day successors may be marginal crackpots, but these were solid, serious men, with public stature and political influence.'

'Okay,' Kennedy said. 'Look, I've probably taken up more of your time than you can really spare . . .'

'I'm happy to help,' Bouchard said.

She got up from the desk and pushed the typescript in his direction, going for broke. 'Then could you explain some of these prophecies to me? The proper nouns, at least?'

Bouchard raised his eyebrows. There were a lot of pages. It was a lot to ask.

'I can perhaps add some annotations,' he said, without much enthusiasm. 'Marginal notes. Here and there.'

It was Kennedy's turn to be surprised. 'Marginal notes? On the only surviving copy of a lost book?'

'No. Obviously not. What you've been reading is not the only copy. It's a copy of the copy, which I made so you could take it away with you.' He raised his hand, forestalling her thanks. 'Thank John Partridge. He pleaded very eloquently on your behalf. Burn it when you're done. And don't, please, tell anyone who gave it to you. We have our reputation to consider.'

Kennedy understood perfectly. She'd had one of those herself, once.

Since there was no second chair, and no room in the narrow cubicle to set one down, Bouchard just sat on the floor and talked her through the prophecies one at a time. Some he just passed on, but on most he had at least a guess to offer – and Kennedy copied in his annotations in the margins or over the actual words of the text.

Münsters Churche was the Überwasserkirche, where a group of religious extremists – Anabaptists – had inaugurated their new government during a short-lived coup.

The faithlesse Soldier was almost certainly Thomas Fairfax, one of Cromwell's generals who had been a friend to Toller and the Fifth Monarchy movement, but had subsequently withdrawn his support for them and backed out of public life entirely.

Ister was one of many old names for the River Danube.

And so on, through all the intricacies and idiosyncrasies of a very intricate, idiosyncratic book. But Bouchard had nothing to offer Kennedy on *the Island that was given for an Island*. 'It could be anywhere. This was a time when all the European powers were annexing territories in the New World as fast as they could be discovered, then fighting endless wars over them, using the native populations as cannon fodder.' He frowned at the text, as though unwilling to admit that he was stumped. 'It would have to be referring to something recent enough that it was still talked about in Toller's day. Then again, he refers to the Münster uprising, and that was decades earlier. It will be hard to pin down.'

Kennedy was only half-listening. Something Bouchard had said had nudged a memory and she was chasing it up on the laptop. The Überwasserkirche. She found the reference and stared at it in mute horror.

And the faithless soldier. A few more clicks brought up a biography of Thomas Fairfax and she knew with a sickening certainty that she was right.

'The ending of days,' she muttered.

'*Qu'est-ce que c'est?*' Bouchard enquired politely.

Kennedy stared at him. 'What all of this is about. The ending of days. The second coming. Armageddon.'

Bouchard nodded. 'Yes, that's the climax of Toller's prophecies, of course. Christ will descend and destroy the unrighteous. Only the just will remain. All of these other events are merely warnings. Harbingers. They tell us that the beginning of Christ's kingdom is imminent.'

'Then He must be on His way,' Kennedy said. 'Because most of these things have already happened.'

40

Rush fretted a lot about how he was going to get his stash of illicitly borrowed books out of Ryegate House. But in the end, he just picked his moment and walked out of the staff entrance carrying them in a black plastic bin bag. If he was stopped, he was planning to say he'd found the bag in a corridor and assumed it was rubbish. But he wasn't stopped.

An hour or so later, and seven miles east in Harlesden, he decanted his haul onto his parents' kitchen table. His mum and dad were in bed already. His mother would have fallen asleep long ago, on half a temazepam, and his dad would probably be sitting up with a book, listening to classical music on his headphones. Neither had heard him return, which meant he didn't have to pretend that everything was normal.

He'd chosen the books quickly, and some of them were no use at all. But Toller appeared in the indexes of most of them. And in one, Rush found a commentary of some kind on the mysterious book of prophecies.

It looked pretty promising at first, but it turned out to have nothing to say about the prophecies themselves. It was more interested in the book as a physical object, and in particular the revolutionary use of a process for the book's few picture plates that anticipated some aspects of lithography.

Rush had no idea what lithography was, so he had no opinion about that. But as he was flicking through the pages he saw another reproduction of the frontispiece: the steep crag, and the town, and the Latin tag. Now he noticed the image had a second caption as well as the one Toller had given it.

It read 'Gellert Hall, *circa* 1640'.

His vision was starting to swim. It wasn't 'Gellert Hall', it was 'Gellert Hill'.

He gave up and closed the book. He'd get up early in the morning and read some more before he went into work. Or maybe he'd pull a sickie and spend the day reading. He was keen to have something solid to show to Kennedy when she got back.

He went into the kitchen, raided his dad's meagre stash of booze and found a half-bottle of cheap brandy that was mostly full, but when he unscrewed the cap the smell of it made his stomach turn. What he really needed was sleep, but he knew that it would take its own not-so-sweet time coming. Whenever he closed his eyes, he could still see Professor Gassan with his hands clasped around the knife that was sticking out of his chest.

Rush put the bottle back and went up to his room, moving as quietly as he could in case his dad had taken off the headphones and turned in for the night. He opened his bedroom door, stepped inside and closed it firmly before turning the light on.

There was a girl on his bed. That registered first, because it was such a novelty in itself.

The gun in her hand presented itself to his mind a half-second or so later, but with even more breathtaking effect.

As a distant third, he realised that she'd been watching

283

TV on his tiny portable, with the sound right down. Cartoon Network. A very old episode of *Courage, the Cowardly Dog*.

'Lock it,' the girl said, with a nod of her head towards the door.

PART FOUR

COUNCIL OF WAR

41

On both sides of the Channel, wherever she could get any internet access Kennedy continued to work through Toller's prophecies, trying to nail down the idea that had occurred to her when she was talking to Bouchard. By the time she was done, she was a few minutes away from St Pancras, and in a slightly surreal daze. She'd thought after meeting the Judas tribe that nothing could ever surprise her again.

She'd been dead wrong.

Her phone rang as the train pulled into the platform. She glanced at the caller ID: Ben Rush. As she was about to answer, Leo Tillman rolled slowly into her field of vision. He was leaning against a pillar halfway along the platform, hands in his pockets, conspicuously waiting for her. The train slowed to a halt, placing him dead centre in Kennedy's window. In her current mood, that was slightly too flashy an effect for her liking. She hit IGNORE on the phone. She'd catch up with Rush later.

Tillman fell into step with her as she descended from the carriage and walked towards the barrier. 'Welcome home,' he said.

Kennedy looked around, first left and then right. 'No marching bands? No parade? Some welcome.'

'Heather, whatever this is about, it's not ancient literature.'

'I never thought it was,' she said. 'Actually, Leo, I think it's about the end of the world.'

He gave her a slightly wary glance. 'I wouldn't have gone that far. But I went looking for your *Elohim* girl and I found—'

'You did what?' Kennedy stopped dead and swivelled to face him, unable to keep the horror from showing on her face. 'Leo, I told you—'

'I know. You told me to sit this out. But I didn't make any promises. Listen, there's something I need to show you. Can you give me an hour or two? I can promise you something you've never seen before.'

'I've heard that from a lot of men,' Kennedy muttered darkly. 'It never comes to anything good.'

And this is no exception, she thought, forty-five minutes later. She was standing in a lock-up in Lewisham, underneath a railway arch, with the gates locked behind her, and she was staring into the back of an articulated truck. The stuff inside it was maybe what you'd get if you asked a terrorist to come up with a vision of the earthly paradise.

She picked up a rifle from a case close to the truck's tailgate that Tillman had already opened. It was a military machine gun – no use for sports, and scarcely better for public order deployment. It was designed to be planted firmly on the ground and set to full automatic, spewing out a few hundred rounds per minute into whatever piece of territory needed to be tenderised.

The next box held grenades, and the one after that, more rifles. They were stacked up against three drums of white phosphorus.

'This is a nightmare,' Kennedy said.

'Or a wet dream,' Tillman said. 'Depending on where you're

standing. There was a warehouse full of this stuff, Heather. Thirty to forty times as much as you're looking at here. The warehouse is mostly smoke and charcoal briquettes by this time. And I'm going to get rid of what's in the truck, too, as soon as I've figured out how. I just wanted you to see it first so you'd know I wasn't exaggerating.'

Tillman ran a hand through his unruly hair, looking more uneasy and uncertain than she could ever remember seeing him. 'Heather, I got a look at the paperwork. The outfit that owned the warehouse – High Energy Haulage – was delivering to a hundred other places. It was a global network.'

'Did you call the police?'

Tillman laughed lugubriously. 'Yeah, I did, for what it's worth. But like I said, this was just a distribution centre. Do you see what we're looking at? We already knew that the Messengers were killers, but this . . .' He threw out his arms in an inarticulate gesture, indicating the truck full of death. 'Unless the London branch just experienced some kind of sudden shared psychosis, we're talking about an incredible escalation of hostilities. They're shipping industrial quantities of small arms, field munitions, high explosive and incendiaries. Moving it all into place. And it's enough to fight a medium-sized war – which I guess is what it's probably for.'

Kennedy shook her head. 'That's not what it's for.'

Tillman stared at her in bewilderment. 'How would you know? Is this something you found in France? Something to do with —'

Kennedy cut across him. 'Not yet, Leo. This is still you showing me yours. How does any of this tie in with the Messenger I met? The girl? You said you went looking for her. Explain.'

Kennedy could tell from his expression as he stared at her that her tone had given too much away. He knew that she was hiding something, and he knew that it was important. How hard would it be for him to put the pieces together and realise who it was he'd been chasing? 'Tell me,' she said again, more urgently.

'She rides a motorbike,' Tillman said, his voice calm, almost expressionless in contrast to Kennedy's. 'Manolis was able to get the licence number, and then he hacked into the UK speed camera networks to see where she'd been clocked. We were looking for clusters. Thought we might get some idea of where she was based. But she saw us coming.'

'*Saw* you?' Kennedy was appalled all over again. 'You mean you met her? You actually—'

'No. I don't mean that. She guessed what we'd do and she turned the tables on us. That's what I'm thinking, anyway. She wanted me to find that warehouse. She used the bike to lead me there. Or she had the place under surveillance herself, and Mano got the wrong end of the stick. But whichever of the two it was, she knows I was there. She was watching me the whole time.'

He took the rifle from Kennedy and put it back in the case, pushed the lid back down hard. Kennedy had forgotten she was even holding it. 'How do you know that?' she demanded.

'Because I tripped an alarm, while I was in there. I made myself a target. I should have been killed, by rights. But I wasn't, because I had a tailgunner. There was another shooter, lying out in the long grass, who laid down some cover fire for me. And as far as I could see, she did it without killing anyone. Beautiful, precision shooting.'

'Not your man?' Kennedy asked. 'Manolis?'

'He isn't a shooter. And he wasn't anywhere near that place.

His wife would skin me and salt me if I asked him to do anything like that. I use him for surveillance, which is his specialty, and that's all I use him for.'

Tillman paused for a second, watching her. Kennedy had to fight the impulse to turn away from him, afraid of what he might be reading in her face.

'Look,' he said, 'I know for sure nobody followed me in. And nobody else was moving out on that waste ground after I got there. That means the shooter was already embedded and hidden before I arrived. It was the girl. There's no other way I can figure it. And she backed my play, which is the only reason I got out alive. If she actually planted that trail for me to follow – if she knew I'd go looking for her, find the bike, and all the rest of it – then she made a lot of right guesses about me based on nothing but thin air and moonbeams.'

'She's a Messenger,' Kennedy said. 'They studied you for years.' *And you share a whole lot of DNA. Maybe that gave her a little bit of an edge, too.*

Tillman nodded. 'Makes sense, I suppose. A little bit of sense. But I've still got a feeling that there's something else going on – and that it might be the something you said you'd tell me about later. Is it maybe time you came clean, Heather?'

'There's ... I think ...' She came to the brink, then hesitated. When she'd first met Tillman, he'd seemed to be on the edge of some kind of breakdown, worn down by years of searching for his lost family. He was doing a lot better now, but if she told him about Diema, and it turned out she was wrong, the harm she might do him was beyond any reasonable calculation. It was almost exactly balanced by the harm she could do if she was right, and Tillman found out from his daughter what had happened to his sons. There were so many reasons for Kennedy to keep quiet, and only one reason to talk. But it was a big reason: it was that she had no right to stand between Tillman and his daughter – the only living person he truly loved.

She shook her head, as much to clear it as anything. Tillman waited patiently for her to speak, but before she could, her phone went off. Grateful for the interruption, she took it out of her pocket. It was Rush again.

'I have to take this,' she lied.

'Okay,' Tillman said. 'I'll still be here when you're done.'

Putting the phone to her ear, Kennedy turned slightly away from him, not so much for the sake of privacy as because she still felt the impulse to hide and the phone gave her the excuse.

'Go ahead, Rush,' she said.

'Kennedy.' His voice was strained. 'How was your trip?'

'It was productive. Did you find out anything useful about Toller?'

'Well, I was going to do some homework on ...' Rush began. But a second voice in the background made him pause. 'I'm not supposed to talk about that,' he muttered. 'She says it will keep for later.'

'*She* says? Who says? Rush—'

'I'm sorry, Kennedy. I'm supposed to stick to the script. Listen to me.' The tremor in his voice was much more evident now, making it hard to understand what he was saying. 'This is an invitation from Diema Beit Yudas. She wants both of you to come and meet her.'

'Both of us?' Kennedy repeated stupidly. Tillman looked like he was about to speak so she held up a hand to stop him and at the same time flicked the phone to speaker. Leo probably had to hear this first-hand. And it hadn't escaped her notice that the girl was going under a different surname from Tillman's former wife, Rebecca Beit Evrom. 'Both of us are to meet her? Ask her who she means by that, Ben.'

Rush's voice sounded out, thin and strained.

'She wants to talk to you, but she wants it to be on her terms. She says she thinks you probably know enough about her by now not to do anything stupid, but in case she's wrong about that, she wants you to know that any move you make against her will mean ... will get me killed. Is that understood?'

'It's understood,' Kennedy said, her heartbeat loud in her own ears. 'Rush, don't panic. We'll come and get you. Give me the address.'

'No, wait. There's more. She says you should bring the book and Tillman should bring the truck. And it's got to be just the two of you. Nobody else.'

'Can I talk to her?' Kennedy asked. 'To ... Diema?' Tillman said nothing, but his eyebrows rose and his lips tightened.

The other voice murmured in the background.

'Yes.'

'Then put her—'

'You can talk to her here. She wants you to come here, so all three of you can talk.'

Kennedy breathed out slowly, finding some stratum of calm. 'And where's here, Ben?'

'A farm. Dovecote Farm. The address is—'

'We know the address,' Kennedy said. 'We're coming. We'll be there soon.'

'Great.'

'Rush, you'll be okay. We're coming right now. She won't hurt you.'

'You think?' His voice crackled with bleak sarcasm. 'She's got me wired up with a bloody—' The phone went dead.

Kennedy turned to Tillman. He was already heading for the cab of the truck. 'I'll drive,' he said over his shoulder.

42

When Ben Rush thought about farmyards – which admittedly wasn't all that much – he tended to think in terms of a big house with a whole lot of barns and stables all around it, chickens scratching at the dirt and a horse looking over a hedge.

Dovecote Farm was basically just a ruin. There must have been an actual farmhouse once, but it looked like it had burned down, leaving only a massive patch of scorched earth where nothing grew. The barns and stables were still standing, but there were holes in the walls where planks had been taken out or kicked in, and the spavined, sagging roofs seemed close to final surrender. Insects buzzed and chirped in the weeds and bullrushes between the outbuildings, but nothing was moving that was big enough for Rush to see.

From his vantage point on the upper level of one of the barns, with the hayloft doors thrown open in front of him, he could look out across the ruined ground towards the road – and be seen from it in his turn, which was probably the point. He was sitting in a wheelback chair, his ankles tied to the front legs and his arms handcuffed together around the back. The chair was rickety, so every time he shifted his weight it lurched either forward and to the left or back and to the right. He was afraid that if he tipped forward too suddenly, he'd fall right out of the hayloft and break his neck. Or maybe he wouldn't break his neck, but the explosives or whatever it was in the package that the girl had strapped to his chest would detonate and blow him apart.

The girl was sitting a few feet away, behind him, with her back against one of the beams. She had her arms folded in her lap and she was looking out at the road. Whatever thoughts were going through her mind, they left no footprints: the girl's face was completely inexpressive.

They'd been like this for a while now, and clearly the girl could keep the silence up for however long it took. So if anyone was going to speak, it was going to have to be him.

He screwed up his courage and went for it.

'You like *Courage, the Cowardly Dog*?' he asked her.

The girl didn't move, but her gaze flicked round and her eyes focused on him. 'No,' was all she said. She said it with a warning emphasis, as though that was fighting talk where she came from.

'You were watching it.'

No answer.

'I prefer the golden oldies,' Rush said. '*The Flintstones. The Jetsons. Yogi Bear*.' Since the girl didn't react, he went on listing old cartoon shows as a mental exercise. At least it passed the time. '*Huckleberry Hound. Hector Heathcote. Funky Phantom. The Hair Bear Bunch. Josie and the Pussycats. Deputy Dawg. Top Cat. Foghorn Leghorn. Tom and Jerry*.'

Still no reaction from the girl. Well, maybe a flicker of interest on Tom and Jerry, but nothing you could take to the bank.

'You want to play a game?' he asked her.

'No.'

'Come on. I bet I can read your mind.'

She stared at him for a long time. Eventually, she said, 'Be quiet.'

'You don't think I can read your mind?' Rush persisted.

This time she didn't bother to speak.

'Think of a number from one to ten,' Rush said. 'Then take away five.'

The girl's forehead creased in a frown. 'A pink elephant from Denmark. It's old and it's stupid. Now be quiet. Or do you want me to cut you?'

And suddenly she had a knife in her hand. It was a weird, asymmetrical thing, with a flat extension like a hook or a bracket to one side of the blade. Rush stared at it, and then at the girl's face. After a moment, she slipped the knife back inside her shirt. There must be a sheath there, strapped to her shoulder: the strap would go down between her breasts, and the knife would sit underneath. And now he was looking at her breasts – and she was looking at him looking at her breasts, which maybe wasn't such a great idea.

'If you cut me, you don't have a hostage any more,' he said. He was just about able to keep the tremor out of his voice.

'No, boy,' the girl said patiently. 'If I *kill* you, I don't have a hostage. I can still cut you.'

That shut him up for a good ten minutes. But he'd read a thriller once where the detective said that psychopaths found it easier to kill you if they didn't have to see you as a human being. So he gave it one more try.

'My name's Ben,' he said. 'What's yours?'

Instead of answering, the girl rummaged in the kit-bag she carried, brought out a narrow strip of straw-coloured cloth and started to twist it into a braid. She looked at Rush expectantly.

He weighed up the pros and cons. It was a good sign, really, that she'd decided to gag him instead of taking the knife to him.

But he really didn't want to be gagged.

But maybe if she got in close enough to put the gag over his mouth, he could do something. Shift his weight at a crucial moment, maybe, and push her out of the hayloft.

He knew that wasn't going to happen. Even if he had both hands free, the girl could fold him into an origami sculpture.

But what the hell was he, anyway? She'd called him *boy*, and he had to be at least a full year older than her, and probably more like two. And he hadn't done one damn thing, so far, besides get smacked around and tied up and questioned and intimidated by her.

'Those are really, really small tits,' he said, after a long and pregnant silence. 'But they look great on you. If you've ever considered plastic surgery, I'd say don't go for it.'

The gag was uncomfortable, and it bit slightly into the corner of his mouth, but Rush was very slightly cheered by the fact that the girl had been blushing when she tightened the knot.

Now I'm human, he thought. *And what's more, so are you.*

43

On the A3100, just south of Shalford, there was a sign by the side of the road that read DEAD PEOPLES THINGS FOR SALE. It stood in front of a windowless wooden shed, whose peeling white paint gave it a leprous look. The first time Kennedy had been driven along this road, as a girl of twelve, she'd mainly noticed the missing apostrophe, and in a priggish way disapproved of the sign. It hadn't occurred to her to wonder who the dead people were, and how their things made their way out here to the arse end of Surrey.

Three years ago, riding as now in the cab of a fourteen-wheeler with Tillman beside her, driving, she'd only been amazed that the sign was still there.

Today, with the sun hiding its face from moment to moment behind sudden, scudding banks of cloud, the unwelcome reminder of death struck her as a bad omen.

When Tillman pulled the truck off the road and onto what was left of the drive of Dovecote Farm, it was death that was chiefly on her mind – her own as much as anybody else's. On that previous visit, three years before, she and Tillman had been trapped on the roof of the farmhouse as it burned, with a trio of *Elohim* on the ground taking free potshots at them every time they stuck their heads up above the guttering. Kennedy had been close to jumping off the roof-ridge, with a vague hope of staying intact enough when she landed to make a run for it, but really, she was just choosing a broken neck over being burned alive.

But Tillman had turned the tables on their attackers, who thought themselves invincible in the dark. Firing from the roof, he'd blown up the gas tank of the truck they'd arrived in with a home-made incendiary round. One of the Messengers had died in that explosion, and Tillman had shot the other when he came running – much too late – to help his friend.

Except it wasn't his friend. It was his brother. They were Tillman's own sons, Ezei and Cephas, who he'd known as Jude and Seth. And because he hadn't seen them since they were four and five years old, and because in any case he'd never been close enough to see either of their faces clearly, Tillman never had the slightest idea what it was he'd done – how his quest of twelve years had finally brought him back to his family just so he could gun them down.

But Kennedy was pretty sure that Diema-who-used-to-be-Tabe-who-used-to-be-Grace knew it very well. That she'd chosen this place where her brothers fought and died because in some way it fitted her agenda for today. And now, as Tillman rolled to a halt on that same sad piece of scorched earth, Kennedy found herself genuinely afraid of what that agenda might be.

Tillman looked a question at her: *ready?* She gave him a curt nod, turned the handle of the door and climbed down out of the cab, holding the print-out of Toller's book under one arm. The blackened substrate under her feet – even after three years, probably as much charcoal as dirt – crunched as she put her weight on it. She looked around, and as Tillman rounded the cab, she pointed wordlessly.

300

Rush was in plain sight. When the farmhouse was still standing, the barn that Diema had chosen would have been hidden from sight behind it: now it faced them across thirty metres of nothing very much. The hayloft doors were wide open, or more likely just gone, and Rush was sitting in what looked like an ordinary kitchen chair, close to the edge, looking down at them. His hands were behind his back, presumably tied or cuffed.

Kennedy wondered for a moment why he hadn't called out to them. Then she saw the gag in his mouth.

The girl wasn't visible at first, but then she stepped forward from deeper inside the hayloft and stood beside Rush, her hand resting on the back of the chair. Her expression was calm and cold. They took a step towards her, but she tilted her head in a warning motion and they stopped.

'Something you should hear before you go any further,' she called down to them. She raised her hand. Something small and white was resting on her palm. She pressed it with her thumb and the digitised chimes of Big Ben wafted down to them. As far as Kennedy could tell, they were coming from Rush.

'This is just the ringer from a wireless doorbell,' Diema told them. 'But I want you to take a good look at your friend.' Kennedy did. Rush was wearing something bulky over his shirt – a sleeveless garment like a life jacket. It was shiny black, and whatever was inside or under it showed in rectangular bunchings on its surface. A suicide vest. And the ringer from a doorbell would make a perfectly good detonator at this range. Diema had just armed the explosives. If she pressed the ringer again, they'd detonate.

'Now we understand each other,' the girl said, lowering her hand to her side again. 'Come on up. I won't ask you to drop any weapons you might be carrying. Just know that any misbehaviour on your part will lead to a more even distribution of this boy across the landscape.'

'Then maybe we should talk down here,' Tillman said bluntly.

Diema stared down at him – and there was something of mockery in her face, or maybe contempt. 'Are you afraid of dying, Tillman?' she asked him.

'I'm averse to it wherever it can be avoided,' he said.

And you want her on ground she hasn't already prepped, Kennedy thought. *But the stakes are too high here, Leo – for you as well as for Ben Rush.*

'We'll come up,' she said aloud. And in a quieter voice, to Tillman, 'Don't push her too hard. When we find out what she wants, then we decide which way to jump.'

'When we're cosying up to forty or so pounds of high-explosive?' he murmured back.

'Move the truck away from the road first,' Diema told them. 'Out behind the barn. Tillman, you do that. Kennedy, come up here. Now.'

They did as they were told. Tillman got back into the truck and the ignition rumbled into life. It rolled on past Kennedy as she walked towards the barn. Then she stepped across the threshold, into sudden shadow.

The loft ladder was off to her right. There was nothing else in the ruined barn, no hay-bales, no rusting farm equipment, no stalls or mangers. If this was an ambush, the ambushers were up in the loft with Diema and Rush. But then, if this was an ambush, the girl was working too hard. She could have left both Kennedy and Tillman to die individually and severally before now, and instead she'd exerted herself to keep them alive.

If the agenda had changed, they'd find out soon enough. But there wasn't anything Kennedy could do about it besides play along; not unless she was prepared to stand by and watch Ben Rush's insides become his outsides.

She climbed up the ladder.

The loft was much better furnished than the floor of the barn. As well as the chair in which Rush was sitting, there were two more chairs set at a fold-up table. A pitcher of water stood on the table, next to a stack of plastic cups. All the comforts of home.

Diema had moved away from Rush and was standing with her back to the wall of the loft, directly facing Kennedy. The detonator was ready in her hand, her thumb poised over it. Kennedy hauled herself up through the trapdoor in the floor, moving very slowly.

'I want to be sure Ben is okay,' she told the girl. 'Can I take that gag off him?'

'You can sit,' the girl said, 'at the table, and wait quietly until I tell you what else to do. Is that the book?'

Kennedy showed her the typescript, which was still unbound and only held together with a thick elastic band. She set it – still slowly, still carefully – down on the table.

'Good,' Diema said. 'Now sit.'

Kennedy sat.

She heard Tillman below, starting to climb.

'If you press that button now,' Kennedy said to the girl, 'you're going to kill yourself as well as us.'

'I'm a soldier,' Diema told her. 'Death in the field is what soldiers expect.'

'In my experience,' Tillman said, his head and shoulders rising through the trapdoor as he spoke, 'soldiers expect that for everybody else, not for themselves.' He kept his empty hands constantly in full view as he climbed up into the loft. Nonetheless, the girl gave him a stare that was full of mistrust.

'Sit down,' she told him.

He sat, but he pulled the chair a little away from the table and angled it towards the girl. He wanted to be free to move if the need arose, Kennedy guessed.

If Diema saw what he was doing, she gave no sign of being troubled by it. 'Is everything you took from the warehouse still in the truck?' she asked him.

Tillman nodded. 'All the incriminating evidence,' he said, 'assembled in one place. Is that what this is about? Are you the cleanup crew?'

Diema gave the question serious consideration. 'Yes,' she said. 'I suppose I am. But you have no idea what it is I'm cleaning up, so you don't know what it is you're saying. That's why you're here, really. To be instructed.' She paused for a moment, as though expecting a question. When neither Kennedy nor Tillman spoke, she said, 'If I meant you harm – if I meant you harm now, today – I'd have come at you in a different way. You realise that, don't you?'

Kennedy looked from Diema to Ben Rush, sitting with his back to them, then back to Diema. She raised her eyebrows. Exhibit A.

Diema met her gaze, unblinking. 'I was doing my best to help you,' she said. 'That's what I was ordered to do. That's why I'm here. But then I spoke to the boy, and now I think I may need to reinterpret my orders.'

She continued to stare at Kennedy with quiet, fierce intensity. 'Some time ago,' she said, 'a secret came into your keeping. A very great secret. When I spoke to the boy ...' her gaze flicked momentarily across to Rush '... I learned that you'd passed that secret on to him. Before we say anything on any other subject, I have to know why. I was assuming you have some sense of honour, some idea of what honour means.'

All of this was addressed directly to Kennedy, seeming purposefully to exclude Tillman, and it was said so solemnly that Kennedy boggled slightly. If this girl had seen twenty, it was a recent memory.

'You tied Ben to a chair with a suicide belt strapped to his chest so you could see if we're honourable?' she said, trying to keep her tone neutral. 'Is that what you're saying?'

'No.' The girl made an impatient gesture – her mouth folding into a grimace before straightening again to the deadpan that seemed to be her default expression. 'That's what *you're* saying. Let's go through this again.'

She pressed down on the ringer and the chimes of Big Ben sounded again. Kennedy gasped aloud and Rush convulsed, but it was only with an access of panic. No explosion came.

In the loud silence, Diema threw the ringer onto the table.

'There's no suicide belt,' she said. 'No explosives. And I gagged him because he was talking about my breasts. I didn't like it.'

Kennedy rose to her feet. Her first thought after *screw me sideways!* was for Rush. She wanted to get him untied and away from that bloody drop. Tillman's initial reaction was different. His right hand swept across his left and suddenly he had a gun in it, centred on the girl's upper body. It wasn't the big and heavy Mateba Unica he usually carried, it was a discreet little Saturday night special, and it looked absurdly tiny in his big hand.

'I'm sorry to do this,' he said to the girl brusquely, 'because I know you saved my life the other night, but there's too much blood under the bridge already for me to trust you. Please move over to the wall. Keep your hands where I can see them, and move like you're walking underwater.'

'Leo—' Kennedy blurted, her heart in her mouth.

'She's *Elohim*,' he said, across her. 'No surprises, Heather. Not beyond the ones we've already had.' And to the girl, 'Please. I said against the wall, and I don't want any argument. Do it.'

Just one damn thing after another, Kennedy thought bitterly. And she knew Tillman was right, on one level. But the level on which he was wrong concerned her more, and she found herself stepping in between the two of them, letting the barrel of Tillman's gun bump against her breastbone, come to rest up against her throat.

'Enough, Leo,' she said. 'Put the gun away. She's done enough to prove her point.'

Tillman tried to step around Kennedy but she gripped his wrist in both of her hands and it was clear that the only way he was going to get it free would be by force.

'What point,' he asked, 'has she proved, exactly?'

'That she's not interested in killing us,' Kennedy said, between clenched teeth. 'So put the gun away, and we'll talk it out. For now, this is neutral ground we're standing on.' She looked over her shoulder at the girl. 'Right?'

'Not right at all,' Diema said. 'Blood was shed here. My people's blood. It's far from neutral. But it's holy, and I'll respect it. You who shed it should honour it, too.' She was looking at Tillman, staring straight into his eyes, a quiet ferocity in her expression. He met that stare with a pugnacious determination that Kennedy had seen in his face before. The back of her neck prickled unpleasantly. She felt, for a moment, as though she'd stepped between Tillman and his reflection in a mirror. *How could he look at Diema, from this close, and not see? And how could he not hear in her voice how much that spilled blood mattered to her?*

'So we're good,' she summed up, knowing that was something a lot worse than a lie. 'We're good for now, and that's what matters. The gun goes away. We talk. Maybe you tell us what the hell is going on, Diema, and where you fit into it. Nobody dies. Nobody dies, Leo.'

He still had the gun raised. Forcing the issue, Kennedy closed her hands over it and tugged. She couldn't have loosened his grip, but Tillman let her take it from his hands.

Kennedy drew a deep, ragged breath. She turned to the girl.

'Could you cut Ben loose?' she asked. 'Or would that be too much to ask?'

The girl gave a half-shrug. 'He's a lot more bearable like this,' she said. But she reached into her pocket and came up with a handcuff key, which she tossed to Kennedy with a disdainful flick of her wrist.

Kennedy manhandled the chair back from the edge before she set about freeing Rush. And before she loosened the gag she leaned down until her mouth was at his ear. 'Don't try anything stupid,' she said. 'Only Leo would be able to slow her down for more than a heartbeat. So just swallow your pride and keep your mouth shut.'

Rush said nothing, even after the gag was removed. When Kennedy had unlocked the handcuffs, he took the strip of cloth from her and wound it around his wrist. 'I said too much already,' he muttered. 'She had a gun, and she said she was going to kill me. I'm sorry, Kennedy.'

'Forget it,' she said. Given that it was her loud mouth that had gotten him into this position, she should be saying sorry to him.

They walked back to the table. Diema faced them across it like a stern schoolmistress.

'It was after Alex Wales died,' Kennedy said. 'I told Rush what he was.'

'Alex Wales?'

'The Messenger at Ryegate House. The one who was undercover there. Rush saw Wales kill a man with a poisoned sica. And he saw Wales cry red tears. He asked me what it all meant and I told him enough so he'd understand. I told him about your tribe and about the Ginat'Dania where you lived before your last move. I didn't do it lightly.'

'Who else have you told?' Diema demanded.

'Nobody.'

'Not even your lover?'

The girl was staring at her with scornful scepticism. Kennedy stared straight back. 'Especially not Izzy. In my experience, anyone who knows too much about you people does pretty badly out of it. I wouldn't do that to someone I love.'

The girl turned to Tillman. 'And you?' she asked him.

He shook his head. 'Nobody.'

'Swear it.'

'My word's good, girl.'

'Your word is water. Swear it. Swear it on something that matters.'

Tillman thought about that for a moment. Then he pointed past her out of the window. 'You mentioned the blood I spilled here. I swear on that blood. I've never told anyone about your people or about Ginat'Dania.'

Diema's face went blank, then filled with powerful, chaotic emotion. She tried several times to speak, and Kennedy tensed, ready to step in, because it looked for a moment as though the girl were going to fling herself on Tillman. But she got herself back under control.

'Why should I believe that blood matters to you?' she asked him, her voice thick. 'You shed it easily enough.'

'They were young men,' Tillman said simply. 'Very young men. And I had to kill them because somebody had filled their heads full of rancid crap. I hated to do it. But if you don't believe that, I'll swear on something else.'

Diema made a formless, unreadable gesture. 'It doesn't matter,' she said. 'I swear – on the same blood – you'll never tell anyone else. Take that any way you like.'

'Well, I'm inclined to take it as a threat,' he said unhappily.

'For the love of Christ!' Rush interjected. 'It was me that was tied up and gagged and wired to a fake bomb. Can we drop this and get to the bloody point?'

'I agree,' Kennedy said quickly, pulling them both away from the danger zone. 'Diema, this meeting was your idea. What is it you want?'

The girl crossed to the hayloft doors and brought back the chair that was there. She set it down in front of her, but didn't sit. 'I want us to share information,' she said. 'And then I want us to discuss strategy.'

'I'll need some convincing,' Tillman said, 'that either of those is a good idea.'

Diema didn't seem to have heard him. She was addressing herself to Kennedy again. 'This was my mission long before it was yours,' she said. 'But I can't make you trust me or cooperate with me. I suggest you pool what you know. Now that you've read the book of Johann Toller, you probably know a lot. Call when you want me. I'll tell you what I was told, and what I've found out for myself, and I'll answer any questions you have. I'll do that without asking you to do the same. I can't think of anything else I can offer. I'll wait in the truck.'

'Which is full of—' Tillman began.

'In the *cab*. You'll be able to see me from here. Wave, and I'll come back up.' Now she turned to look at him, and the depth of her hate was there in her face, for all of them to see. 'Do you know how the *Elohim* are bound, Tillman? Did Kuutma, who is called the Brand, ever explain it to you?'

'You're not bound at all,' Tillman said. 'You're free to kill whoever you like. Your priests give you absolution up front.'

'Free to kill, yes. Or to maim. Or to torture. To steal, where necessary. To damage and destroy whatever might need to be damaged or destroyed, if it will help the People. But not to do any of those things for our own pleasure or profit. And not to lie. So I tell you again that I'm not here to kill you. God kept you alive for this long so you could be useful. So you could be the stick that chastises his enemies. When your work is done, then you'll be free to die.'

She descended the ladder, making no sound at all. A moment or so later, they saw her cross to the truck and climb into the cab, where she sat, arms folded, in the passenger seat.

'Where do we start?' Kennedy asked.

'By checking for listening devices,' Tillman answered quietly.

44

Diema remembered very little about the father of her flesh. Her mother had taken her back to the People before her third birthday, and of course she'd never seen him again after that homecoming. Three years was long enough for some memories to have stuck, but belonging as they did to another world, another life, there was less and less in her mind for those memories to adhere to. So they faded, slowly at first, then quickly and finally. But there were a few isolated moments that had stayed with her:

In one of them, she was sitting at a long, low table, sitting on the ground, so it must have been very low indeed – probably a coffee table of some kind. She was drawing with coloured pencils. Drawing a lion in a jungle. The pencils were new, and excitingly unfamiliar to her hand. They were entirely full of themselves, in her memory; almost luminous with their *thisness*, as new things are to a child.

And she was almost done with her picture, but there was a feeling of urgency in her mind, of a time drawing to its close. Then big, enfolding hands closed around her waist and she felt herself lifted, her legs kicking slightly, off the floor, gathered up into arms too strong to resist.

Her father's face, square-jawed and bristle-chinned, smiled

down at her, his basso voice rumbled at her that it was time for bed, and she was taken away from the pencils and the almost-complete, almost-incarnate lion to be tucked up in white sheets in another room. Probably, being a child's bedroom, it contained things and colours and textures, but in Diema's memory it was white like the sheets, empty like her grieving hands.

Despite the vagueness of the memory, she knew this beyond any possibility of a doubt: she never held the pencils again; the drawing was never completed. That trivial, wonderful thing had been stolen from her.

The father of her flesh was synonymous with loss, even then.

She kept her eyes fixed on the open doors of the hayloft, where nothing moved. She waited for them to call her. And for the lion to be delivered at last.

45

'Ben Rush, this is Leo Tillman. Tillman, Rush,' Kennedy said.

She turned the photocopied sheets so that they faced the two men.

'If we're going to do this,' she said, 'I think we should start with Toller's book. Alex Wales came to Ryegate House to steal this, and then stayed to get a list of everyone who'd read it, going back about sixty or seventy years. The ones that were still alive aren't alive any more.'

Kennedy was standing, both men were sitting – side by side on the same side of the table, facing her. Tillman pulled out the sheaf of paper from the bundle in front of him and read aloud, with Rush peering over his shoulder. '*And the False word wille die, and the True worde live. As on the threshing Floor, when Chaff is sorted from Wheat, that all who worke dilligently and earn their Hire may finally eat ...*' Tillman looked up at Kennedy. 'Any chance of a summary?'

'It's pretty much all like this,' she said. 'Three hundred and seventy two prophecies over sixty or seventy pages – all the signs and wonders that come right before the end of the world.'

'Like in the Book of Revelations,' Rush said.

'Thank you, Rush. I knew I could rely on a good Catholic

313

boy like you to make that connection.' Still chafing under the weight of his earlier humiliations, Rush blushed, and glanced at Kennedy sharply to see if this was sarcasm. 'Exactly like the Book of Revelations,' she confirmed. 'Except that Toller goes into a lot more detail. Look at a few of the prophecies at random, you'll see what I mean.'

Tillman turned the pages and he and Rush both read for a while in silence.

'Why is the book significant?' Tillman asked at last. 'To the Judas People, I mean? Why do they care who reads this? It's not their scripture, is it?'

'Yeah, I think it is,' Kennedy said.

There was a silence while Tillman absorbed this. 'But we *read* their scripture,' he said. 'You did, anyway. It was much, much older than this nonsense – first- or second-century. And it was about the bargain Jesus made with Judas.'

'Which was what, again?' Rush asked.

'Judas helped Jesus to die,' Kennedy said wearily. 'In return, God gave Judas and his kindred the earth. But they would have to wait three thousand years to inherit. Thirty pieces of silver – standing for thirty centuries.'

'So where does this come in?' Tillman asked, jerking his head at Toller's book.

'I think Toller was one of the Judas People,' Kennedy said. 'I think he came out of their hidden city into the world and started or joined a cult called the Fifth Monarchists. They preached an apocalyptic version of Christianity. They were waiting for the fifth and last empire – Christ's – to start, which would bring about the end of history, the end of earthly kings and dominions, the end of the world as we know it.'

'Wait,' Rush said. 'Is this what all the Judas People think or just Toller?'

'They all think it's going to happen,' she said. 'But Toller thought it was going to happen right then, at the end of the seventeenth century. And he went out and spread the word among the heathens, which really isn't the Judas tribe's MO at all.'

'So Toller was what, a kind of Judas People heretic?'

'Good a word as any,' Kennedy said. 'But what matters for us is that he appears out of nowhere in the middle of the seventeenth century and starts to preach and write ...'

'After an accident,' Rush said.

Kennedy and Tillman both looked at him.

Rush seemed a little uncomfortable with the attention, but he went on. 'Toller fell down a ravine in the Swiss Alps. Then an angel started talking to him about the time to come. It was after he came back to England that he started prophesying.'

'Some sort of near-death experience,' Tillman mused dourly. 'You could see where that might change the course of his life. Make him feel like there was something else he needed to be doing.'

'Is there anything else we know about him?' Kennedy asked Rush.

Rush shrugged. 'We know when he died. And we know that he had this weird way of doing the sign of the cross that was more like he was rubbing his stomach.'

'The noose,' Kennedy said. 'The Judas People use the sign of the noose the same way Christians use the sign of the cross. It means the same thing to them. Because some of the early accounts of Judas's life have him dying by hanging.'

'It's circumstantial evidence,' Tillman said.

'But Toller also talks about three thousand years being given to the four kingdoms of Man before Christ returns. It's a close match to the Judas tribe's belief that they get to inherit the world after the children of Adam rule it – for three millennia. Okay, Leo, you asked why Toller's book matters. Why it matters now, to us and to the Judas People. And here's where we get to it. Look at the prophecies on the first page of Toller's book.'

This time it was Rush who read – flatly, without expression. '"The Infidels who soile the Holy Worde will bewaile their Blindness, and repent. Even in the House of the faithlesse Soldier they will repent. And in Münsters Churche, so, and likewise, they will repent. But such repentance wille come too late and Helles Fires will take holde on them."'

'The faithless soldier is Thomas Fairfax,' Kennedy said. 'One of the generals in the English Civil War. He was sympathetic towards Toller's Fifth Monarchists for a while, but then he dropped them. From their point of view, betrayed them.'

'Still sounds like ancient history,' Tillman said dryly.

'Doesn't it?' Kennedy agreed. 'But a few weeks ago, Fairfax's old country seat, Nunappleton Hall, was burned to the ground. Hell's fires, if you want to be melodramatic, in the house of the faithless soldier.

'And Münster's church went the same way. Toller meant a specific church – the Überwasserkirche, which was the site of a famous uprising. The day after the fire at Nunappleton, someone planted and detonated a bomb in the Überwasserkirche. Again, a firebomb.'

Both men were staring at her in grim, perturbed silence, trying to figure out what this could mean. But they hadn't heard anything yet, and Kennedy couldn't spare their feelings.

'With me so far? Okay, look at prophecy number two. "Gods Angel will stand over Zion with a flaming Sworde outstretched in his hand, ready to doe Execution." One of God's angels was called Azrael – I think he might have been the angel

316

of death, but don't quote me on that. When I got home four nights ago, I turned on the TV and heard about an incident where an Azrael ground-to-air missile was fired over Jerusalem. The Israeli government blamed it on an accident. It exploded in mid-air, thank God – no deaths, this time. But the prophecy goes on to say that the angel won't strike with his sword because it isn't the time yet.'

Kennedy paused for a second, waiting for them to challenge her. What she was saying sounded so much like madness, even to her, that she couldn't imagine anyone else swallowing it for a moment. But when Tillman spoke, it was to ask a very practical and logistical question.

'So the order of these incidents,' he said. 'Is the same as the order in which the prophecies occur in the book?'

'Always. I went back and checked. The abortive missile strike was the same day as the Münster bombing, but if you correct for local time, it happened two hours later.'

She looked at the book again. It had almost developed a personality for her by this time, its riddles and ellipses part of a sick game, its dire promises full of psychopathic enthusiasm.

'"Where the Highest bled,"' she read, '"the Lowest wille likewise bleed. Even the vermin, that all shunne and disdaine."' When the Civil War was over, Cromwell's Parliamentarians sentenced Charles the First to death by decapitation. He was executed on Whitehall, in front of a building called the Banqueting House.

'An hour and a half after the Azrael incident, a beat cop found about a thousand rats on the steps of the Banqueting House – all with their heads cut off. Take the king to be the "Highest", and the vermin bled right where he bled. They even died in the same way.'

She met Tillman's gaze, then Rush's, and shrugged. 'And "Ister" is the River Danube. It ran red a couple of hours after the rats were found – not with blood, with aniline dye, but then the prophecy only says "*as* with blood".

'And so it goes on. I didn't manage to match all of them up, but as near as I can tell, we're three-quarters of the way through the book. Toller's prophecies are all coming to pass, one by one, in order.'

Tillman scratched his chin but said nothing.

'Jesus Christ!' Rush protested. 'What are we saying here? Seriously? Toller predicted the end of the world three hundred years ago, and now it's happening?'

'You're not listening,' Tillman growled. 'That isn't what she's saying at all.'

'No,' Kennedy agreed, 'it isn't. But Rush wasn't in that warehouse with you, Leo. And he hasn't seen what's sitting in your truck.' To Rush, she said, 'The Nunappleton fire was arson. The dead bodies the police found in the wreckage – the unbelievers who'd profaned the holy word – had been brought into the house purely so they could die there. The missile attack wasn't an accident either. Somebody infiltrated an Israeli field station and killed four soldiers before setting off the Azrael. None of these were accidents, Rush. And more to the point, they weren't inexorable destiny. These incidents are all being set up, very carefully and very deliberately.'

Rush looked confused rather than convinced. 'But if they're happening all over the world . . . and they're only a few hours apart . . .'

He let the sentence tail off. Kennedy turned back to Tillman.

'Tell him what you found,' she said.

Tillman said nothing.

'Leo, he knows about the Messengers. And the girl had him pegged as my accomplice, so you can bet that the *Elohim* know all about him. Tell him about the warehouse or I will.'

Tillman made a placatory gesture, but it was still a moment or two before he spoke. 'There seems to be a group,' he said, giving Rush a sombre glance, 'that's stockpiling weapons and explosives in very, very large amounts. They're shipping the weapons out to a lot of different places. I found what I hope to God was their main stash, and closed it down, but it's pretty certain that they've got a lot of really lethal kit already sitting in a lot of different places. Maybe if we're lucky, I slowed them down a little.'

'Oh my god,' Rush said. His face was pale.

'Someone is using Toller's book as an instruction manual,' Kennedy summed up. 'Everything that he predicted, they're playing it out, taking a lot of care to get all the details right and to make sure that the disasters happen in the right sequence – the same sequence the book puts them in.'

Something occurred to her, belatedly – maybe because of where she was, and because of what had happened, what she'd seen, the last time she was here. She went to the window and looked down. After a moment, when the two men came to join her there, she pointed to the side of the truck. It bore the name of the company that owned the warehouse, High Energy Haulage, with the initial letters picked out in red and their logo, which was a sort of dolmen shape, two vertical blocks supporting a horizontal one.

'H-E-H,' Kennedy spelled out. 'Heh.' She pronounced it *hay*. 'It's the fifth letter of the Aramaic alphabet. And they used their letters as numbers, too, so that sign, right there – it's a five. As in fifth. As in monarchy.'

'But why?' Rush demanded, although it sounded more like a plea. 'Why would anybody make prophecies come true three centuries too late? It doesn't make any sense.'

'Maybe it's time to call in our expert witness,' Kennedy said into the silence that followed.

46

There was once a man of great virtue, Diema said, to whom all earthly rewards and accolades came early, and easy. Everyone loved him. Everyone believed in him. Everyone wanted him to succeed. But unfortunately, although nobody around him could see it, he was possessed by a demon.

She told it exactly like this, as though it were a fairy story, or perhaps a parable – but in any case, as though it were a narrative already removed from all of them, herself and her listeners alike, into another level of reality, even though she'd made it clear that the man she was talking about was still very much alive.

His name was Ber Lusim, and perhaps, after all, he was no more than the furthest point on a bell curve. The *Elohim* were always chosen young. Diema herself, selected at age sixteen, was coming to her calling late, by the standards of the People. Most of the Messengers were learning the tools and methods of their trade before their thirteenth birthday.

Ber Lusim presented himself to Kuutma – pre-empted the process – when he was nine. His words, according to the story, were 'I want to serve.'

'And what service can you offer?' Kuutma demanded of the little boy, amused.

Ber Lusim opened his hands. In each of them there was a dead bird – a tiny thing, less than four inches from beak to tail. The birds had green flanks and crimson throats. The feathers on their bellies, by contrast, were a drab grey. *Calypte anna*, Anna's hummingbird, one of the fastest creatures that ever lived.

'I want to serve,' the boy said again.

Kuutma adopted him formally into the *Elohim*, there and then.

'This Kuutma,' Tillman cut in, his stare hard and unwavering. 'This was the man we met in Mexico? The one who used to call himself Michael Brand?'

The girl stared back. 'Yes, but why should that matter? It's not a name, it's a job description. All Kuutmas are the Brand. Kuutma means the Brand. And the "el" in Michael stands for the holy one, whose name cannot be spoken. Kuutma is the brand of God on the world of the godless.'

Wordlessly, Tillman waved to her to go on.

Ber Lusim was the greatest of the Messengers. He was given his journeyman posting when he was fifteen – to Washington, where his appearance of youth and unworldliness was a very useful resource. His first kill came quickly, when an American journalist began to take too much of an interest in certain medieval documents whose speculations touched on the existence of a Judas-worshipping sect.

The journalist, a woman, had paedophilic tendencies, so far expressed only through the consumption of illegal pornography. Ber Lusim's Summoner was considering using this fact to silence her, but Ber Lusim took a more direct approach. He presented himself to the woman – a fresh-faced boy, apparently willing; an impossible combination of innocence and wantonness. He was welcomed into her house, into her bedroom, where he killed her in a way that posthumously destroyed her reputation and drew all media attention far, far away from her professional researches.

It was a triumph. But possibly it left the boy damaged, an unacknowledged victim of his own elegant plan. Or perhaps it woke something inside him. The demon that had always slumbered there, biding its time.

Ber Lusim went from strength to strength; from his Berlin apprenticeship to South Africa, and from there to the Federal Republic of Germany. There he proved adept at forestalling potential enemies by stepping in ruthlessly and decisively as soon as a possible threat was identified or even suspected. He did not trouble, as many Messengers did, to lay a smokescreen of suicide notes or decoy suspects: but neither did he leave any trail leading to the People, so his brutal methods were never questioned.

In his twentieth year, he was made a Summoner of Elohim. It was a popular choice. The Messengers with whom he'd served admired him and were loyal to him. His star continued to rise. Was he too fond of proceeding to extreme sanctions? Was the kill count for his station higher than it should have been? Perhaps. And was it only coincidence that male *Elohim* thrived and were rewarded under Ber Lusim's dispensation, while women were assessed harshly and passed on quickly to other assignments? Perhaps not. But it's always easy to see these things in the spotlight glare of hindsight.

As Summoner, Ber Lusim was chiefly responsible for guarding and shepherding the *Kelim* who were in Germany at that time. He was good at this, by his lights. At least, he was good at making sure the women returned, with their families, when the appointed time came. Unfortunately, it turned out to be a task that exposed the cracks in Ber Lusim's personality, and drove a crowbar into them.

Ber Lusim disliked the *Kelim* and the continued business of their sending out. He had spoken, in Council, in favour of suspending the practice, and although he had lost that argument . . .

Another interruption, this time from Ben Rush. 'This is what you were telling me about?' he asked Kennedy. 'The sacred whores? The women who leave the secret city to get themselves pregnant?'

Tense, Kennedy nodded. 'Let's just listen,' she said.

As Diema spoke, Kennedy could see how tightly Tillman's fists were clenched and how white his knuckles were. This subject was far from abstract and theoretical for him. His wife had been one of these women and although he knew she'd been dead for many years, his feelings for her had never adjusted to that reality.

'Go on,' Tillman said to Diema. For a moment, his gaze locked with hers. *She knows what she's doing to him,* Kennedy thought, amazed and unsettled. *Maybe it's even part of why she's here.*

Diema continued. Ber Lusim disliked the *Kelim*, very strongly. Or perhaps he disliked what they implied, which was that the vigour and virtue of the Judas People were not sufficient in themselves – that they needed to be fortified, from time to time, with graftings from other stock.

Or perhaps it was because his own mother had been one of that number, and he felt tainted by the association. Whatever his motivations may have been, Ber Lusim's position allowed him to act on his feelings. The women who came out of Ginat'Dania to lie with Adamite men and then to return home freighted with their DNA passed through his hands on both the outward and the return journeys.

Oh, he took his duties seriously. Nobody could say he

slacked, or failed to exercise due diligence. No sheep went astray on his watch. No holy Vessels returned empty, or failed to return at all.

Some, however, returned damaged. Specifically, they had been beaten. When questioned about this, they said that they'd been punished for disobedience. For taking too long to arrange their Adamite affairs, for weeping at the loss of their Adamite husbands, for taking too much with them or leaving too much behind.

Representations were made in Council. Ber Lusim was not reprimanded – there was a minority point of view that saw his zeal as admirable – but he was requested to put a moratorium on the beatings. In some cases, returning *Kelim* might be pregnant; too harsh a punishment might harm the unborn babies, who of course were the very point and pith of the whole enterprise.

Even that was a divisive judgement. The case of Ber Lusim leaned hard upon the paradoxes that propped up the People's society, and the paradoxes threatened to give. The *Kelim* were necessary, and in theory they were respected. The women who went out were chosen by lot, so the unwelcome mission could fall to anyone. It was a sacrifice, as important to the survival of the Judas People as the eternal vigilance of the Messengers, and the sacrifice was honoured.

In theory.

The reality was more complicated. When a young woman of good family was chosen to be a vessel, it was common (though officially deplored) for her parents to say the service for the dead over her. When she returned, it was often impossible for her to find a husband among the People. There were even some – religious conservatives or just unvarnished misogynists – who would refuse to allow her shadow to fall on them.

Ber Lusim was one of those – and he converted many of the Messengers who served with him to his extreme opinions. But he accepted the judgement of the Council and stopped inflicting physical punishments on the returning vessels.

Until Orim Beit Himah.

Orim Beit Himah failed to present herself and her children to be returned to Ginat'Dania when the time came for her to do so. Ber Lusim had to send out a team of Messengers to retrieve her. He decided to lead the team himself.

He found Orim still with her Adamite husband. It was rumoured that she had explained everything to this man and that he tried to kill the Messengers when they arrived. Then again, and to the contrary, it was said that the husband had found Orim about to leave and had imprisoned her, convinced that she was running away with another man. And one account said that she had missed her appointed date because she was ill and couldn't rise from her bed.

Ber Lusim killed the husband.

And Orim.

And the children.

For the first time in the telling, Diema seemed to be having trouble getting the words out. She had to break off for a few moments and go to the window as if she was checking for traffic on the road below – but they could all hear that the low engine sound she was responding to was that of a plane flying overhead, probably on its way into Gatwick.

The three of them watched the girl in silence as she squatted in the hayloft door, still and silent, staring down at the empty road. Though her agitation showed that she had human feelings, the pose reminded Kennedy of what Diema was. It was the pose of a raptor, scanning for prey with its telescope eyes.

When she came back, she'd recovered some of her composure.

Ber Lusim claimed that the deaths were accidental. There had been a fight with the husband, and he had been armed. The woman and the children had found themselves in the crossfire and had been killed by stray bullets before anyone registered their presence.

Ber Lusim's men backed up his story, in every detail. But curiously, they used almost identical language in their descriptions, as though they had been coached or at least had discussed the matter between themselves in a great deal of circumstantial detail.

It was a terrible thing. Unlike the beatings, it could not be overlooked. No gloss of decency could be put on it. The best that Ber Lusim could hope for would be to be stripped of his post as Summoner. If it was found that he had killed Orim deliberately, with full intent, he would never leave Ginat'Dania again. His life would be lived out in a windowless cell, a foot longer and wider than he was tall.

But when he was recalled to be tried, he disappeared. And his Messengers went with him.

'So that's who we're dealing with,' Tillman said, when Diema had finished her story. His face was cold and inexpressive, but his fists were still clenched and pressed down hard against the table. Kennedy knew how deeply that story would have penetrated into him and how much blood it would have drawn.

And what about Diema? Her own mother had been one of these women. Was that what had moved her or had it been something else? She remembered the girl in action, taking on the two *Elohim* in Izzy's bedroom, beating them down and leaving them for dead.

Leaving them for dead. Not killing them. Since when did the *Elohim* not finish the job?

An answer to that question came to her very suddenly and the more she thought about it, the more she felt it had to be right. It explained so much. It explained that unlikely mercy. It explained why Diema had broken off her story so abruptly just then. And most of all, it explained the impossibly tenuous chain of chance or destiny that had drawn first Emil Gassan, then her and then Tillman into this deepening, thickening mess. Tillman had said you went with coincidence or you surrendered yourself to megalomania – that there was no third way. But there was. And it took her breath away with its sheer simplicity – its almost indecent obviousness.

'The enemy we face,' Diema said solemnly, 'is those renegade *Elohim*, commanded by Ber Lusim. There is another man – Avra Shekolni – who joined them recently and has become their spiritual leader and teacher. We think that Shekolni has strengthened Ber Lusim's extremism. Made him even less inclined to compromise than he was before.'

'Wait,' Rush said. 'If this Shekolni is new on the scene, is he why they went after the book? Was that his idea?'

Diema stared at him thoughtfully for a second or two. She seemed to be deciding whether or not answering a former hostage's questions would compromise her dignity. 'Yes,' she said. 'We think it was Shekolni's idea.'

'They didn't just steal that one copy of the book, did they?' Kennedy broke in. 'There were ashes in the box at Ryegate House.'

Diema turned her head to stare at Kennedy. The intensity of her attention was unsettling. It was as though, when she looked at you, the rest of the room, the rest of the world, disappeared. '*Tephra*,' she said.

'What?'

'The ashes of a sacrifice are called *tephra*.'

'Whatever.' Kennedy couldn't keep the impatience out of her voice. 'They stole every copy of the book they could find. They burned all but one of them. They were taking the holy word out of the hands of the unbelievers.'

'Yes.'

'But why is it the holy word? It was written only a few centuries ago, by – what would you call him? – a heretic? A turncoat? An escapee? It's not your gospel. It's late-breaking news from a religious lunatic.'

Diema nodded. 'Toller's words were lost because we didn't think they were worth keeping,' she agreed. 'It was a long time before anyone even realised that he might have been of the People. One of our Messengers went astray, at that time, and was looked for but never found. It was within my lifetime that a scholar of the People saw the correspondences in Toller's book and came up with the idea that our missing brother had taken a new name and preached to the Nations as Johann Toller.'

'Then why would his word be revered?' Kennedy demanded. 'Why would it even be read, any more?'

'Toller was the first to leave the People without the People's blessing or sanction. Until Ber Lusim and Avra Shekolni, nobody else followed his example. Not in all of the three hundred and seventy years in between.' Diema reached into her shirt and drew out the knife she kept there – the strange, asymmetrical blade that the Judas People called the sica. 'Do you know what this is?' she asked them. Before she spoke, before she'd even completed the movement, Tillman once again had the gun in his hand. But the girl didn't acknowledge the threat or seem to notice it.

'Take that as a yes,' Rush suggested.

'But you don't really know what it is,' Diema insisted. 'To you it's just a weapon. To us, it's two and a half thousand years of history. We carried it and killed with it when we were subjects of the Romans. Now we carry it and kill with it as free men and women.'

'What's your point?' Kennedy demanded. 'And can you make it without that filthy thing in your hand?'

Diema set the knife down on the table, beside the typescript of Toller's book. 'I suppose my point is that we stick to our traditions. Change isn't something that comes naturally or easily to us. Perhaps Avra Shekolni was already interested in Johann Toller before he left the city. Or perhaps not. Now, we know, he's obsessed with the man. Toller is his only real precursor – a man of religion who went alone into the world, carrying what he thought was a great message.'

'So?' said Kennedy.

'So Shekolni believes in that message.'

'But Toller was predicting the end of the world back in the 1660s. It didn't end,' said Rush. 'Or does Shekolni think it did and now we're all living in the Matrix?'

'You don't understand,' Diema said.

Rush flushed slightly. 'No, I don't. That's sort of what I just said.'

'Johann Toller,' Diema said, enunciating the words with the care reserved for deaf people, foreigners and imbeciles, 'said the world would end after all his prophecies were fulfilled.'

'That part I got.'

'Then what would you do if you *wanted* the world to end?'

Rush stared at her. 'If I . . . ?' he repeated.

Then he stared some more. Tillman and Kennedy were staring, too.

'The time of the bargain came,' Diema said. 'And then it went. God didn't appear to us. But over such a very, very long time, mistakes and misunderstandings are possible – not on the part of the Holy Name, but on our part. The Sima, our high council, argued for patience. God's plan would reveal itself, if we waited.

'But Shekolni, who had a voice in that council, disagreed. He said God had never, ever expected us just to wait. That to do nothing was the last thing He wanted from us. After three thousand years, our time would come. But it was exactly that – *our* time. It was up to us to act. And God had already told us what to do.'

'Through Johann Toller,' Kennedy said.

Diema gave a brusque shrug. *What do you think?*

'That's what they're doing.' Kennedy felt an acute sense of vertigo. 'They're making it happen by making all the signs and wonders happen first. They're ringing in the Second Coming.'

'And the signs and the wonders will only get bigger and bloodier,' Diema said. 'Unless you stop them.'

'Unless we stop them?' Rush blurted. 'Why is this down to us?'

Diema pointed at Kennedy, and then at Tillman. 'I meant them,' she said. 'Not you, boy. You weren't planned for.'

'And we were?' Kennedy said, jumping on the words. She was right. She had to be right.

'The boy raises a good point,' Tillman growled, getting to his feet. He didn't seem to have registered Kennedy's words. 'This is your business, not ours. Something you and your people vomited into the world. Why in the name of anything you want to swear by would you come to the very people you despise and hate, and ask them to clear up your mess?'

Diema was silent. With all their eyes on her, she shrugged again. This time the gesture seemed to say she'd made her case and they could take it or leave it. 'It's true that we want Ber Lusim's network closed down,' she said. 'His beliefs are heresy – abomination. And besides, what he's doing puts us at risk. It's too visible. It makes people ask questions and look for patterns. So that's why I was sent. That's why I'm here, now, talking to you.

'But I'd say the stakes are higher for you than for us. Lots of people have already died. But if Ber Lusim gets to the last prophecy, many, many more people will die.' Diema's gaze met Kennedy's. 'You read the book. Toller talks about the thousand thousand who are going to be sacrificed. A million people. I can't believe you want that to happen.'

'But that's not why you came to us,' said Kennedy. 'You don't give a damn how many people die, so long as it's our kind and not yours. We're no better than cattle to you. And the stakes? How could the stakes be higher, exactly? Secrecy is an iron law to you people. Anything that threatens the big secret, you rip it right out of the world. And you want us to believe that this – these maniacs running around loose, making all this noise – is no big deal for you?'

Diema pursed her lips, her eyes narrowing a little. 'I expressed myself badly,' she said, with stolid patience. 'Of course this concerns us. But there's a parable – about a traveller who is set on by robbers as he sits by his campfire at night. He takes a stick out of the fire to fend them off. Then, when his enemies are beaten, he throws the brand back into the flames and lets it be consumed.'

'And we're the stick?' Kennedy said. 'That's sweet. And it's a lot closer to the truth. But you gave yourself away, girl – when you were talking about the death of the woman and her children, and all of a sudden you had to go to the window and breathe some sweet, fresh air. So why is it so hard for you to say?'

'To say what?' Tillman asked. 'What am I missing?'

Diema glanced at him for a moment, then lowered her gaze to the ground.

'You've seen how they fight, Leo,' Kennedy said, her voice sounding harsh and hateful in her own ears: because she really did hate this. The big unspoken lie, the sin of omission. She hated everything that was behind it. 'You've seen how casually they kill.'

'Seen it right up close,' Tillman agreed. 'Like you.'

'But when Diema here dismantled the two Messengers who were about to torture me, she left them both alive. Concussed, bleeding, beaten to a pulp, but alive. And you said at the warehouse . . .' She let the sentence tail off.

'Same thing,' Tillman confirmed.

Kennedy leaned forward, her face right up close to Diema's. Like a scolded schoolgirl, Diema kept her head bowed and her eyes down. 'You can't kill your own, can you?' Kennedy said. 'You put us through all this because you can't do it yourself. There's one commandment you can't break. You're not allowed to shed the blood of the blessed.'

They held the tableau for a few seconds longer.

'Answer me!' Kennedy yelled.

Diema looked up at last. 'You're right,' she said, her voice tight. 'There are two commandments that can't be broken – for which the punishment is exile, for ever. And one of them is . . . what you said. We can't do this without you. We can find Ber Lusim and we can help you to stop him, but . . .'

The silence lengthened.

'But you need us to pull the trigger on him,' Tillman said.

333

Diema drew herself up to her full height, which was a head shorter than his. She stared up at him, her arms at her sides, as unbending as the upright of a cross. 'It should come naturally to you,' she said. 'You talk about how easily we kill. But we kill for survival. You've killed for much less important things, like money, for example.'

Tillman seemed taken aback by the barely contained fury in her tone. He opened his mouth to answer, but Diema hadn't finished. 'The only question,' she snarled, 'is whether you want to work with me and use what I know or cut me loose and go your own way. Either way, I've said what I came here to say. And even though you're my enemies, I never treated you as enemies. I gave you more respect than you gave me.'

A single red tear ran down the girl's cheek. She didn't move to wipe it away.

'No,' Kennedy said. 'That's not the only question. Before I decide whether I can work with you – whether I can even bear to be in the same room with you – I want an answer on something else.'

The girl looked at her in stolid silence.

'What's eating you, Heather?' Tillman asked. Clearly, he could see from her face that it was something big.

'We thought there were only two kinds of emissary,' Kennedy said. 'The soldiers and the mothers. But suppose there was a third kind? Not fighters, exactly, but fixers. People who make things happen. People with connections and resources, who plant themselves in the Adamite world and do with money what the *Elohim* do with knives. Protect the Judas People and serve their interests.'

'Why,' Diema asked quietly, 'would you suppose that?'

'Oh, I don't know. How about because the Validus Trust put Emil Gassan in place to deal with the theft of Toller's book

334

from Ryegate House. Then Gassan brought me in and I met you, and I went to Leo. None of that was chance, and none of it was destiny. It was planned. You just said as much, right now. Someone set us up like dominoes. Anticipated our every move and the money of the Validus Trust was the first domino. Everything else flowed from that.'

Diema didn't confirm or deny the hypothesis, and nobody else spoke. They were all staring at the girl.

'Tell me that didn't happen, Diema,' Kennedy said. 'Tell me we weren't recruited.'

'They're called *Nagodim*,' Diema said at last. 'And they work in exactly the way you just described.'

Kennedy shook her head slowly. The certain knowledge that she'd been manipulated filled her with mixed emotions of outrage and relief. Outrage, because she was being moved around like a playing piece in a complicated game. Relief, because she was being moved around by some ordinary man or woman, not by Nemesis or Fate or God.

All the same, two men had *died* because of these manipulations. Jesus, they'd probably been behind the fortuitous stroke that had taken out Emil Gassan's predecessor. Sooner or later, there had to be a reckoning. Kennedy said that to the girl with her eyes.

Aloud, breaking the heavy silence, she said, 'You haven't earned my trust. Nothing like. I still think your people are a kind of creeping poison, but this has to be stopped. So I say we work together.'

'I agree,' Tillman said. 'With the same reservations. We pool our resources until we've done what we've got to do. Beyond that, we don't make any promises or any assumptions.'

'Do I get a vote?' Rush asked.

Kennedy searched the boy's face for a long second. She

could guess at some of what he was feeling: it had to overlap at least a little with what she'd felt when she was helpless in the hands of Samal and Abydos. The difference was that nobody had suggested she should kiss and make up with Samal and Abydos. If there wasn't so very much at stake, she'd be prepared to give the boy the right of veto here. As it was . . .

'I vote yes,' he said, before she could answer. 'I'm good with it. In case anyone was wondering.'

He poured himself a glass of the water, which nobody had touched, and drank it down.

There was a sense of everyone in the room stepping back from a confrontation whose terms and rules of engagement had never been formally stated. Diema relaxed her stance, letting out a long breath.

Rush reached for the sica to take a closer look at it. Diema's hand locked around his wrist. With the other hand, she took the knife away from his reaching fingers and slid it back into its sheath inside her shirt.

'The blade's poisoned,' she said, matter-of-factly. 'Pick it up in the wrong way and you'll probably die.'

Looking at the red runnel on the girl's cheek, it occurred to Kennedy that that was every bit as true of her as it was of the knife.

47

The talk ebbed and flowed around Rush. He tried to pay attention, but the rigours of the last two days – everything from his fight with Alex Wales and the wounding of Professor Gassan up to his interrogation and kidnapping by the scary girl and the drive down here, bound hand and foot, in the back of what looked like a postal delivery van – were catching up with him. He found himself drifting in and out of a heavy doze, missing the connections between sentences and ideas or else experiencing them as an imagistic jumble.

He kept flashing back to the one time the girl had really hurt him. She was a skilled interrogator, and mostly she just talked the truth out of him. She seemed to know most of it already, so all he had to do to save his life was to agree to one or two of the things she was saying – agree that he knew what she was, and who her friends were, and what she was for.

But when she asked him where she was from, and he said he didn't know, she took his hand in hers and folded his wrist back on itself in some complicated way. It was agonising, and he was terrified that the wrist was going to snap.

'Ginat'Dania,' she said. 'Where is it?'

'I don't know!' Rush had yelled and then bellowed and then

whimpered. 'I don't know I don't know I don't know, I never heard of it, please. Oh, Jesus. Please.'

The night was a morass of fear, leavened with shame, but most of it could be dissolved into soft focus. That moment stood out very clear and sharp. He turned it over and over in his mind as though it were a puzzle box and he was looking for the sequence of manipulations that would slide it open.

That was why he'd voted yes, although he wasn't kidding himself that his vote had counted for much. He needed to prove that he wasn't afraid of her. Hating her would have been okay, but being afraid of her wasn't. The distinction mattered a lot.

And still they talked. Kennedy was arguing now about what it was they were signing up for. 'Leo's a soldier, and you're ... what you are. But this isn't what I do. I've killed exactly twice, once in a police action and once in self-defence. I can't take part in raids or ambushes or executions. I probably can't even watch those things.'

'I've studied you,' Diema said bluntly, 'and I think you're wrong. But it's not for me to say what you can do and what you can't do. It's irrelevant in any case. There are too many of them for us to fight them like that. We need another way.'

Then there was some talk about the two men – the warrior, Ber Lusim, and the priest, Shekolni. Their strengths and their weaknesses, according to Kuutma, and according to the girl's own observations. Rush started to doze, missed some of the conversation.

'... tracked Ber Lusim to safe houses in three different cities,' Diema was saying now. 'Berlin. Tokyo. Santiago. And we think there might be bases in Los Angeles and London, also. But as far as we know, none of those places was a permanent base of operations.'

'Same problem with the paperwork I saw at the warehouse,' Tillman answered. 'They were shipping stuff pretty much everywhere. Singapore. Toulouse. New York. Budapest. No way to know whether any of those places are fixed bases or distributive hubs in their own right. They're setting up hundreds of one-off terrorist acts in a dozen different countries. Ber Lusim could be overseeing the whole programme from any one of those places, or from somewhere else entirely.'

'Budapest,' Rush said. He knew he'd said it because he heard it – with that weird sense of detachment and unfamiliarity you get when you hear your own voice played over a tape recorder.

The other three all looked at him.

'You've got an opinion on this?' Tillman asked him.

Rush blinked a few times, because he wasn't seeing all that clearly. 'It's Budapest,' he said again. 'I think.' He found his gaze drawn to the girl, whose dark eyes and pale face suddenly reminded him overpoweringly of a photographic negative, or an X-ray. As though she belonged to another world that was the anti-matter image of his own. 'What you said,' he mumbled, 'about Shekolni being obsessed with Johann Toller – and about how your people always follow tradition. Stick to what you know.'

'Yes?' Diema said. 'What about those things?'

It was a shock to Rush to realise that he was the only one who knew this. He riffled through Kennedy's typescript until he found the picture of the rock and the town at its base. And the Latin tag in heavy, uneven type.

De agoni ventro veni, atque de austio terrae patente.

He showed it to the others. 'It's Gellert Hill, in Budapest.' He pointed at the little cluster of buildings. 'Whoever captioned it thought so, anyway. And that town there is Buda, I

339

guess. It's the Buda side of the river, anyway. I went there once on holiday.'

He realised at this point that he wasn't at all certain of his ground, but he plunged on anyway. 'Toller put this engraving at the front of his book. So maybe the "I" in the Latin there – "I come from the belly of the beast", and all that – is really him. It's him saying to us, this is where I come from. This is my secret origin.'

'Budapest,' Tillman mused. 'But where does that get us?'

Diema had gone very still, looking down at her hands, which were in her lap, palms-up.

'Not just Budapest,' Rush said. His index finger was still resting on the badly photocopied picture. 'Somewhere around here – the base of Gellert Hill. I know about this place because I did the Blue Danube tour when I was on holiday out there. There's a massive cave inside the hill that the modern city uses as a reservoir. I think that may have been where your Judas People were living, back in the 1660s. Budapest was part of the Ottoman Empire back then, so coming and going would have been a bit of a challenge – but maybe that just made it easier for Toller to get away from his people and not be followed.'

'Is any of this true?' Kennedy asked Diema. 'Is that where your people were living three centuries ago?'

Diema continued to stare at her own hands. 'I told you there were two commandments that couldn't be broken,' she said quietly. 'Now you know both of them.'

'It makes sense,' Kennedy said. 'So if Shekolni thinks of Toller as the great prophet ...'

'... he might want to go back to the source,' Tillman finished. 'But that still gives us an entire city to search. Might take a long time if we have to go house-to-house.'

340

'Our *Elohim* could do it,' Diema said. Clearly they were no longer in the taboo zone and she was able to speak freely again. 'We can access satellite and CCTV footage to map the movements of any trucks with the HEH logo and livery. Any address where a truck goes, we'll know. We should be able to narrow it down in a matter of hours or days.'

'But they wouldn't be delivering weapons to their head office,' Tillman objected. 'This – what we're looking for – is the think tank. It's where the decisions get made. The arsenals are almost certainly elsewhere.'

'We'll make the search, in any case,' Diema said. 'If it comes up empty, we've lost nothing. Also, we'll monitor communications. We have a long list of phone numbers that we've tied to Ber Lusim's people – some definite, some just highly likely. Calls into the city from any of those numbers can be traced.'

'And that's all wonderful,' Tillman said. 'But it still comes down to time. They're working their way down Toller's list. When they get to the end, it's at least possible that a million people will die. We have to find them before that happens.'

Kennedy counted on her raised fingers as she worked it out in her head. 'If they keep working at the present rate, I'd say that gives us four days at most,' she said.

They were all silent for a moment or two as the implications of this sank in. Budapest was a very big haystack, and four days was no time at all. It had taken Kennedy almost that long to find Alex Wales and she'd only had one building to search.

'We need a back-up plan,' Tillman said. 'By all means, girl, let your people go to town on this. But there's no way we should just sit and wait while they work.'

'You have a better suggestion?' Diema asked, her eyes narrowing as she stared at him.

'I do,' Kennedy said.

They all turned to look at her, expectantly.

'I think there's at least a chance that we can make them come to us.'

PART FIVE

THE BELLY OF
THE BEAST

48

Diema, Tillman and Rush flew from Heathrow to Budapest Ferihegy on a red-eye flight that left at half-past midnight. They used false papers supplied by a contact of Tillman's who he referred to as Benny.

It was only a two-hour flight, so there was no question of sleeping. Rush had brought along some of the books he'd swiped from the Ryegate House collection, and used the time to look up Johann Toller in the index of each book in turn.

Diema put on her headphones and selected a cartoon to watch. It was very beautiful to look at, but she quickly decided that she didn't like it one bit. It started with a lengthy sequence in which a man loses his wife and mourns her: the emotional precipices that opened up for Diema as she watched were a long way from what she looked for in a cartoon. She wanted irreconcilable war between cats and mice, violence that bent and buckled the world, and a world so resilient it snapped right back into shape.

Angry and frustrated, she snatched the headphones off and stuffed them back into the seat pocket.

'Can I ask you a question?' Rush asked her.

'No,' Diema growled. She'd noticed how often his glance

stole in her direction and it was irritating her so much that she'd considered moving seats.

'It's not big secret stuff, swear to God. It's about Toller.'

Diema turned her head to give the boy a cold stare. 'One question. Then you leave me alone.'

'Okay, it's this. Toller said he was born in darkness. Was that literally true? Do your people actually live underground?'

She carried on staring at him in stony silence for a few seconds longer. Then she picked up the headphones and put them back on.

'Okay, I'm sorry,' Rush said quickly. 'If you don't want to answer that, fine. I get it. Maybe that does touch on one of your big secrets. Different question. What's the actual passage in your scripture that talks about the three thousand years? The one that Toller based his predictions on? Is it possible he was counting from a different start date?'

Diema suppressed the urge to clamp a hand around the boy's windpipe – both to shut him up and for the sake of emphasis. 'Adamites who read our gospel die,' she reminded him. 'So if that's really your question, I'll answer it. Then I'll cut your throat in the airport car park at Ferihegy. It's your call, boy.'

Rush digested this threat in thoughtful silence.

'Okay,' he said at last. 'Scratch that, then. How about this? Robert Blackborne talks about the weird sign that Toller used to make as a blessing, but nobody else ever mentions it. So I'm wondering how different it is from the sign of the cross. Can I see it?'

Diema scowled. 'You want me to bless you?'

'I want to see you make the sign, that's all.'

It was like pacifying a baby. Disgruntled, she demonstrated the sign of the noose for him, several times over, and he

346

watched her with a certain fascination. Unless it was all just a ruse so that he could stare at her breasts again.

'Can I try,' he asked at last. 'Or would that be blasphemy?'

Diema shrugged dismissively. 'Go ahead.'

He moved his hand as though he were suffering from a stomach ache and was trying to ease it. Amused in spite of herself, and happy to be distracted from the lingering feelings left by the movie, Diema schooled him.

Not the whole hand, with the palm flat – that looks wrong. The forefinger should be extended, pointing inward to your chest.

Don't do it so fast, and only do it once. Not around and around and around.

Imagine a clock, set in your chest. Imagine the hands of the clock running backward. Follow the hands of the clock with your finger.

'I'm not going to get this,' Rush said, but he kept on trying. In the end, he was reasonably proficient.

'Would there be something you'd say, at the same time?' he asked her.

'You could say, "*He kul tairah beral*". "The hanged man's blessing be on you".'

'Ha kul tiara beral.'

'Tairah. Tay-rah.'

'Ha kul tairah beral.'

'He kul. Not ha.'

'He kul tairah beral.'

'*Vi ve kul te.*'

'What's that?'

'And on you.'

'Okay. What else? Yeah, I was wondering—'

'You've run out of questions,' Diema said, cutting him off.

'This one isn't about Toller. It's about you.'

'I never said you could ask questions about me.'

'No, you didn't, but maybe we could swap. I ask a question, then you ask a question. Like an exchange of hostages.'

'That's a wonderful idea,' Diema said.

'Cool.'

'Except that there's nothing I want to know about you.'

This, finally, made the boy back off and give her a respite from his noise. She found another cartoon, a short from 1935 directed by Tex Avery, but she couldn't enjoy it. Her mind was too unsettled.

She left her seat and went to the back of the plane, ostensibly to use the toilet. She didn't really need it, but she did need to be alone with her own thoughts. The boy's presence was intrusive, whether he spoke or not.

Both toilets were engaged and to her further chagrin, Leo Tillman was also waiting there.

He gave her a nod, which in her present mood incensed her more than she could bear in silence.

Leaning against the bulkhead wall, looking out at the unchanging vista of clouds, she addressed him without looking at him.

'Did you understand the plan, as I outlined it to you?' she murmured, her voice barely audible above the engines' constant rumble.

'I think so,' he said. 'Why?'

'Because the whole point of our travelling separately is so that Ber Lusim's people, if they're checking flights into the city, won't realise that we're working together.'

'Yeah, I got that.'

'They're meant to be watching Kennedy, not us.'

'Sure.' Tillman's tone was easy and – insultingly – reassuring.

348

'But you said yourself, we're worried about them checking the passenger manifests on incoming flights. We're not assuming they'll have spies on the plane. That's so unlikely, we might as well count it as impossible.'

But it was still sloppy and thoughtless and she couldn't give him the last word. 'We don't take risks that we don't have to take,' she snapped. 'Only a fool would do that.'

Tillman didn't answer. She looked round. He was watching her with detached curiosity. 'First time on a stealth mission?' he asked.

'No. I've been a soldier for almost a year now. And I've been undercover in enemy territory for most of that time.'

He nodded and his expression changed – became something that she suspected was pity. 'But the whole world is enemy territory for you, isn't it? Apart from that one tiny patch of ground. No wonder you people go squirrelly in the head.'

'Whereas your society is a monument to pure reason,' Diema sneered. How dare this hacked and sanded thug, this slubbering executioner, lecture her? Talk down to her?

'We don't make murder into a sacrament.'

'Yes.' Diema couldn't keep the outrage from showing in her voice. 'You do. Of course you do. Your priests and bishops blessed soldiers and butchers for centuries. They still do. You kill more of your own every day than we've killed in the whole of your history. Half the stories you tell, the novels and movies you make, have killers for heroes. Your whole culture is in love with violence. You embrace your own destruction, all the time. It's what defines you. You ruin the world that was given to you. Treat her like a whore, instead of a mother, and then—'

She stopped herself by force of will, fighting down the anger as she'd been taught. Tillman was still staring at her very intently, but his expression now was unreadable.

'Well,' he said, in a tone that was carefully neutral, 'you got me on that one. Here we both stand, kid. On the moral low ground.'

'I don't think I could get down that low,' Diema said, 'if I dug for a thousand years.'

She left him and went back to her seat. The conversation had done nothing to improve her mood and she was still unable to settle either to work or to diversion. She was relieved when the plane finally landed and she could become active again. Movement and action healed by their very nature.

They went through customs and immigration very quickly. They'd brought only carry-on luggage, and their new-minted passports stood up to scrutiny.

She had been told to go to the third level of the short-stay car park, where she'd be met by a Summoner of Elohim with local knowledge. He would be standing beside a blue Skoda Fabia and he would have with him a range of equipment from which she and her team could take what they needed.

When she stepped out of the elevator on the third level, she saw him at once. Saw both of them, rather. There were two men waiting there, hands in their pockets, stolid and patient. Diema turned to Tillman and Rush, who were right behind her.

'Wait here,' she said. 'I'll speak to them alone.'

'Given what we were saying back in England about trust,' Tillman said curtly, 'I think that's a pretty terrible idea.'

'For a minute, alone,' Diema insisted. 'If this was an ambush, I'd have set it up by phone, before we ever got on the plane. I wouldn't be trying to scrape it together now.'

'A minute,' Tillman said. 'Go on.'

Diema crossed the thirty yards or so of asphalt that separated her from the two *Elohim*. The nearer man smiled and opened his arms as she approached. She embraced him and let him embrace her.

'It's so good to see you, Diema,' he murmured in her ear.

'It's good to see you, too, Nahir,' she said in a neutral tone.

He'd changed a lot since she saw him last, but probably no more than she had. Now that he'd been exposed to sun and weather, he'd lost the characteristic pallor of the People. But where Diema's skin had initially reddened and blotched, and turned gradually to an uninspiring ruddy blush, Nahir's had magically reverted to the rich olive cast that the People must have had when they lived in the air instead of the earth. He'd changed in other ways, too. He seemed to have gained a confidence, a poise, that he'd never displayed in Ginat'Dania. It was perhaps no surprise that he'd already been promoted to the role of Summoner.

The second man, Shraga, who Nahir now introduced, was a complete stranger to her. He too bore the marks of living among the Nations, although in his case, while his skin darkened, his hair had bleached to the colour sometimes called strawberry blond. It would have made him a wonderful exotic in Ginat'Dania.

They gave Diema another set of papers. A new name, a Hungarian passport and driving licence, a bank account to draw on, and weapons. Nahir had assumed correctly that she would have left her knives, her guns, her pharmaca, behind in London, and that she would wish to resupply at the earliest opportunity.

'Kuutma relayed your message,' he told her, as she examined the guns they had brought – dismounting and reassembling them, testing the load and the firing action, weighing them in her hands. It was a slightly risky thing to do right there in the car park, but they were shielded by the raised

351

lid of the boot and Diema wanted to be done and gone from here as quickly as she could. 'He told us to extend every assistance to you and promised us two dozen Messengers in addition to those we have. Some have already arrived. Do you want to brief them yourself?'

'No,' Diema said. 'Not yet. I have other duties to attend to. I assume you made sure you weren't followed here. But I won't be taking that risk again, with you or anybody else. If there's news, tell me by phone or through agreed channels. If there's no news, leave me be.'

Nahir stared at her, both affronted and troubled.

'We understood,' he said stiffly, 'that you'd be leading this mission.'

'That's correct,' Diema told him, still absorbed in her triage of the weapons. Along with six sica blades, and the modified Dan-inject she'd chosen and ordered for Kennedy, she chose a nameless Chinese army-issue semi-automatic and a nine-millimetre hand pistol, which was small enough to carry in her ankle holster. She put both guns into a sports bag that Shraga handed to her. After a moment's thought, she also took a Ruger 44 carbine rifle.

'Follow the brief that Kuutma gave you,' she instructed the two men, helping herself to some boxes of ammunition. 'Look for possible addresses or areas from which Ber Lusim might be operating. Circulate likenesses of his rogue *Elohim* to all your people, and drill them – make them memorise faces and names. Also, look for trucks, vans or cars bearing the name of the High Energy Haulage company, and anyone who travels or books goods or services under their auspices. If you turn up anything that seems positive, or even hopeful, pass the information to me at once.'

'To you?' Nahir asked.

Diema nodded. 'To me. And then wait. I'll decide what action you're to take, if any. Those men standing over there by the elevators are my primary team, for now – along with the *rhaka*, Heather Kennedy. I'm sure Kuutma didn't omit her from his briefing.'

She beckoned to Tillman and Rush, who came over from where they were still standing, in front of the elevator doors. 'Help yourself,' she said to Tillman.

Tillman rummaged among the guns on offer, watched with silent outrage by the two *Elohim*. Finally he held up a retooled Beretta that looked as though it might once have been a competition gun. 'Is this chambered for .380?' he asked the Messengers.

Shraga nodded wordlessly.

'Okay, then,' Tillman said. 'I'll take this. Thanks.'

'What about me?' Rush said. 'Do I get to have a gun?'

'Have you ever fired one?' Diema asked him.

'No.'

'Then no, you don't. You'll be more danger to us than to the enemy.' She looked into the boot of the car again. In among the weapons, there were a great many items of general equipment. Some of them were clearly left over from training exercises, and had no conceivable use for her or her team.

She picked up a small cylinder of black plastic with a tab at one end like the ring-pull on a soft-drink can. She tossed it to Rush. 'Here,' she said. 'You get to have this.'

He turned the object over in his hands, examining it gingerly as though it might go off in his hands. Then he found the label. WILDWAYS GREEN PAINT BOMB. 400ML. SPRAY AREA 8MTRS DIAMETER. 'Funny,' Rush said. 'Really hilarious.'

Diema wasn't listening. She'd turned her attention back to

Nahir and Shraga. She'd said all that needed saying, but she knew that men often took categorical instructions differently from a woman than they did from another man.

So she spelled it out for them. 'You're not part of this,' she told them. 'Your role, for now, is to gather information. When I need more from you, I'll ask for it. I'm speaking with Kuutma's authority in this, and if you doubt me you can ask him. Keep your eyes open and your hands to yourselves. That's all.'

Nahir bristled. 'This is absurd,' he said. 'You need us.'

'I disagree,' Diema said quietly. 'Do as you've been told, my brother. Please. We serve the same god, and the same city. Everything will be fine, so long as you give me the help I need, when I need it.' She paused, holding his gaze. 'If you don't, you'll have enough blood on your conscience to make an inland sea.'

She turned to Shraga. 'These weapons are not traceable to you or to any of your people?' she asked him. She indicated with a nod the guns and other munitions piled in the boot of the car.

Shraga shook his head.

'Good. Then drive the car to Katona József Utca. Leave it there, locked, but with the keys on top of the rear driver-side tyre. Leave all the weapons where they are. If we need any more equipment while we're here, we'll help ourselves. I assume you brought a second car for us to use?'

He gave her a set of keys and nodded towards the car that faced them across the aisle of the car park, a black Audi A4 with a Hungarian licence plate. 'What about you?' Shraga asked, dismayed. 'We were supposed to escort you to the safe house and see you installed there.'

'We'll make our own way into the city,' Diema said, backing

354

across to the other car while still talking to them. 'Good hunting, cousins. And God favour us all.'

'May He watch over you,' Shraga muttered, bowing again.

He'll need to do a lot more than just watch, Diema thought as she got into the car, followed by Tillman and Rush.

'The paint bomb was way harsh,' Rush reproached her, seeming genuinely hurt.

'So is life,' Diema told him.

49

Kennedy took a mid-morning flight and got to Budapest around two in the afternoon. The customs officer who took a cursory glance at her EU passport asked her if the purpose of her trip was business or holiday. She told him she was there to work.

She also told that to the taxi driver who took her from the airport to the Hotel Karoly, on Molnar Utca, directly across the Danube from Gellert Hill and a short walk from the Hungarian parliament. She booked in under her own name and, in answer to the desk clerk's polite query, once again said very emphatically that she was in Budapest because she had a job to do there. Might take one day, might take two or three, but she was staying until it was done.

Then she grabbed another cab and went to the police headquarters building – Police Palace – which was a squat, stepped tower of glass and steel just opposite the northern tip of Margaret Island. She applied for a temporary licence to use legal but controlled surveillance equipment, providing a long and itemised list and giving her profession as 'freelance investigator'.

She walked back along the Pest side of the river. Here the down-at-heel Soviet-era brutalism seemed tilted to a rakish angle, inviting tourists to fantasise that they were taking a walk on the wild side. But the hotel and restaurant owners maintained their frontages in a precisely calibrated state of decorative distress, so clearly the wild side was only as wild as the market would bear. Kennedy grabbed some lunch – *hortobagy* pancakes and a sugared fruit skewer – at a café in a square off Bathory Street, in the extensive shadow of the Magyar Televízió building. She watched the people passing, but made no attempt to interact with any of them.

This was the riskiest part. If everything had gone according to plan, Tillman and Diema had picked up her trail at the Police Palace and were now moving with her through the city, keeping track of her – but they had to stay well away, and out in the open there were too many variables for them to be able to stay on top of all of them. Kennedy imagined information flicking through the air around her: streams of data converging, triangulating, defining her position and her vector.

Or maybe she flattered herself.

She did a lot of things on the way back to the hotel that left a footprint. She drew some money from a cashpoint, signed a petition at the parliament building, used her credit card to buy grapes and a four-pack of Staropramen at a mini-market. Probably none of these things would make a difference, but a little overkill certainly wouldn't hurt.

At the hotel, still thinking about the evidence chain she was leaving, she placed a call to Ryegate House. She spoke to the receptionist there – not Lorraine, who was on extended leave of absence – and left a more or less meaningless message for Valerie Parminter. She called Izzy's flat, too, and told the answerphone there that she'd be out of contact for a few days but would get back in touch as soon as she could. Izzy never checked her voicemail anyway, so she wouldn't get the cryptic message and be panicked by it.

There was nothing more to do but wait. Kennedy turned on the TV and flicked through the menus of pay-on-demand movies. She tried a couple, but the comedy wasn't funny and the conspiracy thriller depressed her by being less implausible than her life had become.

She called room service and ordered a Caesar salad. When it came she felt like the last thing in the world she wanted to do was eat.

The phone in her room rang at about nine o'clock in the evening, as soon as darkness fell – three rings, then silence. Ten minutes later, Kennedy went down to the ground floor and out of the back door of the hotel, where there was a row of five green-painted dumpsters. Between the third and the fourth, there was a large plastic bag carrying the logo of the Europeum Mall. She collected the bag and took it back to her room.

It took a while to familiarise herself with the contents. During her days in the Met, Kennedy had carried a Glock 27 – a true cop's gun, with a forward-canted grip so it seemed to jump into your hand on the draw, and a dead-straight recoil. She'd lost it in circumstances that still haunted her and had only fired one other in the years that followed. She'd certainly never fired anything like the monstrosity she took out of the bag. The Dan-inject had been Tillman's suggestion and Diema had seen the virtue of it.

Kennedy put out her light early, but didn't go to sleep. She sat on the bed and thought about Izzy. Specifically, she thought about sex with Izzy – varied times and places, even more varied sex. It had been sweet at the time, and it was a whole lot sweeter in retrospect.

Kennedy indulged a fantasy in which she was back in the Cask bar in Pimlico, and Izzy was offering – by way of a peace initiative – to take her home and screw her until her brain melted. In the fantasy, Kennedy accepted the offer and brain-melting sex ensued.

In reality, the bedside alarm clock ticked from 11.59 to 12.00 and the world – or the part of it that spoke Hungarian and sprawled around Kennedy on all sides – was silent and sex-free.

She settled back on the pillows, but sat up again at once when she felt herself starting to drift into a doze. That was a luxury she couldn't indulge until the job was done.

50

'I don't see how this is going to work,' said a voice in Diema's walkie-talkie.

It was the boy, Rush, complaining again. That seemed to be the unique talent he brought to this operation. Diema ignored him, but Tillman's voice replied. 'Diema thinks it has a chance, Rush, and I'm inclined to go with her instincts. She knows her own people.'

It was half-past midnight. Diema was up on the roof of a building directly opposite Kennedy's hotel, crouched behind a low parapet wall so she was invisible from the street but had a good view of the window of Kennedy's room. Tillman was watching the small alley where the dumpsters were, and where Diema had dropped off the Dan-inject for Kennedy. Rush was sitting in the parked Audi down the street from the hotel, watching its front door, which was far and away the least likely way for Ber Lusim's *Elohim* to come and therefore the place where the boy could do the least harm.

There was a silence. But not for very long.

'It just seems too obvious,' Rush said. 'I mean, like we're trying to scare them by saying boo or something.'

'Maybe.' Tillman again. 'But we know Ber Lusim's people see Heather as a threat. They've tried to kill her twice already and the second time they wanted to interrogate her, too. They're worried that she knows something important. If we're lucky, losing their warehouse will have made them even more worried.'

'I get that. I just don't see how it—'

'Do your job and be quiet,' Diema snapped. 'You don't need to understand or to agree. You only need to do what you're told.'

This time the silence was longer. There was a click as the walkie-talkie switched frequency – Tillman closing the party circuit to talk to her directly. 'He's afraid,' he told Diema. 'If you want to shut him up – or calm him down – you should explain to him.'

'It would be quicker to cut his throat,' she muttered.

'More time-consuming, though. You'd have to go all the way down to the street and then back up again. And then we'd have nobody to watch the front lobby.'

Diema said nothing. But after a minute, still scowling into the inoffensive night, she switched the walkie-talkie back to the all-parties frequency. 'Heather Kennedy is well known to my people,' she said, in a tone somewhere between terse and outright sullen. 'Mostly we think of the Adamite world as a distraction. A nothing. But she has a reputation. There are stories about her. How she found the Ginat'Dania that was and how she fought one of our *Elohim* to the death. She's the only one outside the People themselves who the Messengers actually respect.'

Almost, she added to herself, a little unwillingly. *Almost the only one.*

'But she didn't do a thing today besides walk around,' Rush pointed out. 'She was acting like a tourist. They've got to see that she has nothing.'

Actually, Diema thought, *that's the real genius of Kennedy's plan*. But perhaps she saw that more clearly than the boy did because the plan was aimed so squarely at the Messenger mindset; of course Diema would have the right reaction to it, because she was in the target demographic. 'What they see is this,' she told Rush. 'If you're right, and Budapest is where Ber Lusim has set up his home, then the *rhaka*, the wolf woman, the bitch, has done it again. She's found them. She comes and camps out on their doorstep, so obviously she knows they're here. Once you accept that, her doing nothing is a lot more sinister than her doing something they can identify and stop.'

Static on the walkie-talkie. 'Okay,' Rush said slowly. 'So then ...'

'Sooner or later they send someone to take her. We intercept and question him instead. We find out where he came from.'

'Okay. I guess I get that. Thanks.'

'You're welcome,' Diema growled. 'Now shut up and watch the door.'

Which the boy did, at last. And at length.

The night wore itself out and the sun came up. Diema saw Kennedy draw back the curtains of her room and open her window a little way to breathe the dawn air. She caught Diema's eye briefly as she yawned and stretched.

The hook still dangling there, in the water. But nobody was biting.

51

'I don't believe this is something we need to act on,' Ber Lusim said.

Avra Shekolni spread his hands. 'You are the Summoner. I bow to your knowledge of your profession and its attendant rituals,' he said, with well-polished humility. 'None of God's Messengers is so mighty as Ber Lusim, nor so clear-sighted.' He paused, as if reluctant to voice what he had to say next. 'But still, I think it is.'

They were in a large, airy chamber in the labyrinthine space that Ber Lusim had chosen for his followers to inhabit. Both had just listened as one of his Messengers, who had watched Heather Kennedy for half a day and all of the night, told them of her movements – or rather, her immobility. Several other *Elohim* were present, including Hifela, who had recently returned from England. He stood at the back of the room, beside the door, ostensibly taking onto himself the role of watchman. In this tightly guarded and barricaded space, and with so many Messengers meeting together, the role was superfluous: it was a mark of discretion and respect on Hifela's part, and reflected all that Ber Lusim found admirable in the man.

The room was close and windowless – which made it, on the whole, comfortable and homely to anyone who had been born and raised in Ginat'Dania. Every man here had spent his formative years underground, absorbing the light frequencies of sunlight only from luminescent panels. Every man here experienced confined spaces as security and was highly tolerant of artificial light and recycled air.

So the claustrophobia that Ber Lusim felt arose from something else. It was a strange thing. Since they had embarked on the plan – since that first night of blood and wonder back in Nunappleton Hall, a feeling had been growing in him. It was that his life, which had at times seemed a labyrinth of complex choices, had been progressively unravelling itself into a single straight line.

Each of the choices he'd made since he first went out into the wider world had paradoxically narrowed the scope of subsequent choices more and more, so that the vast arcades and vistas of the Nations, so unlike the cramped and contained perspectives of his home, were for him a long, straight corridor with no branches.

One of those choices had been to give his trust to Avra Shekolni, and despite the separate and several misgivings of his heart and mind he didn't in any way regret that bargain. His old friend was now become his prophet, the light that guided his soul through the darkness of the world. But about some things, perforce, he was more clear-sighted than the Holy One. Violence and subterfuge were the twin mysteries into which he had been initiated when he joined the *Elohim*, and they were ingrained in him so deeply that his mind knew no other way to work.

Therefore, there were things about the present situation that concerned him. The English warehouse shut down, the intricate clockwork of their plan interrupted and thrown out, and now this – the *rhaka* arriving here, presenting herself to them, like an omen of doom. All women were omens of doom, of course. From Eve onwards, their business and their delight was always to stray from the path and drag others to destruction with them. One did not move to chastise such a one until one was sure beyond all doubt what mischief she was bent on.

He said none of this to Shekolni. 'You know what the mathematician, Archimedes, had to say about levers,' he observed instead. Because he was among his followers, he kept his tone light and accompanied the words with a half-smile, disowning their import even as he spoke them.

'That with a large enough lever, he could move the world,' Shekolni said.

Ber Lusim inclined his head. 'And that is all Heather Kennedy is, blessed one. She moved Ginat'Dania, I know. We all know. And by this we know that she is a very large lever, or else one which on that occasion was very cleverly positioned, so as to exert a greater force than might have been expected.'

'Forgive me, but I thought Archimedes was born of the Nations, not of the People.' Shekolni did not smile and his tone was a little stern. 'I was also given to believe that it was this Adamite man, Leo Tillman, who had found Ginat'Dania. The woman was with him, certainly – but it was Tillman, not the *rhaka*, who killed Kuutma-that-was. And it is doubtless he who hides behind this woman now.'

Ber Lusim turned to Hifela, his refuge in many storms. 'Tell us again what happened at the warehouse,' he ordered him.

Hifela made the sign of the noose. 'One man went alone into the warehouse,' he said, as formally as if he were reading aloud from a report. 'A second remained outside, providing cover fire when he retreated. The man killed three of us and wounded four. None of us saw him clearly enough to identify him, but we believe it was Leo Tillman. Some footage survived from perimeter cameras. Red hair. Tall. Heavy build. Those are circumstantial details – but if you consider them in the light of the way he fought us, it seems almost certain.'

He didn't need to add that for any Adamite man to kill three Messengers was a dark miracle in itself. They all knew that.

'So,' Ber Lusim summed up. 'Tillman, moving against us in England. Depriving us of resources that were already allocated and about to be sent out. Throwing everything into jeopardy. And now, here, the *rhaka*, arriving – as it were – at the gates of our house. Yes, it seems possible that you're right. That these two have made common cause again. It doesn't follow, though, that we have anything to fear from them.'

'Only observe her arrogance,' Shekolni countered, his body leaning forward. 'She comes. She stands full in our sight. She doesn't even try to hide herself from us.'

'Perhaps she does not hide,' Ber Lusim said, 'because she doesn't know that there is anything to hide from.'

Shekolni grimaced, as though the suggestion were something unpleasant in his mouth. 'Perhaps. Yes. That could be. But consider, Ber Lusim, the whole pattern of her movements since you first became aware of her. She begins by searching for the book. She finds your man, within a matter of days, despite two attempts to remove her.'

'I spoke with Abydos,' Ber Lusim said. 'He could not say much, but I pieced together some of what happened. The *rhaka* had help, from another, younger woman. A woman whose identity we still haven't managed to determine.' The familiar fury and hatred rose in him as he said it, as he saw it in his mind – his men, the brothers of his heart, struck down by whores whose very strength and skill were abomination in God's sight – but he still kept his voice perfectly level and the muscles of his face relaxed.

'I believe my point stands,' Shekolni said quietly. 'But I have other points. She finds a copy of the holy book. A copy that should not even exist, if your Messengers had done the work assigned to them. And in this, we see, she is swimming up the waterfall, pressing herself against the very current of our enterprise. How does she do this? How does she find what your *Elohim* missed?'

'Again, Blessed One, with help,' Ber Lusim said. 'Not alone. Not by some superhuman ability or intuition.'

'Then, having read the book, she comes here.'

'And does nothing.'

'And does – so far as we can see – nothing. But what can we infer from that, Ber Lusim? If she came to search for us, why doesn't she search? If she came to confer with someone, why doesn't she meet them and confer? Why does she go from such wild activity to such complete stillness? What is she, perhaps, waiting for? I beg you to indulge me in this. If you're right, you lose nothing by questioning her. If you're wrong, you lose much by leaving her free to harm us. Despite the time you've lost because of events in England – the need, which you have explained to me, to re-route shipments and to source new equipment – we are coming to the final page. I beg you to question the *rhaka* and ensure that nothing she has planned can interfere with that.'

'I will do this thing,' said Ber Lusim, 'if I'm brought to it. But precisely because of that lost time, Most Holy, I would rather not be brought to it. To secure the *rhaka*, and then to question her, would delay us still further. I would rather drive onward with the mission that we've set ourselves.'

'Well, I am unschooled in these things.' Shekolni's voice was freighted with almost subliminal amounts of sarcasm and resentment. 'I'm prey to foolish fears.'

It was necessary to bring this matter to rest, Ber Lusim knew. It was bad for the others to see the two of them at odds, even for a moment. An idea struck him. He caught Hifela's gaze and held it for a moment.

'Tell me this, Blessed One. If you're right, and the *rhaka* knows we're here – if she is about to call down some disaster on our heads – how should I cast my net, for such a fish? How should I bring this woman into my house, so that I can question her? No matter how many Messengers I send against her, she'll merely eat them alive and excrete their bones.'

Nobody laughed. Nobody could be completely certain that their leader was joking.

'Send me,' Hifela suggested.

The words hung in the air. The *Elohim*, awed, waited for Ber Lusim's verdict.

'You, old Skull-bone?' Ber Lusim enquired. 'Well, I said that she was formidable. But if I approved this thing, I'd want her brought to me alive and your natural instincts tend towards death.'

'No,' Hifela said.

'No?'

'No, *Tannanu*. My instincts tend towards obedience. I wait on your will. If you say to bring her alive, I will be as protective of her body's safety as her mother would be. But I will bring her.'

He knows me so well, Hifela thought. It was like a small piece of theatre that they had planned together. Perhaps, as the ending of days came closer, all conversations would feel more and more like this. As though the weight of many centuries pressed on every word.

'Watch her, Hifela,' Ber Lusim said. 'Choose a few who you trust, and watch her close. So long as she does nothing, do likewise. When she moves, move with her. And if she does anything that concerns you, even in the smallest degree, take her. Take her and bring her before me. Let me speak with her and satisfy myself on some few significant points.'

He rose to his feet, signalling that the meeting was at an end. But none of the *Elohim* moved or spoke. They waited on his peroration.

'It may be,' he said, 'that Heather Kennedy's death is meant to be folded into the greater death. It may be that God has brought her to our door for a reason. Because he wishes us to make a sacrifice unto Him that is great in proportion to the greatness of what we do. If that's so, we'll sacrifice joyfully, as the commandment bids us.'

He left the room to the sound of their cheers. He paused at the doorway and put his hands on Hifela's shoulders, staring for a moment into the man's deep-set, almost hooded eyes. Then he walked on without a word. The Face of the Skull was never comfortable with signs of approval, let alone signs of love. But this was a father's blessing bestowed upon a faithful son – and as such, it was holy.

52

The day was hot and humid – uncomfortable at ten in the morning, and by noon hardly bearable. In Kennedy's hotel room, where the AC control on the wall turned out to be a completely empty plastic box, it went by like a river of treacle.

But it was even worse for the watchers. The rooftop opposite the hotel was as hot as a grill pan. Diema slathered her melanin-deficient skin with a zinc oxide preparation and bore it stoically. Rush, still in the car, was far less stoical but was forbidden by Diema to move the car so that he could follow the shade. All he could do was wind the windows down and keep swigging water from the plastic bottles stacked up on the back seat. Only Tillman, bivouacked among the dumpsters, was out of the fierce sun and fairly comfortable.

There was one point in the course of the morning when it seemed as though someone might be walking into their trap – when a windowless van rolled up at the hotel's back entrance and two men stepped out. But they were delivering catering supplies, boxes of individual tea bags and sugar sachets, plastic cups and tiny packs of biscuits. They were done inside of ten minutes and on their way again.

At 1 p.m., breaking protocol, Kennedy called Tillman on the walkie-talkie that Diema had given her.

'What?' Tillman said, without preamble.

'Nothing,' Kennedy muttered. 'Too much nothing. I'm starting to get antsy.'

'I sympathise. But you're supposed to maintain radio silence unless there's an emergency. Is there an emergency, Heather?'

'No.'

'Then we stick to the plan.'

She could tell from his tone that he was about to sign off, so she spoke quickly, forestalling him. 'Leo, I'm not sure the plan is going to work.'

Tillman sighed. 'We agreed on this. Anything we do now—'

'No, hear me out. Say we read them right and everything is playing out the way we wanted it to. Say we got Ber Lusim's attention. He could have watchers camped out around the hotel now, but further out than where you are – or closer in, for that matter. Someone sitting down in the lobby, waiting to follow me when I move.'

'So?'

'So maybe I should move. He might be ready to swallow the bait, but still not feel happy about moving into a space I've had time to fortify. Maybe he's planning to grab me off the street as soon as I step out.'

'All the more reason to keep you off the street, Heather.' Tillman's tone was dry. 'We're in control here. Out there, not so much.'

'I'm looking out of my window at the dumpsters, Leo.'

'I know. I can see you.'

'So give me a wave.'

'No. And don't look out of your window at the dumpsters.'

'Listen, if there was less at stake, I'd agree with you,' Kennedy snapped, all her tension coming to the surface at once. 'But if he's waiting for us to do something, and we're waiting for him to do something, he wins. Because presumably, he's still got his merry band of lunatics out there setting incendiaries and decapitating rats the whole time – and getting closer to whatever it is they're going to do that will leave a million people dead. I don't want that on my conscience, Leo. I seriously don't. I can't just sit here and wonder how high the body count is getting.'

'But we can protect you here,' Tillman objected, stolid and patient. 'If they come in, we come in right behind them. Out in the open, it's different. Not to mention the fact that if you start wandering around again, it doesn't look purposeful. It looks random. We want them to think you're up to something that threatens them.'

'I know. So let me do something purposeful.'

'Such as?'

'Such as a meeting.'

There was silence on the line while Tillman considered this.

'Diema could set up someone for you to meet with,' he admitted reluctantly. 'One of her *Elohim* . . .'

'I don't mean a real meeting. Especially not with someone they might recognise. I mean an imaginary someone. I go to a place where there's a crowd, but only a few ways in and out – a place where it's still easy for the three of you to come in close to me.'

'And what does that give us?'

'Leverage, maybe. If they think I'm up to something – delivering something or hooking up with my contact – maybe that's when they decide to play out the hand. Maybe they feel they need to stop it from happening.'

She waited. The silence was a lot longer this time, because Tillman was thinking through all the implications. 'I'll talk to Diema,' he said at last.

'It's not for her to decide,' Kennedy said sharply.

'No, it isn't. But she's got people who know the ground. If we do it, we need to pick the right place.' There was a pause, but he didn't turn off the walkie-talkie, so she knew he hadn't finished speaking. 'But you could be right,' he said at last. 'This is meant to be a provocation. It becomes less provoking the longer you sit there and do nothing. I'll talk to the others and get back to you.'

He signed off. Kennedy tossed the walkie-talkie onto the bed and made herself a cup of really uninspiring coffee.

Diema didn't even argue the point. 'She's right,' was all she said. 'We should probably have done it earlier. Give them a changing situation to react to, instead of one that seems stable.'

'Jesus, please,' Rush broke in. 'Anything that gets me out of this car. It's like a sauna in here.'

'So where should she go?' Tillman asked Diema.

'I'll ask.'

'You mean you'll confer with your people?'

'Yes.'

'And how long will that take?'

'As long as it takes.'

She closed the channel. A moment later, the walkie-talkie vibrated again. It was Rush.

'I need to pee,' he groaned.

'Use the empty water bottles,' Tillman said. 'That's what they're for.'

'Okay, then I need to breathe.'

'No, you don't. It's just a habit people get into.'

'I need to use my legs before I get a deep-vein thrombosis and die.'

373

'Keep the channel clear,' Tillman grunted, 'and your eyes open. We're still working here.'

He switched off the walkie-talkie. His shoulders were stiff so he massaged them, one at a time, always keeping the walkie-talkie ready in his free hand, and never taking his eyes off the hotel's rear door.

Maybe a little more than half an hour later, Diema got back to him.

'My people say we should use the Országház,' she said. 'The parliament building.'

Tillman was dubious. 'Did they say why? Lots of security, presumably, so lots of risk. Plenty of reasons for Ber Lusim not to want to go anywhere near Heather in a place like that.'

'And plenty of reasons why he'd be afraid of who she might be meeting there,' Diema countered. 'The high risk cuts both ways. Ber Lusim thinks that, perhaps, this is why she came. Perhaps she's been waiting for an appointment with someone high up in the government and it just came through. He'd need to know who that is and what's being planned. Most likely, if he makes a move, he'll do it as soon as he figures out where she's going – either when she's in the front lobby or before she even gets into the building.'

'I don't like it,' Tillman said. 'There'll be armed guards in there. If Ber Lusim's people come for her, Heather could get caught in a crossfire.'

'Heather's in this conversation,' Kennedy said on the walkie-talkie. 'No pain, no gain. I follow the reasoning, Diema, and I'll do it.'

But Tillman was still thinking it through and he still had questions. 'How many exits has that place got?'

'More than a dozen,' Diema conceded. 'But I had a thought

about that. My people are going to drop something off – something that gives us a bit of an edge.'

'What kind of something?' Kennedy asked.

'A GPS chip. It's about the size of a pinhead, and we can implant it under your skin. Once it's in place, we can establish your location to an accuracy of half a metre – which means if we lose you for any reason, we can still keep track of you. They'll be dropping it off to me in the next few minutes. I'll need to get it to you. The easiest way is if I just walk right in there, looking like I'm visiting someone or delivering something. Leave your door unlocked.'

The channel went dead. But only for a couple of seconds.

'Tillman?' Rush said.

'Lad, either use the bloody water bottles or hold it in until we—'

'It's not about that. It's about this whole thing. Taking the Heather Kennedy show on the road.'

'Well? What about it, Ben?'

'I think I might have a better idea.'

Kennedy did as she was told – unlocked the door and left it on the latch, so it could be pushed open from the outside. For a few minutes after that, she paced up and down the room, unable to keep still. Finally she went back to the window and stared out at the dumpsters, trying to identify where exactly Tillman had secreted himself. Wherever he was, he was well hidden. But he could see her, so she ought to be able to see him. At any rate, it was interesting to keep looking, like playing a chess game with only one move.

The door whickered momentarily against the thick pile of the carpet and a breath of air touched her back. She turned and saw Diema closing and locking the door.

'Okay,' the girl said. 'Let's do this.'

She was carrying a shoulder bag. She took something like a Bic lighter out of it and threw the bag on the bed.

'That's it?' Kennedy asked.

'This is the applicator. And this,' she held up her other hand, in which she was holding a small, unlabelled tube like a tube of toothpaste, 'is a topical anaesthetic plus anti-bacterial agent. You need to rub it on the spot and leave it to work for half a minute. Take off your pants and sit on the bed.'

'Take off my *what*?'

Diema was matter-of-fact. 'There'll be an implant wound – tiny but noticeable. If we had time for it to heal over, anywhere on your body would be fine. As it is, our best bet is to implant the chip internally, so there's no visible mark. The supplier said the inside of your cheek would do, but he also said there might be swelling on your face, which would look suspicious. So I think we should go with his other suggestion, which was to place the chip in your vaginal wall.'

Kennedy folded her arms and stayed exactly where she was. 'I think we should stick with the cheek,' she said, deadpan.

Diema stared hard at Kennedy, clearly surprised and a little impatient. 'We know Ber Lusim's men are female-averse,' she said, in an *I'll-keep-on-saying-this-until-you-get-it* tone. 'If this goes wrong, and they succeed in taking you, they may search you. But the two rogue *Elohim* you met in London were reluctant even to undress you fully, so I think we're safe in assuming that they wouldn't give you a full orifice search.'

She waited for reason to prevail and for Kennedy to do as she was told.

'Sit down, girl,' Kennedy said.

Diema seemed bemused at the suggestion. 'There's no time,' she said curtly. 'If you insist on the cheek, then let's—'

376

'Sit down,' Kennedy said again. 'We have to talk.'

'No,' Diema said, not even bothering to hide her contempt for the older woman. 'We don't have to talk. We only have to work together. I thought that was clear.'

'Clear to you, maybe. I'm going to sit down anyway. You can stand there, if you want to, but you will talk to me. Because if you don't, this ends here.'

Diema's eyes widened. 'You're lying,' she said. 'There are too many lives at stake.'

'A couple more than you know, maybe.' Kennedy went and sat, not on the bed but on the room's one chair. She waited in silence for the girl to join her.

Diema stood irresolute for several heartbeats. Finally, rigid with tension, she crossed the room and sat on the bed facing Kennedy. She put on a sardonic expression. *I'm waiting.*

'Why did you change your name?' Kennedy asked.

Diema blinked. 'What?'

'It's not that tough a question. Why did you change your name?'

'For no reason that you need to know about.'

The girl's tone was flat and final. Kennedy waited her out.

'Because I changed my life,' Diema said at last, in the same voice.

'Yes,' Kennedy agreed. 'I can see that, Grace. I'm just trying to work out how deep the changes go.'

The girl's expression didn't change, apart from a barely perceptible flicker of her eyelids. 'I was Tabe,' she said. 'I was never Grace. Grace was just what the father of my flesh called me.'

'The father of your flesh? Is that how you think of him?' Diema opened her mouth to speak again, but Kennedy held up a hand. 'Never mind. I don't pretend to understand your

377

customs, but you're wrong about that and you need to know it.'

'My name is—'

'Your *mother* named you Grace. And she named your brothers Jude and Seth. Normally you'd have kept those names when she took you back home, because none of them were offensive to your people's beliefs. The tradition, as far as I was told, is to rechristen children if they've been given names that are too ... what would you call it? Too Adamite. But Jude and Seth were good, biblical names – and who could argue with Grace?'

'I said,' the girl repeated, through gritted teeth, 'my name is Diema.'

'But your Michael Brand, your Kuutma, he seemed to feel that your past, and your brothers' past, needed to be more thoroughly erased than that. Perhaps because he loved your mother, Rebecca, and wanted her family to be his family, too. But she killed herself. She didn't want to live without your father. I mean, the father of your flesh. Leo Tillman. And after she was dead, Michael Brand gave new names to the three of you. He called you Tabe – and your brothers Ezei and Cephas.'

Diema seemed completely unmoved. 'You seem to think I should care what I was called out here in your world,' she said to Kennedy, her lower lip twisting. 'I don't. It's never been my world and it isn't now. It's just a place where I work.'

Kennedy nodded. 'I know,' she said. 'Your world is a big cave somewhere, with the sky painted on the underside of the roof. I can't imagine what that would be like, but I know you didn't ... don't ... think of it as a great hardship. You never missed what you never had. But doesn't it seem terrible to you, now that you've seen what the real world is like, that anyone should grow up in that way and live in that way? In the dark?'

Kennedy heard the tremor in her own voice. She was trying to speak to the young woman, but she kept seeing the child imprisoned inside her, the child entombed, and it was so terrible she felt a sort of sympathetic panic – a feeling of vicarious suffocation.

'It's not dark,' Diema said. 'It was only dark when you saw it, *rhaka*. And that was because you saw your own darkness.'

'No,' Kennedy said sharply. 'No. Believe me, I know the difference. And I know there's nothing I can say that will change you now. I can't push back the weight of all those years. But at least think about it. Please. Why did they send you? Why you, of all people? Why did they even think to turn you into ...' she pointed at the girl with a hand that trembled slightly '... into this? I can't forget what Kuutma said to Leo, the only time we ever met him. "Your daughter is an artist. She paints. There's such beauty inside her that it spills out of her fingers into the world." He said that! And then they turned around and made you into one of their murderers.'

Kennedy felt tears welling in her eyes and fought to hold them back. She knew that the girl would only see them as signs of weakness. But in spite of all she could do, a tear ran down her cheek. She was weeping for Grace, and for Tabe, both of them gone without a trace.

Diema was not contemptuous of the tear: she was outraged by it. 'Nobody made me do anything!' she said, her voice rising. 'This was my decision. Kuutma saw the potential in me. He gave me the choice – to serve my people.'

Kennedy shook her head. 'And he sent you to me, knowing I'd see Leo's face in yours. Knowing I'd have to go to Leo, against every instinct I had, and bring him back into this. Don't lie to yourself, Diema. If you were ever an artist, you probably had that gift that artists have of seeing exactly what's in front of your eyes. So look at this picture and see what it says to you. They took you up, and trained you, and sent you out to enlist us, because they knew you were the only one who could. Not an atom of chance or coincidence. Not an atom of choice, for any of us.'

Diema lurched to her feet. She looked as if she might run, but she stood her ground, her fists clenched. 'It doesn't surprise me,' she said, her voice almost back under control now, 'that you'd try to turn me against my own people. It's exactly what I'd expect from you. I'm only surprised you waited until we were all the way out here. You should have done it at Dovecote Farm, where you and Leo Tillman killed my brothers.'

It was Kennedy's one remaining hope – that they'd spared the girl that, at least. She sank her head into her hands, succumbing to a moment of sheer despair.

'Oh yes,' Diema sneered, glaring down at her. 'Did you think you could lie to me, Heather Kennedy? Did you think they'd let me meet you – and *him* – without telling me what it was you'd done? You say I've been lied to, and manipulated, by people I love. But you forgot to mention what Leo Tillman did to me. What he took from me. Perhaps it slipped your mind.'

Kennedy forced herself to look the girl in the eye again. It was an effort. She was really afraid of that scorn and that hatred: afraid of what it might be capable of doing. 'Diema,' she said, her voice thickened by her crying, 'did you ever ask, or did your teachers ever tell you, why Leo and I went to your Ginat'Dania?'

'To destroy it,' the girl said promptly.

'No, it wasn't that at all. And it was already destroyed, as far as that went. We came too late. I went to make an arrest.

380

But Leo was looking for his wife, and his children. He was looking for you. He'd been looking for you for twelve years. Ever since the day he came home and found the house empty. He loved you more than anything else in the world. He couldn't live without you. So he kept on searching, for you, and for Rebecca, and for your brothers, even though it had been so long, and nobody else believed you could even be alive—'

'We *weren't* alive!' Diema shouted. 'My mother was dead by then. My brothers were dead, because he'd already killed them, back in England. I was the only one left.'

'He didn't know that. He still doesn't. Oh, he knows about Rebecca. Michael Brand told him how she died. But he doesn't know about Ezei and Cephas. It would break his heart if he ever found out.'

Diema leaned down and thrust her face into Kennedy's face, gripping the lapels of the woman's jacket tightly. 'Then when this is over,' she growled, 'I'll break his heart.'

The fury passed through the girl, almost like a visible wave, and left her weak and sickened. She turned away from Kennedy with a gesture of surrender: not surrender to her arguments, just a desire to be done with all these words, all these thoughts.

'Put the chip into your cheek, *rhaka*,' she said hoarsely, after a while. 'I want to get out of here.'

'Keep it,' Kennedy said.

'We need you to—'

'I know what you need me for. But talking to you just now, I had another thought about that. I think it might be a really bad idea to have something implanted in my body that lets your people find me whenever they want to. So forget it.'

Diema stared at her. 'It's your choice,' she said coldly.

'Yeah, isn't it?'

The walkie-talkie, still set to vibrate, jumped and writhed on the bedside table, raising a burring clamour like a dentist's drill hitting enamel.

Kennedy picked it up and opened the main channel. Diema drew out her own set and turned away as she pressed it to her ear.

'Are you two almost done?' Tillman asked.

'Yes. No. Almost,' Kennedy mumbled. 'Can you give us a couple of minutes, Leo?'

'Take as long as you need. But listen to what Rush has to say before you go anywhere.'

'What the boy has to say?' Diema snapped. 'Why should anyone care what the boy has to say? He knows nothing about this.'

'Actually,' Tillman said after a moment, 'he makes a good case. Heather, you shouldn't go to the parliament building.'

'Then where should I go?' It didn't seem possible that it could matter right then: she asked mechanically, because he seemed to be expecting her to ask.

'To the baths,' he said.

53

The Gellert Hotel stood right at the foot of Gellert Hill, on the Buda side of the Szabadság Hid, or Freedom Bridge. It was an art nouveau palace, dressed in cool white stone and with Turkish minarets at its corners, even though the Ottomans had bailed on Budapest several centuries before the hotel was built.

On the top of the hill, 235 metres above Kennedy's head as she walked across the bridge, a weathered bronze statue of Saint Gellert stood at the edge of the precipice, one arm raised above his head in valediction, as though he were about to jump.

The hotel, with its huge bath complex, was a major tourist attraction, and on a day as hot as this there was a line right out of the side door and down the steeply sloping street. The front door, and the whole of the piazza between the hotel and the river, was taken up with a massive open-air market.

Kennedy joined the line and stood on the scorching pavement, tuning out conversations in English, Hungarian, German and Italian. The shoulder of Gellert Hill rose behind her, its rugged face softened on this side by the mature vines and fig trees that sprawled down from its peak almost to the river.

Out of the belly of the beast.

'This is what I'm thinking,' Rush had said. 'Toller used that picture as the frontispiece of his book, right? So I'm betting that his house is actually right there in the picture. What else would he be showing us? And if Shekolni is trying to model himself on Toller, maybe he's in that same house – or as close to it as he could get. So there's no point Kennedy going up to the parliament. It's the wrong side of the river and too far north. She should go to some place that's actually in that picture – or a place that stands where the houses in the picture used to be.'

With a certain degree of smugness, he'd unveiled his front-runner: the Gellert Hotel. He remembered it from the holiday he'd taken in Budapest a few years before. It would have been in Toller's picture, if it had been built back then. It was big enough and crowded enough to make a plausible spot for a meeting, but it had only two main entrances. And it had no armed guards, no lock-downs, no pack drill. 'Elementary, my dear Watsons.'

Diema hadn't liked it at first – hadn't wanted even to discuss it. The confrontation with Kennedy had left her sullen and withdrawn – regrouping herself, Kennedy thought, along the interior battle lines that seemed to mean so much to her. But Diema hadn't been able to fault the argument and finally she'd gone along with what was basically a fait accompli. It was clear by then that both Kennedy and Tillman preferred Rush's version of the plan, and had withdrawn their consent from hers.

So Kennedy crossed the river and waited in the sweaty heat of the afternoon until the line moved forward enough for her to get through the doors into the vast entrance hall with its wooden pillars, its light wells, its elegant nude statues and geometrical mosaics. Some of it was original, approaching its hundredth birthday. The rest had been seamlessly reconstructed after 1945, when the Russian shelling of retreating German columns had reduced most of Buda to loose chippings.

The ticket window Kennedy was slowly approaching was flanked by massive wooden notice boards – one in Hungarian, the other in very bad English – advertising an array of treatments and services. In addition to the main public access and spa pools, there were dry and steam saunas, massage booths, manicures and pedicures, mud packing, carbonic acid tubs, weight baths, stretch baths and cold dive-pools. And a bar, she couldn't help noticing.

Trying not to scan the faces around her, or meet anyone's gaze for more than a fleeting second, Kennedy took the open day pass. It would get her into all the pools and saunas: specialist services involving heavy weights, mud or mild corrosives would cost extra.

She was given a towel, a wrist band and a set of instructions in rapid Hungarian to which she just nodded along. There were separate entrances for men and women: Kennedy's Hungarian was just about equal to following the arrowed signs marked *Nök* to a gleaming steel turnstile standing incongruously under a decorative arch, whose carved woodwork echoed the grape vines on the hill outside. A stony-faced woman with the hotel's logo blazoned in red across her white T-shirt showed her how to use her wristband to swipe herself in.

Looking neither to right nor left, Kennedy went on, down a long flight of steps and through an underground tunnel into the main bath complex. A lot of it, she realised, was underground, although there were signs everywhere pointing up towards the outside pool.

Kennedy went into a one-person changing room, where she

took off her light jacket, shirt and trousers, replacing them with T-shirt and shorts. The few things she needed to carry went into a string purse that she wore on her shoulder.

She looked innocuous. Unarmed. A lamb to the slaughter.

She exited the changing room and sauntered through the seemingly endless aisles and alleys of cubicles until she found one of the spiral staircases that led to the outdoor pool.

The pool area was vast and heaving with bronzed or lightly broiled bodies. Kennedy had read once – admittedly a good few years before – that the whole human population of the world could stand shoulder to shoulder on the island of Zanzibar. It looked as though most of them had chosen today to try to stand in the Hotel Gellert's bath complex.

She sat down on a deckchair and anointed herself with sun-block, putting the bottle back in the shoulder bag afterwards. Then she checked her watch, not ostentatiously but visibly, and leaned back in the chair, hands folded demurely in her lap.

If it was going to happen at all, it would probably happen soon.

Kennedy's three watchers had had to cross the city in lock-step with her, which prevented them from choosing their stations in advance. There was a brief, hurried conference at the western end of the Freedom Bridge, where Diema was able to use the hotel complex itself, looming in the middle distance, as a visual aid.

'I'm going to be on the hill,' she said. 'That way I can see the front and side doors of the hotel, so I'll be your early warning if anybody shows. Tillman, you go inside, in the lobby space. You can watch the entrance to the baths, and you'll be on point if anyone gets past me.'

'What about me?' Rush asked, without much hope.

'Watch the front doors, from the outside, and the steps up from the river,' Diema said. She didn't go to any effort to make it sound like a job that had any real importance.

'Are they likely to come up from the river?' Rush asked.

'They could,' Diema said.

She was already walking away when Tillman caught her by the arm and brought her to a halt. It was an electrifying moment, and it made Rush swallow the complaint he was halfway to voicing.

'Do you have a problem?' Diema asked, in a tone that said *do you want to lose that hand?*

'The GPS receiver,' Tillman said.

'What about it?'

'No offence, girl, but I think I might have Heather's interests more at heart than you do. Why not let me hold onto the base unit?'

They locked eyes for a long, dangerous moment.

'Protector of women,' Diema said. 'Defender of the weak, and the weak-minded. Is that your brief, Tillman? Or do you just want to get into her pants?'

'If you want to know about Heather's pants,' Tillman said equably, 'you should probably ask Heather. Meantime, I'll take the tracker. Unless this is something you actually want to fight about.'

Diema reached into a pocket of her black leather jacket, found something that looked a little like a TV remote, and tossed it to him. 'No,' she said. 'You take it, with my blessing. It won't do any good, though. She changed her mind about wearing it. You should teach your bitch a little discipline, some time. God knows, she could use it.'

The girl walked away before he could answer her, heading

for the east side of the hotel and the rugged hillside beyond. She didn't look back.

Tillman turned to Rush, who was giving him a slightly dazed stare.

'Did I just hear right?' the boy demanded. 'Kennedy's in the wind?'

'Not if we do our job right,' Tillman muttered gruffly. 'Pick your spot, lad. And keep your channel open. This might be our last shot.'

'It might be hers,' Rush said.

And since Tillman had no answer to that, they parted without any further exchange of pleasantries.

Rush stayed where he was, out on the pavement in front of the hotel's main entrance, with the street market right at his back. Tillman went into the lobby and up into the gallery set into the circular dome at its mid-point.

Once again, all they could do was wait. And Tillman was starting to feel that if they waited much longer, this so-called plan would founder on the reefs of their divergent agendas.

He was also wondering, if they happened to succeed in locating and neutralising Ber Lusim, for how long after that the Judas People would let them live.

Sitting under the rotunda dome at the centre of the Hotel Gellert's lobby, wearing a gaudy shirt and with a camera around his neck, Hifela watched Heather Kennedy pass through the turnstile and considered his brief. *If she does anything that concerns you*, his commander had said.

He could refer back to Ber Lusim, but this seemed to fit the definition very well. For the *rhaka* to come so shockingly close to their base of operations was still an ambiguous act, but it admitted of very few interpretations – and in all of them, the woman or one of her associates had somehow succeeded in locating them. Possibly she was planning some kind of raid, but it seemed unlikely she'd do that by day. It was only too plausible, though, that she was reconnoitring the ground for a later incursion.

Hifela decided that this was a good moment to intervene. But he didn't want to overstep the bounds of his commission, even then. He took out his phone and texted a message to Ber Lusim. 'The woman is close to you. Horizontal distance, two hundred and fifty metres. Vertical distance, eighty metres.'

He sent the message, and while he waited for a reply he sauntered around the lobby, casting a critical eye on the statuary. But he could not relax, and he was all too aware that he looked as though he were inspecting the nudes on a parade ground.

He thought back, at this crucial juncture, to his life's other major turning point, to the moment when he had decided to follow Ber Lusim into exile. That had been an act of blind faith. They had had no idea, then, of the part they were to play in human history. They hadn't even known that they were chosen. Then the prophet had arrived and made sense of everything. He had promised to show them a miracle and he had delivered on the promise. He had shown them how every one of their own actions was a stone in a mosaic, not random but perfect and necessary and interconnecting. When Shekolni spoke, there was perspective.

So the other *Elohim* said, anyway. For Hifela, it was always more a matter of personal loyalty to his chief – love, even, for what he felt for Ber Lusim was more fervent and intense than anything he had ever felt for a woman; just as the intimacies of the battlefield were deeper than the intimacies of the bedroom.

His phone pinged once, the discreet sound of an elevator arriving. He glanced at the screen, then opened the text, which consisted of a single word.

Execute.

Hifela stood slowly, set the camera to flash and took a photo of the nearest nude.

That was the prearranged signal. Although there was no visible sign of it in the random movements of the crowd around him, the word was being passed down the line and the Elohim assigned to him were going in.

Not against the woman. The woman would wait, a little while.

Until they'd disposed of her three guardian angels.

54

Ben Rush survived the first attack for one reason only: he was in Diema's line of sight.

Rush was watching the hotel's front entrance, which faced onto the river. Diema was watching from the south, where the hotel faced the hillside, and as always she favoured a high vantage point. In the absence of a building backing onto the hotel, she'd chosen a massive fig tree at the base of the hill, whose upper branches were on a level with the hotel's fifth-floor windows. Tillman was inside, in the lobby, close to a window that looked onto the outside pool where Kennedy had positioned herself.

It was some trick of body language that made Diema focus on the man who was crossing the road, heading towards the front entrance and – as though coincidentally – towards Rush. She couldn't say what it was she recognised, but she found herself staring at the man, registering him instantly as one of her own tribe. Then, as he drew the sica from the back of his belt, she realised belatedly that his left hand had just traced an ellipse against the light-coloured fabric of his suit jacket. It had seemed as though he were just smoothing out a crease, but it was the sign of the noose.

The distance was about two hundred metres – already long

for the nine-millimetre, but the nine-millimetre was in her hand while the Chinese cannon was in the satchel sitting on the branch beside her. She was sure she could place a bullet in the man at that distance, but she couldn't with any confidence gauge where it would hit – and he was of the chosen, so she couldn't risk killing him.

Squaring the circle, she fired off five rounds in quick succession, aiming very low. Three pedestrians went down, shot in the knee, calf or foot. Screams and bellows rose from the street, and consternation burgeoned visibly from the seeds of pain and panic she'd just created. It was a rough and ready solution, but it made people flee across the knife-man's path. It might also make Rush look in the right direction and catch sight of him.

It was the best Diema could do and it took a heartbeat longer than she would have liked. Because she knew for certain that she was blown. There was just no way Ber Lusim's *Elohim* would come for Rush and not for her. And no way, given enough time and patience, that they wouldn't have made her, sitting up in the tree, and gotten into position to take her.

The satchel was an arm's length away, with all her kit – apart from the nine-millimetre and the walkie-talkie, still strapped to her belt – inside it. It might as well have been on the dark side of the moon. She straightened her legs, slid forward and let herself fall straight off the branch. Rifle fire shredded the foliage above her and reduced her former perch to a threshing floor.

Diema used the canopy to slow her fall, turning it into a cascade roll, and caught herself on another branch ten feet lower down. She'd been able to gauge the direction of the gunfire, at least roughly, and had angled her fall to the left, away from the flank of the hill. Now she scrambled a few feet further over, even though it meant crawling out towards the thinner end of the branch she was on. The branch dipped precariously under her, but the bole of the tree was between her and the shooters.

For now.

She snatched up the walkie-talkie, but before she could open the channel, let alone speak, more shots smacked into the bark right above her head.

She was pinned from at least two directions. And they could see her.

Tillman saw the knife first, already in the air, the knife-man a half-second later. It was much too late by that time, and though he turned and dropped by subliminal reflex, that only meant the sica caught him higher up on his side and at a shallower angle. Sharper than a razor, it went into the angle of the pectoral and deltoid muscles on his right side and embedded itself deeply. Along with the pain came the shock of realisation that the hurt he'd just received was probably his death warrant. The anti-coagulants the *Elohim* used to coat their blades could render even a shallow graze deadly, and he'd just taken a deep wound at a nexus of two major arteries.

Two men – presumably Messengers, given their choice of weapon – were coming at him from two different directions around the circular gallery, intentionally cutting him off from the stairs and the lift. Tillman's gun was tucked into the back of his belt and there was no time to get to it – especially with the protruding knife impeding his movements. Any of the *Elohim* would already have the advantage over him in speed. The man who'd already thrown was drawing another blade. The second assassin, marginally closer because he hadn't taken the time to aim and throw, was coming towards Tillman at a run.

He carried the knife in his right hand, the left hovering above it seemingly en garde – but then he let the two hands draw apart, the knife-hand stabbing low while the supposedly defensive hand darted up to jab at Tillman's throat.

Tillman walked right into the attack. Being wounded already freed him from that particular concern, although not from the danger of being disembowelled. He struck down with his own right hand to knock the knife aside and leaned to the side so that the throat-jab went wide.

He clamped his left hand onto the assassin's shoulder. Still advancing, still turning, he ducked to transform the lock into a throw. He took the man's knife-arm just above the wrist, pulled him around and down in a clumsy but quick *kitap*, but since he maintained his grip on his opponent's forearm the weight of the man's own body ripped his arm out of its socket.

And gave Tillman a knife.

He brought it up in time to fend off a slashing attack from the second man, the two knives clashing once, then twice, as though they were swords and this was a fencing bout. Tillman was aware that every movement was forcing more blood out of the deep wound in his side, but there was no time to think about that.

More worrying was the fact that he was facing a knife-fighter far more experienced and comfortable with this weapon than he was. He was giving ground with each feint and guard, backing towards the wall. He was going to lose, and he was going to die.

So he did the only thing he could think of. He bought a half-second with a wild horizontal slash, used it to back away another step – leaving his knife way out of line, his torso unprotected.

The assassin took the invitation, moving in with terrifying

speed, but Tillman was already angling his body away from the blow, and because he had to make the call he decided it would be a high thrust to the heart. Luck was with him: his opponent, over-committed, leaned in past him. By this time, Tillman had dropped his knife. He grabbed the man in a two-handed embrace and pivoted on his left foot, adding his own momentum to the lunge.

They went through the tall window together, but the *Elohim* assassin was the lead partner in this short, ugly waltz.

Tillman kept the other man beneath him as they fell the twenty feet to the ground. They landed on bright blue tiles, in a shower of glass shards, and gravity delivered the *coup de grâce*.

Where they landed was a decorative apron next to the out-door pool, in the middle of a dense crowd of sunbathing tourists – who screamed and leaped to their feet, scrambling to avoid the hard rain of broken glass and then to get away from the blood-boltered madman who reared up, staggering, in front of them, standing over a pulped corpse like a lion over his kill.

As they backed and ran from him, Tillman's walkie-talkie vibrated on his belt. He thumbed the ACCEPT key and heard Diema's voice.

'Tillman! Rush! The plan's shot. They were waiting for us. They'll kill us first, then go after—' Her voice was drowned out by the white noise of gunfire. An automatic rifle, from up close.

Tillman snatched up the walkie-talkie, already moving. He had plenty of empty space to move into, suddenly. The bathers were fleeing away from him on all sides as quickly as they could.

'Where are you?' he yelled.

He heard a single word. It sounded like 'hill', or maybe 'kill'.

He hoped the boy would survive. He hoped they all would. But he did what he had to do.

Kennedy heard the gunshots first – the precise, hammer-on-nail iterations of Diema's handgun, followed by the nerve-shredding road-drill roar of an automatic rifle. A moment later, and much closer, a window shattered.

From where she was, the side of an awning hid the falling bodies of Tillman and the Messenger, and the first screams drowned out the sound when they hit. She only knew that violence was erupting all around her – and from this, that their plan had both succeeded and failed. The *Elohim* had taken the bait, but somehow they'd missed the target. Or else they were choosing to take her out in a way that involved a lot of collateral damage.

She took three steps in the direction of the sounds, but that was as far as she got. The people closest to her backed into her, turned and started to run, infected with the panic of those at the epicentre of the disturbance. Except that it wasn't really running. In the space of seconds, as hundreds of people surged towards the few available exits, the crowd congealed into a single, struggling mass. Kennedy couldn't swim against that tide: she tried to stand her ground and let it sweep past her, but even that was more than she could manage. She was carried with it.

Men and women with the hotel's red logo on their chests – lifeguards, presumably – were trying to divert the tide and stop people from being crushed against the walls. One of them was shouldered aside by a fleeing man and pushed into the pool. *Probably the safest place to be right then*, Kennedy thought, but she had to find out what was happening, and she had to do it quickly.

She let the crowd carry her. Once she was downstairs, in the changing area, it would be easier to peel off and go her own way.

'*Itt!*' the lifeguards were shouting. 'Here! This way!' Two of them, a man and a woman, were holding a door open against the crowd's barging, stumbling turbulence. Kennedy went through it and down the stairs beyond. Each step was a fight to stay on her feet and avoid being trodden under by the sheer press of people.

At the bottom of the stairs, emptying into the wider space of the changing area, the crowd spread out a little and the crush was lessened. Here, too, though, urgent men and women ushered them onward – '*Itt! Itt!*' – and pushed them if they stopped.

A man stepped into their path and yelled into Kennedy's face. '*Itt kell mennem, asszony – itt!*' She went the way he pointed, through another door off to one side and into a white-tiled corridor that was mercifully empty. She'd already taken several steps along it when she realised that the man who'd just spoken to her hadn't had the house logo on his chest. He hadn't been wearing a T-shirt at all, but a plain white shirt and a linen-weave suit.

She stopped and turned, just in time to see the man pull the door closed and draw a bolt across, locking himself in with her.

55

As soon as he saw the man walking towards him with the knife in his hand, Ben Rush turned and ran. The street market was right there beside him and it was pretty much the only way that wasn't blocked by shouting, screaming people, so that was where he headed.

But the knife-man was running too, and after one frantic glance over his shoulder, Rush knew that he wasn't going to win this race on the flat. Jesus, this guy was *fast*!

So his only chance was to make it into a steeplechase. He vaulted over counters, to the indignant bellows of the stall-holders, barged through clothes racks and stacked boxes, swarmed under tent flaps, and generally did his best to get out of his pursuer's line of sight. But every time he thought he'd shaken him off, the bastard hauled into sight again, dogging Rush's heels so closely that there was never any chance for him to go to ground.

Rush was young, and reasonably fit, but he knew he couldn't keep this pace up for long. And it was getting harder to manoeuvre as stallholders and shoppers stopped what they were doing to watch the chase. They formed a semi-solid wall now, blocking him from most of the bolt-holes he might have used and giving the assassin – with their attentive, curious stares – a signpost that pointed towards Rush in real time.

If Diema had only given me a gun, he thought wildly. But how could he have started a firefight in the middle of a thousand innocent bystanders? And besides, he'd never fired a gun in his life. The only thing that was certain if he'd tried it here was that he wouldn't have hit the one man he was actually aiming at.

He rounded a corner, legs and elbows pumping, and skidded to a halt. No more road. The market went all the way to the river, and that was where he was. There was a low parapet wall ahead of him. A long way below, the broad ribbon of Zela Utca, the river road, stood between him and the Danube. Not even an Olympic athlete could have jumped across that distance.

Rush thought furiously. He did have the paint grenade and he took it from his pocket now. Maybe he could let the guy get up close and then blind him with it? But he'd seen people messing with these things on YouTube – they sprayed paint in thin streaks, not in waves. They were a nuisance, designed for drunken prats who think damage to property is hilarious in itself.

The inspiration hit him when it was almost too late to be of any use. He still had a second or two before the assassin turned the corner and saw him again. He staggered right up to the nearest stall, which was selling sweet and savoury strudels, held the grenade above his head and pulled the pin. 'Debreceniiii!' he yelled, his voice ragged. 'Debreceni are a load of *bollocks*. Polecsik is a *wanker*. Liverpool shagged you up the arse!'

The grenade kicked in his hand and the world went green.

*

The gunfire was coming from at least three directions and Diema could only think of one way to respond. She couldn't return fire: she couldn't even see where the shots were coming from, and if she fired at random she might kill one of her own race – the sin that would bar her from ever going home.

So she kept on dropping and sliding down through the branches of the tree, hiding herself from one shooter or another, trying to find a space that would offer her cover from all quarters. As a strategy, it was only a little bit better than praying.

As soon as that thought crossed her mind, she realised that she had at least one more option.

Diema began to sing. She knew a hundred blessings, and most could be sung as well as spoken. She started with the funeral hymn, which for obvious reasons was uppermost in her mind. Forgetting cadence and harmony, she shouted it at the top of her voice, hoping that it would carry to where Ber Lusim's *Elohim* were.

The gunfire slackened and then stopped.

Yes, Diema thought. *Home-town girl. Now you know.*

Somewhere close by, a shrill, rising voice screamed out an order in bastard Aramaic. *'Y'tuh gemae le! Net ya neiu!'* The order was utter blasphemy: *never mind who she is, complete your mission*. For a moment, and then another, nothing happened. But the speaker had pronounced Diema's death sentence.

The branch she was squatting on was barely able to support her weight – but the one above it, to which she was clinging with her hands, was longer and thicker. As the shooting began again, she hauled herself up onto it, found her balance and began to run.

She was still maybe ten feet above the ground – clearly visible from below now as she broke out of the tree's thickest canopy into semi-open air. But these trees were old: centuries ago, they'd linked arms in solidarity against the city's incursions, tying their extremities into a lovers' knot.

At the end of the branch, Diema jumped. She wasn't aiming for any particular part of the neighbouring tree, just using its foliage to soften the impact and then its branches to allow her to complete her controlled fall to the ground.

She landed on her feet, which was a welcome miracle. There was a man directly in front of her, already turning – a rifle in his hands. Diema shot him in both legs, and then as he toppled towards her she swung the handgun up to meet him, driving the butt into the side of his head. He was unconscious when he hit the ground.

She took the man's rifle and retreated up the hill, darting quick glances into the trees around her. There was movement there, and another shout: '*Be hin et adom!*' *Yes*, Diema thought. *She's on the ground. Maybe you'll be a bit less free and easy with the rifle fire when you might hit one of your own.*

Meanwhile, her own rifle fire would sound like theirs and make it harder for them to track her. It also lent itself very well to her new tactics. She cut another man off at the knees with a short, sweeping burst, and left him screaming – then she waited until one of his comrades came to check the damage, and shot him too. She was happy to keep this up until Ber Lusim didn't have a single Messenger left who could walk.

She kept on moving, always upwards – which she hoped would draw the *Elohim* along with her, away from the others. The plan was moot now, but they still needed a living

Messenger to question. Kennedy had the Dan-inject, so she had the best chance of landing that fish.

Of course, the slopes of Gellert Hill were now full of *Elohim* who were in no fit state to walk away, but their comrades would collect them as soon as they'd dealt with Diema, and for all her efforts that couldn't take long now.

Even as she was thinking that, she heard a soft, thudding impact on the ground close by. Looking down, she saw a grenade rolling to a halt against her foot. She kicked it away down the hill and threw herself flat on her stomach.

Or started to.

She was still in mid-air when the shockwave took her.

Kennedy had encountered the *Elohim* before and survived the experience – mostly by means of luck or outside help, and once (in Santa Claus, Arizona) by the time-honoured device of bringing a gun to a knife fight. She knew enough to be certain that if she let this man get in close to her, she was probably finished.

As he advanced, she took the Dan-inject out of her bag. Then she threw away the bag, dropped her free hand to her side like a duellist in a Victorian novel, and took aim with the flimsy, almost weightless device – one-handed and with her arm straight out in front of her, a stance she'd never have used with an actual gun. But this wasn't a gun, it was a modified version of the dart-launchers that zookeepers use to sedate dangerous animals. Instead of bullets, it fired flechette darts with a payload of three millilitres of fentanyl. Recoil would be minimal, too small even to feel.

The assassin was on Kennedy in three strides. In that time, she fired off both of the pre-loaded darts, aiming for his chest. But the darts were slower than bullets, as well as lighter. The

Messenger, whose addiction to the drug kelalit profoundly altered his perceptions of the world, walked around them, tilting his body first to the left and then to the right.

Which kept his mind occupied while Kennedy brought up the jabstick and stabbed him in the shoulder.

The jabstick was manufactured by the same company that made the dart gun. It was gas-and-spring loaded, modifiable to release the sedative payload either automatically or on depressing a trigger. The one Kennedy was carrying – illegally customised and cut down from its original two-metre length to just under five inches – was set to automatic. And because it was a weapon of last resort, it carried five millilitres of fentanyl instead of three. The assassin's eyes registered a momentary shock as the drug hit his system.

But he didn't break stride. He swatted the jabstick out of Kennedy's hand and at the same time punched her hard in the stomach.

She didn't see the punch coming, so she had no chance of leaning into it and lessening the impact. She doubled up, the breath leaving her in a huffing bark of agony. The follow-up blow to the back of her head made her crash down onto her knees, her sight strobing black and white.

Fentanyl was a relatively recent addition to the line-up of commercially available sedatives, a synthetic ethyl compound discovered in the 1960s and at first used almost exclusively for emergency pain relief. Its spectacularly quick action made it perfect for use by paramedics on burn and trauma victims, and that instant knock-out effect was one reason why Diema had chosen it. The other was a chemical oddity that the drug's inventor had noted enthusiastically at the time: even long-term drug addicts whose habit had made them too tolerant of opioids to be treated with morphine would respond to fentanyl.

But long-term users of kelalit seemed to be able to shrug it off with impunity. The Messenger was on top of Kennedy now, rolling her onto her stomach and twisting her arms behind her. He was much stronger than her and trained in immobilising techniques. He held both of her hands in one of his, and his grip didn't even seem particularly tight, but she couldn't move an inch without searing agony shooting up her arms.

She screamed for help, but he ignored her. There were enough screams echoing around the building that one more wouldn't even be noticed. With his free hand, he took a plastic gardening tie from somewhere she couldn't see and fastened it around her wrists, pulling it tight.

Then he hauled her to her feet, pressing her hard against the white-tiled wall. He drew a knife – a sica – and waved it in front of her eyes.

'You see this?' he muttered in her ear. 'Just nod.'

Kennedy nodded.

'The blade is poisoned. If I cut you with this knife, you'll die. You understand?'

She nodded again.

'At the end of the corridor, there is a door. Beyond the door, a small parking area. We will walk across that space to the van that's parked there and you will climb into the back of the van. Do this without a word, without a sound, and without trying to run. Otherwise I'll kill you. Do you understand?'

'Yes,' Kennedy said.

With a hand on her shoulder, he turned her and launched her.

When Diema clambered to her feet again, she found that she was deaf.

Two men were running towards her down the hill, but dirt and leaves were still raining down from the explosion and the air was thicker than soup, so they hadn't seen her until she stood up directly in front of them. She let the first man run into her, ducked under him and threw him high and hard. But doing that laid her open to the second man's attack, a vicious combination of kicks and punches that sent her staggering backwards on the treacherous ground until she fell, fetching up with a jarring impact against the bole of a tree.

The Messenger brought his rifle up to chest height, his free hand steadying the breech. His gaze met Diema's.

'*Aikh kadal*,' Diema murmured, staring deep and pleadingly into those dark eyes. *Older brother.*

The man's resolution faltered, for a heartbeat. Diema fired twice, which emptied the handgun's clip. One shot went wide, the other hit the man's right hand, shattering the rifle's stock and blowing off two of his fingers.

He was drawing a sica from his belt, left-handed, when Diema rushed on him, leaving the ground in a desperate leap to kick him in the chest. He went down hard and took a second longer than she did to struggle upright again. By that time she'd snatched up his rifle – which was still just about serviceable as a club. Her wild swipe slammed into the under-side of his jaw and the shuddering impact knocked him out cold.

Her hearing was starting to return now, but her whole body throbbed with pain – and against that dull background ache, every movement caused flares of bright, localised agony from her left side. Probably she'd cracked a rib when she'd fallen after the grenade went off.

But she had her prisoner. If the others had survived, this could still count as a success. Diema looked around for something to tie her attacker's hands with. His belt would probably do. She knelt down and unfastened it, rolling the man onto his side so she could drag it free.

But as she bundled his wrists together, he stirred under her hands and opened his eyes. '*Dekai?*' he mumbled. *Alive? You're taking me alive?*

'To question you,' Diema told him, though she shied away from explaining what that might mean. 'We want to know about Ber Lusim and about the work you've done for him.'

The man grimaced. The muscles of his jaw contorted and his pale face flushed suddenly red.

Diema didn't realise what he was doing until it was too late to stop him. She wrestled briefly with his jaws, but even as she forced his mouth open, a shudder ran through him. He stiffened, eyes wide, and all his muscles locked in a body-wide rictus.

The idea of a suicide capsule – for one of the People – was as obscene to her as the idea of the People killing their own. *Costly in the sight of the Lord is the blood of his servants.* Their lives were precious because there were few enough of them to be counted. But Ber Lusim had taught them new ways of thinking.

Grim-faced, fighting back tears, Diema used her thumb and forefinger to force the dead man's eyelids closed over his bulging eyes.

As she did so, something cold and hard touched the back of her neck.

'*Akhot ha'aktana*,' Hifela said softly, raising the Sig Sauer so that the tip of its barrel touched her cheek. 'Little sister.'

Kennedy walked in front of the Messenger, but when they got to the end of the corridor he reached past her to push the door open. Bright sunlight flooded in, making her blink and squint.

'There,' the man said, not pointing but pushing her where he wanted her to go. There was a red van, parked about twenty feet away. On its side, in black script printed to look like a military stencil, were the words 'High Energy Haulage', along with the dolmen logo.

Kennedy stumbled towards it, dragging her steps in the vain hope that someone might come around the corner of the building and see what was happening.

Nobody did. They reached the van and her captor threw open the back doors. 'Inside,' he ordered. Kennedy stared at him. His voice had definitely been slurred and there was an asymmetric lean to his stance.

She backed away a few steps. The Messenger lunged for her and caught her by the arm, but almost fell over in the process. He blinked rapidly a few times, as though to clear his vision.

'Inside,' he said again, pulling her towards the van. He held the sica close to Kennedy's throat and though he was careful not to cut her, she was terrified: his hand didn't look that steady.

She climbed into the van, with great difficulty because of her bound hands, and swung herself around so she sat facing outward.

As the Messenger pushed the doors to, Kennedy threw her upper body flat, bracing herself against the floor of the van, and kicked the doors into his face. The knife flew from his hand, bouncing end over end across the ground, and he stumbled backward, going down on one knee.

Kennedy squirmed and rolled out of the van, aiming to hit the ground running. But the assassin was already scrambling to his feet again, blocking the only way out of the narrow cul-de-sac. She feinted left, then when he took a step towards her she sprinted past him on the right. But even doped and confused he was faster than her. He swivelled and turned, tripping her.

Kennedy rolled as she landed, and managed to get her feet back under her. The Messenger moved around her, putting himself between her and the exit again. Blood was brimming behind his clenched teeth and his eyes were glazing over, but the look on his face was one of murderous rage. He fumbled inside his jacket and came out with two slender wooden rods like the handles of a tiny skipping rope. A moment later, as it caught the light, Kennedy registered the almost invisible wire suspended between them.

The man advanced on her and Kennedy retreated before him. But a handful of baby steps left her with the wall pressing against her shoulders. She looked left, then right: she had nowhere to go. As the Messenger raised his strangling cord, she bowed her head and turned her back on him.

He dropped the cord into place around her neck and she stepped back into his embrace as though welcoming her death.

The sica, which she'd snatched up from the ground when she'd fallen, was clutched tightly between her bound hands. The assassin walked onto its blade, which sank hilt-deep into his stomach. Kennedy twisted, moving her hands up, down, across. *Seppuku* by proxy.

The dying man made a choking sound of pain and protest. She heard the muted impact as he fell to his knees, and only then turned to look. He was folded around the obscene wound, probably already dead, although his staring eyes seemed troubled by some unfathomable realisation. Kennedy told herself that the fentalyn must have taken away most of the pain. The strangling cord remained around her neck, its wooden grips dangling like the loose ends of a bow tie, as she addressed herself to the problem of freeing her hands with a poisoned blade.

Diema dropped her hands to her sides and waited. She recognised Hifela's voice, of course: recognised it twice over, from the tapes she'd studied in Ginat'Dania and from the shouted command she'd heard when she sang her blessing from the top of the fig tree that she should be killed, no matter who she was or where she came from.

So she knew what was about to happen, apart from the precise details. The gun was pressed into the hollow at the base of her skull, perfectly positioned for an execution shot.

'I have a question,' she said.

'So do I,' Hifela told her, his voice relaxed, almost casual. 'Two questions, in fact. How did you find us and who else knows? Obviously we'll ask the *rhaka* the same things, at greater length and with more emphatic punctuation. But since we have this moment, little sister, answer me truly. Are the four of you alone here or will I have to kill again tomorrow?'

'We're alone.'

Hifela made a half-swallowed sound like a snort or a chuckle. 'Fascinating. Perhaps we should have let you come, then, and visit us at home. It might have been cheaper, in terms of lives lost.'

Diema stiffened. 'I killed no one,' she blurted.

'Not you. But your burly friend killed at least one of the men I sent against him and maimed another. And the grenade that failed to kill you took down one of ours. So. Now I've got half an answer. The other half, please. How did you find us?'

'The frontispiece of Toller's book. It showed this hill. We guessed the rest.'

'A prodigious guess. But yes, I see. There is a trail of logic there and we should not have placed ourselves so squarely at the end of it. Elegantly done, sister. Your question, now, before I fertilise this soil with your bone and blood and brains.'

'You'd do that?' It sounded weak, childish even, like a plea for mercy. But it wasn't, it was a plea for the world to make sense and be as it was meant to be. But then, perhaps only a child would expect that.

'Didn't this soldier do as much, when he killed himself?' Hifela asked her. 'Didn't his life, his death, weigh as much as yours?' Diema saw the flaw in that reasoning, but with her mind in turmoil, she couldn't articulate it. Hifela didn't seem to need an answer. 'In growing older,' he said, as though he'd read her mind, 'I've become impatient of excess baggage. The sacred, the solemn, the binding, these things are terrible weights. I travel lighter now. So yes, I'll kill you without a thought. I'm a killer, after all. Why set limits to such a clean and simple thing? And now, this is your last chance to ask your question.'

'I withdraw my question,' she murmured.

'Really?' For the first time there was something like interest in the man's voice. 'Then tell me, little girl, just for the sake of curiosity, what would it have been?'

'It would have been this. Why did you follow him? Why did you go with Ber Lusim when he spat on his duty and forsook his people? Did you really think his conscience outweighed the whole of Ginat'Dania? But I think you already answered me. If nothing is sacred, what would stop you from doing those things?'

'Ah, but I didn't say that *nothing* was sacred.' Hifela tapped her lightly on the nape of the neck with the barrel of the gun, as if he was a teacher rebuking a thoughtless child. 'Did I?'

She turned her head, very slowly. She knew this might

410

provoke him to shoot her, but since he was going to shoot her anyway she didn't feel as though she had very much to lose – and she wanted, perhaps because of that contemptuous tone, that contemptuous tap, to stare him down as she died. 'Then that can be my question,' she said, trying to find the same tone, trying to spit at least a little of his contempt back in his face.

He tilted his head a little to one side, but the gun – now pointing at her throat – didn't waver by so much as a millimetre. He frowned. 'I'm sorry?'

'What's sacred to you, Hifela?'

'Ah.' He smiled – a sad, bleak smile, a little twisted at the corner. 'I thought that was obvious. *He* is, of course.'

The moment lengthened. Diema closed her mouth, which had fallen open. Hifela laughed out loud – and though when he smiled he was mocking himself, now he was mocking her. 'Oh, child, if you'd lived longer, you'd have had a lot to learn. But perhaps God lets us die when he thinks we've reached the end of our learning. When our minds close, and all we can do is live, the way animals and vegetables do. Shut your eyes.'

'No,' she said.

'If you close your eyes, it will be easier.'

'Then you close yours,' Leo Tillman suggested.

The boom of a single gunshot, from very close, deafened Diema all over again.

56

If Tillman had been shooting with his right hand – if his right hand had still been functioning – he would have tried for the kill shot, even though Diema and the cadaverous killer were so close together that they were practically touching.

He'd approached the two of them from down the slope, from the direction of the hotel. He had the GPS signal to go on – Diema had kept the pellet in her pocket when she gave him the tracker – but even without that, the shredded foliage, bullet-torn bark and spilled blood made a trail that an idiot could have followed. Twice he'd encountered seriously wounded Messengers, crippled by leg shots but still in the fight, and twice he'd had to exchange fire with them, leaving them dead behind him.

Once he was close enough, he tracked Diema by the sound of her voice, and the other voice that was speaking to her. Tillman had learned stealth in the jungles of three continents, and besides, Diema and the pale man were thoroughly engrossed in their conversation. They didn't hear his approach.

But he was carrying – in his left hand – a gun he'd never fired. Only a lunatic would have relied on a weapon like that when friend and foe were standing cheek by jowl. So he got in as close as he could without alerting the skull-faced man to his presence, fired into the air and threw himself forward in a headlong charge.

The gunshot did what it was meant to do. It told the assassin there was a clear and present danger, shifting his attention from the girl to Tillman.

But there were still ten feet of ground to cover. Enhanced by kelalit, Hifela brought his gun around and fired before Tillman had travelled half that distance.

Enhanced by kelalit, Diema slammed the heel of her hand into the assassin's wrist, pushing the gun even further in the direction in which it was already moving. The shot went wide.

Then Tillman hit Hifela like a tank.

But in the split-second before that impact, Hifela had assessed the changed situation and, it seemed, made a decision. He had two enemies now, instead of one. Order of preference had become an issue.

He dipped and pivoted, and though Diema saw the kick coming she couldn't do much more than roll with it. The heel of Hifela's foot struck her in the side of the head, slamming her backward and down the slope in an uncontrolled sprawl.

There was a price to pay. Hifela was off-balance when Tillman hit him and had to take the big man's attack head-on. Tillman's left hand swept down, clubbing the gun loose from Hifela's grip and he followed up with a scything blow to Hifela's stomach. The Messenger simply endured it, noticing that his opponent's fist had slowed in the instant before impact, suggesting some sort of injury to his right arm. With Tillman now well within his reach, he hit back hard and fast.

A storm of kicks, punches and jabs rode down Tillman's guard in an instant and he staggered back, dropping his own gun and taking damage even as he blocked. Hifela followed him, keeping up the pressure. Tillman knew at once that he was outclassed. He wasn't going to win this fight, and barring outside factors he wouldn't even be able to draw it out all that long. One of those outside factors was stirring on the ground behind Hifela. Tillman tried to move round in the opposite direction, forcing the assassin to turn his back on Diema, but it was all he could do to stay on his feet.

The girl made her move, but Hifela could see her out of the corner of his eye. He leaped over her dive, turned as he came down and launched a kick at Tillman's midriff, blindsiding Tillman and forcing him to turn and take the kick on the thigh as the only possible defence. There was no opening, no hole in the terrifying virtuosity of his violence.

Diema tried again. Her movements were sluggish – the blow to the head had left her hurt and dazed – but she struggled up onto hands and knees and gathered herself for another lunge.

Without seeming even to look at her, Hifela scraped dust and gravel into her face with a sweep of his heel, then wheeled on the spot to kick her in the exact same spot, on the side of the head. As she fell, he shifted his balance and did the same thing again. This time Diema raised her hands in a block, but too slowly. Hifela's booted foot went through her guard without slowing and slammed into her temple.

It was a taunt, as much as anything, a demonstration of his absolute power over the two of them. But there was an opening this time, the last kick obliging the assassin to angle his body a little away from Tillman. Tillman launched himself into the gap, fists flailing, but Hifela was gone – falling out of reach, rolling, coming up with Tillman's gun in his hand. He had anticipated the move, probably invited it. He was ahead of them all the way.

Staring down the barrel of the Beretta, Tillman – who counted his shots obsessively – knew that this was the best chance he was going to get. Probably the only chance. He walked into Hifela's attack as the slide of the empty gun jammed open with a flat thud, and wrapped the other man in a tight bear-hug.

It was scarcely a tactic. He was able to trap the assassin's right arm against his body, but his left arm was free. He was only hoping to hold the man more or less immobile while the girl got her act together and attacked him from behind.

Hifela responded by hammer-punching him in the head with jarring, agonising force. Tillman saw stars – then the darkness between the stars. He leaned in close, burying his face in the assassin's shoulder, forcing him to bring his arm down at an oblique angle and so taking some of the force out of the second punch, and the third.

There was no fourth. Trying to break Tillman's hold, Hifela's groping, testing fingers had found the hilt of the sica that was still embedded in Tillman's shoulder. He pulled it out and drove it in again, higher and at a more oblique angle.

The shock of agony, and the near severing of his trapezius muscle, caused Tillman to release his hold. Leaning away from him, Hifela brought the knife up in a diagonal slash across the other man's chest. Then he drew it up and back for a final thrust into Tillman's heart.

Taking the risk that Tillman had shrunk from, Diema shot the assassin in the head. The bullet went obliquely through Hifela's skull, entering via the left occipital lobe and exiting through the orbit of his left eye.

Hifela's body – that exquisite instrument – rebelled against him. He froze with the knife still in the air, though his hand trembled violently as though he were still trying hard to bring it down. Then the spasm passed and he lunged.

Tillman caught Hifela's wrist in mid-air and turned him,

slowly, inexorably, so that they were both sideways on to Diema. He could see her on her knees, her face stupid with concussion, her eyes glazed, the gun – Hifela's own Sig Sauer Pro 2022 – held before her like an offering at an altar nobody else could see. The head shot must have been a one-in-a-million chance, but this was a gift and she took it.

In fact, since the gun had eleven bullets left in its magazine, she took it eleven times.

Hifela crashed down onto his knees in the dirt, then fell full-length. Tillman fell beside him, unable to hold himself upright any more. He ended up staring into Hifela's slack, haunted face.

'*Bilo b'eyet ha yehuani*,' Hifela wheezed. '*Siruta muot dil kasyeh shoh*.'

The words had a liquid undertow, but they were distinct, forced out of him along with the last of his spirit.

57

Kennedy found them first – following the same trail that Tillman had followed – but she knew she couldn't be far ahead of the pack. The local police – it was the *Çevik kuvvet*, the anti-terrorist squad – had gone directly to the hotel, because dozens of witnesses had seen shots fired there and there were bodies, one lying face down next to the outdoor pool and the other in the staff car park. But shots and explosions had been heard in the parkland on Gellert Hill, too, so that would be their next stop.

Tillman was unconscious and almost certainly dying. The ground around him was so saturated with his blood that Kennedy's shoes sank into it. Blood was still welling from deep wounds in his shoulder and across his chest – but weakly and fitfully, like the last knockings coaxed from an almost empty barrel.

The man lying next to him was dead. A dozen bullet wounds, each a black disc ringed with red-brown crust, stood out like withered flowers on his dead white skin.

Then there was another man, also dead, but with no wounds on him apart from a damaged hand – and Diema, trying to stand and failing. The front of the girl's shirt was drenched with vomit and her bloodshot eyes seemed unable to focus.

Kennedy supported her weight and helped her into a sitting position, her back to a tree. 'You're concussed,' she said. 'Don't try to move.' Kennedy's gaze kept sliding back to Tillman, his ashen face and the red ruin of his shirt. She had to do something. It was probably too late, but she had to try.

She took out her phone and started to dial the emergency number. If Hungary was in the EU, it ought to be 112. If not she'd try the operator and ask to be put through.

Diema's hand locked on Kennedy's wrist and dragged her hand down. 'Channel zero,' she slurred.

'I'm calling an ambulance,' Kennedy said, pulling her hand free. 'Try to stay awake.'

'Channel zero!' The girl fumbled with the walkie-talkie and unhooked it from her belt on the third try. But then she just stared at it, unable to see the keys clearly enough to operate them.

Kennedy took the walkie-talkie from Diema and reset it. 'What's channel zero?' she asked.

'Tell them … where we are.' The girl's hands were at her belt again. Kennedy opened the channel, heard the crackle of a live line.

'*Ayn?*' It was a man's voice, clipped and clear.

Kennedy's scalp prickled. 'We're on Gellert Hill,' she said.

A pause. 'Who is this, please?'

'Diema is here,' Kennedy said. 'Diema. Diema Beit Evrom.'

'*Pere echon!*' Diema cried, sounding like a drunkard. '*Pere echon adir!*'

'I said—'

'I hear her,' the man said quickly. 'On Gellert Hill. North side or south?'

'North. Just above the Gellert Hotel.'

'Keep the channel open. We will come.'

Kennedy lowered the walkie-talkie and stared at Diema – or rather, at what Diema was holding in the palm of her hand. A small hypodermic, of the kind that diabetics use to dose themselves with insulin, and a snap-in ampoule of clear liquid. They fell into the dirt as the girl's hand swayed.

'*Dal le beho'ota*,' Diema said.

Kennedy took the needle, waved it in the girl's face. 'Diema, what do you want me to do with this?' she yelled. 'In English! I speak English!'

The girl's eyes swam briefly into focus.

'Put it in his heart,' she said.

58

There was a time of pain, and of regrouping, but it was a short time. There was a great deal still to be done.

Nahir's team of local *Elohim*, loyal to the People and the oath they'd sworn, took Tillman off Gellert Hill in broad daylight, in the hollow interior of a gurney rigged to look like an ice cream cart. Diema and Kennedy walked beside them, their battered faces hidden behind masks in the likeness of Punchinello, the comical child-murderer and wife-beater from the Italian *commedia dell'arte*. The bodies of the *Elohim* who'd died on the hill were also removed, by some other means into which Diema and Kennedy were in no condition to enquire.

In the nearest safe house, behind the boarded-up frontage of a former florist's shop on Stollár Béla Street, Diema was examined by *Elohim* medics. Her concussion was mild, and already passing, but she had two cracked ribs, which they bound up, and a broken finger that she didn't even remember acquiring. She impatiently refused the pain relieving drugs offered to her, and – as soon as she could think straight – asked after the health of her team.

The prisoners, Nahir told her, were in safe keeping. The Englishman would probably die, but the others were in relatively sound condition and ready to be questioned at her convenience.

Diema stood on tip-toe to bring her face as close to Nahir's as possible, and told him that it would be inconvenient for the Englishman to die. So inconvenient, in fact, that if it happened she would see that Nahir spent the next few years in the main cloaca of Ginat'Dania, cleaning out sewage conduits with his tongue.

'I am still Kuutma's emissary,' she reminded him, with ferocious calm. 'And as long as I'm here in your city, you answer to me.'

Doctors were summoned and assigned. Leo Tillman's condition was looked to and addressed.

Next, Diema had them find Ben Rush and bring him. He was in Uzsoci Hospital, serving as a sewing sampler for a nurse with well-muscled arms, several yards of suture and a robust work ethic. Thoroughly worked over by fists, boots and many ad hoc implements, the boy was unrecognisable. He had already had seventy-three stitches put into various wounds in his face, scalp, shoulder and side. The nurse was optimistic about the sight in his left eye, but only in the long term. For now it was swollen shut and ringed with thirty-five of those stitches.

When two strange men turned up at Rush's bedside and told him that Diema had sent them, Rush assumed they were there to kill him and refused point-blank to go with them, struggling to maintain control of his bladder. 'She says,' Shraga added, delivering Diema's message with scrupulous care, 'that nobody besides you has ever complained about her breasts, and that a little boy who likes big breasts probably has an unhealthy sexual fixation on his mother.' Rush changed his mind and agreed to accompany them, although he was still scared of having his throat cut right up to the moment when he saw her.

He told Diema what he'd done, and how he'd survived. The paint bomb had masked his face, or rather it had given his face at least a passing resemblance to the faces of the two dozen other people who were within its effective radius when it went off. And since most of those people were already piling onto him, each of them eager to be the first to push his teeth down his throat, the confusion was compounded. The Messenger sent to kill him, finding himself on the fringes of a spreading mêlée, and with the sound of police sirens already tainting the summer breeze, had quietly withdrawn.

Rush also remembered to thank Diema for the warning she'd given him when the knife-man first appeared. She told him she resented the bullets she'd had to use up, and that on future occasions she wouldn't waste a second of her precious time on his survival. Privately, she was both surprised and (reluctantly) impressed that the boy had come out of the battle alive – and that he'd done it using the paint bomb she'd offered him as a mark of contempt. She remembered one of her teachers telling her, after she'd fluked a perfect score in a test, that it was better to be lucky than to be good. The boy was probably too stupid to realise that he'd just used up a lifetime's luck in one go.

By this time, Diema had extorted further concessions from Nahir's people. Kennedy had been moved to a cell with a bed in it, and Tillman to a thoroughly disinfected room in which a full trauma suite had been painstakingly assembled.

Diema demanded a report and the doctors obediently provided one. The Adamite, they told her, had lost more than two litres of blood – close to the maximum that a human body can shed without shutting down for good. The anti-toxin that Diema had had Kennedy give him had probably prevented, by a hair's breadth or so, his slipping into clinical shock, and

422

allowed him to survive long enough to be given a transfusion, but his wounds were terrible. The damage to his right arm, particularly, was likely to be irreversible, and they wouldn't be able to tell whether there'd been any brain damage until he recovered consciousness – for which the doctors could offer no realistic estimate.

She went to see him. A doctor was examining Tillman's pupillary responses, but he stepped back from the bed when Diema entered the room and waited with his arms at his sides.

'Go outside,' Diema told him. 'Stay there until I call you.'

The doctor inclined his head and retreated.

She went to the bed and looked down at Tillman. He looked old and weak, and more than a little ugly, his skin mottled red and white with broken blood vessels, his cheeks sunken. Tubes for fluid and wiring for diagnostics decorated his flesh or tunnelled into it. A faint smell of sweat and disinfectant rose from him: the smell of bad news delivered in well-lit rooms.

Diema wrestled with the riddle, but she couldn't solve it without a clue of some kind, and everybody who could have given her the clue was dead. Her mother, Rebecca, who had taken her own life. Kuutma-that-was, who in the end died because he grieved for Rebecca too much. And her father – the father she remembered, lifting her and carrying her away (as she cried and kicked) from her half-finished drawing. The father who lived mostly in the scorched earth between the thickets of her memory, and who had torched most of that ground himself.

Are you him?

The red-and-white thing on the bed, trailing strings and wires like a marionette, couldn't tell her. She thought of Punchinello. No matter what the question might be, Punchinello's only answer was to grab his stick, which he cradled like a child in his two folded arms, and commit another murder. And she thought of Wile E. Coyote, whose implacable enmity for the Roadrunner was the core of his being.

She had wanted Tillman to be like that: a cartoon creation, simple and predictable and easy to hate. That was how she had always seen him, even before she knew what cartoons were. She could still see him that way, with only a little effort.

But here was someone else, who had come to her when she needed him instead of trying to save the *rhaka* who was his friend and ally, who had faced down Hifela, the Face of the Skull, with his arm all but useless, and let his chest be sliced like pork rind while he did what he could to give her a clear shot.

Hifela's words echoed in her head. *Y'tuh gemae le. Net ya neiu.*

One of the People had tried to kill her. And the father of her flesh had saved her. She had to acknowledge that paradox, and deal with it.

Or become a cartoon character herself.

It was time to stop putting off the inevitable. She went to see Kennedy – who went off like a bomb as soon as the door was opened.

'Where's Leo? What have you done to him?' The woman took a step towards Diema, not in the least deterred by the two *Elohim* who stood, stoical and watchful, to either side of her. 'If he's dead—'

'He's alive,' Diema said. 'But only just. Sit down, Heather. Please.'

Kennedy obeyed – perhaps because hearing about Tillman's condition had taken some of the strength from her, or perhaps because she'd registered that Diema had just used her Christian name and knew from this that something significant had changed.

Diema sent the Messengers away with a curt gesture and closed the door behind them.

'Tell me,' Kennedy said, her voice tight. 'Tell me how he is.'

Diema recapped the blood loss, the chest and shoulder wounds, the continuing coma. It was a concise, full and factual summary. Her teachers would have been proud of her.

'But he'll recover,' Kennedy said, not quite asking, still less pleading. 'This is Leo. He's going to get back up again.'

'They think so,' Diema said. 'Everything except the shoulder. They say the damage to the muscle was very severe. They did what they could to knit it back together again, but they can't promise.'

'And who are *they*, Diema?' Kennedy demanded savagely. 'The doctors you trusted his life to? This place isn't a hospital. It's a prison. So where in God's name do you source your doctors from?'

'It's not a prison,' Diema said. 'It's just a safe house. The doctors are on staff here, but they're in touch with other doctors in Ginat'Dania. They've spoken to the most skilful of our healers, taken advice. And those other doctors are on their way here, now. I asked for them to be sent and they're coming.' This wasn't a boast: it was just a statement of fact. Kuutma had promised her all the support she needed, without question. She had told him she needed this.

'I want to see him,' Kennedy said.

'He's unconscious. He won't know you're there.'

'I want to see him.'

Diema nodded. 'All right.'

'And Rush. What happened to Rush? I want to see both of them.'

'Yes,' Diema said. 'I promise. But I've got something else to ask you first. The mission has reached—'

'Oh my god,' Kennedy raged. 'Don't. Don't even talk about that. We did what we could. We did everything we possibly could, but we were outclassed. We should have known that before we went in. It was *not* our fault that the mission was a fiasco!'

'No.'

'If it had been anyone but Leo, I would have *known* it was madness.' Kennedy was speaking to herself now, rather than to Diema. She shook her head in dismayed wonder. 'I thought he was some kind of bloody Superman. I thought he couldn't fail. And so I let him go up against those . . . those monsters, and I went up against them myself. As if we had a chance. But we didn't. We failed because we had to fail, Diema.'

'We didn't fail.'

'Because nobody could take on a whole—'

'Heather, we didn't fail.'

Finally, Kennedy wound down, assimilating what she was being told. 'What?' she muttered, confused. 'What are you saying? They all died. Or else escaped. We got nothing.'

'We got everything we needed. I know where Ber Lusim is. And we're going in. We're just waiting for the equipment. That's why I came here. To ask you if you want to come. I think you've earned that right. And I think . . .' She hesitated. It was hard to frame the words, around the bulky, ugly concepts that they covered. 'I think you'll be safer if you stick with me than if I leave you here.'

Kennedy's unwavering stare was full of surprise and mistrust. Perhaps there was an accusation there, too.

'I'm not asking you to kill anyone,' Diema said. 'You already told me that wasn't something you felt you could do.' She'd seen the police reports from the Gellert Hotel by this time and knew what Kennedy had done with a sica to a trained assassin, but she felt that might be a conversation best left for another time. 'For your insights. I need you as a detective.'

Kennedy was implacable – and bitter. 'To detect what? Something you say you've already found? Do you think I just fell out of a tree, girl? Do you think I don't know how you spoon-fed us all the way down the line? You let Leo get a fix on your bike so he'd follow you to that factory. You let us find Toller's book for ourselves and then went ahead and told us what was in it. You only needed Leo to cut throats – and you only needed me to bring in Leo. Which, God forgive me, I did. But I'm all done, now. You go on and play your games.'

'But it was you that brought us here,' Diema said. 'You and the boy. You put together all the things you knew and made sense out of them. Gave me a direction. I want you to be with me when I go into Ber Lusim's house, in case that's needed again. Whatever's in there, whatever he's still got planned, it might help me if I can see it through your eyes.'

'That's a pity. They're staying right here, along with the rest of me. Along with Leo.'

Diema's impatience made her reckless. She slapped Kennedy hard across the face.

Kennedy's response, before she'd even registered the pain of the blow, was to slam her fist into Diema's jaw. Diema took the blow without a sound, without even wincing.

'Your pain,' Diema said, feeling the thin trickle of blood running down from the corner of her mouth, 'and my pain. Are they the same?'

Kennedy had stepped back, arms raised, readying herself for a fight. It didn't seem to bother her that it was likely to be a very short fight. But the question troubled her. She dropped her

427

hands again, nonplussed. Then after a moment she shrugged it off, making a gesture of disgust and dismissal.

'Please get out of here,' she told Diema. 'Let me see Leo, or get out. I've got nothing for you.'

'Answer the question. Your pain—'

'How do I know if they're the same?' Kennedy yelled. 'I'm not inside your mind, am I? I don't know what you feel. Or *if* you feel. I don't know anything about you except your name, and even that's kind of a grey area.'

'But we're all the same,' Diema said. 'Under the skin. That's what you believe, isn't it?'

Kennedy stared at her, angry and incredulous. 'Never mind what I believe. It's not what you believe. You believe in a separate creation – your people and the rest of the world. The chosen ones and the dregs at the bottom of the barrel.'

'So which of us should care the most about a million dead?' Diema asked.

She didn't expect an answer, but she was pleased when the woman reacted – a succession of emotions appearing briefly in her face, like a slide show. At home in Ginat'Dania, Diema was used to saying what she thought, and even more used to refusing to do so. But in the Adamite world, talking was like fighting. You said what would give you advantage.

'You don't need me,' Kennedy said. 'You've got everything you need.' But there was no conviction in her voice, and a moment later she spoke again. 'Did you manage to take one of Ber Lusim's people alive, after all? Have you been interrogating him all this time?'

Diema was certain that she'd won, but she didn't let that awareness show in her face or her tone.

'There'll be a meeting,' she told Kennedy, 'in half an hour's time. By then, the equipment I've asked for will have arrived and we'll be ready to go in. I'd like you to be there. You can make a final decision when you've heard me out.'

She left, nodding to the *Elohim* to lock the door behind her. There was no need to talk any more.

Except to Nahir, who was still uncertain about what she was asking him to do and would need to be argued with. And to the boy, who would just have to do as he was told.

The boy.

Ronald Stephen Pinkus, risen from the grave yet again to haunt and torment her.

'We set up an ambush, but it didn't work. In fact, we got ambushed ourselves.'

Diema's voice rang out, almost too loud in the small, crowded room. Along with Nahir, there were more than forty Messengers, many of whom were recently arrived. They sat in silence on folding chairs, flimsy things of stainless steel and black plastic, dressed in the hand-woven linen of their home. They were vectors of terrible violence, eerily suspended. Birds of prey, somehow brought to earth and persuaded to pose for a group photograph.

In their midst sat Kennedy and Rush, ringed by empty seats. Nobody wanted to sit next to the *rhaka*, the wolf-woman, and take the taint of her proximity.

Diema stopped, alarmed, and cleared her throat. There had been a shrill, rising note to her voice. She sounded like an idiot. Worse, she sounded like a child. The palms of her hands were hot and moist.

For all the things that she had done, and had had done to her, over the last three years, she had never been called on to speak in public. She feared now that it might lie outside her skill set.

She tried again. 'The idea was to lure one of Ber Lusim's Messengers into trying to capture Heather Kennedy – as they'd already tried to do in England – by making it appear that we might know where their base was.' She looked from one grave face to another. 'That part worked. Except they didn't just come for Heather Kennedy, they came for all of us. And they didn't send one Messenger. They sent many.'

'They only sent one after me,' Rush said. 'Turned out to be a mistake.' Given the state of his face, and the fact that his muffled, distorted voice was coming out of one side of a hideously swollen jaw, it could only have been intended as a joke. Forty *Elohim*, with no sense of humour when it came to their holy calling, stared at him in grim silence.

'There were more than a dozen in all,' Diema said, hastily pulling their attention back to her. 'We can't say for sure how many, because they waited until we were separated and attacked us in smaller groups. The last to fall was Hifela, who all of you know, or at least have heard of.'

The room was suddenly sibilant with a dozen whispered conversations. Diema waited them out. She'd used that phrasing deliberately and she wanted her countrymen to reflect for a moment on what it meant – that twelve *Elohim* had been sent against three Adamites, two of whom were sitting in front of them, still breathing.

'We fought Hifela, on the slope of Gellert Hill,' she said. 'By we, I mean myself and ... and Leo Tillman, known to the People because he was once ...' Her throat was dry and she had to clear it again. 'Known to the People in other times, and other contexts. Hifela fought hard and might have won. Some of you have seen his body, so you know. It took a dozen bullets to kill him.

'And as he lay on the ground, beside us, he spoke these words. "*Bilo b'eyet ha yehuani. Siruta muot dil kasyeh shoh.*"'

More murmurs around the room. Most of the Messengers looked puzzled or disconcerted. Nahir frowned. 'He cannot have said that,' he told Diema.

'I was ten feet away from him, brother. I tell you what I heard.'

'Then he meant the teacher. The apostate, Shekolni. The ground where he walks.'

'That's not what he said.'

'Some of us,' Kennedy said, cutting in loudly, 'are Aramaically challenged. If there's any point in our being here, someone's going to have to translate.'

Nahir glanced at her once, coldly appraising her, then turned back to Diema. '*Is* there?' he asked. 'Any point in their being here? Many of us have wondered.'

Diema answered Kennedy's question, ignoring Nahir's. 'Hifela said, "Take me to my Summoner. Let me die on holy ground."'

'And why is that significant?' Kennedy demanded.

'Because the only holy ground is Ginat'Dania,' Diema said.

There was a sense, rather than a sound, of the assembled *Elohim* drawing in their breath, of the tension in the air ratcheting itself up a notch more, and then maybe another notch on top of that. Diema met Kennedy's gaze. The boy would be clueless, but the *rhaka* would know how thin this tightrope they were walking was – as thin as the edge of a blade. You didn't talk to the children of Adam about Ginat'Dania. Out of all the things you didn't do, it was perhaps the one you didn't do the most. In a society that lived at the cusp of the catastrophe curve, the instinct for self-preservation ran very deep, and subsumed all other instincts.

'In spite of the latitude granted to you,' murmured Nahir softly, 'you will be careful what you say.'

Diema looked him in the eye, without flinching. This was a moment that had to be walked through, the way you walk over fire. 'The woman, Heather Kennedy,' she said, 'and the man, Benjamin Rush, already know that Ginat'Dania exists. Moreover, they know that it used to exist here. It was necessary to tell them these things in order to follow Ber Lusim's trail as far as we have – which you, Nahir, for all your resources, weren't able to do.'

'I have a knife,' a woman in one of the rear ranks of the Messengers called out. 'And a conscience. Tell me why I shouldn't exercise them both.'

The woman was sitting directly behind Kennedy. Kennedy didn't look round: she knew this was Diema's play, and she had better sense than to get in the way of it.

'Exercise your brain, sister,' Diema said coldly. 'That's the part of you that you're neglecting. The woman knew for years and Kuutma spared her. More. Kuutma sanctioned her involvement in this. She has Kuutma's blessing – the first Adamite in a hundred lifetimes to be so blessed. All *you* have is a wish that things could be like they used to be in the old days. But the old days are dead. And if you cling to them now, you'll die, too.'

It wasn't – quite – a threat. It was hard to say what it was. The Messenger opened her mouth, but closed it again without speaking. Blood had rushed to her face, and she bowed her head to hide it, discomfited.

'Ginat'Dania,' Diema said, to the room at large, 'the living and eternal Ginat'Dania, is far away from this place, and from Adamite eyes. But three hundred years ago, Ginat'Dania stood here. In the caves under Gellert Hill and Castle Hill, and under the river Danube itself. That's where Hifela was asking to be taken. That's where Ber Lusim has set up his house – in a maze

432

of tunnels and chambers vast enough to house a million people. It's the perfect hiding place, if you're hiding from Adamites. But not if you're hiding from us. We have maps of the city dating back to the time when it was alive and we can mount a search that will bring them into our hands.'

'I thought your hands had to be empty.' Ben Rush shrugged in mock-apology as the holy killers all turned to stare balefully at him again. 'I mean, I thought that was the point. Human lives are expendable, but you can't kill each other. And you don't have Tillman to hide behind any more. So what, did you push through a rule-change? You've got a hunting licence now?'

Diema ignored the sarcastic inflection: the boy's jibe was as good a set-up line as anything she could have scripted.

'The Adamite mind,' she said to the *Elohim*, smiling, inviting them to smile at Rush's idiocy. 'You see how little they can grasp, even when we put the answers in their hands? This is why we don't have to be afraid of what they know. In the end, what they know always adds up to nothing.'

'I know this much—' Rush blurted, but Kennedy's hard grip on his arm stopped him right there.

'No hunting licence,' Diema said, opening one of the boxes and reaching into it. 'The rules – the rules that actually mean something – don't change. But when a new situation arises, we apply the rules in different ways.'

She showed them the dart-rifle – the bigger, meaner brother of Kennedy's Dan-inject – and how it worked. She told them that it would topple Ber Lusim's *Elohim* without any risk of killing them. She omitted to mention the fact that the bullets that had slain Hifela had been fired by her, rather than Leo Tillman, that she'd already breached that final taboo.

Once they learned that, her life would be over.

59

Ber Lusim was grieving, alone in his room – a monastic cell carved into solid granite, without a window and with only a natural fissure in the rock for a door.

His *Elohim* absented themselves from his grief, recognising that it was not their property; not part of their leader's public self at all, but an outpouring from his innermost soul.

Avra Shekolni showed less compunction. He came to the door of the cell and sat down there, with his back to the wall, tapping at the rock with his silver-ringed hand in a simple, repetitive rhythm.

After some little while, Ber Lusim came out to him.

'Avra,' he said, 'I'm poor company right now. Please, take your music and your consolations somewhere else, for a while, and I'll come to you when I can.'

Shekolni looked up at him from under lowered brows, stern and humourless. 'Have I offered you consolation, Ber Lusim?' he asked.

'Blessed one, you have not. I assumed you came here—'

'Because you've lost your friend and you find the loss hard to bear,' Shekolni said. 'Yes, of course. But it doesn't follow, Ber Lusim, that I came to tell you how to bear that loss.'

Ber Lusim was puzzled and unnerved by this speech, and by

the tone in which it was delivered. He didn't know from which direction to approach it. 'Hifela was not my friend,' he said at last. 'He was my servant, and the first among my *Elohim*. I relied on him in everything.'

'He was your friend,' Shekolni snapped. 'Ber Lusim, God is not a lawyer or a politician. He knows the love you felt for Hifela, and he knows that his loss weakens you as a man, not just as a leader of men.'

The prophet's voice rose, and he rose up with it, climbing to his feet to face Ber Lusim, with one hand raised as though he were preaching in a pulpit.

'But to mourn him? To mourn him now? Are you mad, Ber Lusim? Has this loss turned your brain?' He clamped his hands on Ber Lusim's shoulders, stared with wide eyes into his.

Ber Lusim drew a deep breath. 'Avra, I know my duty. Nothing that has happened today will stop me from completing—'

'No! You misunderstand me!' In his exasperation, Shekolni shook the *Elohim* Summoner as a mother shakes a child. 'Think about what we're doing, my dear friend, and what will come of it when we're done. In ordinary times, to cry for a dead friend, a dead wife or husband, these things make sense. Even for someone who believes in the reality of heaven – you weep for the separation, and for how far away heaven is.'

The prophet's eyes burned and Ber Lusim felt something within him take fire from that fire. 'But now,' Shekolni growled, 'heaven is imminent. Heaven hangs just above our heads, like fruit on the lowest branch of a great tree. Do you cry, because Hifela has walked before you into the next room? Then how absurd your tears become! Hold faith now or Hifela will laugh you to shame when you meet next.'

Such was the force of the words that Ber Lusim saw, as

though in life, the face he knew so well staring at him from the heights or depth of some interior space. He nodded, blinking to clear his dazzled eyes.

'Yes,' he said. 'You're right, Avra. You're right. What must I do?'

'I've already told you what to do,' Shekolni said more gently – more like a man to another man, and less like the voice of God or Fate. 'Enact the last prophecy and take your reward. The reward of God's most faithful servant.'

The words struck home. It was – almost – all that Ber Lusim had ever wanted.

Rapid footsteps on stone made both men turn. The man who ran into view, full of urgency that bordered on panic, was Lemoi, the youngest of those who'd been foresworn with Ber Lusim and followed him into exile. He stumbled to a halt in front of them, made the sign of the noose to the prophet, but addressed his words to Ber Lusim.

'Commander, the scouts in the lower levels … The alarm has been raised. There's a breach!'

'What kind of a breach?' Ber Lusim demanded. 'Speak clearly, Lemoi. Is it Adamites? You're saying the city authorities have found us?'

'Not Adamites,' Lemoi blurted. '*Elohim.* It's an army! They've brought an army against us!'

60

Diema's Messengers, with Kennedy and Rush in tow, entered the Gellert caves through a doorway built into the back of a house.

Rush was in the rear as they descended the stairs into the house's sub-basements. Not all the way to the back, obviously. There were armed Messengers behind him, their guns casually at the ready, and more on either side of him, subtly conveying the suggestion that he was fine so long as he didn't stop, slow down, take a wrong turning, or look too much like an Adamite.

The house had stayed in *Elohim* hands ever since the city's medieval heyday, so nothing had been changed. In the lowest cellar there was a hand printing press, which looked like a rack waiting for a customer, and on the wall beside it a massive wooden compositor's frame, with hundreds of pigeonholes for movable lead type.

Diema's Messengers slid the frame aside, with some effort because the iron tracks on which it had been mounted had rusted almost solid in the damp air. As the pale men and women put their drug-boosted backs into it, there was a sound like the bellowing of bulls – and gradually, an inch at a time, the frame was moved aside and the dark tunnel beyond opened itself to their eyes.

Each of Diema's Messengers wore an AN/PVS autogated night-vision rig that turned midnight into cloudless noon. And each of them had been equipped with the new guns, in both rifle and handgun configurations.

Rush had been given a flashlight and an apple.

On the whole, he was kind of touched by the apple. Unlike the paint-bomb, it was an insult that Diema had put some thought into. She would have had to go out somewhere and buy it, or at the very least pick it up off a plate in passing and save it for him. It did something to help his bruised ego recuperate after the briefing session.

'So the flashlight's for finding my way in the dark, obviously,' he said to her now, as the *Elohim* opened the gate. 'And the apple's for if I get hungry. So what do I use for a weapon?'

The girl fixed her dark, intransitive gaze on him. 'The apple,' she said, 'is to remind you that you don't *have* a weapon. Which in turn is to remind you that you're not here to fight. If you find yourself about to get into a fight, look at the apple and it will jog your memory.'

'And then?'

'Go and hide somewhere until the urge goes away.'

As Diema turned away, Rush saw Kennedy checking the action on the M26 – the gun Diema had carried during the hotel raid. But Diema now had one of the new guns. Only Kennedy, out of all of them, had a regular handgun and Diema's permission – under certain very strictly defined circumstances – to use it.

'It's okay for you,' Rush muttered.

Kennedy smiled, without a trace of humour. 'We're going to fight in a cave, Rush,' she said. 'Against people who've lived in caves their whole lives, and have probably had years to fortify this particular cave against anything we can bring against it. So "okay" isn't the word I'd use, exactly.'

She tucked a couple of spare magazines into her belt, the gun into its holster inside her jacket. 'Diema is right, though,' she said.

'About what?' Rush demanded.

'About this fight. It's not yours, and it's not mine. Our time is going to come, and it'll be soon, but I don't think it's going to be today. So we should both of us hang well back and let them do what they've got to do'

'Then how come you get a gun and I get an apple?'

'Because I know how to shoot and you don't. Stay close to me.'

'Why?' he grunted. 'So you can patronise me some more?'

'Because you're the only one who won't be tempted to cut my throat in the dark,' Kennedy said. 'We can watch each other's backs.'

The gate was open now, the heavy wooden frame pulled all the way to the side to reveal a wide corridor that sloped down into the ground at a shallow angle. The first few yards were lined with royal blue tiles that shone with a faint, rich lustre even in the dim light of the cellar. Beyond that, there was bare granite.

Diema raised her hand in a pre-arranged signal. Six *Elohim* launched themselves into the dark at a rapid, even jog-trot.

Diema gave them thirty seconds, then signalled again. More assassins peeled away from the mass and stepped through the gate.

Rush positioned himself off to one side and watched them go. The sight made his skin prickle, and when he tried to swallow he found his mouth was dry. What was so scary about them? Or rather, what was scarier about them now than when he was in that room, surrounded by them, and they were looking at him like they were trying to decide whether killing him

439

merited the trouble of cleaning the blood off the floor afterwards? Maybe it was the night-vision goggles, which made them look like armoured owls. But no, he realised, it was something else.

It was because you expected the dominant predators in any ecosystem to hunt solo: to see these killers moving in formation, like synchronised swimmers, was like seeing the violation of some kind of physical law.

Rush was part of the last wave, with *Elohim* flanking him on either side and Diema running just ahead of him. He'd been expecting a steep descent – partly because of the angle at which the tunnel opening was set, but mostly because, well, they were going into a cave. But the house was at the foot of the hill and after the first hundred yards the corridor ended at a flight of stone steps leading upward. At the top of the steps was a broad arcade with stone pillars around its edges like a cloister. Many arched openings led off it on all four sides.

Diema and her people didn't slow down as they moved out into the larger space. They'd planned their approach already, using the old maps of the place, and each squad had learned a route from which it was not expected to deviate except in emergencies.

The team Rush was with took the third opening on their left and kept on going, through narrow tunnels with ceilings so low they had to bend their heads and vast arcades like underground cathedrals. Every few yards, it seemed, the passage they were in was intersected by others, a few angled downward but most leading up towards the heart of the hidden city, still hundreds of yards above their heads and more than a mile away in horizontal distance.

At least it wasn't totally dark. Every so often there were shafts sunk through the rock that must have been set there as lightwells, centuries before. A grey light filtered through them, presumably trickling down from the sides of the hill. Rush wondered what was at the other end of them. Rabbit holes? Wayside shrines? Probably just innocuous gratings that passers-by thought must be part of the city's drainage network. The lightwells were irrelevant to the night-sighted *Elohim*, but Rush welcomed each one as it approached and missed it as soon as it was past.

Long before they got to the upper levels, they met the first show of resistance. Rush missed it, because it was over before he realised it was happening. They ran out of the mouth of a long, straight corridor into a space that was completely unlit, and there was a flurry of movement from around them. Not even breaking stride, the *Elohim* fired in all directions, the quiet reports of their guns like the sound of a gentle rap on a door. Heavier sounds of falling bodies created a stuttering counterpoint. Not one of Ber Lusim's men got close enough to go hand-to-hand with the invaders.

Diema had taken Tillman's idea and run with it – into some pretty dark places. The weapons she'd issued to her people were modified versions of the Dan-inject dart gun she'd given to Kennedy, and the modifications were utterly terrifying. These were configured for repeating fire, and they spat multiple darts on the principle of a shotgun or scatter-gun. Diema had also taken into account how long the Messenger tagged by Kennedy had taken to fall: she'd ordered the darts to be topped off with four times the highest dosage legally available. Experiments on volunteers from among her own people had established that a single hit would put down most opponents instantly. If you took more than three or four, you'd be in serious danger of death from respiratory depression. So medics followed behind the fighters, checking the condition of the fallen and administering intravenous ampakine where needed.

The second skirmish was longer than the first, but it had the same outcome. Cornered in their rat runs, outgunned and out-manoeuvred, Ber Lusim's *Elohim* gave as good an account of themselves as they could, but though they tried to sell their lives dearly, Diema's stone-cold mercy had ensured that they couldn't find a buyer.

Other squads began to rendezvous with theirs as they progressed, having checked out the areas assigned to them and either come up empty or cleared them of opposition. The third confrontation was a massed battle lasting fully twenty minutes. Rush and Kennedy were kept well back from it, but when it was over they walked across the wide, low-ceilinged hall where it had been fought, stepping over the prone bodies of dozens of *Elohim*. Blood slicked the white stone floor, so obviously Diema's forces hadn't prevailed by dart-guns alone.

They crossed that room, and the two more, and that was as far as they got. Half an hour after they began their journey into the hill, they found their way blocked by a massive steel door that didn't look anything like an antique. One of Nahir's people examined it, and he didn't seem happy with what he found. Rush casually ambled closer to eavesdrop as the Messenger straightened and turned to Diema, but he only got an earful of Aramaic for his pains.

Diema rapped out questions, then orders, and three *Elohim* headed back the way they'd come.

'What have we got?' Kennedy asked.

'A Mosler-Bahmann safe door, apparently,' Diema said. Her tone was distant: she was thinking as she spoke. 'Shraga says the company has been bankrupt for well over a decade, so it's possible that someone else put it here. Or else Ber Lusim acquired it from a bank that had no more use from it, and brought it down here. But Shraga also says it's likely to be three feet thick and weigh forty tons. They wouldn't have been able to carry it far.'

'So you're going to burn through it?' Kennedy asked.

Diema shook her head. 'Three feet thick,' she said again. 'And the core is concrete – only the shell and frame are steel. We're going to use plastique.'

Kennedy looked shocked. 'How *much* plastique?' she asked.

'A lot. But we don't have to break through it, we just need to loosen it from the surrounding rock. Then we can tear it down. It should be simple enough.'

'Then why are you looking like you swallowed a wasp?' Rush asked.

Diema gave him a disapproving look – as though being reminded that he was still alive did nothing to improve her day. 'Because it will take time,' she said sourly. 'And the more time they buy, the less we're going to like what we find on the other side of that door.'

Avra Shekolni preached a sermon to Ber Lusim's remaining Messengers. It was short and simple, since time was pressing on all of them.

His theme was the difference between the earthly and the eternal, and how hard it is, from behind the veils of the world and the flesh, to comprehend what is everlasting and incorruptible.

'For now,' he intoned solemnly, 'we see as through a glass, darkly. But then we will see all things clearly, as they are. Now we understand in part, but then we will know and be known. As your teacher, I have tried to bring you to that glass, not so that you could peer through it, but so that you could feel how

443

close the eternal world is – how thin and fragile is the barrier behind which He waits for you. But today my purpose is lost. Today you'll step through the veil and see for yourselves what was hidden. And because of your courage, your faith, your love for each other and for the light of truth, the veil will soon be parted for ever. See, I bow my head before you. The fool has said in his heart that there is no God. But I look at you, and I know that there is. No demiurge or lesser spirit could have made anything so beautiful, so perfect as you. Give me your blessing, my sons, my angels. Your blessing, and then – if I may ask this, if I am worthy – your lives.'

Some of them wiped tears from their eyes as he walked among them: some let them fall down their cheeks, unashamed. Some of them reached out to touch his hands or the hem of his robe. All were preparing themselves, mentally, for what was to come.

Ber Lusim came to Shekolni, and they embraced briefly.

'It should not have happened like this,' Ber Lusim said. He didn't say whether he meant the invasion, Hifela's death, or what was about to come.

'It happens as God wills, Ber Lusim. I don't need to lecture you on predestination. You are predestination's agent. This is no tragedy – and indeed, it seems to me that we've had this conversation already, only a short time ago. The only thing that would be tragic, now, would be if these final, most necessary things were left undone. It would be as though we climbed a great mountain, and turned around when the summit was in sight. We would be fools, when we thought to be saints. And I think that God probably finds fools harder to love than sinners.'

'I hadn't looked to be either,' Ber Lusim said. 'Go well, Avra.'

'And you, my dear friend. I'll see you soon.'

*

444

It took ten minutes to put the explosives in place. Diema used the time to satisfy herself absolutely that there was no easier way. She had had some hope that one of the adjacent walls might have been built during the time of the city, but they were all original rock – and far thicker than the vault door. That, of course, was why the door had been placed here rather than somewhere else. Ber Lusim had chosen his ground, and chosen it well.

'Does this seem a little crazy to you?' Rush asked Diema, as they jog-trotted with the *Elohim* back through several chambers to what Shraga had designated as the safe distance.

'As compared to what?' Diema asked dryly.

Shraga passed out earplugs and told them to breathe through their mouths from the start of the countdown right up to the detonation. It wasn't unusual for a powerful shock wave to rupture eardrums, but if you had your mouth open, the Eustachian tubes should equalise the pressure and stop that from happening.

He offered the detonator to Diema, but she shook her head. 'You're the expert,' she said. 'Go ahead.'

Shraga counted down from ten, both aloud and with his fingers. Then he pressed the button.

Even with the earplugs, and the distance, the sound of the explosion felt to Diema like a physical blow, like a wrestler with two fistfuls of rings punching her temples. Then the shockwave hit, in two stages, making the floor buck and the air crack like a whip.

She didn't realise she'd fallen until she felt the cold stone under her back. She picked herself up again and shouted out the command to go in. She knew nobody could hear her, but they could see her mouth form the words and her hand pointing.

Nahir's men rushed into the chamber beyond the door, from which smoke was pouring like a river. They were carrying ropes and pulleys, but Shraga had placed the explosives like a maestro. The door was already down. Detached from the solid rock by perfectly shaped detonations, it had toppled under its own weight.

Nahir stepped out again, waving smoke away from his face, and gave the *clear* signal. Diema relayed it. The Messengers advanced, covering each other's flanks and blind spots, alert for any movement from beyond the ragged opening in the rock. From moment to moment, as the smoke roiled, they stepped in and out of Diema's sight.

'Stay with me,' she told Kennedy. Then she glanced across at Rush. He still looked shaken and disoriented by the explosion, but he waved his flashlight in a satirical show of readiness. 'You too,' she said curtly. She went forward, and after a moment they followed.

They had to clamber over the fallen vault door and the rubble that surrounded it. It had stayed miraculously intact through the blast, though the steel sheeting, inches thick, had been ripped away in places from the concrete core. It was as though some animal had clawed the metal – but it would have had to be one of the beasts of the Apocalypse.

That association was an unpleasant one. Diema stepped down and hurried on. A short corridor gave onto a roughly circular room much smaller than the gallery they'd just left, but with so high a ceiling that it was lost to the eye in the shadows overhead. *No room at all*, Diema thought: most likely it was a rock chimney that had stood at the heart of Gellert Hill since it reared its head up out of the earth, and greeted the Judas People when they first came here to build.

Around the curved walls, two dozen *Elohim* lay still. All were men, and not one wore the night-vision rigs or body armour of Kennedy's people. Blood pooled visibly around the heads and

446

chests of most of them, and a few had fallen on their backs or sides, so she could see that the blood came from their slit throats. They had kept their knives in their hands when they fell.

Diema's own people hung back, guns trained on the man who sat at the centre of the room. He was dressed in black robes, bare-footed and bare-headed. He too held a sica in his hands, which were pressed to his chest as though he were praying. The tip of the blade pointed to his bare throat. His face wore an expression of beatific calm.

'Avra Shekolni,' Diema said. She raised a closed fist, signalling her *Elohim* to hold position and do nothing without her order. 'Where is Ber Lusim?'

'I am afraid,' Shekolni said, 'that this is not a question I am able to answer. He is gone to enact the glory of the ages and the end of time. The fifth and final king is coming, to reign for evermore. But He waits to be invited, and Ber Lusim must open the way for Him.'

'I want to be there, too,' Diema said. 'I want to see this thing. Please, *Tannanu*. Tell me where this will happen.'

Shekolni stared at her for a long time. Then he stared at the knife around which his two hands were clasped.

'Midnight,' he whispered. 'Sunday. Greenwich meantime.'

He leaned forward a little and drove the sica up to its hilt into his throat. With a curse, Diema ran forward as he toppled, and wrestled the knife from his grip, but there was nothing to be done. Shekolni was already drowning in his own blood, his airway as well as his jugular completely severed.

His right hand rose, trembling violently, and found her arm. It was as though he were trying to console her.

61

'For Christ's sake, could you please switch to English!'

Kennedy had said the words three times already, but this was the first time that the seemingly unending torrent of Aramaic was interrupted and the other people in the room – every last one of them *Elohim* – deigned to look at her. Not even Diema looked friendly.

She and Rush had been all but forgotten in the rapid retreat from Gellert Hill. The assassins had become removal men, taking up everything they could find – including the fallen, the few dead and the many wounded on both sides – and running flat-out with their heavy burdens back to the old print shop through which they'd entered.

From there, with the evacuation still in progress and the sound of sirens rising on all sides, Diema had had them taken back to the safe house in one of a phalanx of ambulances – real or fake, Kennedy couldn't decide – driving with their own sirens full-on, against the swarms of emergency vehicles converging on the Buda side of the river. Earthquake or not, the fact that Gellert Hill had just shrugged massively and shaken down some of the houses on its slopes was being taken in deadly earnest. Kennedy prayed that no one had been killed as a result of the blast – then realised how futile that prayer was, with a million lives hanging in the balance.

Or were they still hanging? Thinking about the expression of peace and calm on Avra Shekolni's face when he died, she had to wonder whether they'd just blown their last chance to stop Ber Lusim from turning Toller's three-century-old visions into cold, hard fact.

At the safe house, Diema requisitioned a room and went into conclave with Nahir and his deputies. But at the last moment, just as she'd done down in the tunnels, she indicated with a flick of her head that Kennedy should come along too. Rush was led back to his cell, protesting bitterly.

But Kennedy's presence at the crisis meeting mattered about as much as a fart in a windstorm, because the Judas People locked her out anyway – not with a door but with their language. And listening to the increasingly urgent and furious exchanges between them, Kennedy yielded to her own impatience at last and stepped in.

'I'm not following this,' she said now. 'If you speak in English, I can be part of the conversation. Believe it or not, I might know something that will turn out to be useful.' Nobody answered. The assassins all stared at her with a mixture of longing and hatred.

'Why is she here with us?' Nahir asked Diema. But he said it in English, allowing Kennedy to get the full benefit of his scorn for her. 'Why must we endure this again?'

Diema stared him down. 'For the reason she just gave you. She was involved in the earlier stages of this hunt. Her knowledge is relevant. I thought it was sensible to keep her close to hand.'

Nahir raised his eyebrows, politely sceptical. 'If she has knowledge, I can have my people interrogate her.'

'She worked as a detective. Her insights have been useful to me.'

'Yes,' Nahir said. 'So you told me. And I wait, enthralled, to see that wonderful mind in action. But that doesn't mean I want to sit at the same table as her or have her speak to me as though we are equals.'

Diema turned to Kennedy. 'Don't speak unless you're spoken to,' she ordered her.

'And I won't use her gutter tongue just so she can hobble along beside us.' Having made his point, Nahir reverted to Aramaic and continued to talk to Diema in a loud, hectoring tone for a further minute.

When he was done, Diema glanced at Kennedy once and – seemingly with bad grace – nodded. Two *Elohim* rose and approached Kennedy.

'They'll take you back to your cell,' Diema told them. 'We'll talk later.'

Kennedy stood, bowing to the inevitable as the girl had just done. But at that moment the doors opened and a man she'd never seen before walked in. He was a little on the short side but very solidly built, his upper arms bulging with muscle to such an extent that they slightly spoiled the lines of his light tan suit. His bald head gleamed with sweat, and he wiped his face with a linen handkerchief. Two women had entered with him and took up their stations to either side of him. Both were about six feet tall, dressed identically in dark grey pinstripe two-pieces that were probably intended to make them look like lawyers. But they didn't: they looked like the angel of death and her sister. They watched the room with eyes that defied anyone to move.

But the *Elohim* moved anyway. One by one – starting with Nahir – they pushed their chairs back and sank to one knee, bowing their heads. Diema was last.

'Bless us, *Tannanu*,' she murmured. 'And give us your counsel.'

Kennedy wondered why she'd switched back to English, and who the VIP was. But the second question was answered at once when the stranger's gaze, sweeping the room, came to rest on her.

He didn't speak, but it was obvious that he recognised her. And from that, her mind made the leap. This must be Kuutma, the *Elohim*'s supreme commander – the man who sometimes took the name of Michael Brand. The angels were scowling at her, eyes narrowed. Probably it was some kind of *lèse majesté* to look Michael Brand in the eye, but Kennedy was damned if she was going to give him a curtsy. She owed this bastard nothing but harsh language.

Kuutma turned his attention back to his own people. With a brusque gesture he signalled to them to stand. 'I'm sorry I arrived too late to take part in your recent action,' he said. 'I'm also sorry that its outcomes were mixed. You seem to have comprehensively derailed Ber Lusim's operations – and that was very well done – but I gather that the man himself evaded you.'

He crossed to the table, where Nahir instantly and without a word surrendered his place at its head. 'Please bring me up to date on what's happening now,' Kuutma said. 'What steps have been taken to find Ber Lusim?'

Nahir looked profoundly nervous, but spoke clearly. Kuutma had followed Diema's lead and spoken in English, so he did likewise. 'We've closed Ferihegy airport, by planting a small explosive device there and phoning in a warning. Follow-up threats were phoned in at Debrecen, Sármellék, Györ-Pér and Pécs-Pogány, so we're assuming that flights have been grounded there, too. We're also watching the mainline stations and the roads out of the city, but it's impossible to stop all traffic there. We're backtracking from phones and ID found on

Ber Lusim's *Elohim* to addresses in the city to which they were registered. We're hoping we might find a safe house where he has gone to ground.'

Kuutma nodded. 'And you've questioned the *Elohim* you captured in the caves?'

'They refuse to speak,' Nahir said. 'We considered torture, but —'

'But that's out of the question, for anyone of the bloodline,' Kuutma finished. 'I agree. The precautions that you've taken are good ones, but we have to assume he's been able to escape from the city and is now on his way to wherever it is he's going. So where is he going?' Not waiting for an answer, Kuutma turned to Diema. 'You believe he's still working his way through the prophecies in Toller's book?'

'As far as we can tell, *Tannanu*, yes,' Diema said. 'Leo Tillman's intervention in London bought us a little time, but there's no reason at all to think that it derailed the overall plan – which is to enact all the prophecies in sequence and force God's hand.'

The blasphemy, so bluntly spoken, sent a frisson through the ranks of the Messengers.

'And how far has he got?' Kuutma asked calmly.

'That's what we're trying to determine,' Nahir said. 'I have people looking at the book now.'

'People?' It was Kennedy who spoke. She was sick of standing by and listening – and she didn't even try to keep the sardonic edge out of her voice. Nahir gave her another look of dyspeptic hatred, but Kuutma laughed – long and loud, throwing his head back. The *Elohim*, including Diema, stared at him. Twice Nahir seemed about to speak, but hesitated, waiting for Kuutma's huge amusement to run its course.

'She makes a point,' Kuutma said, still smiling, and wiping

the corner of his eye. 'What people do you have, Desh Nahir? Put the lady's mind at rest.'

Nahir clearly didn't get the joke and just as clearly hated having to explain himself to an outsider, a *rhaka*. 'Interpreters,' he said, his gaze glancing off Kennedy before returning to Kuutma. 'Priests. Textual exegesists. People who might be expected to have some skill in navigating a book of prophecies. But the prophecies were deliberately written in opaque and elliptical language. They support many different interpretations, and it's hard – impossible, even – to say which if any is correct.'

'So you don't know,' Kennedy concluded. 'You don't have any idea how long you've got or which prophecy Ber Lusim has reached. Which prophecy he'll be looking to fulfil.'

'This pains me,' Nahir said to Kuutma. '*Tannanu*, I was about to exclude her. Please permit me to do so. I don't see what we gain by letting her hear our proceedings. If you want to interrogate her later, I'd be happy to provide a room and some suitable—'

'It's the last prophecy,' Kennedy said.

'—some suitable implements for—'

'He's reached the last prophecy. Didn't you see what Shekolni did down there? Did he slip it past you while you weren't looking?'

Nahir was forced to acknowledge her now. He snarled what was presumably a curse word in ancient Aramaic, then swivelled to face her. 'You're talking about things you don't understand,' he said. 'There are mysteries that will never be revealed to you – even if you were to spend a lifetime studying them.'

And that was meant to be a killer put-down, Kennedy thought: if there hadn't been so very much at stake, including her life, she might have laughed in Nahir's face. He was only a year or so older than Diema, Kennedy realised now. Of course, the *Elohim* tended to be young. Apart from Kuutma, she was probably the oldest person in the room. 'And that's your problem, right there,' she said to him, her tone of condescension matching his. 'You're looking for revealed mysteries. All I'm looking for is an evidence trail.'

'And you found one?' Kuutma asked. He was staring at her keenly, expectantly. 'Share it with us, please.'

'Has someone got the text?' Kennedy demanded.

Diema had learned it by rote, and to Kennedy's surprise she recited it. 'And the stone shall be rolled away from the tomb, as it was the time before. Then will a voice be heard, crying "The hour, the hour is at hand" and all men will see what heretofore was hidden. The betrayer will condemn a great multitude with a single breath. On the island that was given for an island, in the presence of the son and of the spirit, he will speak the names of the thousand thousand that will be sacrificed. And from his throne in the heavens, the Lord Jesus who is our glory and our life will speak the names of the few that will be saved.'

The words were met with a faintly awed silence from the other *Elohim*. Kennedy just nodded. 'Avra Shekolni used his last words to name a time. Midnight on Sunday, GMT. He was being the voice – fulfilling Toller's prophecy. And he roped us in, too. When we blew that door, we all became part of the scenario. Rolling away the stone from the mouth of the tomb. That's the only reason why he waited for us.'

'That place was not a tomb,' Nahir said angrily. 'It had been used as a granary.'

Kennedy turned to stare at him. 'Wow, you got me there. Unless it became a tomb when he got a whole lot of his men to cut their throats in it. What do you think?'

'And the door was steel. Not stone.'

'Steel filled with poured concrete. You're going to argue semantics with a dead prophet?'

'No,' Nahir said. 'With a live whore.'

Kennedy shook her head in sorrowful wonder. 'Did you skimp on your research, sweetheart?' she asked. 'Or are you scared you won't be able to say *dyke* without blushing?'

She returned her attention to Kuutma, but she was speaking to the room at large. 'Shekolni was pulling a trigger,' she said. 'We'll probably never know, now, whether they had it planned this way all along or whether he killed himself rather than let you take him and question him. But by dying, he lined everything up – he fulfilled the conditions that would let Ber Lusim enact the last prophecy. And wherever he went when he left here, the place he's heading for is the island – the "island that was given for an island". Find that, and you'll find him.'

She paused and looked from face to face, meeting an endless gallery of hostile stares and one quizzical frown.

'And how,' Kuutma said, 'are we to do that?'

'I'd suggest doing it fast,' Kennedy answered.

A hubbub of voices arose, with Nahir and a dozen of his *Elohim* all shouting out at once. Kuutma held up a hand, calm and commanding, and the voices died away.

'Enough,' Kuutma said coldly. 'I need to be completely briefed on your recent actions.' Diema began to speak, but he continued over her. 'Desh Nahir has rank and oversight in this city, so I'll speak with him first – and then with my special emissary, Diema Beit Evrom. Time is short. We'll speak in your command room, Nahir, and then we'll meet again here immediately afterwards. The rest of you will wait for us to return.' He glanced at Kennedy. 'Except for the *rhaka*, who can be placed in whatever receptacle you deem appropriate.'

'Take her back to her cell,' Nahir said. The two Messengers who had started to close in on Kennedy earlier, and had stopped in their tracks when Kuutma entered, took hold of her now.

They turned Kennedy around and led her to the door. Their grip on her shoulders was tighter than it needed to be: one of them also had a fist jammed against her lower back, presumably prepared to get her in a full lock if she stepped out of line. Nahir looked away, done with the whole business. So did Diema.

If I wasn't dead before, Kennedy thought, *I'm sure as hell dead now*.

62

For about a quarter of an hour after he was thrown back into his cell, Rush just sat on the cot bed with his head sunk onto his raised knees. But gradually, boredom and frustration won out over fear and unease.

He whiled away some time carving obscene graffiti on the walls with the edge of a coin. Then he hammered on the door for a while, demanding something to eat and drink – until he remembered the apple that Diema had given him, and ate that. It quenched his thirst a little, but mostly just reminded him of how much he wanted a hamburger or a chicken madras.

He tried not to be afraid, but he'd seen how Nahir and his posse had been looking at him and Kennedy down in the caves, and he was pretty sure he knew what those looks meant. They'd outlived their usefulness – not that there'd been much usefulness to outlive, in his case. The *Elohim* would figure out the prophecy without their help, or else they would blow it. Either way, he and Kennedy – and Tillman, assuming Tillman wasn't dead already – would be taken out behind the barn. Even if Diema wanted to protect them, there probably wasn't a lot she could do about it. And as far as he could tell, Diema was going along with the whole—

The bolt on the outside of the cell door rattled and then clanked as it was drawn back. Rush turned around, expecting to see the Messenger who'd brought him here – but it was her.

Diema closed the door behind her, quietly but firmly. She stared at Rush hard, her expression intense but unreadable.

'So how was your day?' he asked.

'Shut up,' Diema said.

'Okay.'

'And lie on the bed.'

It wasn't what he was expecting to hear, so the snappiest comeback he could dredge up was 'What?'

'The bed,' Diema snapped, walking up to him and pushing him towards it. Her body was rigid with tension. 'Lie down. Lie down on the bed. Quickly!'

Bemused, Rush obeyed – but this just seemed to get the girl angry. 'Not with your clothes on!' she exploded. 'For God's sake, have you never had sex before? Your pants. Your pants!'

He stood up again. 'Is this a joke?' he asked. 'Because I'm really not in the mood. The apple? Okay, the apple was funny, but this—' A thought struck him, and he wound down in mid-sentence. It wasn't a joke. It wasn't a joke at all, it was—

Poison on a sugar lump.

A hypnotist's pocket watch, set swinging.

Being asked to count down from ten, so you wouldn't feel it when the needle slipped into your arm on the count of seven.

'Hey,' he said, his voice shaking a little. 'Let's not do this, okay. I swear I'm not going to tell anyone about you. Nobody would even believe me if I did. You don't have to . . .'

Diema exhaled – a loud huff of exasperation – and breathed in again deeply and slowly. On the in-breath she magically produced a knife, one of those evil-looking sica things, and pressed it to Rush's stomach.

'Oh shit,' he blurted.

With a single sweep of the knife, she sliced clean through his belt and took his fly button, too. Then she pushed him again, tangling up her foot with his in a complicated way so that he slammed down onto the bed.

Diema kicked off her boots and undressed from the waist down. With the knife still in her hand, she climbed on top of him. She tapped the blade of the knife against his chest. Her face, as she contemplated him, was solemn, even severe.

'We've got ten minutes,' she said. 'Can you get there in ten minutes, Rush?'

'Can I—'

'Because if you can't, I'm not going to be responsible for the consequences. But I can pretty much guarantee there'll be a lot of blood.'

She reached underneath her, found him with her hand and rubbed him with a lot more vigour than tenderness. When he was hard enough, she guided him in.

It was reminiscent of Dovecote Farm, in a lot of ways. Except that being beaten up by her at Dovecote Farm hadn't involved performance anxiety. It took him a long while to get into any kind of a rhythm, and a couple of times along the way he almost lost his erection. Diema was pushing back against him brusquely, but there was no trace of pleasure on her face.

As soon as he reached his climax, Diema uncoupled from him and tucked the knife away. She began to dress again without a word.

'Was it ... was it good for you?' he asked dazedly.

Diema snorted in derision. 'No!'

He raised himself a few inches to stare at her. 'Then why did we do it?' he asked.

She tugged her trousers up over her hips, then stepped into her boots and knelt to tie up the laces.

'Why?' Rush insisted. He was afraid of what the answer might be, but he really needed to know.

Diema was already walking towards the door, hauling it open, but she paused for a moment in the doorway and glanced back at him.

'Because I don't trust you to lie,' she said coldly. From the tone of her voice and the look on his face, a casual observer would think Rush had just run over Diema's dog, rather than that they'd just shared a moment of physical intimacy.

The door slammed shut behind her.

He slumped back onto the bed and closed his eyes, overwhelmed by a feeling of helplessness and despair.

Maybe every condemned man felt like that after his hearty meal.

Diema was oppressed by the feeling of time running out – except that the image her mind gave her wasn't of sand falling through an hourglass. It was of a lit fuse, like the fuse on a bomb in a Tex Avery cartoon, burning down to the final, irrevocable KABOOM.

She found Nahir sitting at the desk in his command room, deep in discussion with Kuutma. She waited in the doorway to be noticed, prepared to walk away again if Kuutma ignored her, but he beckoned her in.

'—monitoring live data feeds from scanners at airports and border checkpoints,' Nahir was saying as she entered. 'But there's nothing yet. We're checking against all of Ber Lusim's known aliases, but of course we're not assuming that we know every identity he has. Since we closed the airports, the knock-on effects have led to security checkpoints being set up along all the major roads into and out of the city. We can't say for sure that we've stopped Lusim, but I'm confident we've slowed him down.'

Kuutma nodded. 'Sensible steps to take, certainly,' he said. 'Diema, your opinion?'

'My opinion? I don't think it can do any harm,' Diema said. Her slow, considered tone left vast amounts unspoken.

'What would you do that I've left undone?' Nahir asked, receiving the insult with a face frozen into immobility.

'Assuming that you've also stationed Messengers at the Keleti and Nyugati Pályaudvar railheads—'

'Of course.'

'—and that you're monitoring take-offs from private airfields, then I'd say you've done all you can to prevent Ber Lusim from leaving the city.'

'Thank you.'

'So what I would do, Nahir, is assume that you've failed, and do my best to find out where he's going.'

She was standing before him now, and he stood up too, maybe to assert the advantage of his height.

'Do my best,' he repeated, with cold politeness. 'That's a rhetorical exhortation, Diema Beit Evrom, rather than a piece of advice that I can actually act on.'

'Then act on this,' she said. 'Wake Leo Tillman.'

Nahir looked from her to Kuutma and back again. He shook his head, not in refusal but in bafflement. 'Tillman was enlisted as a killer,' he pointed out. 'Surely his usefulness is at an end.'

'We need what's in his head. He was the one who went into Ber Lusim's warehouse, back in London. He saw the documentation on the weapons and equipment that Lusim had already shipped.'

'We're starting to retrieve similar information from the computers we found down in the caves.'

'Good.' Diema's tone was clipped. 'I'm not saying those efforts should stop. Just that we should use every option that's open to us. Kennedy is right that as Adamites, she and the others come at the Toller prophecies from a different angle than we do. She proved that just now – and justified your decision to enlist her, *Tannanu*. I want to use Leo Tillman's expertise, too. His tactical intelligence, which was great enough to allow him to find Ginat'Dania that was.'

Kuutma rubbed his cheek with his thumb. 'Could this be done?' he asked Nahir. 'Could you wake him? Or is Tillman too far-gone?'

Nahir made a non-committal gesture. 'I don't know, *Tannanu*,' he admitted. 'I was thinking of Tillman as a spent asset, so I haven't asked the doctors to report to me on his condition. I'll do so now.'

'Thank you, Nahir,' Kuutma said. 'Take my bodyguards with you. They both have a good grounding in field medicine. Perhaps they can be of use. We'll join you shortly.'

'I want the others there, too,' Diema said quickly. 'Kennedy and Rush.'

Kuutma frowned. 'They were not, I believe, present in the warehouse with Tillman,' he observed.

'No. But they were both researching Johann Toller and his prophecies. Again, it's a case of using all possible assets. If any of them has an insight we can use, we need to squeeze it out of them now.'

'Very well,' Kuutma said. 'Nahir, please have them fetched.'

Nahir made the sign of the noose, which Kuutma returned, and then he left. Diema read extreme tension in the set of Nahir's back and shoulders. He wouldn't forgive her for the indignities she'd put him through today. But in a way, that made what she had to do easier: he was so relentlessly focused on his own hurt feelings that she didn't need to give them any thought herself.

Alone with Diema for the first time, Kuutma gave her a brief but warm embrace. 'I'm pleased with all you've accomplished,' he told her. 'Pleased and proud. The operation here was brilliantly handled.'

'Thank you, *Tannanu*.' Diema assumed the same tone of simple humility she'd used when she spoke with him in Ginat'Dania, and her heart swelled as it always had when he praised her, but there were other emotions in the mix now, and she chose her words with care. 'But I think I could have done more, and done it more quickly. And in any case, the plan was yours.'

'Yes,' Kuutma agreed. 'The plan was mine. I said you should bring Tillman and the *rhaka* into the orbit of our investigation, and use their talents. But I knew how much I was asking of you. I knew that this thing, which was so easy to say, would be very hard indeed to carry out. You carried it out immaculately.'

'Thank you, *Tannanu*.'

'What I'm concerned about, is how you yourself may have been hurt in the process – especially in meeting Leo Tillman and being forced into close proximity with him. No Messenger has ever had to bear that burden.'

Diema knew that she couldn't plausibly counterfeit indifference, so she let him see some of the tension she'd been hiding, letting the mask slip as though with relief. She grimaced. 'It hasn't been easy. Sometimes I see my brothers in him. Myself, even. It's hard, at those times, not to let him see how much I hate him.'

'Walk with me,' Kuutma suggested.

He bowed, and with a sweep of his arm invited her to go before him. As they left Nahir's command room, he fell in at her side, hands clasped behind his back, moving at an easy amble that belied the urgency of their situation.

'Your hate, then,' he said. 'It's as great as it ever was?'

'His crime is as great as it ever was.'

'Of course. It's important that I know your heart in this, Diema. Very important. You've served the city more in a year than many do in a lifetime. Your well-being matters to me.'

'I know.' She looked at the ground.

'Well,' Kuutma said. 'I'm answered. And really, I shouldn't even have needed to ask. It was your suggestion to wake Tillman and speak to him, despite the severity of his wounds. You're obviously not troubled at the thought of compromising his recovery – or accidentally killing him. The drugs that will be used will be very potent. So we'll be putting a strain on his heart, when it's already weak.'

Diema swallowed hard. 'So long as he lives long enough to talk to us,' she said, as carelessly as she could.

'And here we are,' Kuutma said. They had reached a door that was like all the other doors they'd passed. How did he know? Diema wondered. Had he studied the layout of the house before he arrived? Had he arrived earlier and remained in the background during the raid on the caves? Was there some system of signs in the safe houses that he knew about and she didn't?

Was her face equally easy for him to read?

Diema knew that prolonged use of the drug kelalit could induce amphetamine psychosis. Paranoia was its chief symptom. She reached out and opened the door, bowing for Kuutma to precede her into the room. She didn't even look over the threshold.

'*Tannanu*,' she murmured.

'Thank you, Diema.'

He went in, and she followed him, steeling herself. Killing, when she'd been brought to it, had been much harder than she expected it to be. But what she was about to do now would be harder still.

She had to bring all three Adamites out of here alive.

63

When Kennedy got her first look at Leo Tillman, she had to fight back a cry of dismay. She'd seen his injuries when they were fresh, so she thought she was armoured against anything she might find when the Messengers thrust her and Rush in through the door of the medical room and told them brusquely to wait there.

But she'd reckoned without the vagaries of *Elohim* psychology. Tillman's wounds had been bandaged, and he'd been given the blood transfusion he so desperately needed. In fact, it looked as though he'd been given scrupulous care. Diagnostic machines had been brought in from somewhere and hooked up to his body wherever there was a space between the drip feeds and catheters. His dressings were clean, and so were the sheets.

But someone had remembered, at some point in all these clinical proceedings, that they were dealing with an enemy. At that point, they had shackled Tillman's hands and feet to the bed frame with four sets of sleeve cuffs tied so tightly that his body was almost being lifted from the bed.

A doctor was checking Tillman's blood pressure with a pneumatic sleeve, his expression bland and calm, as though this were all in a day's work. Kuutma's two angels also stood by, coldly indifferent, watching him work.

'Jesus frigging Christ,' Rush exclaimed.

Kennedy turned to the four *Elohim* who'd brought them there. 'Cut him loose,' she said. She had to force the words out. The blood was pounding in her temples and she felt like she was choking on an anger – close to panic – that had been rising in her since the first time they'd been brought to this place.

The Messengers affected not to hear her. Clearly they didn't take orders from the likes of her.

Kennedy switched her attention to Nahir, who was standing in the corner of the room, watching them in silence. He hadn't moved since they arrived, which was why she hadn't seen him up until then. His expression was less detached than those of the doctor and the guards, but what was showing on his face was mostly curiosity – an interest as to which way they might jump.

'What,' Kennedy said, 'are you scared he might pick a fight with someone? Cut him loose!'

'No,' Nahir said.

'This is a human being.'

'Is it?'

Kennedy went to the bed and started to untie Leo herself. When the Messengers moved in to stop her, she swivelled on the spot and punched the nearest one full in the face.

They had her immobilised before she could draw another breath. Actually, it was the man she'd just punched who put her in the arm-lock, inside of a second and without the aid of his three colleagues. Rush stepped forward to help her and ran into a human barricade: a male and a female *Elohim*, standing shoulder to shoulder, daring him to raise a hand against them.

He took the dare, but unlike Kennedy he didn't have the

advantage of surprise. One of the two dropped him with a punch that he didn't see coming and couldn't even reconstruct after it had hit. He was left in a foetal position on the floor, struggling to draw in a breath through a solid wall of agony.

'You better not give me an inch of slack,' Kennedy gasped.

'I won't,' her captor promised her, sounding almost amused.

'A human being,' Nahir said, musing. 'Would you claim that status for yourself? I wonder. I imagine you would. And that you'd do so without the slightest sense of irony.'

'You want irony?' Kennedy snarled. 'I'll tell you what's ironic. That you people are so prissy about killing each other when killing is the only thing you're any good at!'

Nahir signalled to the Messenger to release her – a negligent wave of the hand. Kennedy could see from his face and his posture that he expected her to attack him, and was ready for her if she did.

'This is personal for you, isn't it?' she asked him, clutching her numbed arm to her chest.

Nahir's mouth pinched in a minute grimace. 'Not in the slightest.'

'I'm just trying to figure out why,' Kennedy said. 'Is it because we found your Ginat'Dania? I can see where that would hurt.'

'Nothing you can do could ever make the smallest difference to us.'

'And yet here we are.' Kennedy forced a grin. 'Saving you from yourselves. Because three thousand years turned out to be nowhere near long enough for you sorry sons of bitches to get your act together. You saying you don't need us is a really bad joke after you went to so much trouble to get us here.'

Nahir put a hand to the back of his belt. 'Say another word,' he invited Kennedy. 'And find out for yourself how much I need you.'

She opened her mouth – and the creak and swish of the door at her back interceded, probably saving her life.

'Good,' Kuutma said. 'Everybody is here, and everything, I assume, is in place.' Diema entered the room behind him and closed the door. For a moment, her gaze was locked on Kennedy's – a wordless catechism. Then she looked away.

'Doctor?' Kuutma said.

The doctor, a man of the same age and with the same physique as the Messengers, bowed perfunctorily and made the sign of the noose. 'I've completed a physical evaluation of the patient,' he said. 'He seems to have been in excellent health before he received these wounds. His system is massively compromised now, but I believe I can wake him by injecting adrenalin and methylphenidate directly into his heart. Obviously there are a number of risks involved in this procedure. But if time is of the essence ...'

'Time,' said Kuutma, 'is very much of the essence. Do it, please.'

The doctor turned to the racks and trays against the walls and began to select from the bottles there.

'What risks?' Kennedy asked.

Assembling the hypo, the doctor answered over his shoulder. Possibly he hadn't noticed that he was being questioned by an Adamite. 'Haemorrhaging within the heart is possible, but not very likely. The main risk is *tamponade* – massive, uncontrolled vaso-constriction that will starve his system of oxygen. I'll have a stand-by injection of benzamine ready in case that happens.'

'Don't do this,' Kennedy said. She was speaking to Diema.

469

'Restrain her,' Nahir ordered. 'She's capable of disrupting the procedure.'

Two *Elohim* took Kennedy's arms. The remaining two stood over Rush, who by now was sitting up but hadn't managed to stand.

'Proceed,' said Kuutma.

The doctor used an epidural needle that looked more like a duelling sword. Kennedy forced herself not to look away as the doctor, without preamble, inserted the point between Tillman's fourth and fifth ribs and pushed the needle in slowly and smoothly, to a depth of about three inches. He thumbed the bulb at the end of the syringe, and the plunger inside the hypodermic slid across, instantly, like an eye blinking shut.

For a split-second longer, Tillman's body remained calm and motionless. Then it quaked, riven by a massive interior shock. A powerful muscular contraction went through him, making the restraints tighten and his body lift clear of the bed – then slam down again with enough force to make it rock.

'Hold him!' the doctor said, to the two angels, and they stepped in on either side to enfold Tillman in a rigid embrace. There was a second contraction, then a third, not so severe as the first but more protracted.

Tillman's eyes and mouth gaped open. His throat worked and so did his chest, but there was no sound of indrawn breath. Quickly, the doctor gave him a second injection into the side of his neck. Sputters and gasps came from Tillman's throat, as though he were doing a bad mime of a coffee percolator. They peaked, then died away.

The doctor turned to look at Kuutma, tense, seeking instruction or permission. 'He's barely breathing. I need another chemical antagonist to fight the adrenalin. But there

470

are none here. This house is not so well stocked as my own surgery. I didn't think to bring—'

'Glyceril trinitrate,' one of the angels said.

The doctor blinked, his mouth dropping open. 'But that's ... that's the chemical composition of nitroglycerin. It's an explosive.'

'And a vaso-dilator.' The woman looked to Nahir. 'Do you have any?'

Nahir shrugged. 'Almost certainly.'

One of the *Elohim* went in search of it. The rest of them were summarily ejected from the room so that the doctor could prep Tillman for an emergency ECMO. If necessary, they would force oxygen into his blood using cannulae and membrane oscillators.

Kennedy was still in the grip of the two *Elohim* who Nahir had told to guard her. But she'd stopped struggling against their grasp, and they were holding her loosely. If Leo died, she intended to try to tear loose from their grip, but she had no idea whether she was going to attack Nahir, Kuutma or Diema. She just felt that leaving a mark on one of the three would be a memorial that she owed Tillman, even if she died trying.

Her gaze kept going back to Diema, who stood with her arms folded, her expression sullen and guarded. Everything that was happening here was being driven by her. She could still stop this, but she said nothing, engaged with nothing, let it flow around her while she stood and thought.

The nitro was brought. Kennedy was expecting a gelid brick, wrapped in grease-proof paper, like a package of C4, but it came in a bottle, looking a lot more like medicine than explosive. The *Elohim* took it into Tillman's room and closed the door behind them.

'You know the one thing I regret, in all of this?' Rush asked. He was speaking to Diema, who turned to stare at him, startled out of her reverie.

'That I let you touch me,' Rush said.

She didn't answer. Kuutma frowned, and looked at Diema – a look of surprise and deep thought.

The door opened, and the doctor looked out at them. His bland expression gave nothing away, but he nodded. 'He's ready for you,' he said to Kuutma.

They filed back into the room. Tillman's eyes were open and he was breathing – not normally, but deeply, with an audible rasp on each in-breath like the blade of a hacksaw dragged through cardboard. Kennedy tried to go to him, but the Messengers who held her arms wouldn't allow her.

'Leo,' she said.

His wide eyes flickered, swivelled and found her. He tried to speak, eventually producing a sound that could have been the start of her name. 'Heh . . .'

And a second later, '. . . ther.'

Kuutma wasted no time. 'As you wished, Diema,' he said to her, with a wave of his hand. 'Please continue.'

Diema stepped forward. 'We found Ber Lusim's base of operations, underneath Gellert Hill,' she said, addressing herself to Tillman. 'But he escaped us. And now, we think, he's aiming to fulfil the final prophecy in Toller's book. So we have to go there, too, and stop him. Our goal is what it's been all along – to save a million lives. If we can do that, then everything . . . everything that's happened along the way will have been justified.'

The tone of her voice was strange. So were her words, Kennedy thought. She sounded as though she were pleading a case rather than carrying out an interrogation.

Tillman nodded. He swallowed deeply before he tried to speak again. 'The island,' he said, his voice slurred but comprehensible.

Diema nodded. 'The island given for an island. We've all had time to think about it. If you've got any ideas – if any of you have anything at all – this is probably our last chance to figure it out.'

Nobody answered. Diema looked at each of them in turn.

'Please,' she said. She sounded desperate. 'Anything. It's not about our feelings. It's not about whether we trust each other or not. Think about the living, who will soon be dead.'

Nahir winced, and shook his head. He seemed to think this whole spectacle was beneath his dignity.

'There were treaties,' Rush said, with deep reluctance.

Diema turned to him. 'Go on.'

'In the seventeenth century. Sometimes countries would give away or trade ownership of colonies, either to prevent a war or to share out the proceeds after one. I found a whole bunch of them.'

Diema was still looking at him expectantly. So was Kuutma. Rush shrugged. 'I don't think I can remember.'

'Try,' Diema said tightly.

Rush scowled and stared at the floor. 'The Spice Islands,' he said. 'West Coast of ... India, I think. They were given to England in the 1660s. It's the right time for Toller, but there wasn't a swap involved. I mean, they weren't given for an island. They were part of a dowry. When Catherine of Braganza married Charles II.'

'Then they're probably out,' said Diema. 'What else?'

Rush thought some more. 'The Azores kept changing hands between Spain and Portugal, all through the sixteenth and seventeenth centuries. So did the Madeira archipelago. There were a whole bunch of treaties where they swapped control over one island or another, abandoned forts, leased land, that kind of thing. You could probably say that any one of those islands had been given for another island at one time or another.'

'Not enough people,' Kennedy said, remembering Gilles Bouchard's sleeve notes. 'Even now, Madeira doesn't top a quarter of a million. And the Azores are even smaller.'

'Okay,' Rush said. 'Well, there's Paulu Run, in Indonesia. Britain gave it to the Dutch in 1667 and got Manhattan – which is when New Amsterdam became New York. Martinique is possible. That was French, then British, then French again, all around the time when Toller was writing. Grenada. The French took the indigenous population out of there in the 1640s, which again is about right for Toller, and pushed them onto the smaller islands in the Grenadines. So you could say they gave an island for an island. And there are others. I can't remember the details, but Aruba fits. So does Tasmania. Abel Tasman was resupplying his ship in Budapest at a time when Toller might still have been here.'

Rush shook his head. 'The truth is,' he said, 'you could make a case for any island you want, pretty much. The big European powers back then, they had big, colony-swapping parties where everyone put their car keys in a bowl. We're not going to get there this way.'

They absorbed this in silence. Diema let her hands fall to her sides, then balled her fists. An image flashed into Kennedy's mind, suddenly and powerfully: Alex Wales, in the boardroom at Ryegate House, in the moment before he exploded into violence.

'It's ... Manhattan,' Tillman said.

A change came over all the *Elohim* in the room. They tried to hide it, and it was gone as quickly as it came – their ferocious self-control reasserted itself that quickly. But for a moment they looked the same way they'd looked when Diema had made her comment about forcing God's hand.

'Why?' Kuutma said quickly.

Tillman stared at him, his eyes swimming in and out of focus. 'Because High Energy Haulage ... shipped there.'

'We have that information,' Nahir said. 'From the computer files Ber Lusim left behind. High Energy did send a shipment there – but it wasn't weapons. It was food products.'

'Manhattan,' Tillman murmured again, more weakly.

'What food products?' Kuutma asked Nahir.

'Beans.'

'Beans?'

'Castor beans.'

'Those aren't food,' Diema said savagely.

'Natural ... natural source ...' Tillman mumbled.

'Of the ricin toxin,' Kuutma finished. 'I salute you, little sister. And you, Mr Tillman. Nahir, you've closed the local airspace. Open it again. Do whatever it takes. Diema and I will leave for New York at once.'

He opened the door and stood aside for her to step through. Diema remained where she was.

And took a breath.

PART SIX

THE THRESHING FLOOR

64

The Borough of Manhattan extends beyond the Island that gives it its name, carving out a foothold on the mainland in the shape of Marble Hill – 'the Bronx's Sudetenland'. But on the island itself, if you keep on going north about as far as you can, just before you hit the Harlem River you hit Inwood.

It's a seriously schizophrenic neighbourhood, anyone will tell you that, but there's some disagreement as to exactly where the divide comes. Some people claim it's East-West, with Broadway separating a larger East Side full of mostly Dominican families, maybe two or three generations out of the Republic and as aspirational as hell, from a smaller and more Bohemian West Side full of artists, writers and second-stringers from the city's many orchestras. Others say the distinction that matters is up-down. Inwood is either your first beachhead in Manhattan real estate, with a view to going south along with your rising fortunes, or else it's your swan song before you hit the boroughs.

And then there's a third distinction, of which most of Inwood's general population are entirely unaware: between those who live above the ground and those who live under it. Because from Isham Park in the North to Fort George Hill in the South, from 10th Avenue to Payson, and from 30ft to

700ft below the street, Inwood is the current location of Ginat'Dania, the peripatetic homeland of the Judas People.

Within that volume of space, whose combined ground area across all of its levels is close to five hundred square miles, the entire population of the People, apart from the tiny diaspora already defined, live and work and dream and die. Six high-rise blocks wholly owned and staffed by the People's guardians, the *Elohim*, form its periscopes and its guard towers, but most of the citizenry never visit these above-ground extrusions. They're accustomed to the rhythms and logistics of life underground, to the point where 'underground' ceases to be part of their frame of reference.

Ginat'Dania, the Eden Garden from which the rest of humanity was long ago expelled, is where they live.

And to Ginat'Dania Kuutma now returned, in order to begin its defence in depth.

By the time he touched down at Newark and went through customs, it was nine minutes after 11 a.m. Since Eastern Standard Time is five hours before Greenwich Meantime, that meant that there were seven hours and fifty-one minutes left on the clock. Zero hour would be seven that evening. Kuutma was already giving orders to his Messengers as he was being driven through the streets of New Jersey, and the first Messengers were mobilising and moving out by the time he reached the island of Manhattan and descended into his home.

The first and most important consideration was to seal and guard the borders. To this end, Kuutma gave orders for the surface streets at Thayer, Nagle Avenue and along the eastern limits of Inwood Hill Park to be undermined with earthworks so that they would start to collapse. The New York City authorities promptly closed the affected streets for repairs, re-routing traffic via the bridge at University Heights. Cars could still come and go along the full length and breadth of the island, obviously, but if Ber Lusim was carrying his poison in trucks, they wouldn't be able to pass directly into the territory under which Ginat'Dania lay.

That left air and water as potential approaches. *Elohim* were sent to search all known private airfields around the city, looking mainly for microlight aircraft small enough to be exempt from safety inspections and federal monitoring. Satellite footage was being examined in order to identify any potential runways whose location was disguised.

As far as the water went, dockside warehouses were being searched at the same time, as well as ships on the river that were in fixed moorage. The factory in which Ber Lusim had extracted and refined his poison had already been identified from archived satellite footage, which showed the red liveried trucks of the High Energy Haulage company making a delivery there more than a month before. But it had clearly been abandoned for some time. There was nothing there now except some industrial waste, sacks of raw chemicals and several hundredweight of castor beans that had not been pulped and processed. The location of the factory was a calculated insult: it was in Marble Hill, looking directly across the Harlem River towards the northern tip of Manhattan Island. Ber Lusim, who they had sought around the world, had built his weapon of mass destruction within walking distance of Ginat'Dania itself.

It was true the *Elohim*'s search was hampered by their having no idea of what that armament might be, and what it might look like. But it was also true that they could rule out some possibilities and concentrate on others that were more likely. Ricin was extremely difficult to weaponise. It had a high

481

toxicity, but it was most effective in solid form, either as a pellet or as a poisonous coating on some form of scatter munition. The amount required to kill a million people would be measured in tons, and each of the victims would have to be directly exposed to the toxin: there was no way its effects could be transmitted from one person to another.

All of these factors worked in their favour. But Ber Lusim had known these things, too, and had still chosen ricin over a wide range of other toxic agents such as sarin, botulinum, smallpox or anthrax, which might have been more convenient or more efficacious. It followed that he had a plan for delivering the poison across the city, or at least across enough of the city to kill a million of its inhabitants.

Would he really attack Ginat'Dania itself? The thought was terrible, but it had a monstrous logic of its own. Shekolni had believed completely and fervently in Johann Toller's divine inspiration, and Toller, in his book, had described God *choosing* those who would be saved. Who else would he choose but the Judas People? And therefore, where else could the final atrocity be unleashed?

So Ginat'Dania was in a state of siege, all of its citizens in lockdown, all of its entry and exit points fortified and guarded, all of its Messengers answerable directly to Kuutma himself, who sent a constant stream of instructions and queries from his rooms in *het retoyet*.

Or almost all.

Coming from a tiny commercial airfield much further out from the city, a good hour behind Kuutma because of the complications involved in transporting one of its passengers, an armoured truck bearing the logo of a well-known security firm was also headed for Manhattan. In its innards, not quite imprisoned and yet not quite free, was the small group that had been deputed to Diema's command. It consisted of Diema herself, Desh Nahir, Kuutma's two bodyguards Alus and Taria, and the three Adamites. Tillman. Kennedy. Rush.

Kuutma frowned as he thought about them. The memory of that last hour in Budapest still troubled him. He had heard Diema out – he owed her that, and more. But he was far from sure that he had made the right decision.

'I need the three of them to come with me,' Diema had said. 'You see that, *Tannanu*, don't you? The reason why you sent me to them – it wasn't just because they can kill where we can't. It's because they see things differently from the way we see them, and we need their expertise. It was with their help that I got this far. It would be blind stupidity to give up that help now, while we still might need it. Let them come with us, to New York.'

Nahir made a sound of disgust, deep in his throat.

'You disagree, Nahir?'

'It makes no sense, *Tannanu*. If you need their input, speak to them by phone or address your requirements to me and I'll speak to them for you. There's no need for them to accompany you. It would even be better that way, since Tillman is probably too weak to be moved. You'd risk killing him in transit – which Diema Beit Evrom surely wouldn't want, if he's such a valuable asset.'

'We can't predict what we'll find and what we'll need,' Diema countered. 'It may be that we'll need Tillman to accompany us, as weak as he is, and give us his insights. It's not about safeguarding his health. It's about keeping him where he can do the most good.'

'And Kennedy, likewise?' Kuutma asked.

'Yes. Exactly.'

'And the boy?'

Diema didn't answer. Which was an answer in itself.

'Very well,' Kuutma said. 'We'll take the *rhaka*. And Tillman, too, though I find it hard to believe we'll use him in the way you suggest. But the boy stays. Once we're gone, Nahir can dispose of him as he sees fit.'

Diema tensed visibly, as though she was steeling herself for some intense physical effort.

'Benjamin Rush is the father of my child,' she said, 'who is not yet born.'

Kuutma's shock at hearing this was as great as Nahir's, but unlike Nahir, he was able to keep the shock from showing on his face or in his actions.

Nahir, by contrast, cried out, a wordless yell of disgust and protest. He took a step towards Diema, his hand raised as though he intended to strike her. She took a combat stance herself, ready to defend against the attack.

'What is this?' Kuutma asked her coldly. 'What is this thing you say? You're *Elohim*, not *Kelim*.'

'Now I'm both,' she said.

'You're a whore!' Nahir bellowed. 'A filthy whore!'

She gave him a look of cool derision. 'You need to learn some new curse words, Desh Nahir. Vary your repertoire. It would be terrible if you became dull.'

'Desh Nahir makes a reasonable assumption,' Kuutma broke in, grinding out the words. 'If he's wrong, tell me why. How did this happen?'

Diema stared into his eyes. 'It happened, *Tannanu*, in this wise,' she said. 'I gave myself to the boy in order to win his trust – and through him, the trust of Heather Kennedy. It was part of my mission, I took no pleasure in it, but neither did I hesitate. Other *Elohim* have done such things, many times. But

I miscounted my days and fell pregnant. And in that, obviously, I was at fault.'

'At fault?' Nahir almost screamed. 'This foulness—'

Kuutma silenced him with a curt gesture. 'Go on,' he said to Diema.

'And so,' she said, 'I was faced with a choice. I could have terminated the pregnancy. It would have been no shame. But the wombs of the daughters of the People are the portals through which the Blessed enter the world. I decided to be delivered of the child, if I can carry it to term. And once that decision was made, I was thenceforth *Kelim* and Ben Rush was my partner, the man with whose seed I must be sown. Three times, the laws say.'

'The laws do not cover this!' Nahir shouted. 'The laws are silent on this!'

'It is without precedent,' Kuutma said.

'It's filth and abomination!'

Diema had said her piece. She stood with her head slightly bowed, awaiting Kuutma's verdict.

And for the first time since he took the mantle of command – his own personal holy of holies – Kuutma was at a loss.

'Bring me the boy,' he said at last.

Nahir turned to the nearest of his *Elohim*, but Alus and Taria, the women who served Kuutma as his bodyguards, had already detached themselves and were gone.

'Say nothing to him,' Kuutma warned Diema. 'I'll question him myself.'

The women returned, a few seconds later, leading Ben Rush between them. Rush looked anxiously at Diema, who looked pointedly away, then at Nahir, who glared at him like an ogre in a pantomime.

'Keep your eyes on me,' Kuutma snapped. Startled, Rush obeyed.

'If anything has passed between you and our sister,' Kuutma said, 'tell us now. Only honesty will save you. A lie dooms you, and ruins her. So speak.'

The boy took a long while to get a word out. And since he was an Adamite, when he did it was a lie. 'I didn't touch her,' he said. His gaze flicked sideways at Diema again.

'At me,' Kuutma growled. 'Only at me. So there was no physical congress? She's clean? Clean of your pollution?'

The boy was clearly terrified now. Perhaps he had some inkling of what was at stake here; of how close he was to death.

'I . . . obviously I came on to her,' he stammered. 'I thought, you know, I might be in with a chance. So if . . . yeah. Anything that happened was down to me. But it wasn't much. She . . . Diema wasn't interested. She smacked me in the head, and that was that.'

Kuutma reached out and gripped the boy's face in his broad hand.

'You're saying you didn't lie with her?'

'No,' Rush mumbled. 'I mean, yes. That's what I'm saying.'

'So if she were pregnant, the child could not be yours?'

The boy's face gave him all the answer he needed. The wonder and terror and stark astonishment that warred there could not be counterfeited.

'*Tannanu*, I beg you,' Nahir said, his voice thick. 'Kill the Adamites here and now, and be done. The three of them. Nothing is gained by this . . . this humiliating alliance.'

Kuutma released his hold on the boy and made a brusque gesture. Alus and Taria took Rush away, handling him a good deal more roughly than before.

Nahir's face, now, was almost as transparent as the boy's had been. The whole course of his affections for Diema, his hopes, and the crisis into which he was now thrown, could be read there.

'I will not pronounce on it,' Kuutma said, speaking mostly to Diema herself. 'Not yet. The time is too pressing. Diema, I will allow you to bring your Adamite menagerie to New York, and I will guarantee their safety until this threat is dealt with. After that, we will speak further on these matters. For now, we set them aside.'

But Nahir wasn't quite done. His whole body shaking, he spat out the *hrach bishat*, the formal execration that made him Diema's accuser.

'Are you sure you want this?' Kuutma asked Nahir.

Nahir made no answer. There was nothing to be said: too much had been said already.

'You will return with us,' Kuutma told Nahir. 'Make the arrangements.'

He pondered that decision now, alone in his room in *het retoyet*, while in the city around him, his Messengers moved in and out among the Adamites, weaving their invisible skein. Surely so great a concentration of *Elohim* in one place had never been seen before, in all the ages since Christ's death. Perhaps Ber Lusim was right: perhaps these were, after all, the end times.

Or perhaps he was just growing old.

Old men, past their prime, were wont to second-guess their own decisions.

There was no doubt in his mind as to what Diema's performance was meant to achieve. She had chosen a course of action – perhaps the only course of action – that would bring Tillman, Kennedy and the boy out of Budapest alive. Because she'd reasoned, correctly, that leaving them behind in Nahir's hands would mean consigning them to their deaths. So she'd demonstrated that Tillman and the *rhaka* were still valuable alive, and then she'd extended to the boy the temporary but binding status of an out-father.

It was clever and deeply troubling – that his protégée, his agent, his almost-daughter should waste so much effort to such an end. As though she had lost the *Elohim*'s necessary indifference to Adamite lives. As though she had forgotten, all at once, the rules that licensed and governed her.

But it wasn't so sudden, he corrected himself. There had been the boy she killed, and her inability to put his death behind her. The warning signs had been there from the start.

Kuutma knew he had been right, in any case, to bring Nahir back to Ginat'Dania. If they all survived this, the *Sima* would hear Nahir's accusation against Diema, and pronounce on it. It would mean exile for one of them. This needed to be done at once. It couldn't be allowed to fester.

But to place Nahir in Diema's team – to force them to work together – that was unnecessary cruelty. It showed Kuutma the mirror of his own failings. He had put too much faith in the girl, allowed her inside his guard, and now he felt a sense of grief and anger that was largely personal, when he should be entirely Kuutma, the Brand, his individual emotions sublimed away by the heat of righteousness.

He had never had a family. The women he had known had never been as real to him as his vocation, his life of service, and he had let them drift away with no sense of loss.

For the first time, now, he found himself thinking about what Tillman had lost. Then about what Tillman had destroyed, with his own hands. It would not be possible to imagine two men who had lived more different, more

488

opposed lives than himself and that man. The Adamite's purely private, purely selfish quest, as against his own public life, his relentless self-abnegation.

But he knew what it was he was feeling, and the facile comparison didn't blunt the force of it. Nahir's jealousy, so blatant and indecent, allowed him to see his own for what it was – but it gave him no clue as to what he should do about it. Perhaps he would be fortunate. Perhaps the decision would be taken out of his hands.

Perhaps the world would end.

65

Three miles out from Manhattan, breaking the speed limit in the back of a truck that had air conditioning but no suspension, Kennedy held on tight to a balance rail and to her kidneys, and tried not to think about the situation they were all in.

Rush was sunk in introspective misery. The two female *Elohim*, Alus and Taria, sat in perfect stillness, seeming indifferent to their surroundings but, Kennedy was sure, supremely aware of them. Tillman was awake but very weak – and strapped onto a bench at the front end of the truck so that the incessant jolts and bounces didn't send him sprawling. There was still a danger that they would open his wounds, and Kennedy could see from the expression of concentration on his sweat-sheened face the effort it was costing him to keep himself from fainting every time they hit a bad stretch of road. Diema stood a few feet away from him, her feet bracing her into a corner, staring at her father with an expression of deep thoughtfulness. Nahir watched them all, the way a cat watches a mousehole.

The journey from Hungary hadn't given Kennedy any real time to talk with Tillman or with Rush. It had been a chaotic, seemingly endless ordeal involving a breakneck drive out of

Budapest on narrow, crowded streets, across the Slovak border into the ragged industrial outskirts of Levice. And then a night flight out of a private airfield near Podluzany that turned out to be no airfield at all, but a newly laid runway in the middle of nowhere – just fresh tarmac poured over grass and weeds and smoothed with garden rollers while it cooled. Their feet, as they walked to the plane, had stuck to the still-wet surface and come up again with audible pops and smacks.

On the flight, they'd torn out a row of seats and adapted the row behind into a makeshift travois for Tillman, strapping him in with seatbelts and duct tape all along his body's length. He was drifting in and out of consciousness: the *Elohim* doctor seemed to favour a pain-control regime that was basically a chemical sledgehammer. But in one of his brief periods of lucidity, Kennedy was at last able to ask him how he was feeling.

'Fine,' was all he'd said. 'I'm good, Heather. Only hurts when I laugh.'

'She sold us out, Leo,' Kennedy had said, leaning close to murmur the words in his ear. 'As soon as you were down, on Gellert Hill, she took us home to meet the folks. They're running this, now. Running us.'

Tillman had smiled at that, a little lopsidedly because his system hadn't purged itself of the sedatives yet. 'I'm her folks,' he said.

Which startled and appalled Kennedy, because she thought it must have been her that gave it away. 'You *knew* that?'

'Yes. I knew that. That was why I followed her signal, back there on the hill. I knew there was a possibility you might be in trouble, too. And the lad. But I heard ... gunfire, explosions, all around her. I couldn't leave her there. I'm sorry about leaving you to fend for yourself.'

'Don't be,' Kennedy muttered. 'How did you know, Leo? What did I say?'

He shook his head, very slowly. 'Nothing. Well, you said at Dovecote that you only came to find me after you'd met Diema. You didn't say it was *because* you'd met her, but that seemed to be the implication.'

'Damn,' Kennedy said bitterly.

'But I would have known, anyway. She's the spitting image of her mother.'

'I think the resemblance ends right there.' She had to say it, however much it hurt him. Otherwise, he'd only be hurt worse later. 'She doesn't give a good goddamn about any of us. She got them to stick a needle in your heart to wake you up, so they could question you.'

Tillman winced – pain from his wounds or from the words. 'Good,' he said.

'Good?'

'She doesn't know me from Adam, and Adam was a piece of shit in her book. A million dead, Heather. That's what's about to happen. She plays the hand she's dealt, which is what I'd want her to do. What I'd do.'

The conversation had to stop then, because they were coming in for a landing. It was Diema who loomed suddenly at their shoulders to tell them that – and in retrospect, there was no way of knowing how long she'd been listening.

How they'd gotten into the USA at all was still a mystery to Kennedy. Probably they hadn't, officially. The plane had had to clear customs, of course, but there had been no inspection of its contents and – in her case, and Tillman's, and Rush's – no passport checks or immigration procedures. Kennedy's best guess was that the remote field where they'd landed was mostly used by drug runners and that the Judas People were

492

just taking advantage of an existing network of bribes, bungs and semi-professional courtesies. As far as US Customs were concerned, they were all airfreight. Whoever pocketed the kickback didn't care whether they were sex workers, terrorists or camera-shy rock stars.

So they'd never had a chance, at any stage in the proceedings, to cut loose from their *Elohim* handlers and ask for sanctuary. They were here on Diema's terms, and at her mercy, as they had been ever since the battle on Gellert Hill. They'd fallen off the edge of the world, and into another world that ran along next to it. Now their fate was in the hands of lunatics and children.

And it was a little after nine on a misty, sunny Sunday morning, which meant that there were ten hours left to Armageddon.

The truck took a turn very sharply, rocking on its base like a boat on a rising tide. One of Kuutma's women – *Alus*, Kennedy thought – spoke through a security grille to the other, who was driving. Both had changed into security guard livery in case the truck got stopped at any stage. Everyone else had been given a change of clothes before they left Budapest, so they were now dressed in smart casual clothes that wouldn't attract a second glance. Except that Tillman looked like a dead man walking and Rush's face (though the swelling had gone down) was crossed and recrossed with ant-tracks of surgical suture.

'Where are we?' Diema asked Alus.

'*He vuteh*,' the woman answered shortly. 'The tunnel.'

Diema looked at Kennedy, then at Tillman, ignoring Rush. 'We've reached the Lincoln Tunnel,' she said. 'We're crossing into Manhattan. We have to decide where we want to go first.'

'The factory,' Tillman muttered. His voice was indistinct.

'Up in the Bronx. Where Lusim milled the ricin. I want to see it.'

'The factory's already been searched by our people,' Alus said. 'You won't find anything they missed.'

Tillman didn't waste energy arguing with her and Kennedy knew why. It was still Diema's operation and her voice was the one that counted.

Diema spoke to Alus – it sounded like a single word – and Alus spoke through the grille to Taria.

'This is foolish,' Nahir said to Diema, in a low, fierce voice. 'A waste of time. Everyone else is searching the north end of the island.'

'You see a point in us doing what everyone else is doing?' Tillman asked him.

Diema said something else to Nahir, in quick-fire Aramaic, and he fell silent. *Do as you're told*, Kennedy guessed. So Diema trusted Tillman's instincts, whatever else. So did she, for that matter. Everyone needs a rock to cling to when the flood comes.

Nothing to do now until they got through the Uptown traffic to the Henry Hudson Bridge, and over into the Bronx. Kennedy crossed to Rush, who was still lost in his own fathomless thoughts, and put a hand on his shoulder.

He looked up at her, his face tired and bleak.

'Hanging in there?' she asked him.

'I'm okay,' he said. He even tried a smile.

'I don't think any of us are okay, Rush. But you haven't said a word since Budapest. Did something happen there?'

'Lots of things happened there.'

'That's true,' Kennedy acknowledged. 'But you gave a good account of yourself. Faced a stone killer and came away alive, which is one-nil for the home team. You're not going to have to do that again, if that's what's worrying you. If we figure out where Kuutma's going to make his strike, it's Kuutma's people who will go in. Not us.'

'It's not that,' Rush said. 'It's ... I ...' He seemed to wrestle with the next word for a long time. Kennedy realised that Nahir was watching them both from the other side of the narrow space, and moved to block his line of sight. The sound of the traffic and the rumbling of the truck's diesel engine would drown out any sound they were making.

'What?' she asked him.

'She's in trouble with her people,' Rush said. 'Diema. And I think it's because of me.'

The thought that he might be concerned about the girl had never occurred to Kennedy and it blindsided her completely. 'What?' she asked stupidly.

'It was something that happened at the safe house. I think she might be under arrest, or something. The shithead over there, Nahir – he was mouthing off at her, and then the scary bald guy got a turn, too, and then he said he'd make a judgment.'

'A judgment about what? Do you have any idea?'

He shook his head. 'I wish I hadn't come here,' he muttered bleakly. 'I haven't made the slightest bit of difference. I don't know why I thought I could. All I've done is screw things up.'

'This – what we're doing right now – it isn't your area of expertise,' Kennedy said gently. 'Or mine.'

He looked up and met her concerned gaze. 'Heather, I haven't got an area of expertise.'

Kennedy took the typescript of Toller's book out of her handbag and handed it to him.

'Yeah, you do,' she said. 'Same as mine. We're the detectives, Ben. That's why they need us.'

The truck rolled to a halt at last, and Taria unlocked and opened its rear doors from the outside. They stepped out into daylight for the first time in two hours. Taria and Alus, with surprising care and gentleness, helped Tillman down off the tailgate of the truck. Kennedy had to remind herself that they'd be just as happy to cut his throat, if the order came down. You couldn't lower your guard around these people.

Any of them.

The factory was a shell, most of its windows broken or boarded, graffiti climbing its walls like moss. It stood on an apron of asphalt that was being ripped apart in slow motion by bramble and knotweed. Pigeons nested on the ledges of the higher windows and in holes in the walls where bricks had fallen out. The air was heavy with their insinuations. There was a sign, also streaked with birdshit. It read PARNASSUS IRON AND STEEL COMPANY, with a stylised picture of a mountain behind it like the Paramount logo.

Beyond a sagging chain-link fence, the waters of the Harlem River lapped at a concrete pier on which an ancient sofa sat, mildewed and foul. There was a small, dense cluster of empty beer bottles standing next to the sofa and a cairn of polystyrene boxes bearing the McDonald's logo. Further in the background, but dominating everything, the towers of Manhattan rose like a dream: the land of milk and honey, just across the water.

One of Kuutma's Messengers, who looked to be about the same age as Diema or maybe a year older, had been stationed at the factory's main doors to await their arrival. He was dressed in torn jeans and a faded STROKES T-shirt, but he came to attention as Diema approached and greeted her with the sign of the noose, instantly on his mettle. She seemed to know him.

'Raziel,' she said.

He blushed with pleasure at being recognised. 'Ready to serve you, sister,' he said. He stood aside for her without a word and fell in behind her. The rest of the party, apart from the driver, followed her inside the building. Tillman, leaning heavily on Kuutma's two angels, brought up the rear.

'Where are the vats?' he asked. 'I'd like to see them.'

Raziel looked to Diema, who nodded. 'Do as he says.'

Raziel led them to a massive room that seemed to take up most of the factory's interior space. Certainly its ceiling, far over their heads, was the underside of the building's roof, buttressed with massive steel beams and festooned with looped and dangling cables. The pigeons flew to and fro up there, and everything in sight was speckled chalk-white with their droppings. The beating of their wings reminded Kennedy very suddenly and strongly of a bike she'd had when she was seven. She'd slipped playing cards through the spokes of the rear wheel, and the sound when she rode it was exactly the same, she realised now, as the sound of pigeons taking startled flight.

In the centre of the room, obviously much newer than anything else in the place but already mottled with guano, stood seven massive tubs. They were of yellow plastic and they came up to Kennedy's shoulder. In each, there was an inch or so of thick green slurry or paste.

'Get me some of that,' Tillman said. 'But don't touch it with your hands.'

Taria found a length of wooden slat and used it as a spoon, scooping up a little of the muck. She held it out to Tillman, who leaned his weight against a cement pillar before he took the slat and sniffed at the gooey mess.

'Is that the toxin?' Kennedy asked him.

'No, it's too wet,' Tillman said. 'This is just cake. Ber

Lusim's people would have crushed the beans here, expressed the oil, and then filtered the residue a whole bunch of times. But they'd still have needed to precipitate the ricin. That's a two-stage process. We're looking for a room with a lot of wide, flat trays in it.'

'Why are we looking for it?' Nahir asked, with sarcastic emphasis.

Ignoring him, Diema barked out a terse command. Raziel and the angels made the sign of the noose and got moving at once. Nahir stayed where he was.

'*Na be'hiena se ve rach* chain of command,' Diema said to him. Her tone was mild, but her eyes were narrowed. Nahir met that gaze for a second or two longer, then joined the search.

That left Diema and the three of them. She turned to Tillman. 'You've seen a place like this before?' she asked him.

'Twice.' He held up two fingers, counted them off. 'The first time in Afghanistan, the second time right here in America. Texas. Small-scale outfits, both times, and as far as we could tell, neither of them processed enough ricin to hurt anyone. Except themselves, maybe. This looks to be a slicker operation.' He pointed at some bags of chemicals stacked up next to the vats. 'Sodium sulfate. Carbon tet. Lots of both. And seven vats means they had batches refining and drying all the time. A real assembly line.'

He reached up a hand to scratch his chest, but was defeated by the thick layers of dressings and gave up after a moment or two. 'It's the delivery system, every time,' he murmured.

'What is?' Diema asked.

Tillman looked at her, shrugged one shoulder: the other was holding most of his weight. 'The problem with ricin. It's really nasty stuff. Kills if it's inhaled, or swallowed, or if you get any of it inside your system some other way. But you need more than a grain or two. You need a thick aerosol spray or a solid pellet. Did you ever hear of Georgi Markov?'

Diema shook her head.

'A Bulgarian writer, and a political dissident. Lived in London in the 1970s. He was saying harsh things about the Soviets, and they wanted to shut him up, so someone got an assassin to stab him with the sharp end of an umbrella. Three days of agony, then he died. The umbrella had been rigged to deliver a pellet of ricin about a millimetre in diameter.'

'Which is fine if you want to kill one Bulgarian,' Diema said.

Tillman nodded. 'But you can't bomb New York with poisonous umbrellas. You need a delivery system that will flood the streets with millions of those pellets or with billions of smaller solid particles in suspension. If we figure out the system, we'll know where to find Ber Lusim. And whatever it is he's come up with, this is where he put it together, so there might be a clue here.'

Nahir and Raziel returned, followed a few minutes later by Taria and then Alus. 'Nothing,' Nahir said. 'No trays, and no obvious surface on which trays might have been ranged or racked. You appear to be mistaken.'

Tillman turned – slowly, carefully, shifting his weight with some difficulty – to look at the Messenger. 'Maybe about the logistics,' he said. 'Not about the chemistry. This process would have produced a pulpy mass, and once it's dried the ricin is skimmed off the surface. You lay it out flat in a shallow tray because you want a big surface area. If Ber Lusim didn't do that here, then he took the refined pulp away and skimmed it somewhere else.'

'A secondary processing plant,' Kennedy said. 'Maybe over in Manhattan itself. Would there be any way of identifying it?'

Tillman shook his head reluctantly. 'No, it's a pretty stream-lined operation. This is the biggest and the hardest part of the job. Pressing the beans, extracting the oil and processing the pulp. That takes time, manpower and a lot of powerful chemical solvents. But when you're skimming it, all you need is a blade.'

'And gloves,' Diema said. 'Presumably.'

'Well, you wouldn't want to touch the stuff, certainly. Or breathe it in. You'd have your harvesters in protective body suits with their own air supply. But unless they go out for a cigarette break and forget to change into their street clothes, I don't see where that helps us.'

'In any case, the skimming wouldn't still be going on now,' Kennedy pointed out. 'Whatever Ber Lusim intends to do, we've got to assume he's got it all in place and ready to go.'

'The trucks that dropped the castor beans and chemicals off here,' Taria said. 'Where did they go afterwards?'

Kennedy had never heard Taria speak before and she was surprised that the woman's voice was light and soft rather than sonorous.

'I don't know,' Diema admitted. 'And it's a good question. Nahir, find out.'

Nahir took out a cellphone and dialled, without protest or argument. *The earlier conversation about the chain of command must have struck a chord*, Kennedy thought.

While he spoke, either to Kuutma or more likely to some subordinate, Tillman made his own painfully slow circuit of the factory. Kennedy went with him, supporting some of his weight.

There was nothing in the main room that caught his attention, but at the back of the space, furthest from the door through which they'd entered, there was a double-door that had once been padlocked. A length of chain still hung from one of the two handles, and the wood of the doors themselves was splintered around the edges. At first, Kennedy thought that Kuutma's *Elohim* must have forced the door when they searched the place. Then she realised that the broken chain was welded to the woodwork with immemorial deposits of pigeon shit. It had been there a long time.

In the space beyond, they found a grease pit. Tillman examined it closely, even though he had to kneel down to do so. It was a massive space, about twenty feet by ten in area and five feet deep, with two parallel bars of pitted, rusted iron laid across the bottom. 'There would have been some kind of hydraulic lift here,' Tillman thought aloud. 'Back when this place was still up and running, I mean.'

'Are you wondering whether Ber Lusim could have laid trays or racks out down there, to skim off the ricin?' Kennedy asked him.

'Thought had crossed my mind.'

It looked unlikely, at first glance. The floor of the pit was filled with a thick, foul sediment of oil and slurry.

But Kennedy tapped with her foot at the edge of the pit. Tillman looked where the toe of her shoe was pointing: fresh scuff and scrape marks showed light against the ingrained oil stains at the edge of the pit, and a bisected crust of pigeon shit indicated where a piece of rusty sheet metal had been moved.

'Something got done here, anyway,' Kennedy said. 'Maybe he threw a cover over the pit and set the racks out on that.'

Tillman scanned the bare room slowly, with intense and silent concentration. Then he made a circuit of the pit, which took a good ten minutes, and finally rejoined Kennedy.

'Plenty of evidence of movement,' he said. 'Heavy stuff

501

being dragged around. I think you're right, Heather. Ber Lusim processed the ricin right here, and then he hauled it out. What I'm looking for is some kind of clue as to what else he might have done with it first. Whether it's still just loose powder or it's been packed into jackets or containers of some kind. Aerosol sprayers is a possibility, but then we ought to find some more chemical residues. He'd have been messing with propanes or ether compounds to make a propellant, and the smell would be all over here.'

Kennedy looked at her watch. It was 14.48. Four hours and twelve minutes left. 'Let's go see if Nahir found anything on those HEH transports,' she suggested.

They found that the others had returned to the truck. Rush was sitting on the tailgate, leafing through the typescript of Toller's book, while Diema was speaking to the other *Elohim* in their native tongue.

She turned to Tillman and Kennedy as they approached, and switched to English. 'The trucks went from here to a rented lot at Locust Point,' she said. 'Four miles east. They're still there. Nobody's used them since, as far as we can tell.'

'Okay,' Tillman said. 'Did you check for—'

Nahir rode right over him. 'They're empty, and they've been stripped clean. Nothing to go on. Nothing we can use. And the site rental was paid through a front company in Belgium. It was a dead end.'

'But there's something else,' Diema added. 'Kuutma has been working through the satellite images, and he found something. The time we know about – when they delivered the castor beans – that was the *second* time this place was visited. HEH trucks came here another time, a week earlier. So there could be something else, besides the ricin. Another threat.'

'No,' Rush said.

Nahir shot the boy a look of sheer exasperation and muttered something in Aramaic.

'It doesn't make sense, that's all,' Rush said, with a defensive shrug. 'The prophecy talks about one thing. One breath, killing a million people. Not multiple attacks.'

'He's right,' Kennedy said. 'Whatever was in the first delivery, it has to relate to the ricin. It's all got to be tied together, somehow. Can we find out what it was?'

'We're trying,' Diema said. 'The information could be in the computers we took in Gellert Hill. We just can't afford to wait for it. We've either got to find Ber Lusim or else we've got to cover every base.'

Kennedy felt a wave of fatalistic despair sweep over her, like a sudden paralysis. There was too much ground to make up and too little time. Ber Lusim had set the agenda all along, and everything they'd done had achieved nothing more than getting them ringside seats for his command performance. Under the circumstances, it was hard to make herself believe that anything they did now could matter.

But Diema was still pacing, her face fierce with thought. And Tillman, watching her, was wearing an expression that was both more complicated and more painful. His desire to help her, to make her mission succeed, was palpable. He'd almost died trying, and it wasn't over yet.

What was left? What had they missed? What could they still hope to do, in the dog end of time they still had?

'You said your people checked the water already?' she asked Diema.

'Yes,' Diema said tersely. 'There's nothing out there now that shouldn't be there. And there are *Elohim* stationed at the confluence of the rivers. If anything unscheduled comes down into this stretch, they'll keep a watch on it – and fire on it if they have to.'

At the confluence of the rivers. That meant at the northern end of Manhattan, right across the water from where they were now. Kennedy wondered whether Diema knew how much she was giving away here, and decided that the answer was almost certainly yes. Whatever else she was, the girl was no fool.

Ber Lusim's big finale was also his homecoming. Where else would one of the chosen expect the Messiah to descend? So now Kennedy had found Ginat'Dania twice – and this time she hadn't even been looking for it. It was one more problem that would have to be faced at some point: whether there was any way the three of them could get out of this alive, knowing what they now did.

'Okay,' she said. 'And you've got the street traffic covered. Air dispersal seems like the best bet – maybe the only bet – but there's no way he's going to get in close by diverting a commercial flight. Nine/eleven closed that loophole.'

'And we've got effective lockdowns on all private airfields,' Alus said. 'Nothing can get into the air without our *Elohim* seeing it. And if they don't like what they see, they'll swat it down before it even gets off the runway.'

'Subway trains.' Kennedy didn't even believe it as she said it, but there was no point in missing the obvious.

'There's only one station in what we think is the target zone,' Diema told her. '207th Street, at the top of Broadway. It's the northern terminus for one of the main underground lines, so there's no through traffic to worry about. But Kuutma has stationed Messengers on the platforms and in the streets around, just in case Ber Lusim tries to bring anything in that way.'

504

'That way? Meaning in a train? Okay, but suppose he's setting something up in the tunnels? Maybe it's worth sending a team in to check.'

'You're not thinking of the numbers,' Nahir told Kennedy scornfully. 'At the end of the line, there will be the lowest concentration of people. The whole New York subway and Metropolitan transit network – across all the boroughs and outlying areas – handles about four million passengers in the space of a day. Perhaps more, but not many more. What percentage of those do you think will visit 207th Street and Broadway, *rhaka*? I guarantee you that it's not a quarter of them.'

Kennedy did her best to ignore the anger that rose inside her. It didn't help that Nahir was right.

'Maybe we should forget about the maps, for a while,' she suggested.

'And do what?' Nahir's politeness was even more scathing than his contempt.

'And go back to the book. Rush, could you give us the last prophecy again?'

Rush glanced at her, nodded, and turned to the final page of the typescript. She wondered what page he'd been reading, if it wasn't that one. He began to read aloud. 'And the stone shall be rolled away from the tomb, as it was the time before—'

'We know what it says,' Diema said. Her tone was tense, strained. They were all getting close to the ragged edge.

'Sure,' Kennedy agreed. 'But have we accounted for all the variables? The stone and the tomb, and the voice crying out – yes. That all happened when Shekolni died. And presumably "the time before", when the stone was first rolled away, is the time of Jesus's death and resurrection. Toller seems to be saying that at least some of the circumstances of Christ's second coming will be like the first one.'

'Obviously,' Nahir said.

'And then there's the breath. "He will condemn a great multitude with a single breath." If Ber Lusim is as literal-minded with this as he's been with the other prophecies, he'll have turned the ricin into some kind of gas.'

'That's what we're assuming,' Diema said. There was still an edge to her voice, as if this were a distraction from more important things.

'How high does he have to be to get the stuff out on the wind?' Kennedy wondered. 'Has anyone done the maths?'

'It's not a question of height,' Nahir said. 'With a microlight aircraft, he could cover an area of—'

'I'm not thinking of aircraft. I'm thinking of window ledges. Rooftops. Terraces. Suppose he's just relying on the wind? Ricin spreads best as a powder. If he's refined it into that form, he could have tons of the stuff ready to shovel out into the air. You're thinking crop sprayers and microlights, but maybe he'll use a low-tech solution.'

Diema had already picked up her phone. A second later, she was having a conversation, either with Kuutma or with someone else in the hierarchy.

Locked out again, Kennedy gave the typescript back to Rush.

'I think we may be about to hit the road,' she said. 'Get ready.'

Diema lowered her phone. 'The prevailing wind is westerly,' she said. 'But only for the last couple of hours. It's predicted to be from the north, which is where it's been for most of the last three days. Kuutma is sending spotters up to the tops of the tallest buildings. They'll look for suspicious movement. But we're talking about thousands of windows and hundreds of rooftops. He's. . .' She hesitated, picking her

506

words with care. 'He's going to try to draft in some additional *Elohim*.'

'He's asking for volunteers,' Tillman translated. 'Raising a posse of concerned citizens.'

There was another pause. Diema nodded.

Nahir muttered something savage and Diema shut him up with a terse '*Ve rahi!*' She'd just confirmed that Ginat'Dania was right here and the fact had not gone unnoticed by the other Messengers.

Kennedy tried not to think about that. 'Correct me if I'm wrong,' she said. 'But a wind out of the north will be passing right through here, won't it?'

'Yes,' Diema confirmed. 'Kuutma already made that point. He'll send some people – as many as he can. But we're stretched very thin now. It's possible that we can't check every possible location in time.'

'Then let's get started,' Kennedy said. 'We can work outward from this place in semi-circular sweeps, doubling back on ourselves every time we hit the river.'

'Two hours left,' Tillman mused. 'I'm not saying you're wrong, Heather, but maybe this is the wrong time to be putting all our eggs in one basket.'

'The only basket we have,' Diema countered. 'Unless anyone can think of anything better, that's what we're going to do.'

She waited, looking from face to face. Nobody spoke.

'Then it's agreed. We pair up, with a Messenger in each pair, so that we can stay in touch with each other and with Kuutma.'

'Can I be paired with you?' Rush asked her.

'No,' Diema said.

Rush tried again, tentative but stubborn. 'I'd like ... I need to talk to you about some stuff. Please. Let me go with you.'

507

'We'll talk later, Rush. For now, you go with Taria. Alus, you're with Kennedy. I'll go with—'

'I'm staying here,' Tillman said. 'This is a tall building. If I can find my way up to the roof, I can get the lay of the land from here. I'll just slow you down, in any case. You'll get twice as much done without me, and I can keep in touch with you by phone. If anything else occurs to me, I'll pass it along.'

'He'll need to be guarded,' Nahir said, ignoring Tillman and speaking directly to Diema. 'More than ever now, after your incautious words. He can't be left alone, to speak to others of his kind, or leave messages. Someone has to watch him, from now until—'

'Then watch him,' Diema snapped.

'Yeah,' Rush said. 'That'll work.' He stood up, whacking the rolled typescript against the side of the truck and producing a bass-drum boom. They all looked at him – much as they'd looked at Taria when she'd proved she had a voice. His face was full of anger and confusion and hurt pride. 'I mean, it's not like your friend there will kill us as soon as your back is turned. It's not like he was trying to persuade your boss to finish us off back in Budapest. He's a reasonable man. I bet he'd never even dream of sharpening his knife on Leo's kidneys.'

Diema was rigid with impatience, standing on the balls of her feet. 'He'll follow his orders,' she said tightly. 'Kuutma said he'd give a ruling. You're safe until he's pronounced on you.'

'So you say. If Leo stays, I'm staying too. And I'll be watching your friend the whole time he watches us.' He stared at her, looking close to tears, and she looked back at him with a face like a closed fist. If it was a staring contest, Rush lost. He held up the typescript like a shield in front of his eyes. 'Anyway, Kennedy said the answer's in here and I believe her. So you do what you want. I'll stick around and catch up on my reading.'

508

'As you like,' Diema said curtly. 'We'll spend an hour on this, then regroup here. And we'll stay in touch by phone, in the meantime. Those who are coming, come.'

Along with Alus, Taria, Kennedy and Raziel, she headed out. Diema and Kennedy took the truck, since somebody had to. The others took to the streets on foot.

66

A feeling of despair welled up inside Rush as he watched Diema leave.

Brief as it was, their lovemaking had left him feeling more bruised and blown open than he'd felt at any time since the death of his ex-girlfriend, Siobhan – the one who'd killed herself.

Then Kuutma had shone a light on the whole thing that was crazy but plausible. Diema had done that to him – seduced him, or raped him, or ricocheted off him – because for some reason she wanted to get pregnant. Maybe it was like that tired bullshit you heard about single mothers and council flats. Girls having babies so they could jump the queue. Maybe Ginat'Dania had a housing shortage.

But when he got that far, and tried to imagine Diema – who he thought of as an unexploded bomb in human form – knitting woollen booties, breast-feeding, pushing a stroller, it was like trying to paint the two sides of a Moebius strip in different colours.

If that was all, if she'd needed a quick delivery system for some DNA, he'd still feel stupid but he could let it go. What was hard was the not knowing: the feeling that his pocket had been picked, somehow, while his attention was elsewhere, and that he couldn't figure out what had been taken.

But the more Diema ducked away from talking to him, the more certain he was that it was something that mattered.

As soon as they were out of sight, Tillman turned to Nahir.

'So is she right?' he asked. 'Are you going to stick to your orders and work with me? Or are we going to have to fight this out? I know you don't lie, so I figure it's worth asking. It would be useful to know if I can turn my back on you.'

The Messenger stared at him – stared at both of them – with stony calm. The hate was still there, too, but it was a good way back and under control. And something else was working under the uncommunicative surface of his face. *Maybe he's afraid*, Rush thought. Diema had as good as told them that this was her home town – Ginat'Dania, the great mysterious refuge. He hadn't figured out yet how you hid a city in the middle of New York, but if that was what they'd done, Nahir – along with all the *Elohim* – might be about to become a homeless orphan. Under the circumstances, it was pretty much of a miracle that they were keeping it together as well as they were. Maybe being batshit crazy was protecting them from the worst of it. Rush knew that the only reason he was staying so calm himself was because his mind couldn't make the phrase *a million dead* mean anything: it just kept slipping off at an oblique angle.

'There would be no fight,' Nahir said with chilly dignity. 'If I were to decide that you and this boy should die, I'd kill you. But I would hardly have waited, in that case, until you stood on this holiest of ground. I would have killed you out among the Nations. I could have dealt with you while Diema was leading us into Gellert Hill. I thought about doing that. But I take the oaths I've sworn seriously. Obedience in a soldier is what chastity is in a marriage.'

Tillman raised his eyebrows at the comparison. 'You mean it's precious because it's so rare?'

511

'I'm getting tired,' Rush said, 'of being called a boy. Just thought I'd throw that out there.'

'I want to get up to the roof,' Tillman said. 'Take a look at the neighbourhood from up there. Supposing you're still feeling chaste, I'd appreciate some help with that. Are there any stairs in this place?'

It turned out there were, and with both Nahir and Rush taking some of his weight, Tillman was able to climb them. A steel door, hanging halfway off its hinges, gave onto a narrow walkway with the main pitch of the roof above and behind it. There was a parapet wall just high enough to trip over and a congregation of pigeons that scattered when Rush pushed the door open.

Gravel crunched under their feet as they stepped out. The Bronx was laid out before them, wearing the beauty of the evening like a garment – a peephole bra, maybe, or something similarly sleazy and enticing. Warehouses and office blocks close to hand gave way to streets of low-rises and row houses further to the north and east.

A thousand terraces, rising like the steps of an amphitheatre. New York's vast, vertical concatenation.

A thousand places for a madman to sit and watch the sun go down, and throw his poisoned confetti.

Nahir and Tillman began to discuss wind speed and elevation. Rush left them to it, certain that they didn't need him and wouldn't see him go.

He went back down the stairs, into the big room with the vats. He found a patch of sunlight coming through a hole in the roof and sat to read Toller's book one final time.

Diema let Kennedy drive, because she trusted her own instinct and observation more than she trusted anyone else's. But the hopelessness of the task began to sink in before they'd gone half a mile. The possible launch points for an aerial release of the powdered ricin were pretty close to infinite – and unless they happened to see Ber Lusim loitering at a window or looking down from a roof, there was almost nothing to make any one stand out from the next.

Higher was better. Upwind was essential. They were searching a vast cone of three-dimensional space with the northern end of Manhattan Island as its base – and they were searching it from the ground.

Except that Kennedy wasn't. She'd allowed the truck to roll to a halt, and she was looking south. Diema followed her gaze. They'd reached the end of a cross street – the sign told her it was 225th. Highway 9 was ahead of them, with a stretch of elevated railway rising like a rampart over the surface street. Beyond was just more of what they'd already seen, factories and marshalling yards and sheds, with occasional rows of shops whose windows were so grimy you couldn't guess from this distance what it was they sold.

But just south of them, beyond the glittering arc of the Henry Hudson Bridge, Broadway opened up like a lover's arms.

'What's the matter?' Diema asked. 'Why have you stopped?'

'I'm just thinking of an old joke,' Kennedy said. 'When you're buying real estate, what are the three most important things to bear in mind?'

'I have no idea. Please keep moving.'

'Location, location and location.'

Kennedy turned to look at her hard, and Diema understood what it was she was saying.

'Ber Lusim's factory,' she murmured.

'Exactly. Why here? Presumably he didn't want to transport

the poison a long way. Every time he moved it, he was risking being stopped, and found out. So he wanted to be close. But this close? I mean, that's Ginat'Dania down there, isn't it? A half-mile south of us?'

Diema said nothing.

'Oh, for God's sake,' Kennedy exploded. 'Just nod!'

Slowly, with a prickle of superstitious dread, Diema forced her head to move – down once, then up again.

'So I'm guessing he was well within the radius of your border patrols. There's no way you wouldn't keep a watch on your own front doorstep. He's way too close, and way too visible.'

'Perhaps it pleased his ego to play with us.'

Kennedy drummed the steering wheel with the heels of her thumbs, thinking. 'Maybe. But is that what he was like, as a Messenger? Did he grandstand or did he get the job done?'

'Mostly,' Diema admitted, 'he got the job done.'

'Then I think we're missing something. We've got to be. Otherwise—'

Diema's phone rang, and although the *rhaka* seemed disposed to carry on talking, she silenced her with a raised hand. That tone meant Kuutma. And if Kuutma was calling her, he had something important to tell her or to ask her.

Rush had got sick of the final prophecy. They'd worried it to pieces and there didn't seem to be any new insights to be gleaned. So he'd flicked back to the first page and started from scratch.

He was struck all over again by how ludicrous it was to read this crap as though it contained sacred truths. Toller wasn't just barking, he was barking and boring – so hung up on the minutiae of his own time that he couldn't talk about the

514

eternal without making six or seven veiled references to the strictly contemporary.

Which, when you thought about it, was strange for one of the Judas People. Getting so caught up in local politics – Adamite politics – seemed like worrying about the weather forecast for the moon.

Something was nagging at Rush. It had been nagging at him when he read the scholarly accounts of Toller and the other Fifth Monarchists on the plane, and when he'd talked it over with Diema. It was the blunt end of an idea, but it wasn't making enough of an impression to stick. It was just that general sense of wrongness or incongruity, combined with something really tiny and specific that he'd already noticed and wondered about, a discrepancy between the written accounts and the observable here and now.

A second later, as he got into the meat of the prophecies, it fell out of his head altogether, because something else struck him much more forcefully. It was sitting in the book's opening paragraphs, and the only reason he hadn't seen it before was because he'd been focusing on the actual text, rather than on the annotations that Kennedy had written in the margins or over the words. That French guy's sleeve notes.

And so I stand upon the Muses' Mountain, asking Inspiration of all, though my true Muse be Godde the Higheste. And here He doth deliver, through me unworthy, His final Judgment.

That was Toller. And over the words 'the Muses' Mountain' Kennedy had written in neat black biro a single word.

Parnassus.

The word produced the image: the picture of a mountain on

the sign they'd passed as they walked in here. Parnassus Iron and Steel.

Rush got to his feet. The nape of his neck prickled like someone was standing right behind him and breathing on it. Would Ber Lusim – or his Obi Wan, Avra Shekolni – have missed that reference? They'd taken everything else in the book literally as gospel. So it made sense that they would have felt the book had directed them to this place.

Which was empty. There was nobody here, and nowhere for them to be hiding. Kuutma's Messengers had searched the building and found nothing.

But Rush felt that the silence around him had changed, somehow, and he didn't feel like sitting down again. It was only a conditional silence, in any case. Just like anywhere in New York, the air carried the roar of traffic from the middle distance. This emptiness was in the heart of a great city. Rush was standing at the still centre of the turning world.

He stepped out of the sunlight and did a slow circuit of the room, with the manuscript rolled up in his hand. He moved quietly, because the echoes of his footsteps sounded disconcertingly loud. Whenever he stopped, he listened. But nothing was moving any closer than the traffic.

When he moved out of the main factory floor into the smaller rooms around it, Rush admitted to himself that this had become a search. He still didn't know what it was he was looking for, but the uneasiness was eating at him and he wanted to be absolutely sure there was nothing there.

He found himself at last in front of the double doors that led through to the grease pit. He'd seen Kennedy and Tillman looking it over earlier, so he was pretty certain that there wouldn't be anything to see here, but he went in anyway.

The pit was foul. Probably it had been left that way by the

previous owners. The walls and floor of it were thick with industrial residue that might have been oil, tar, paint or most likely all of the above. There were puddles of water with an unhealthy, nacreous sheen to them, and a stink of baking bitumen hung over everything like the breath of a motorway on an August morning.

He looked up at the ceiling. There weren't any obvious holes in it, but that didn't mean anything. Water finds its level. The rain could have come in somewhere else and ended up in the pit because the pit was the lowest point.

There was no way of getting down there without ruining your clothes. If you sat down and lowered yourself in, the seat of your pants would get covered in the oily muck. If you jumped, you'd raise a splash.

He walked around the pit instead, feeling like an idiot and yet relieved at the same time that there was nothing to see.

Except that there was. Halfway around the rim, he walked into a shaft of sunlight that came in through a broken skylight high above him and hit one of the pit's walls. Part of the wall must have been raised a little proud of the area around it, because there was a shadow – perfectly square, and about five feet on a side. It looked like there was a trapdoor in the wall, except that it was only the outline of a door. The colours and textures of that area of wall were exactly the same as the colours and textures to either side of them. It had to be a trick of the light, but it was a disconcerting one, and once he'd seen it he couldn't trick himself into not seeing it again.

He stood irresolute at the edge of the pit. This was ridiculous. If there was something here, someone else – someone who knew what they were doing – would have found it by now.

The sun went behind a cloud, the ray of light disappeared

517

and the imaginary door went with it. Rush turned away. But at the last moment before he walked out of the room, he remembered Diema's words back at Dovecote.

Not you, boy. You weren't planned for.

Bugger it.

Rush launched himself into the pit with an ungainly jump, landing heavily and sending up, just as he'd feared, a shower of variegated filth. He almost lost his footing, but saved himself by holding onto the wall.

One baby step at a time, scared both of what he was treading in and of what he was breathing, he crossed the pit to the wall where the tell-tale shadow had been. There was nothing there. No sign of a hinge or a handle, or of a physical break in the wall where a door might begin or end. But then, the oily residue that had been sluiced over everything made a pretty effective camouflage.

It was pretty fresh, too, and splashed a little thicker, here, than elsewhere on the wall.

Suppressing a shudder, Rush reached out and pushed his fingers into the thick muck. He ran them from right to left and back again, feeling for a break point, a crack in the structure. There was nothing like that.

But there was something else. Around about his chest height, there was a raised spot, rounded and about an inch and a half in diameter. A boss or the head of a rivet, maybe. Rush scooped the oily mess away from it and found a circular plate made of some dull, weathered metal.

It was pivoted at the top, so you could slide it sideways. Rush did so now.

'Son of a bitch,' he whispered.

He was looking at a keyhole.

*

Kennedy got out of the truck and walked to the corner of the street. Diema's conversation with Kuutma didn't look like ending any time soon, and since they were talking in their own language there was nothing to be gained from eavesdropping.

There was a lot of traffic on the main highway, but nobody walking anywhere in sight. The corner store had been a Blockbuster, but not for a while now. Displayed in its window were the upcoming movie sensations of a few years back. *Wild Hogs. 300. Zodiac.* A poster offered two movie rentals plus popcorn and a large bottle of Coke for $12.99. Underneath the poster lay a dead bird, something small and nondescript, like a sparrow or a dunnock, that had gotten itself in there and couldn't get out again.

Two hours and some odd minutes to go, and they were treading water. But she couldn't think of anything else they could do. In a city-wide game of hide-and-seek, the hider had it all over the seeker.

But she was right about the location. She knew there was something there, if she could only think it through. Ber Lusim had extracted and purified his toxin in a place that increased his own risk enormously. Why would someone who was supposed to be a master strategist do something that was so stupid on the face of it?

Maybe the answer was something really banal. When he first became a Messenger, Ber Lusim might have been sent out to patrol these streets. He could have found the old steelworks back then and kept it in mind. Except that back then, he'd still been sane and – you had to assume – wasn't contemplating mass murder even as a distant possibility.

So make a different assumption. He chose the location later, nearer to the present time. He was looking for a specific feature and this place had it. And whatever it was, it was worth the risk of sending his highly visible bright-red trucks here twice, and maybe spending time here himself, within walking distance of the homeland where he was a wanted man.

Twice. The trucks came here twice. And the poison was the second shipment, not the first. But in that case...

Diema appeared at her shoulder without a sound, making her start violently. 'Shit,' she exclaimed.

The girl didn't waste any time on apologies. 'They found out what the first shipment was.'

'Go on,' said Kennedy.

'It was conventional explosive. Ten thousand tons of octocubane and five kilos of acetone peroxide.'

Kennedy thought through the amounts. 'Is the peroxide a primer?'

Diema nodded.

'So how big a blast is that? Not big enough to kill a million, right?'

'Big enough to take down most of a city block. Depending on where you placed it, you could easily get ten or twenty thousand casualties.'

It was clear that the girl wanted to head back for the truck. She made a feint in that direction now, looking at Kennedy expectantly, but Kennedy was fishing out the earlier thought about the trucks. Something was falling into place, and the explosive was the piece that made sense out of everything else.

'Earth and air,' she muttered.

Diema got the reference. 'Toller's book,' she said. '"God will speak in fire and water, and last in earth and air."'

'We screwed up,' Kennedy said. 'I think we screwed up.'

'How? What did we miss?'

'We were thinking Ber Lusim had to release the ricin into the air.'

'He does,' Diema insisted. 'That's the only way you could get casualties on the scale the prophecy calls for.'

'But microlights? Crop dusters? This is the most fiercely defended airspace in the world. He could never be sure of getting through. And my idea about balconies and rooftops – if the wind changes, he's nowhere. He can't wait. We know that much. Shekolni told us an exact time, not a vague ballpark.'

Diema's mind was running parallel to hers now. 'If earth and air were one thing, not two things . . .'

'That's it,' Kennedy agreed. 'You remember Nine/Eleven? You'd still have been at school, but—'

'We remember,' Diema said tightly.

'When the towers fell, there was a dust cloud like nothing on earth. Thousands and thousands of tons of dust, racing through the streets on the shockwave, running the length and breadth of Manhattan. People got sick, just because of the dust. Some of them are still sick.'

'*Berukhot!* He uses the explosive to blow up a building . . .'

'To pulverise a building. Smash it into atoms. So you get a massive shockwave and a massive dust cloud. And the ricin is inside the building, so the dust cloud becomes a vector. It spreads out from here along the lines of the streets. Earth and air, all mixed together into a poison cocktail. It kills everyone who takes a breath.'

'But where?' Diema demanded. 'Which building would he choose?'

'The trucks only came those two times, Diema. They never came back.'

The girl stared at her, bewildered. 'So?'

'So he didn't choose that factory because he liked the décor. He chose it because it's right at the north end of Broadway. That's his delivery system right there. He's got himself a gun barrel thirteen miles long and eighty feet wide. I don't think the poison ever left the building.'

Rush was having a hard time persuading Tillman and Nahir to come and look at what he'd found. In fact, he was having a hard time making them listen to him at all. Nahir's feeling, when he finally let Rush say his piece, was that 'found' was probably the wrong word to use.

'The building was searched by *Elohim*,' he pointed out. His tone suggested that only a moron would need to have this explained to him. 'Anything you've seen, you can be certain that they've also seen it and investigated it.'

'But you can only see it from certain angles,' Rush explained, trying hard to sound calm and rational. 'And even then, only when the light hits it full-on. It's camouflaged.'

'Against amateurs,' Nahir said. 'Not against professionals.'

'Where is this, Rush?' Tillman asked.

'In that empty swimming pool thing.'

'The grease pit? Out toward the back of the building.'

'Yes. That.'

Tillman looked doubtful. 'I checked that over,' he said. 'With Kennedy. We think that was probably where Ber Lusim had his skimming trays. But there was no sign that he'd been there recently.'

Tillman's tone was milder than Nahir's, but the same assumptions were behind it. 'Shit!' Rush yelled, 'I am not making this up and I'm not stupid. I know what I saw. Now will you just come down and take a look at it?'

'Later,' Nahir said loftily. 'We don't have time for this now.'

Rush looked at his watch, which was showing forty-five minutes to zero hour. 'Later?' he repeated.

The two men had gone back to their discussion and neither

of them answered. Nahir was evidently relaying whatever they were talking about to the *Elohim* out in the city. He had his phone to his mouth and was switching between muttered English and muttered Aramaic.

'Sorry,' Rush said. 'Later's no good to me.'

He swiped the phone out of Nahir's hand and threw it over the parapet wall.

The look of surprise and rage on the Messenger's face was pretty damn satisfying – but only for about a half a second. That was how long it took for Nahir to explode into violent motion and slam Rush to the ground in an agonising, total lock.

'Are you mad?' he hissed. 'Do you want to die?'

'Nobody's killing anyone,' Tillman said quietly – quietly enough that the click when he thumbed the safety of the Beretta sounded indecently loud. It was just as well that he took the reins of the conversation, because Rush's windpipe was crimped tightly by what felt like Nahir's elbow, and he couldn't either talk or take a breath. His face was pressed flat against the gravel of the narrow walkway, without him having much idea of how it had got there, and none of his limbs were free to move. The ball was very much in everybody else's court.

'You should put the gun away,' Nahir said to Tillman. 'Or this will end badly.'

'I'm happy to,' Tillman told him. 'But let the kid up. He was just trying to get our attention.'

'He has my attention. And I can break his neck whether you fire on me or not.'

'Works better if you let him up and I put this away.'

There was a short, painful silence. At least, it was painful for Rush.

'I'll release him,' Nahir said. 'But if he speaks again, I'll break both of his arms.'

The immobilising pressure on every moving part of Rush's body was suddenly eased as Nahir rose. Nonetheless, Rush stayed where he was. He could only be thrown down again if he made the mistake of getting up.

'Come and see the frigging door,' he said, his voice slightly strangulated.

'You have been warned, boy.'

'No,' Tillman said. 'Let's go and see the door. You've convinced me, Rush. Whatever it is you've found, you just put your neck on the line for it.'

'Whatever it takes,' Rush wheezed, picking himself up.

They took the stairs even more slowly going down. Tillman seemed to be cramping up a little and needed a lot more support. He was okay over the flat, though, so Rush led the way to the double doors and pointed through them towards the pit.

'There,' he said. 'Far side. Under the skylight.'

Nahir entered first, and Rush stood aside to let Tillman precede him, too. He wanted them to see for themselves. Then, belatedly, he noticed that the sun had gone in again, so they might not see the outline of the door at all. 'Okay,' he said, hurriedly stepping between them. 'Let me show you.'

He needn't have worried. The discontinuity in the wall of the grease pit was clearly visible, despite the poor light, because the door was standing open and the darkness beyond it was much deeper than the darkness on either side.

But it wasn't the door that Nahir and Tillman were looking at.

It was the man standing on the opposite side of the pit, directly facing them.

'This is unfortunate,' the man said. His tone was calm, almost solemn.

'Ber Lusim,' Nahir gasped. He seemed frozen to the spot, unable to process what he was seeing.

And Rush felt something that was almost like vertigo. They'd come so far to attend this meeting, he felt for a split second as though maybe there was such a thing as predestination after all.

Ber Lusim was looking from one to the other of them, with cool, detached appraisal. If he felt threatened or alarmed at their being there, it didn't show in his face or his stance – which when Rush thought about it was pretty frightening.

'In these closing moments of the old order,' Ber Lusim said to them, 'it's still possible for men to die. But after this last, great dying, death will end for ever.' An incantatory quality had crept into his voice. 'I feel, therefore, that it might be presumption on my part if I were to kill you. Arrogance. As though I asserted my citizenship of this time, this world, even as I usher in the next world, the world everlasting. I have no great desire to do that. Therefore, if you wish to die, you must express an explicit preference – or volunteer yourselves for death by some unambiguous action.'

Nahir crossed his hands over his chest and suddenly had two sica blades between his fingers.

Ber Lusim laughed, as though this were a joke that he richly appreciated.

'Yes,' he said. 'Something like that.'

67

Nahir's hands flashed outwards and up in a movement so fluid and graceful that he looked to Rush, for an insane moment, like a flamenco dancer striking the pose that begins the dance. The two knives, leaving his fingers at the same time, drew parallel lines in the air.

Ber Lusim barely seemed to move in response, but now there was a knife in his hand, too, and it met each of Nahir's thrown blades along their separate trajectories. Two high, ringing notes sounded, like the chiming of a bell. Nahir's knives leaped away to right and left, the right-hand one glittering like a Catherine wheel as it hit a sudden shaft of sunlight.

Nahir was drawing again and so was Tillman – presumably a gun rather than a knife – but Ber Lusim was faster than either of them. He crossed the grease pit in a standing long jump, landing between the two men, and he didn't seem to mind very much that he was now fighting a war on two fronts.

Nahir thrust at Ber Lusim with a third sica, aiming for his chest. Ber Lusim leaned away and his own hand came up inside Nahir's guard. The knife he held, unexpectedly reversed, slashed deeply into Nahir's wrist, almost severing his hand.

By this time, Tillman had his gun out and aimed, but his movements seemed almost comically slow compared to those of the two *Elohim*. Ber Lusim didn't even turn to face him. He just took the gun out of Tillman's hand with a near-vertical kick, then returned his attention to Nahir.

A series of lightning-quick sweeps of the blade forced Nahir – who now only had one hand to defend with – to give ground hurriedly, and took Ber Lusim, as he followed, out of Tillman's reach.

Tillman lumbered after him. Rush, who up to this point had stood frozen in shock, recovered himself enough to yell, 'Leo, don't!' He launched himself forward, but in the three seconds it took him to reach them a whole lot of things happened.

Ber Lusim stopped dead, letting Tillman run against him. The Messenger took a solid punch to the side of the head, but it didn't seem to affect him – and at the same time he hammered his elbow into Tillman's throat.

Nahir pressed a desperate attack, jumping into what he presumed was a gap in Ber Lusim's guard. Ber Lusim blocked, feinted, blocked, and then sliced Nahir's other wrist, in a deliberate, mocking echo of the earlier attack.

Nahir's charge faltered, pain and alarm flickering across his face. Ber Lusim bent from the waist to deliver a roundhouse kick to Nahir's stomach, then slammed the hilt of the knife into the side of the other man's head as he folded. Except that it wasn't a hilt, because a sica didn't have a hilt, as such, just a sharp end and a blunter end. The blunt end was still a narrow wedge of steel, which bit into Nahir's skull with a sound like a cleaver dissecting a watermelon.

And Ber Lusim still had time, before Rush reached him, to bring the knife around so that the tip of it pointed at the centre of Rush's chest. Rush stumbled to a halt with the razor-sharp blade touching his skin, having parted the thin fabric of his shirt as though it wasn't even there.

'Think on it,' Ber Lusim said calmly, as Nahir fell full-length and Tillman crumpled to his knees. 'They had weapons, at least. You have nothing. But if you wish it, then come.'

Tillman was fumbling for his fallen gun. Ber Lusim kicked him in the face with brutal force, sending him toppling sideways into the grease pit. There was a moment when Rush could have dodged around the knife and attacked him. But he couldn't make his body move: rooted to the spot with terror, he stared down at Tillman's unmoving body. Leo was face-down in the muck and ooze that covered the floor of the pit. If he wasn't dead already, he was probably about to drown or suffocate.

Rush forced himself into motion. He turned his back on Ber Lusim, while his hindbrain screamed at him to duck and cower and fall into a foetal huddle, and jumped down into the pit.

This time he didn't manage to keep his footing. He went over on his back in the rancid oil and floundered grotesquely for a second or two before he could roll over and right himself. He crawled across to Tillman, pawed at him with hands now thick with grease and finally managed to turn him onto his back. The big man was profoundly unconscious, but he was breathing.

Rush got his hands under Tillman's armpits and hauled on him. Tillman was a dead weight, but Rush managed to move him an inch at a time over to the wall of the pit. He propped Tillman up there, wedged into the corner, so that he couldn't easily slip down again.

Rush was conscious of Ber Lusim's presence above and behind him – the Messenger's utter silence probably, but not necessarily, meaning that he wasn't moving.

'Have you come a long way?' Ber Lusim asked.

Small talk, from the saint of killers.

'London,' Rush said. 'Budapest. New York. I'm sure you can fill in the dots.' He was going for bravado, but his voice – in his own ears, at least – sounded high and weak.

Ber Lusim laughed, as though Rush had said something funny, and jumped down beside him – then walked on, past him, towards the open door.

'We expect to walk a straight line,' he said, looking back at Rush over his shoulder. 'I'm not sure where that hope comes from. Experience should teach us that there are no straight lines in nature. God doesn't draw with a ruler. What's your name, boy?'

And Rush took the insult on the chin this time, because what else had he just been, while the men fought it out?

'Ben,' he said.

'That's half a name. It means *son of*. Where is the rest?'

'Rush. Ben Rush.'

Ber Lusim looked momentarily startled. 'Ben Rush,' he repeated.

'Yeah.' Rush swallowed hard and looked down at Tillman. 'Look, he's in a bad way. Will you let me go, so I can get some help for him?'

'Of course not,' Ber Lusim said. 'What help could there be, in any case? In twenty minutes' time, this building will be a crater. And after that, all reckoning of time will stop. Leave him. I want to show you something.'

He indicated the doorway.

'What?' Rush said.

'Go inside,' Ber Lusim ordered him.

'I . . . what's inside? Why would I go in there?' Rush hadn't been afraid of the dark since he was seven years old, but right then that square opening seemed to be full of inimical promise.

'You came a long way to find me,' Ber Lusim said. 'And you succeeded, where everyone else failed. That was a striking and exceptional thing – and obviously it was meant, as all things are meant. The prophet taught me that, when I had forgotten it, or learned to act as if it weren't true. I'm going back inside, Ben Rush. I can't leave you behind me, on your feet and free to leave. If you insist on staying here, I'll respect that. But—' he raised his hand and the knife stropped the air as he flicked it back and forth with terrifying dexterity '—I'll have to make sure you're unable to move. The quickest and easiest way to do that would be to sever your spinal column and the nerve stem that runs through it. The decision is yours. I'll give you a few moments to consider it.'

'No, I . . . I'm good. I mean, I'll go inside. I pick that one.'

Ber Lusim nodded and indicated with a sweep of the hand that Rush should go first.

Choking on fear and humiliation, Rush stepped into the dark.

To get to the factory's front gate meant driving around three of the four walls of the compound, but Kennedy just dropped the truck down a gear and took it straight through the fence. A length of the wire-mesh weave remained wrapped around the windshield, and one of the cement posts was ripped out of the ground and went bounding along the ground behind them like a dog.

Diema had used the time while they drove to call Kuutma, but she was answered with the brutal bathos of a voicemail message. She told him in a few terse sentences what Kennedy had guessed, and put the phone down just as Kennedy took the fence.

The *rhaka* slewed the truck around, raising a tidal wave of gravel, and was already jumping down out of the driver's side before the heavy vehicle had stopped rocking on its axis. She sprinted ahead of Diema into the building, but slowed once inside to get her bearings.

'There!' Diema said, pointing. It wasn't hard to see where they needed to go: the X that marked the spot was Nahir's crumpled body, sprawled just inside the doorway that connected the main factory floor to the smaller room beyond.

Diema drew both a gun and a sica, and approached Nahir cautiously. Nothing moved on the other side of the doors. There was no clue as to what had struck him, and no sign of the two Adamites.

She let Kennedy examine Nahir, standing guard over them both while she did so. To her surprise, it was apparent as soon as Kennedy turned the man over onto his back that he was alive. He'd fought and lost, and in that process taken a horrific beating. Blood saturated both of his arms and was still pumping weakly from his gashed wrists. He'd taken an injury to the head, too – an attack that had destroyed the orbit of his right eye. Kennedy flinched from the sight of that wound. Diema didn't. A buried part of her reflected on how the matter of the eye itself had become tears, spilling down Nahir's cheek, and how that effect might be rendered in oil pastels. Another part, shocked and protesting, reminded her that she had lain with this man. And a third part, that embraced both of the others and then subsumed them, noted that Nahir's condition proved the validity of Kennedy's guesswork. Ber Lusim was here. Now.

Nahir was trying to speak.

Diema knelt beside him. 'Nahir,' she said. His lips worked, but the sounds that came from them were formless and atomised.

'Ber Lusim,' Diema prompted. 'Where is he? Where is he now?'

531

Nahir's good eye flicked to the grease pit and his finger jerked twice – *down*.

Diema gathered herself and was about to stand. But Nahir's forearm bumped against hers. He was trying to grip her arm, but the fingers of his hand were incapable of responding to his brain's commands. All they could do was twitch in tiny, random saccades.

'Too … quick…' Nahir whispered. 'Too … too … quick … to …' He took a deep, shuddering breath and tried again. 'Don't … fight. Too …'

'We'll be back soon,' Diema said. She was still staring into that one good eye. It pleaded silently, wide with unaccustomed shock and fear. She slipped off her leather jacket, folded it over on itself and slipped it under Nahir's head. Kennedy went to the edge of the grease pit, drew a deep, startled breath and clambered down into it, out of Diema's line of sight.

'We'll be back soon,' Diema said to Nahir. 'We'll get help for you.' Or else, she thought, *this whole place will be ripped into loose molecules by a ten-kiloton cubane explosion*. Either way, Nahir wouldn't have to suffer long.

She crossed to the pit and surveyed its interior before climbing carefully and quietly down to join Kennedy. Kennedy had found Tillman, propped up in one corner of the pit, and was checking on his condition. His face was masked with blood and he was profoundly unconscious, but his injuries looked to be less severe than Nahir's. Weakened as he was, he would have presented far less of a threat.

Kennedy opened her mouth to speak, but Diema hushed her with a raised hand and pointed towards the open door. Kennedy nodded. She touched Tillman's cheek with the fingers of one hand, kissed the top of his head. Then she stood.

Diema took the Chinese semi-automatic from the back of her belt. She was about to offer the nine-millimetre from her ankle holster to Kennedy, but Kennedy stepped past her, moving slowly so as to minimise the squelching sounds her feet made in the thick ooze, and picked up Tillman's fallen gun from where it lay at the edge of the pit. She examined it briefly, seemed satisfied, and responded to Diema's questioning glance with a curt nod. *Ready*.

They moved to the door, taking opposite sides without needing to confer. Standing stock still, they listened.

Two voices, both male. A serious – if slightly bizarre – conversation was being conducted just below them.

'He *is* a piece of bread.' That was Ben Rush's voice. And another voice answered, 'God is one. Only fools deny that.'

There were seven wooden steps, which were dangerously slippery with the same grease and filth that filled the bottom of the pit. Then Rush's feet touched down on gritty, dry cement.

There was a click from above him, followed by the whickering rattle of strip-lights waking up. Rush blinked and shielded his eyes as the dark space around him was suddenly scoured brighter than daylight with remorseless neon.

He was standing in a wide but low-ceilinged room, buttressed with rough-cut wooden beams. All around him were big bags like sandbags or sacks of fertiliser, stacked all the way to the ceiling, with a broad aisle between them. They all seemed to be identical. They bore the legend HIGH C8(NO2)8 EXPLOSIVE in stencilled letters on their sides.

At the far end of the room, facing him, a laptop computer sat on a trestle table. Two long leads connected it to a bizarre modernist sculpture consisting of a handful of steel rods and several dozen fat parcels wrapped in greaseproof paper.

Despite the foul state of the steps, the floor was reasonably clean. A broom was propped incongruously against some of the sacks of high explosive, and once Rush had noticed that, he saw a whole raft of domestic touches in quick succession: a kettle and a carton of milk on an upturned packing crate. A pair of speakers with an iPod nestled between them. A reading lamp on the table and a book lying open next to it.

Ber Lusim was waiting for the end of the world with all the comforts of home.

He appeared beside Rush and put a hand on his shoulder to steer him over to the table. Remembering what else Ber Lusim's hands had just done, Rush shuddered and backed away hurriedly, turning to face the Messenger.

Ber Lusim was staring at him with quizzical interest.

'Look,' Rush said. 'I . . . I don't know what you want from me. I shouldn't even be here.'

'Yes,' Ber Lusim said. 'You should. Of course you should. You had no choice. Please, sit down. I won't hurt you.'

'I'm fine right here,' Rush said.

Ber Lusim nodded. 'Very well.' He walked past Rush to the table and picked up the book that lay there. He held it up for Rush to see.

The book was very old, its corners foxed and furled, its cover as roughly ridged as though someone had dropped it into the bath. On the cover, in a plain, uneven font, were the words *A Trumpet Speaking Judgment, or God's Plan Revealed in Sundry Signes*.

'You know this?' Ber Lusim asked.

Rush thought about lying, but only for a moment. Why else would he be there?

'Yes.'

Ber Lusim smiled warmly, as though he'd extracted a

confession that would be good for Rush's soul. 'I want to thank you,' he said.

The tone – serious, conversational, friendly – shook and scared Rush. He said nothing, only staring at the other man as he flicked through the pages of the book and handed it to him. Rush took it and saw that it was turned to the last page. The centuries-old paper, dry and brittle, rustled between his fingers.

'That paragraph troubled me,' Ber Lusim said. 'Specifically, when Toller says that the son and the spirit will be present when the end comes. It smacked of the meaningless liturgy of the Roman church. The dividing of God into three, as though God were a piece of bread.'

'He *is* a piece of bread,' Rush said. 'Did all that stuff about the Eucharist not get to you yet?'

He heard his own voice saying that and wondered at it. Did he want Ber Lusim to break his arms and legs into loose kindling? Or was he flapping at the mouth purely because of that earlier promise that he wouldn't be hurt? Either way, Ber Lusim didn't react to the flip tone, or even seem to hear it.

'God is one,' he said. 'Only fools deny that. So this referencing of the son and the spirit always struck both of us – Avra and me – as strange. Enigmatic, rather. But time and providence make all things clear. Do you know what your name means?'

'You already told me it means "son of".'

Ber Lusim nodded. 'Yes. That's what "Ben" means. But I meant your family name. "Rush".' He went on, not waiting for Rush to answer. 'It transliterates the Hebraic word *ruach*, which means "spirit". You are the son, Ben Rush, and you are also the spirit. God told Johann Toller that you would come, and Johann Toller told me. In this way, he reassures me that all is well. That what I'm doing is right, and exactly as he intended. I can hear your breathing, by the way.'

He raised his voice on those last words and looked over Rush's shoulder towards the stairs. 'By all means, join us,' he said. 'There's no point in hiding up there. And no time left, now, for anything you do to affect my plans. Although I will, of course, kill you if you try.'

Despite Ber Lusim's words, Kennedy was nearly certain that it wasn't their breathing that gave them away.

She'd discovered that Tillman's gun – a retooled Beretta – had a grip safety, rather than the thumb toggle she was more used to, and she'd chosen a moment when Ber Lusim was talking to squeeze the front of the grip and cock the gun. The click was slight, barely audible even to her, and she'd thought it was completely hidden by the sound of Lusim's voice – but something about the way he paused immediately afterwards made her think she'd put him on his guard.

Then he invited them to join him and there was no longer any doubt. Kennedy mimed to Diema, putting her hands together and then drawing them apart again. *Split up and give him two targets.* Diema nodded.

They came down the stairs, Diema leading the way and Kennedy hanging slightly back.

Ber Lusim watched them with narrow attention as they came into his line of sight.

'I was expounding scripture to your friend,' he told them. 'Which is amusing. I never thought of myself as a preacher. You should perhaps drop those guns, in case you feel tempted to use them.'

'In a roomful of explosives?' Kennedy said. 'That would be a little stupid, wouldn't it?'

Ber Lusim looked at the ramparts of sacks all around them. 'You can't set off octocubane with a bullet,' he said. 'And the primer is behind me, on the table. You'd be shooting through Mr Rush, here, who would be unlikely to thank you. There are also, over there in the corner—' he pointed with the barrel of his gun '— a number of plastic buckets filled with the extremely potent granular poison, ricin. If you were to puncture one of those, the air would fill with highly toxic dust. Of course, the explosion that is about to take place will kill you long before the poison starts to work on you, so that's a matter of less consequence than it would otherwise be.'

'Why are we still alive?' Diema asked. 'Have you lost your taste for killing, Ber Lusim?' She was drawing away from Kennedy, making it harder for the rogue Messenger to keep them both in view at the same time and giving his gun a few more degrees of arc to travel through if he decided to shoot. He held up his hand for them to stop.

'That's far enough. To answer your question, I'm about to kill a million people, which scarcely suggests excessive squeamishness in the taking of life. But that's in the nature of a sacrifice, rather than a murder – fundamentally, a religious observance. Individual deaths, on the other hand … here in this place, at this time, they smack of impiety. But I'll do it, unless you stand where you are and disarm. I'm happy for you all to wait with me, for the moment to come – but I know what's in your hearts and I won't allow it.'

'There's still time to stop this,' Kennedy said. She knew that Diema would be able to aim and fire far more quickly and accurately than she could, so she reasoned that it was up to her to be the diversion. 'Too many people have died already.'

Ber Lusim's gaze flicked to her, but went back to Diema. He

537

seemed to have made an accurate assessment of the relative dangers.

'Everybody who ever lived has died,' Ber Lusim said. 'Apart from the few who are still living now. But today, everything changes.'

'Because of a few lines in a three-hundred-year-old book?' Kennedy asked. 'I don't see that.'

'You're not required to. And this absurd dance must stop, now. Stand where you are. Drop your weapons or place them at your feet. I don't want to spill your blood here. I don't see the need. But I won't let that stop me, if you're determined to force my hand.'

Kennedy slowed and stopped.

'Okay,' she said. 'You win.'

She turned her gun in her hand to point it at the ceiling and bent, very slowly, from the knees, to lay it on the ground.

Diema picked her moment and fired.

68

Once again, just like during the fight beside the grease pit, the action accelerated to the point where Rush had real trouble with crucial things like cause and effect.

He saw Diema's arm move and he heard gunshots – three of them, back to back, so loud that the sound felt more like a physical pressure, pushing against his skin.

Then something flew whirling from Diema's hand and Diema herself was punched backwards so that she hit the wall.

The sound had seemed to come from all directions at once in the confined space, so it was only from this collateral evidence that Rush was able to figure out that Diema hadn't fired at all. All three shots had come from Ber Lusim.

By the time he came to that realisation, the whole thing was over. Diema had slid down the wall to the floor and Ber Lusim had his gun pointed at Kennedy – who was frozen to the spot in a tight crouch, her hand still on her gun which was still on the ground.

'Don't,' Ber Lusim advised her.

Diema breathed out, a long, shuddering gasp. She was lying full length on the cement floor, clutching her side. Blood oozed thickly from between her fingers, and as Rush watched a red stain spread across the leg of her jeans. At least two of Ber Lusim's three bullets had hit their target.

No, all three, he realised. Diema's gun lay on the floor ten feet away from her, the barrel bent into an L-shape.

'I wish that had not been necessary,' Ber Lusim said. 'But you're still alive, at least. Sadly, that's the last courtesy I can do you.'

Rush's heart was hammering in his chest and he felt like he was about to throw up. He saw Kennedy's shoulders tense, which surely meant that Ber Lusim had seen it, too. She was about to make her move, and her move was going to get her killed. There was nothing else she could do.

But there was – there might be – something *he* could do.

If only there was time left to do it in. And if only he could find the words.

'Wait!' he said. Actually, he didn't say it at all; he yelled it, way too loud and way too high. And he raised the book – Toller's book – in his hand as though he were about to preach.

Ber Lusim turned to stare at him and he waved the book in the Messenger's face.

'I'm in here, right?' he babbled. 'You said that. I'm part of the big picture. God sent me, to bring you a message. That's what you said.'

'Yes,' Ber Lusim said in a voice whose calm and quiet made Rush's panicky yelping seem even more absurd than it was. 'I did say that.'

'Okay,' Rush said, fighting down the trembling in his legs, his arms, his voice. 'Then right here, right now, for however long the world's got left, I'm what you are. I'm one of God's messengers. I'm not just some Adamite idiot swimming out of his depth.'

Ber Lusim frowned. 'So?' he said. 'Where is this going?'

'I'll tell you where it's going. If I'm a messenger, Ber Lusim, my message is for you. Are you willing to listen to it?'

Ber Lusim made a gesture, turning both hands palm-up. *Go ahead.*

'Okay.' Rush swallowed. So far so good. He risked a look over his shoulder. Diema hadn't moved at all, except to prop herself up on her left elbow. She was still pressing her hand against her wound, trying without much success to stanch the flow of blood. She was watching Ber Lusim with dulled eyes, or at least she was trying to, but her head kept drooping. Kennedy still looked like she was looking for an opening. Rush met her gaze and moved his head through the tiniest arc. *Not yet.*

He turned back to Ber Lusim.

'Everything you're doing,' he said, 'you're doing because of Toller. Isn't that right? Because of the predictions in this book. It's like he wrote the book for you. Like he saw you coming, three hundred years back, and he spoke to you across that gap.'

'He saw the end of the world coming,' Ber Lusim corrected him. 'But yes, he spoke to us. He told us what we needed to do to bring history to an end and initiate the reign of Messiah.'

'Okay. But I wonder if you know who was talking to you? I mean, if you ever found out anything about Johann Toller's life.'

'More than you can imagine.'

'You think you know him.' Rush felt like he was picking his way through a minefield. But more than that, he felt like he was in a courtroom and he was cross-examining a witness. Trying to make a case, out of nothing except the barest hunch.

'Yes,' Ber Lusim agreed. 'I believe I know him.'

'I'm going to have to disagree,' Rush said. And in the silence

541

that followed, he plunged on. 'I think you're right that God sent me here, Ber Lusim. I think he wanted you to listen to what I've got to say. Because you've made a big mistake. You've killed a lot of people and you're about to kill a whole lot more, and it's all on the basis of a ... a stupid ... you messed up. You messed up so badly.'

Ber Lusim stared at him in complete silence. Rush saw his own death weighed and measured in that stare. The only thing he had going for him was an accidental letter of introduction from Johann Toller, and he had no idea how long that get-out-of-jail-free card was going to last.

'There's something you don't know,' he said, his voice wobbling a little on the last word. 'About Toller. Something you got wrong.'

'Something I got wrong,' Ber Lusim repeated, his tone dangerously mild. 'Really?'

'Really.'

'And what would that be?'

'Who he was.'

Ber Lusim pursed his lips. 'I'll overlook your irreverence,' he said to Rush. 'I still believe there must be some point to your being here. Some reason why you've been placed in my path, at this most solemn and auspicious time. But you must be very careful what you say. Johann Toller was divinely inspired. To speak ill of him is to blaspheme against God.'

Rush kept his gaze fixed on the gun in Ber Lusim's hand – although probably if Ber Lusim decided he needed to be killed, he wouldn't waste a bullet on someone who was in easy reach of his hands. 'Is it speaking ill of Toller to say he wasn't who you think he was?' he asked. 'I don't want to blaspheme. I just think you misread the evidence.'

Ber Lusim raised an eyebrow. 'Yes? How?'

'Well, you think Toller was your missing prophet. The one person who walked away from your hidden city without official sanction. I mean, the one person who did that before you and your people did it.'

'I don't think this. I know it.'

'Because Toller talks about the secret beliefs of the People.'

'Yes.'

'And his book shows the location of Ginat'Dania.'

'Yes, that too.'

'And because he blessed his friends and followers with the sign of the noose instead of the sign of the cross.'

'Of course.'

Rush was standing on the edge of the precipice now. He didn't dare to look around again, to see whether either Diema or Kennedy was tracking his moves. If they weren't, this was going to come to nothing anyway. All he could do – the best he could do – was give them a window.

'Well, in spite of all those things, Ber Lusim, I think you've been cheering for the wrong team. Toller was never one of the Judas People. He was an Adamite.'

Diema used two things to stay conscious: the pain from her wounds and the countdown on her watch.

The pain was constant static along the thousands of unravelling miles of her nervous system.

The countdown stood at seven minutes.

Ber Lusim had his gun pressed against Rush's temple now. Rush was leaning sideways, away from it, his whole body arced like a strung bow, but he didn't dare to step back or to try to push the gun away.

'I see your death,' Ber Lusim said to the boy. 'Without the benefit of prophecy.'

543

'No, just listen,' Rush quavered. 'Listen to me. I can make you believe.'

'I already believe.'

'Then I can make you doubt. Why did God send me?'

'To test me. To put my beliefs to the test.'

'Then ... then you have to take the test, don't you? You have to listen. Blowing my brains out is just going to piss God off.'

Neither of them moved, for a moment or two longer. Then Ber Lusim lowered the gun, very gradually, to his side.

'This is nonsense,' he said heavily. 'But say what you like. Nonsense can't hurt me.'

'Okay, look at the documentary evidence,' Rush said, starting to babble again. 'In your version of the story your man comes out of Ginat'Dania, heading west. Then a good long time afterwards, Johann Toller arrives in England and starts to preach. And you can tell he's your guy because of all the stuff he says. He knows about Ginat'Dania. He knows about the three-thousand-year cycle. And how else could he have found that out?

'But what happened in the meantime? What made him abandon his mission and his people and go native like that?'

'An angel,' Ber Lusim said, his voice almost a growl, 'spoke to him.'

'Right.' Rush nodded. 'An angel spoke to him and gave him the secrets of heaven. And Toller wanted to share the amazing things he'd learned. He felt like he had to share it with the whole world. So he goes to England.

'And this is where I kind of lose the plot. It's the Civil War. The political scene in England is a snake pit, but Toller jumps in like it's a swimming pool. He makes all kinds of friends and enemies in Cromwell's government. He rallies the religious dissenters – becomes one of their spokesmen, kind of. He joins the Fifth Monarchy movement. Gets a seat at the table. And I'm asking myself: *why?* What is the point of it all? If you've seen the eternal truth, why would you care whether Cromwell or Fairfax keep their promises, or whether bishops get to speak in parliament? It's a sideshow. The world is going to end, the kingdom is going to come and that's all that matters.'

Diema pulled her attention away from the doctrinal argument and looked for her gun. It was far enough away that she'd have to crawl to reach it and it looked as though it had taken a direct hit in any case.

But she had the other gun, in her ankle holster: the tiny, modest little M26 that she'd taken from Nahir and Shraga almost as an afterthought.

She groaned and rolled over as though she were in agony, using the movement to curl her legs up and bring them closer to her left hand. It felt as though her right wrist might have been broken when Ber Lusim shot the gun out of her hand – an outrageous feat, even at this short a distance.

'Time is contained within eternity, like the grit in a pearl,' Ber Lusim was saying. 'Toller saw all things, both close and far away. And he cared about all things.'

Rush held up the book, his hand shaking even more noticeably. 'Okay, maybe. Maybe it happened like that. But here's another scenario: Toller was nobody. Just some guy. But he was British. He came out of England, maybe doing the whole grand tour thing, or maybe because he was a merchant or a diplomat.

'So he's travelling through the Alps, and he has an accident. Only he's not alone when he has it. And he's not the only survivor. There's another man, lying next to him – injured, probably dying. That's your prophet, fresh out of Ginat'Dania.

And that's the moment when everything changes for Toller. That's where his life turns upside down.

'Because the injured man is hallucinating, and he can't stop talking. Or else it's just that he knows he's dying. He's got to tell his life story to someone before he goes, and Toller's right there. Toller's listening. Listening with every ear he's got.'

'This is grotesque,' Ber Lusim said.

'So Toller gets the whole story. The holy betrayer. The secret city. The end of the world. It's a revelation. No, it's a whole book of revelations. And it's got to be the truth, because who's going to waste the last hours of his life spinning such a crazy story? It's as though God put this man just in the right place, just at the right time, so that Toller's eyes could be opened.

'And when it was done, and the man was dead, Toller went home to England and picked up his life again. Except now he was a prophet. A man with a message. And he wanted to give the message as much authority as he could, so he came up with the angel's visitation. Or maybe that was how he actually remembered it by this time, I don't know. Maybe he really thought your man was an angel.'

'Why should this thing be true?' Ber Lusim demanded. 'Where is your evidence?'

Diema had pulled the leg of her jeans up three inches from her ankle, exposing the holster. The gun was lying ready to her hand. But now another problem presented itself. Two problems, in fact. How was she going to get through Ber Lusim's guard any better the second time, now that she was using her weaker, slower hand? And how was she going to draw and fire on him without hitting Rush, who was directly in the way? She saw that Kennedy was watching her, ready to move when she did.

'It's not about the evidence,' Rush said, 'although I do have some. A little, anyway. But think about it. Doesn't my version make more sense? In your story, a Messenger decides out of nowhere to betray his sacred trust and go preach to the heathens. In mine, he only talks because he knows he's dying.'

'He didn't just decide,' Ber Lusim said. 'You're forgetting that he had a visitation from God.'

'And this visitation somehow gave him a complete who's who of English politics? And it made him think that English politics actually *mattered*? Because he spent the rest of his life there, Ber Lusim. He was executed for trying to murder some kind of government clerk. What the hell was that?'

Ber Lusim took a step towards Rush, but Rush backed away. He held the book in his two hands, ready to tear it down the length of its spine. 'You better back off,' he warned Ber Lusim. 'Or I'm going to commit some serious blasphemy.'

Ber Lusim raised his gun again and pointed it at Rush. 'The book will be destroyed in the explosion in any case,' he said. 'Its physical integrity isn't of paramount importance to me now. I would just like to die holding it. In any event, I've heard you out and I have not been swayed in the smallest degree. If you were meant to test me, boy, I've passed the test.'

'But I've got evidence,' Rush blurted. 'I told you I had some evidence, right? Well, here it is. Forget about the angel and the accident, and all the rest of it. Forget about what Toller knew or where he got it from. Remember the one thing that he did that marked him out as one of the Judas People.

'He used the sign of the noose.'

Diema had her hand on the grip of the M26 and had eased it halfway out of the holster. But Rush was still in the worst possible position, blocking most of her line of fire but almost none of Ber Lusim's line of sight.

'Toller used the sign of the noose as a blessing,' Rush said. 'His followers didn't know what it was and he never explained it to them. But he did it anyway.'

'I know this,' Ber Lusim said.

'You don't know anything. Toller never used the sign of the noose even once.'

Ber Lusim's eyes narrowed.

'What?'

Rush shrugged, showed his empty hands. 'I know, right? I thought that, too, the first time I read it. But then I saw Diema make the sign and something didn't feel right. I got her to talk me through it. Then I went back and I read it again, and there it was. *He put his hand to his throat, thence to his heart, and his stomach, and so in a circle back to where it began.*'

'I have read the passage,' Ber Lusim snarled. 'Do you take me for a fool?'

'So if you had a clock face on your chest,' Rush said, stealing the metaphor that Diema had used on the plane to Budapest, 'that's the way the hands would turn. Look. Like this.'

Diema could see that Rush was making the sign, just the way Robert Blackborne said Toller had made it. And she could tell from the way Ber Lusim's eyes widened that he got the point.

'It's the wrong way round,' Rush said. 'As though Toller learned it by looking in a mirror. Which I think is more or less what he did.'

'No,' Ber Lusim said. It wasn't a disagreement: it was a warning.

'Yes,' Rush insisted. 'Not a mirror, obviously. But he saw someone else doing it and he copied it, exactly the way he saw it. He just forgot to turn it around.'

'No,' Ber Lusim said again.

'It's kind of funny, in a sick way,' Rush said. Bluntly. Brutally. 'You going to all this trouble, I mean.' He gave a slightly hysterical laugh. 'Pity Avra Shekolni is dead. I bet he'd have loved this.'

Maybe it was the laugh that sent Ber Lusim over the edge. He lunged forward, his hand shooting out to grip Rush's throat.

It was the only moment they were going to get.

'Now!' Diema bellowed. 'Do it now!'

Kennedy rose to her feet, gun in hand.

Ber Lusim turned.

And Diema fired.

Ber Lusim drew in his breath in a tremulous gasp. He looked down at his chest – at the small round hole that had appeared there, like a mysterious punctuation mark. A full stop, inscribed directly onto his heart. It went from black to red, and blood welled out of it. Ber Lusim had stiffened, his eyes wide as though from some awful realisation.

But it was Rush who fell, toppling from the ground up as his knees buckled under him.

Left-handed, out of position, Diema had taken the only shot she could: through Rush's right shoulder and into the left side of Ber Lusim's chest.

And now the way was clear. She and Kennedy fired again and again, emptying their guns into the assassin. Ber Lusim bowed his head and took the punishment, as though a man could endure gunfire in the same way as he endured heavy rain.

But this weather took a greater toll. Ber Lusim sank to his knees, as though by choice, then lowered himself by gradual degrees into a posture of prayer, which was how he died.

Kennedy began to approach the dead man slowly, covering him with her now-useless gun.

'No!' Diema shouted. 'The timer, Kennedy! The timer!'

The woman ran to the desk, but hesitated. The smaller bomb that was the primer for Ber Lusim's WMD was a baroque, ramshackle thing with wires and metal rods connecting to packets of acetone peroxide and clusters of industrial blasting caps. 'What do I do?' Kennedy yelled.

The timer on the screen showed twenty-three seconds. Kennedy turned to look at Diema, desperate, urgent. But Diema had no more idea than she did and it must have showed in her face.

With a wordless cry, like a paratrooper jumping out of a plane, Kennedy ripped the laptop out of the circuit.

It continued to count down in her hands.

To ten.

To five.

To zero.

Diema held an in-breath until her chest ached. Then slowly, soundlessly, let it out.

69

'I'm bleeding,' Rush said plaintively, from the floor. 'Oh Christ. I'm bleeding all over the place. Help me.'

Diema crawled across to him slowly and painfully. She checked Rush's wounds: both of them, entry and exit. The entry wound was small and neat and wouldn't give any trouble at all. The exit wound was a lot bigger and the bullet had taken meat with it.

By the time it hit its intended target, the bullet would have spent at least a third of its initial velocity, most of it inside of Ben Rush. No wonder it had stopped Ber Lusim dead. The slowing bullet, lacking the energy required to leave his body once it had forced its way in, had sent a widening shockwave ahead of itself, pulping his internal organs like a steak tenderiser.

'You did well,' Diema said to Rush, as she patched him up.

Kennedy knelt down beside her and helped by tearing more strips of cloth as Diema knotted the makeshift dressing into place. 'You did brilliantly,' she confirmed. 'Rush, how in the name of God did you figure that stuff out?'

'I didn't figure it out,' he mumbled. His face was ashen. 'I made most of it up. It's probably all wrong. Except for the sign. I was pretty sure about the sign.'

'You prevented a million deaths,' Diema said. 'You were a shield to my people. And to some of yours, too. You might amount to something one day after all, little boy.'

'And you ... aah, shit ... you might grow some breasts,' Rush countered. 'Dream big.'

Diema turned her attention to Kennedy. 'I'll finish here,' she said. 'You go and check on my father – and get the truck into position. We're leaving.'

A look passed between them. Kennedy nodded and left them to it, going rapidly back up the stairs to the grease pit.

Diema carried on knotting the dressing more firmly in place until Rush took hold of her hand to stop her. 'When we had sex,' he asked her, 'was that just so you could get pregnant?'

'I'm not pregnant, Rush.'

He stared at her, nonplussed.

'You're not?'

'No. I said that to stop Nahir from cutting your throat.'

'Oh. Okay.' He thought about that a little longer as she tested the tightness of the dressing. 'Uh ... why?'

Diema was silent for a long time.

'Do you mean, why would that stop him from killing you or why would I care whether he killed you or not?'

'Either. Both.'

'It's hard to explain,' she told him. 'My people have some pretty odd ways of looking at things sometimes.'

Rush winced as some random movement sent a wave of pain through his torn shoulder muscle. 'You don't say? Well, thanks for the heroic self-sacrifice, anyway.'

Diema said nothing, pretending to check Ber Lusim's greying body for signs of life.

It wasn't over yet.

'Do you feel up to moving?' she asked Rush.

He tried to get upright, but every movement hurt him. It took the two of them, finally, Diema bearing the boy's weight whenever a twinge of agony froze his muscles. She raised him like a banner – a flag of surrender, because that was how it felt. As though she were giving in, suddenly but far too late, to the logic of an argument that had first been put to her three years before, when her hands were around the throat of Ronald Stephen Pinkus and the light disappeared from his eyes.

'Ready?' she asked Rush.

'Ready for what?' he panted. 'You want to dance?'

'I need you to walk.'

'Okay.'

It took an eternity for them to get up the stairs. Kennedy met them at the top, her face grim.

'Leo's just about awake,' she told Diema, 'but I think some of the wounds on his chest have opened up. I'm scared of moving him.'

'We don't have any choice,' Diema said.

They both looked towards Tillman. He was on his feet in the corner of the grease pit, his two arms stretched out along its edge to either side. His head was sagging onto his chest. He looked like a boxer who'd only just made it through the previous round.

Diema turned back to Kennedy.

'Heather, we have to go,' she said. 'This is—'

'I know what it is.'

'It was part of the plan, always. You take the stick out of the fire, you beat your enemies, and then you throw it back. You let it be burned.'

'I got that, Diema. I got that the first time.'

'I can walk,' Tillman said. His voice was a ghastly, gallows thing.

553

'Prove it,' Diema said.

But first they had to get out of the pit, which was so protracted an agony that Diema felt nostalgic for the stairs. She and Kennedy had to prop Tillman up against the side of the pit, then drag and push at his limbs one at a time as though they were trying to reassemble the faces of a Rubik cube. When they were done, he was lying on his back at the edge of the drop, exhausted by agony, drawing breaths so shallow that the front of his shirt, stiff with fresh blood, didn't even move.

Then they had to do the same thing with Rush.

Finally they had both men up and moving, Diema supporting Tillman because she was the stronger of the two, Kennedy following with Rush.

They made their way, like the last teams standing in a marathon three-legged race, out onto the factory floor and across the obstacle course towards the main doors.

They passed Desh Nahir along the way, lying unconscious in his blood. Diema murmured a blessing, but didn't stop or slow. The doors were in sight now, and she could see the tailgate of the truck. Tillman slipped in the algae-slick of a dried-up puddle, almost fell, but Diema held him upright by getting her weight under him and pushing him upward – the *tsukuri* part of a judo throw, with the follow-through indefinitely suspended.

The doors were directly ahead of them. Her eyes on the ground, because she was forced now to treat each step, each shifting of her weight, as an exercise in logistics, Diema saw her feet, and Tillman's feet, enter the slanting beam of sunlight that spilled across the grimed cement. They were emerging into the world outside in tortuous slow motion.

Kuutma stepped through the doors, with Alus and Taria to either side of him, and met them there. Other Messengers were standing on the asphalt outside, still and silent, awaiting Kuutma's order.

He stared at Diema, who had stumbled to a halt. His expression was complex and unreadable.

'Report,' he suggested to her, with dangerous mildness.

Diema tried to speak, but the words fled away from her flailing mind.

'I ... we ...' she tried.

'Ber Lusim is dead,' Kennedy said. 'It's over. But you need to dismantle the bomb. And your man, Nahir, needs medical attention.'

Kuutma's gaze flicked to her for the smallest fraction of a second, then back to Diema. 'Is this true?' he asked.

Diema nodded, still mute.

'Then the threat is removed? There's no longer any danger?'

'There is ...' Diema tried again. 'The bomb. As Kennedy says. We removed the detonator, but the bomb needs to be dismantled. And Nahir ...'

Kuutma turned to Alus and Taria. 'See to him,' he ordered, and they were gone from his side in an instant.

'*Dan cheira hu meircha!*' Kuutma shouted. Obedient to his command, the Messengers filed in through the doors to surround the small party.

With Rush leaning on her right arm, Kennedy tried to get her left hand inside her jacket to reach her shoulder holster. Diema reached out, snake-swift, to grip her wrist and keep the hand in plain sight. If Kennedy succeeded in drawing the gun, she'd be dead before she drew another breath.

Kuutma had been staring at Diema throughout these manoeuvres. 'It was well done,' he said to her. 'It was very well done. You may stand down, Diema Beit Evrom. What remains to be done here, others will do.'

Diema made no move. The muscles of her chest seemed to be squeezing her lungs, so that it was a great effort even to draw a breath. '*Tannanu*,' she said, 'I need to speak with you.'

'No,' Kuutma said. 'You don't.'

'Yes,' Diema insisted. 'To report.'

'I've heard your report, Diema. And now this is in my hands. Step outside. I've deliberated, in the matter of your pregnancy, and I've reached a verdict. The only verdict possible, if you're to escape censure. The boy's death protects your honour. The other deaths were already agreed on before you ever left Ginat'Dania. But there's no need for you to be present for this. I understand that it might distress you to see these people, who've fought at your side, lose their lives. Go. Go to the gates of the compound and wait for me there.'

Sour bile rose in Diema's mouth and she swallowed it down again.

'*Tannanu*,' she said, the words scouring her throat like gravel, 'I wish to speak. My testimony is pertinent to these matters. Hear me out.'

They held the tableau for some seconds. If Kuutma saw the tension in her posture, and if he understood what it meant, he gave no sign.

'Very well,' he said at last.

He gave clipped commands. Messengers came forward to remove Tillman from her grasp and to take hold of Kennedy and Rush.

'Son of a bitch!' Kennedy yelled. She threw a wild glance at Diema, who ignored it. Their fates rested with Kuutma now.

He walked aside a little way, beckoning her to follow him. Diema obeyed.

'I'm listening,' Kuutma said, dropping the mantle of

formality. 'But there's no way of stopping this, little sister. You must know that.'

'Brother,' Diema said, staring full into his eyes, 'there is. You're Kuutma, the Brand, and what you say will happen here is what will happen. Nobody will argue with you.'

Kuutma shrugged brusquely. 'That's irrelevant. I can't gainsay what I've already said. They're going to die.' He breathed out slowly, a breath that was almost a sigh. 'I can see that these three have come to mean something to you – I saw that back in Budapest. And I grieve for you. You've known enough loss in your life already. But Kennedy's death, and Tillman's, were part of the task you accepted. Be strong, now, and see it through. As for the boy, even if you love him, you'll forget him soon enough. Take another lover. Take a husband, even. Desh Nahir would embrace you in an instant.'

Diema ignored this grotesque suggestion, and stuck remorselessly to her point. '*Tannanu*, Leo Tillman is my father.'

'No, Diema, he is not. He's only—'

'He is the father of my flesh and the father of my spirit. He is the only father I acknowledge. I cleave to him, as his daughter, and I will stand by him. The hand that's raised to hurt him becomes, with that act, my enemy's hand. On Gellert Hill, he fought for me and would have died for me, though we had but an hour's acquaintance. I knew then that he had loved the child he lost, and that therefore he could not knowingly have killed my brothers. That was some terrible mistake, as the *rhaka* Kennedy told me it was. The monster whose death I assented to never existed – and to my father's death, *Tannanu*, I do not assent.'

Kuutma listened to this speech with a look of sombre concern. When it was finished, he said nothing for a long time.

557

Finally, he reached out and put a hand on Diema's shoulder.

'I've done you no service,' he said heavily. 'I see that now. I love you and honour you, Diema, but I put you in the way of this hurt, and now I don't see how to make it pass from you.'

'Let them live.'

'I can't do that. I'm not free to choose.'

'Then neither am I,' Diema said. She drew a sica from its sheath against her breast and placed it so that the tip of the blade touched her stomach. 'Kill Leo Tillman and I'll die, too.'

Kuutma's eyes widened in horror. 'Diema,' he said, his voice almost a whisper. 'You can't mean it.'

'I mean it.'

Many emotions crossed Kuutma's face. The one that was most clearly visible was pain. 'A blasphemy,' he said.

'I'm damned already. On Gellert Hill, I shot Hifela, of the *Elohim*, and watched him die. And I lied to you in Budapest, *Tannanu*. I'm not pregnant. I said that to save the boy, and the boy just saved us all.' She wrestled with words, with reasons, trying to explain something that had come to her without the benefit of either, as a rising tide of revelation. 'If I let them die,' she said, 'I become less than they are. Less than I thought they were, when I didn't know them.'

Kuutma's face still bore the same expression of dismay and suffering. 'I could disarm you,' he pointed out.

'Possibly. But you couldn't keep me disarmed.' She put the knife away, to reinforce the point. 'I don't have to die here or now, *Tannanu*. I've got all the time in the world. If I decide to kill myself, the only way to stop me is to kill me first.'

Silence fell between them. They stared at one another, intransigent, immovable.

With no more sound than a whisper of fabric, Alus and Taria appeared to either side of Diema.

'Desh Nahir will live,' Alus said.

'And he has withdrawn his execration,' Taria added. 'He wishes no harm to Diema Beit Evrom.'

Kuutma nodded. 'Thank you,' he said. 'Secure Diema Beit Evrom and confiscate her weapons.'

The two women did as they were told. Diema made no protest and she didn't struggle, as Alus held her hands behind her back and Taria methodically searched her for weapons. The tall woman's eyes met hers and she could see how little they liked to treat one of their own in this way.

'Guard her,' Kuutma said.

Taria nodded. 'Yes, Kuutma. What about the *rhaka* and the others? Should we—'

'Do nothing,' Kuutma said. 'I wish to speak with Leo Tillman.'

Following Kuutma's curt instructions, his Messengers overturned one of the plastic tubs, tipping out the thin paste at the bottom of it, and rolled it to a distant corner of the room, far from the others. Tillman was half-dragged and half-carried across and set down on the tub, where in due course Kuutma joined him.

Tillman was still in a great deal of pain, but Alus's medical skills had once again been called into service. She had made up a cocktail of drugs designed to help him manage the pain and stay conscious. His fully dilated pupils and the morbid tension of his posture suggested that they were just starting to kick in.

Kuutma stared down at the Adamite, with the puzzled frown of a mathematician considering a problem in formal logic.

'I had a plan,' he said, 'that included your death. Yours, and the woman's.'

Tillman nodded.

'It's true that your death was only a detail,' Kuutma continued. 'It was a way of dealing with a situation that my predecessor had allowed to arise. The main thrust of the plan related to much clearer and more present dangers.'

He hesitated a moment, then sat beside the Adamite man. It enabled him to lower his voice a little further: all of the Messengers present had recently taken prodigious doses of kelalit, which enhances the senses, so there was a possibility, despite the discreet distance, that they were being overheard.

'I wish,' Kuutma said, 'that I'd killed you first and found some different way to solve my remaining problems.'

Tillman laughed shortly – a single snort. 'Yeah,' he said, 'well, that just sums you people up, it seems to me. You always over-think these things, and you always make the same mistake.'

Kuutma scowled, but kept his tone even and controlled. 'And what mistake is that, Mr Tillman?'

Tillman ran a hand over his sweating face and blinked several times, rapidly. The drugs he'd been given were interfering with his perception, or his thought-processes, or both.

'She's pretty amazing, isn't she?'

'What?' Kuutma asked, thrown.

'My little girl. She's a real piece of work. I'd hazard a guess that maybe that goes for all the women in her family. She reminds me a lot of my wife.'

'Rebecca Beit Evrom was not your wife.'

'No?'

'No. The relationship between a *Kelim* woman and an Adamite out-father is not characterised as marriage, in our laws. What mistake is it that you think we make, Mr Tillman?'

Still blinking, Tillman turned his head to stare at Kuutma. 'There's a kind of a proverb. You must have heard of it. It says if you've only got a hammer in your toolbox, everything looks like a nail.'

'I'm familiar with that observation.'

'You've spent two thousand years killing anyone who gets onto you or gets too close to the truth about you. Playing ducks and drakes with history.'

'We do what we have to do.'

'No,' Tillman said, his voice slurring a little. 'You do what you already *know* how to do. You don't change your repertoire, even when you can see that it's not working.'

'It's worked well enough so far,' Kuutma said.

Tillman laughed again. 'Then why do you even exist? If it worked, Kuutma, if it had ever worked, they wouldn't need you. Thousands of years of surreptitious murder, and every time, every damn time ... as soon as you finish one operation it's all got to be done again. Hundreds of *Elohim* with their ears to the ground, all across the world, trying to keep track of a whisper line with seven billion voices on it. Of course you're going to make a pig's breakfast out of it.'

'You're saying there's a better way?' Kuutma asked sardonically.

'Yes.'

'Teach me, *Tannanu* Tillman.'

'Well, for starters,' Tillman said, 'you don't squash the story. You shout it. Flood the world with rumours about the Judas People, about Ginat'Dania. Tell everyone about the secret book, the lost gospel. Tell them if they read it, pale men who weep blood will find them and kill them with knives that were last seen twenty centuries ago. Tell them about the beautiful women who'll sleep with you and then disappear, leaving you

561

to grow crazy with searching for them. Tell them about the underground city, and all the rest of it.'

'Why?' Kuutma demanded, mystified. 'Why would we do these things?'

'Because the world's full of lies,' Tillman said. 'Full to the brim and slopping over. And when your story's out there, it looks like one more lie. It has its hour, and then it's stale, and then it's dead, and everyone moves on to the next big thing. "You're still trying to sell that Judas People bullshit? Seriously? There's this new book says Jesus was a woman!" That's what you need. That saturated, been-there, heard-it feeling. And it's so easy to get. All you've got to do is face the same way everyone else is facing, so you get lost in the crowd. Whereas what you're doing now is pushing against the grain the whole time. Not only is it a lot harder that way, but every time you move, every time you do anything, you make another trail that somebody could follow.'

The speech seemed to have used up all of Tillman's remaining strength. He bowed his head onto his chest and closed his eyes.

Kuutma stood, and – after a moment's irresolution – moved away.

'Let me speak to her, one more time,' Tillman said.

Kuutma paused. 'Why?'

'To say goodbye.'

'She doesn't need to say goodbye to you. She's made her peace with your death.'

Tillman made a weary, broken gesture with his hand. 'If you say so. I know you people can't lie.'

No, Kuutma thought, staring down at the wounded man, *we can't.*

Except to ourselves.

70

The flight back to London was funereal. And the fact that they were in business class just made it surreal, too.

Any time that Rush could think of anything to say, Kennedy replied with monosyllables. And he didn't blame her, because the things that he could think of to say were all wrong. Small talk. Desperate verbal swerves, taking them away as far as possible from the one topic that they couldn't discuss.

Why did we let them do that to him?

Why didn't they do it to me?

The stewardess came by and offered them champagne. Kennedy didn't even seem to hear. Rush shook his head emphatically.

'We're good,' he lied. 'We're fine. Thanks.'

71

Kennedy didn't phone ahead and tell Izzy that she was coming. The fact was that she was scared to. Scared of words more than anything, at this point, because the first thing she'd done when she finally touched down at Heathrow was to catch up on a whole week of Izzy's texts.

She'd never been an archaeologist, but she'd met some. It felt like archaeology.

Unearthing the evidence of a vanished way of life.

Izzy's tone going from chatty to bitter to resigned to valedictory.

And the dark ages, which was Tuesday and Wednesday and today, when there were no messages, no signs of life at all.

She took the train up to Leicester. She didn't trust herself to drive. A taxi took her from the station to Knighton, the driver bending her ear about something or other the whole way, except that she didn't hear a word, so technically her ears were unbent.

She told him to wait. She might not be here long.

Caroline answered on the third ring. She was surprised to see Kennedy, and judging from how thin the line of her lips got, it wasn't the kind of surprise that makes you squeal for joy.

'Hello, Heather.'

'Hi, Caroline.' Kennedy considered and abandoned various feeble conversational gambits. 'Is Izzy there? I . . . I'd like to talk to her. Just for a minute.'

Caroline nodded and withdrew. Kennedy stood on the doorstep in a light summer drizzle, listening to footsteps echo through the big house, fainter and fainter.

She didn't hear Izzy's footsteps approaching, because Izzy was in her socks. She was just there, suddenly. The door was flung open and she was up in Kennedy's face, in Kennedy's arms, kissing her with a ferocity that was going to leave bruises.

They stayed like that for a long time. Caroline came into the hallway behind them and watched for a moment or two in stony-faced silence, like Lot's wife looking back at the cities of the plain. Then she went away again.

'I screwed up,' Kennedy said, when Izzy finally allowed her the free use of her mouth. 'But I love you, Iz. I can't imagine not having you in my life. If you give me another chance, I'll never push you away again.'

'I knew it,' Izzy murmured in Kennedy's ear.

'Knew what?'

'That if I held out for long enough, you'd find some way that it was your fault I shagged that boy. You're a genius, babe. That's why I need you.'

They kissed some more, but then Izzy pulled her face away from the lip-lock to stare down the drive towards the street.

'Have you got a taxi waiting?'

'Oh,' Kennedy said. 'Yeah.'

'Thank God. Let's go.'

72

That the eyes should be red was licence, of a kind. It was a way of saying something that needed to be said, even if it wasn't what she was seeing.

But there was a problem with the blacks, Diema decided.

Both of the women had such lustrous hair that she couldn't catch the richness and the fullness of it with the pigments and the techniques she knew.

By way of a partial solution, she drew them in stylised form, their hair solid black with solid bars of white for the highlights, their muscles limned in feathered greys on the perfect whiteness of their skin.

'I've got to move,' Alus moaned. 'My nose is itching.'

'Your nose probably isn't in the picture,' Taria said. 'The canvas isn't that big.'

When she finally let them see the picture, they were baffled. 'It looks like something a little kid would do,' Taria said. 'But ... it works, somehow. It's like the way you'd say something, and everyone would know you were exaggerating, but they'd see the truth underneath the exaggeration. It's like that, but in a picture.'

Diema blushed. 'In the Nations,' she said, 'they call a drawing in this style a cartoon.'

'My two-year-old son paints just like this,' Alus said. 'You think I could call it a cartoon and sell it?'

Diema might have bridled at the insult, but she laughed and let it pass. She was still amazed that they had agreed to pose for her, and she was anxious not to do anything that might make them change their minds. Not only was she finally getting to paint them, as she'd wanted to do ever since she first met them, but they were also her only source of news about her father.

They talked about him now, as she prepared a meal of bread and olives for her two models, who were putting their clothes back on in a corner of the studio. It was a very large studio. Space wasn't so much sought after down here in *het retoyet*, at the bottom of Ginat'Dania.

'He's going on about windows now,' Alus said. 'Why can't he have any windows? It's driving him crazy that he doesn't have a view. He's four hundred feet underground and he wants a view. So Kuutma, instead of telling him to shove it up his arse, says "What view would you like, Mr Tillman? What is it that you want to be looking at?" And Leo goes "I don't know, maybe a lake or something." And the next time I go in, Kuutma's fixed up a live video feed from Lake Michigan. And you know what Leo says?'

'He says, "There's no sound!"' Taria broke in, stepping on Alus's punchline. 'He says he likes the water, but it's not real without the sound. So Kuutma turns around and says to Alus—'

'Call Michigan. See if there's any way they can put a microphone in.'

Both women were laughing uproariously. This was their favourite kind of story about Tillman – the kind where he did something outrageous or curmudgeonly or inexplicable. The

567

kind where he was like an exotic pet, with exotic needs and neurotic, high-maintenance habits.

In Ginat'Dania at large, Diema knew, her father was seen very differently. He was the prisoner in the tower, the monster caged, the trophy that Kuutma had brought back after vanquishing Ber Lusim and saving the city. And more, he was the former enemy forced now to toil at the wheel, to labour for the People though it broke his proud heart and gravelled his spirit.

Tillman was the brilliant Adamite tactician who had once found Ginat'Dania and forced it to flee from him. But now his insights, squeezed out of him by Kuutma's merciless interrogation, served Kuutma's agenda and the People's. They had been instrumental in switching the main thrust of *Elohim* activity from concealment to white noise and disinformation.

It was a new age, and Leo Tillman was a prized resource.

Within the *Elohim*, it was known that he was also a hostage for the good behaviour of the *rhaka*, Heather Kennedy. And for the killer of Ber Lusim, Benjamin Rush. These two had saved the city in its hour of greatest need and so were allowed to live out their lives among the Nations, as an act of sublime mercy on Kuutma's part, on condition of profound and eternal silence. If they spoke a word of what they'd done, or what they'd seen, Tillman would die on the instant.

'Over time,' Kuutma told Diema, 'we'll adjust the emphasis, little by little. We'll say that the light of truth, the power of the word, can pierce even a darkness as profound as Leo Tillman's. We'll say that he works for us willingly, seeing the value of what he builds and the error of his former ways. We'll say he wants to be remembered for good, not for evil, and hopes to buy some small degree of redemption by serving something greater than himself.'

Diema understood the strategy, but was impatient of ever

seeing it implemented. Kuutma moved so slowly, seeming content to defer the decision from month to month while he sounded the waters of public sentiment in an endless, open-ended process of triage. 'When can I see him?' she asked, on the occasion of each brief, inconclusive progress report.

'Soon,' Kuutma said each time.

But not yet. That Tillman had been an out-father, and that his child still lived in the city, was the most problematic, the most scandalous aspect of his being there at all. What if he came to learn of the child's existence? What if he tried to assert some imaginary right of access, of guardianship? What if – God forbid! – the child should accidentally come into contact with him?

So not yet. The People were contemplating, now, many things that would once have been anathema to them. But there were still some lines that could not, must not, be crossed.

She wrote him letters, though words had never come easily to her. Then, once she'd heard that story from Alus and Taria about him demanding windows, she began to send him pictures. Imaginary landscapes. Woods and fields, desert mesas, mountains. And a vast lake stretching to the horizon, with islands floating in its grey, choppy waters.

She dreamed, some nights, of the two of them walking there, on its endless, contested margins. Talking about the past until the past lost its power to hurt them and the shoreline turned into a bridge that took them home.

She waited to meet him.